Poppy's Seed

Bethany Askew

Matador
9 Priory Business Park,
Wistow Road, Kibworth Beauchamp,
Leicestershire. LE8 0RX
Tel: 0116 279 2299
Email: books@troubador.co.uk
Web: www.troubador.co.uk/matador
Twitter: @matadorbooks

ISBN 978 1785899 195

British Library Cataloguing in Publication Data.
A catalogue record for this book is available from the British Library.

Printed and bound in the UK by TJ International, Padstow, Cornwall
Typeset in 11pt Aldine401 BT by Troubador Publishing Ltd, Leicester, UK

Matador is an imprint of Troubador Publishing Ltd

For Anthony,
with my love and thanks

About the Author

Bethany Askew is the author of four other novels: *The Time Before*, *The World Within*, *Out of Step* and *Counting the Days*.

She has also written a short story, *The Night of the Storm*, and she writes poetry.

Future projects include a new short story, this one for the young adult market, and another full-length novel.

www.bethanyaskew.co.uk

Chapter One

"I still feel like I'm on holiday," Emily says.

"So you keep saying," Peter says, tersely. "I wish we were. Then I'd be going back to work on Monday."

"It *is* Monday."

"That's exactly what I mean. I don't even know what day of the week it is now. Every day the same. The bloody boring same."

"We could go for a walk…"

"It's raining."

"I don't mind…" But she knows how much Peter hates even the slightest drop of rain. "A drive in the car?" she says.

"No point in the rain. Anyway, where would we go? We've been everywhere…"

"We could unpack some of those boxes…"

"Don't start that again. There's no rush…"

"It's just you said you were bored…"

"Well, I am. But I don't want you nagging me into doing something I don't want to do. Now if you don't mind…" He turns back to the newspaper.

"Okay, okay. I've got loads to do anyway…"

Emily switches her laptop on, leaving it to search for the Internet, which takes ages down here, then runs up the stairs and strips the sheets off the bed.

"I don't know why you're doing that," Peter says when he sees her bundling them into the washing machine.

She stops and looks up. "What?"

"Making work for yourself like that."

"It's got to be done, Peter."

"But you're always doing something. Cleaning, washing, ironing. I thought you'd stop all that now you're not working."

Emily laughs. "Don't be silly. It still has to be done."

"You said it would be easier down here."

"Well, it is. Of course it is. But there's still things to do…"

She switches on the machine, then checks her laptop. She's tempted to type, *Fed up with grumpy husband* on her Facebook status, but of course, she doesn't. *Retirement. One long holiday*, she writes. A comment pops up almost immediately. Jane.

Don't rub it in, she writes. *We're still slaving away here. Quiet without you*.

I miss you all, Emily writes. She scrolls down, glancing at posts, photos, the odd comment about the lousy weather, then closes the lid of her laptop.

Peter has moved from the kitchen and is now in the sitting room flicking through the *Radio Times*.

"I've got to do some shopping later," she calls through to him. "You can come with me if you like."

He glances up at the window. "It's still raining," he says. "We only went the other day. We're always shopping, nowadays."

"Nothing's changed, Peter. We're not eating any more than we used to. I'm not shopping any more than I did before. You just never noticed before, shut up in your ivory tower."

"We could go tomorrow…"

"We need stuff today. And it might still be raining. And if it's a nice day you'll want to go for a walk or a drive or…"

"I only meant…"

"I know what you meant. You meant you don't want to come out and get wet, just to help me carry the food that we need for your dinner. You'd rather stay in and complain about being bored…"

2

"Oh for God's sake!" he explodes.

"Well, it's true! Look at you! Can't you find something to do? What about that painting you were going to start?"

"Don't keep going on at me! I'll do it when I'm ready…"

After lunch, a silent meal, punctuated only by polite requests to pass the salt or the cheese, Emily puts on her coat and heads out. Alone in the suddenly silent house, Peter stands at the window watching her retreating back guiltily. He knows he's being unreasonable. Argumentative even. But then so is she. He hates it when she tries to organise him. He goes into the study, looks at the easel, the half-finished oil painting of the Cobb. When this was only their holiday home, Lyme Regis only a distant dream of retirement, he had looked forward to spending more time on painting. But he had never really been any good at it, always a better teacher than an artist, and now he has no appetite for it at all. He sees only the errors: the reflections on the water are all wrong, the clouds unrealistic, the people out of proportion. He searches for his coat among the pile in the hallway, picks up an umbrella and sets off after Emily. She isn't surprised when he catches her up by the Regent Cinema.

"Hang on," she says, putting down her umbrella, diving under his and linking her arm through his.

"I thought we'd have shepherd's pie tonight," she says. "We haven't had it for ages. So if we can go to the Stores first, then we need some fruit and veg. Then we can do Co-op last for the milk on the way back…"

"Okay." He gives the hand under his arm a gentle squeeze. That's the good thing about Emily. No recriminations. No long arguments, no sulks, no having to say sorry or beg forgiveness. That was why he had married her this time around, and not one of his flighty art students like Anusia, his first wife, with her distant Asian heritage, her coffee-coloured skin, almond eyes, chiselled nose and the dead straight, jet black hair he had loved to feel brush against his balls. Their daughter Jasmine is a carbon copy of her, so little of him in her that he sometimes wonders if he is indeed her father, or whether her biological father was one of the many other men Anusia slept with.

"'Do get over it, Petey,' she groaned sarcastically the first time he found out. "Monogamy isn't for people like us. We're free to do what we like...'"

Emily is so different from them she could be another species. Blonde, where they're dark; fair skin, blue eyes, distinctly English colouring. The only similarity is the willowy build that attracted him to her, but Emily is small breasted in the English way, where Anusia was full-bosomed and voluptuous; a figure most women would kill for: big breasts, slim waist, pert bottom.

"Maybe we could have steak tonight," Peter says as they queue at the meat counter.

He raises his eyebrows and she knows he's asking if they can afford it. But they both have good pensions so she says, "Lovely. You choose it."

Emily watches Peter as he points out the steak he wants, and the female assistant behind the counter blushes as he speaks to her. She can't be more than thirty and Peter's old enough to be her father, but he has that effect on women. His hair may be greying, receding at the front, his face lined from too much sunbathing, but his dark eyes are vibrant, his body still firm, his stomach flat (though he never takes any exercise); more importantly, he has charm, he knows how to make a woman feel special. The assistant ('Lucy' it says on the badge above her left breast) is wearing an unflattering, pink, nylon overall, but it skims tightly over her bust and hips, gaping slightly at the front when she moves. Peter's gaze slides over her body,

4

comes to rest on the rounded cleavage that shows when she bends forward. "This okay?" she asks.

"Very nice," he says. His meaning is obvious and the woman's blush deepens.

Emily allows him this innocent flirtation. She might have been jealous at one time, but they have been together twenty years now. She knows him. He likes to flirt, and she knows he wouldn't actually be unfaithful, though he has certainly had plenty of opportunity over the years and his pick of girls from the wild and willing art students he used to teach. So she pretends not to notice the wink he gives the woman on the way out. At least he's in a better mood, and while she hasn't forgotten his earlier outburst and hasn't fully forgiven it, she realises they can't keep bickering all the time like this. They have to try and get on.

They've been like this since they have been down here, not helped by the weather: day after day of rain that leaves them cooped up together in the tiny house, which is so much smaller than their three-storey townhouse in Clifton where they could disappear into rooms miles away from each other. Here, the only room Peter can escape to is what he calls his study, and it's little more than a cupboard under the stairs. Maybe they'll be better when the weather improves and they can go out in the open-top sports car that they convinced themselves they could keep, although they really only need one car and it has to be garaged out of town: only one parking space being allowed per resident in the car parking area behind their block of maisonettes.

Evenings are the best time. Except that they can't talk about what they've been doing all day, they can pretend they've both just come home from work. Peter cooks the steak, then they watch television (a film they recorded earlier), then bed. Peter initiates sex and as he undresses her she wonders if he's fantasising about the woman from the meat counter. The idea is so ridiculous she feels an absurd giggle rise in her throat and has to pretend she's caught her breath. Peter, put off his stride, finds his erection waning, something that happens more often nowadays, and Emily reaches for him, stroking him until he's hard again. He has drunk too much wine at dinner though, and a whisky at bedtime, and he doesn't last long, finishing with one huge grunt. But he's a good lover and he brings her to a shuddering climax with his expert fingers before falling asleep, one arm heavily across her. She pushes him away gently and he grunts again and falls asleep on his back, snoring gently until she nudges him and he turns over and all is quiet.

They sleep badly. Another problem they've had since they retired. Not doing enough during the day to tire themselves out. Peter wakes first, needing a pee. When he goes back to bed he can't settle. Everywhere he turns is uncomfortable. Then his back starts aching. Then his mouth is dry. A cup of tea would help. His stomach rumbles. A cup of tea and a biscuit. He goes downstairs. He's on his second cup and the third chapter of the book he has been reading, and is just thinking of going back to bed when Emily comes downstairs.

"Are you okay?" she asks.

"Hungry and thirsty," he says. "I was just going back up. How about you?"

"Can't sleep, that's all. Another cup of tea?"

He shakes his head. "No, thanks. I'll go back up."

This is the usual pattern. Like ships that pass in the night. She makes the tea, takes it into the sitting room, takes out her book. But her mind wanders. She's worried about Peter. He didn't want to retire. "I'm too young," he said. But he had no choice. The college compulsorily retires everyone at sixty-five. And it's not the sort of job he can go on doing. Not like her friend Annabel's husband, a doctor, who can do locum work.

No, he's retired for good. Emily didn't want to retire either. She's only fifty-seven; she could have gone on for years yet. But this was their long-term plan. She would retire when he did. They would move into their holiday home. Make it their permanent home. They had talked about it for years. Looked forward to it. It was their dream. The reality somehow isn't quite living up to the dream.

★

The next morning she wakes to the sound of Peter putting a cup of tea on her bedside table. She knows he's been up for hours. He still wakes early, however badly he has slept: up and out of bed at six thirty. Forty years of habit hard to break.

"What time is it?" she asks.

"Nine thirty."

"God, I should've been up hours ago."

"Why? Nothing to get up for. It's pouring with rain again."

"I know. But still… I should get up. It's awful staying in bed like this."

They drink their tea, then both doze for a while until Emily, feeling guilty, throws back the bedclothes.

"I'll start breakfast," she says to Peter's sleeping back.

It's another half an hour before he comes down. Breakfast is a leisurely occasion and it's eleven thirty by the time she clears the table.

"We must get into some sort of routine," she says.

"Why?" says Peter. "What does it matter?"

But Emily misses her routine. She had only worked part-time but on her days off, while Peter was safely out of her way, she had put the washing on, then systematically cleaned the house (the kitchen and bathroom on Tuesdays, sitting room and dining room on Thursdays), then gone out to exercise classes in the afternoons. She popped out in her lunch hour for fresh stuff like milk and fruit and veg, and Peter used to come with her on Saturdays to do a big food shop. Here, they have a tiny freezer, scarcely room for more than a couple of loaves of bread and a tub of ice cream. The nearest proper supermarket is in Axminster, fifteen miles away. There's a Tesco Express and a small Co-op, not even a proper butcher's, just the meat counter in the Lyme Stores. She has to go out nearly every day. And with Peter home she never seems to be able to get on with the housework.

"I just need to wipe the table," she says.

He lifts his newspaper up with a sigh. She manoeuvres past him in the tiny kitchen to wipe the other surfaces.

"I'll take it in the other room," he says.

She watches him settle down with the paper, wondering how he can complain about how bored he is and then just sit down and read.

She finishes in the kitchen and takes the damp cloth in to wipe down the surfaces in the sitting room. Then she gets out the Hoover.

"Do you have to do that now?" Peter says as she wheels it in.

"Well, yes. I do. Why not now?"

"It doesn't need doing," he says, looking around.

"I haven't done it for days, Peter. It's a state..."

"Looks fine to me..."

"Not to me."

"You're always fussing around..."

"I'm not! The housework needs doing!"

Determined not to get into another pointless argument, she switches on the Hoover. Peter throws the paper down in a heap and leaves the room.

In his study he switches on the computer, scrolls through

the news items; he spent hours on there this morning while Emily was still in bed and there's nothing new. He opens his folder of photographs. He could edit some of them. But he can't summon up the energy.

"I'm making a cup of tea!" Emily calls. He turns the computer off, wanders into the kitchen. Emily's laptop is on. A pile of post sits next to it.

"The car insurance." Emily gestures to it. He picks up the letter, gasps at the amount.

"I was just about to search for a better quote," Emily says. "You can do it if you like."

"No, you do it. You always do…"

"I don't have to now. You've got time to do it yourself. I only did it because you were working…"

"You'll be better at it. You know what to do…"

"But I've got loads of other things to do."

"Like…?"

"Oh, you know. All those things that annoy you so much. The washing, the house…"

"Okay, okay. But you can still do it."

"But Peter…"

"Look. I don't want to. Okay? I'm fed up with you trying to find me things to do…"

"But you keep saying you're bored…"

"I am! But I don't want to be nagged and ordered around by you as if I was a child! I'll make up my own mind about what I do and when I do it. God, I wish I was back at work…"

"So do I! I'm fed up too! Fed up with you moping around like this! It's not *my* fault you can't find anything to do!"

Her voice breaks on the last few words. Childish tears come to her eyes. She turns away so Peter can't see, busies herself with the kettle and the teacups. When she turns back Peter has disappeared.

She takes his tea into the study, touches his shoulder lightly as she puts it down next to him. He's staring at the computer screen. "Thanks," he says briefly, but not unkindly.

She goes back to the kitchen. *Am I a nag?* she asks herself. She has never asked Peter to do the housework or gone on and on at him about something. But she can't deny they are at loggerheads the whole time. They're not used to being together all the time. If only Peter would *do* something. He needs a hobby. But he has never been a great one for hobbies. He likes photography and spends hours arranging and editing the pictures he takes when they go out, but that's something he does at home here at the computer; he needs something to get him out of the house, to involve him with other people. She had always known it would be a problem. She had tried suggesting things in the past. But Peter's never been a clubby man, no Round Table or Lions or Rotary. He doesn't have a burning desire to raise money for good causes. He's not keen to immerse himself in the town in any way, to be a parish councillor, or school governor, or do any sort of voluntary work. He doesn't play sport or go to the gym.

"You could take up golf," she said once when they were driving past the fantastic sweeping greens of Lyme Regis Golf Club.

"We could get lessons," he said.

"Good idea," she said readily, pleased he hadn't dismissed it out of hand like all her other suggestions; yet her heart sank. This wasn't what she wanted at all. She wanted him to go off on his own, disappear for hours to the golf club like other people's husbands and give her time to herself.

She picks up the letter from the insurance company and turns on her laptop. She's scrolling through the Internet, jotting down names and prices, when Peter comes in with the empty teacup. He leans over her, rests his hand on her shoulder. "Which ones have you done? I'll have a go at it if you like…" he says.

"Okay," she says quickly, too quickly for his liking. He was hoping she might say she would do it herself now she had started it. "Here." She passes the scribbled list of names and quotes to him.

It takes him ages. He hears Emily vacuuming again, wonders irritably why she has to do it day after day like this. Then she runs up and downstairs several times in a row and he hears the washing machine churning. Her voice floats through to him: odd snippets of songs, muttered words as she races from one room to the next. "Where the hell did I leave the spray polish?" Exclamations of annoyance as she knocks her elbow or falls over the vacuum cleaner hose. He hears the back door open, sees her carrying out a basket of washing to peg on the line in the paved yard at the back. Why the hell does she bother? It's dry at the moment, but heavy, grey clouds hang in the sky. It'll rain again soon. Why doesn't she just shove it all in the tumble drier? She'll be running out to get it all in when the rain comes. He had never realised how much she did all the time. She's like a dynamo. She never stops. There's very little for him to do down here: no grass to cut or borders to weed. Oh, he could look for jobs: the window frames could do with painting, the fence needs a coat of creosote, there are weeds growing amongst the paving stones in the yard, and they could do with repointing. But he doesn't want to do any of them. He wants to do what they talked about when they imagined their retirement: take the MGB out, drive around with the top off, visit little villages, walk on the cliffs, have lunch in a pub. In that perfect dream it never rained; Emily didn't need to do all those hundred and one things she seemed to need to do that he had never known about before, and he very definitely wouldn't have been bored and frustrated, lacking any purpose or motivation, too dejected to think of doing anything at all, except maybe sitting and reading.

The car insurance websites blur in front of his eyes. He minimises them, goes on to Google Earth, zooms in on Europe. Maybe he and Emily could take the sports car on a rally, over on the ferry, drive down through France and Germany. The cameras show blue skies, sunshine, wide open roads…

"How's it going?" He jumps as Emily comes in, quickly minimises Google Earth, gazes at Direct Line Insurance.

"Bloody awful," he replies, grumpily. "It's a minefield…"

"Which ones have you done? D'you want me to finish off?"

"No, no!" he snaps. "I'll do it myself. Don't keep hassling me."

"Okay, okay. Lunch in ten minutes…? Homemade soup…"

She's just thinking of calling him again when he appears.

"All done," he says proudly.

"What. You've paid?"

"No, I've got some quotes for you. I put both cars in my name. It was easier."

"But what about my no claims bonus? You always said I have to have my own insurance on the Audi so I can build up my no claims discount…"

"You mean I've done all that work for nothing?"

"No. It's just the Audi you'll need to do again."

"Well, you can do it yourself next time…"

He walks out of the room. Emily feels a pang of pity for him. Poor Peter. He tried so hard.

"Peter…" she calls after him. No reply. She turns the heat down under the soup, goes out into the hallway. "Peter!" she calls more loudly. "The soup will be spoilt!"

Peter pretends he can't hear her. He stares morosely at the

blank computer screen. Emily comes in. "Lunch is ready," she says. "Come on." She puts her arm around his shoulder. He throws it off impatiently.

"I'm not a child!" he snaps.

"Sorry."

"You're treating me like some sort of imbecile!"

"I'm not. Look, let me have a look at the quotes. I'll ring up this afternoon. It's easier on the phone."

"Well, why did I have to spend hours online then?"

"I always do that first. Just to get some quotes. Then I ring the cheapest. I'll do it, don't worry."

"No, I'll do it. I'm not incapable, you know…"

"I didn't say you were," she says, quickly.

"Well, that's how it sounded." He follows her through to the kitchen. "You're more used to it, that's all," he says defensively. "You know what to do…"

"I know," she says, again. "It's just you've always said…"

"I know what I've always said," he snaps. "I forgot, okay? I haven't done it for ages."

"Okay. You do it." But she sounds doubtful.

"You don't trust me."

"Don't be silly."

"You think I'll get it wrong."

"I don't. It's just…"

"Just?"

"Just, like you said, I'm more used to it nowadays. I just thought I could check it over."

He says nothing. He feels stupid. Old and stupid. Useless. At least in the old days he could contribute something. He earned a good salary. He worked full-time. He could justify leaving everything else to Emily to do. She only worked three days a week. She had time. He didn't. He hadn't realised just how much she had taken over. He scarcely knew the state of their bank account or their savings; certainly didn't know how much pension they were both getting. It was Emily the accountant spoke to when they went through their pensions; Emily the financial advisor dealt with at their six-monthly reviews. He could take an interest, *should* take an interest, but finances had never interested him. As far as he was concerned, Emily could do the lot.

They finish lunch. Peter helps Emily clear the table and stack the dishwasher, then he goes back to the study. She wipes the table down, and is just mixing margarine and sugar for a chocolate cake when he comes back in.

"Here," he says. "I've rung them. £500 cheaper. Look. With the Audi in your name. They're emailing it through…"

She puts the wooden spoon down, reads it through. "It's fine," she says, resisting the temptation to add, "Well done!" She watches him as he takes back the piece of paper and folds it up, that same wave of pity and love washing through her. When he's gone though she feels a sudden stab of impatience. Is she losing respect for Peter? She had never realised how lazy he is; how willing to use work as an excuse not to do the things he doesn't want to do. Annoyance follows swiftly on from impatience. It isn't as if he didn't know he was going to retire. He could make a bit of an effort. She shouldn't have to nag him. Instead of sitting around doing nothing he could find something to do, something to channel his energies into, something, anything that would get him out of the house.

Chapter Two

Things improve, of course, as they have to. Not instantly, but gradually, imperceptibly, the way things do in any relationship, in any situation. Peter stops waking up at six thirty, expecting the alarm to go off for work. They both stop getting up in the middle of the night. They establish a routine of sorts. Peter's still up before Emily and brings her a cup of tea around eight thirty. Then they lie in bed for half an hour or so while Emily dozes and Peter reads the paper. They linger over breakfast and it's often gone ten before they've finished. After that, Peter sits down with the paper or a book, or goes into the study to spend hours on the computer while Emily does the housework and the washing, checks the emails and deals with any post. After the business with the car insurance she hasn't bothered to involve Peter again and he leaves her to make any telephone calls, book the cars in for servicing and MOTs, pay the bills and sort out the direct debits.

She takes him in a cup of coffee and a biscuit around eleven thirty. If he's not reading, he's either editing photos, or on Google Earth or just browsing aimlessly, looking for websites or news stories that take his fancy. She finds it incredible the way he can while away the hours doing so little. But he seems happy enough, even though it irks her, especially when she thinks of all the hundred and one things she could find for him to do, things he said he would do when he retired, like painting the window frames, clearing out the attic, sorting out the piles of motoring magazines he insisted they bring with them, and she doesn't dare say anything in case it leads to another row. Maybe he'll do it when he gets bored enough.

Peter feels honour-bound to offer to help with the housework. Like all couples, they have always had certain chores, and not always the most obvious ones. Peter always makes the bed; she empties the bins and puts them out for the weekly collection, something she did in Bristol because the bin men came while Peter was out at work. She always brought them back in as well, having given up asking Peter to do it, and fed up with the sight of the bins standing at a drunken angle on the roadside long after everyone else had taken theirs in.

Down here, there's the recycling to contend with as well, something she never used to bother with in Bristol, easing her environmental conscience only by rinsing and putting out wine bottles and plastic milk containers. Now she's retired, however, she feels honour-bound to fill the different coloured and sized tubs supplied by the council with carefully sorted bags of paper and card, tins and foil. Peter never knows what to throw out and what to put for recycling, and the odd times he has offered to help he puts everything in the wrong place and she has to go through it again.

When he first suggested, in a sort of half-hearted way, that he could run the Hoover around, Emily jumped at it, but she couldn't believe it when she saw him winding up the hose and putting it away.

"You finished already?" she said.

"Well, it doesn't take long, does it?"

"Okay," she said, doubtfully. "Thanks for doing it."

Peter disappeared into the study with a self-satisfied smile and she went into the sitting room. None of the furniture had been moved. She pulled up the rug from in front of the fire: bits of dirt and fluff litter the floor. She sighed and took out the Hoover again.

"What on earth are you doing?"

She jumped as she heard Peter's voice above the sound of the vacuum. She switched it off.

"I've just done that!" he said.

"You didn't move the rug…"

"Why should I need to do that? Who's going to look under the rug?"

"You need to clean under it…" she began.

"Well, don't ask me to do it again!" he snapped. "God, no wonder you're always doing things. Why can't you just relax…?"

But Emily doesn't want to do nothing. She likes being busy. She can fill the day quite happily. This is the life she always promised herself: time to do things properly, not dash around trying to fit everything in around work. She bakes cakes, flapjacks, biscuits; prepares meals from scratch, using fresh vegetables and making pastry for pies; instead of relying on convenience foods like she did when she was working. When she's done the washing, she hangs it out on the line if it's not raining, enjoying the novelty of seeing it blowing in the breeze, rather than throwing it in the tumble drier for speed. She takes it down, folds and sorts it with equal care. Sometimes she has a swift mental image of herself as she does this, remembering how, when she was working, she used to just shove it in any-old-how, as long as it was out of the way. She irons clothes she would never have considered ironing before, sheets and pillowcases even, listening to the radio while she does so: books and plays and programmes she has never heard of before. In between times she goes on Facebook and Twitter, posting and tweeting to keep in touch with all her old friends.

"Alex got that job," she tells Peter.

"How d'you know?" he asks, incredulously.

"Izzie said. On Facebook. If you were on Facebook too you'd know for yourself what was going on with your friends…"

"You can tell me, can't you?" Peter says. He can't understand what it is with women. They always need to know everything. If Alex wanted to tell him about the job, he would ring him.

They go out most afternoons, Emily doing her best to ignore Peter's grumbles about the rain. If they don't have shopping to do they walk by the brook that runs along the end of the road, or brave the crowds on the seafront. Lyme Regis in the summer, even in a rainy summer, is chock full of visitors. Nowhere to park in town, the shops full of people aimlessly wandering, looking at nothing in particular, dragging moaning children along with them. "I'm bored, Mum! Can we go back to the flat? We can watch telly…" The gift shops are worst, but even the backstreets are bad, with the more intrepid visitors exploring the parts of Lyme others don't find: the Mill with its artists' galleries and the quaint little backstreets. Even the supermarkets are horrendous, with long queues of holidaymakers stocking up on provisions for their holiday homes. Emily watches one couple as they stand looking at the cheese.

"You're not going to get the same choice down here…" the woman is laughing. "This'll do. We're only here for a few days…"

They could be her and Peter a few years back. What made them decide that a few days in Lyme Regis once or twice a year wasn't enough? They often joked, in that romantic way people do, about 'retiring to the seaside', but when did it become more than a joke? Which one of them said, "We could, you know…"? When exactly did that become a very solid plan, then a viable proposition? The final piece fell into place, of course, five years ago when Peter's Aunt Helen, someone he scarcely remembered, let alone ever visited, left him all her money. They had both stared at the solicitor's letter, unbelievingly.

"There must be some mistake," Emily had said, finally.

It wasn't Peter's first inheritance. His family were well off; Peter was an only child and the money his parents had left him, wisely invested, now formed part of their retirement income. If it wasn't for his divorce he would be very comfortable indeed. But Anusia's settlement, coupled with Jasmine's education (at a private school of course, in London, with uniform, sports equipment and expensive school trips) had taken its toll over the years.

But Jasmine was grown up now, an independent woman. This money was Peter's and Emily's, to do with as they wished. And as soon as they were sure the money was theirs they started looking for properties.

They had stayed in many and varied places over the years they had been coming here: different hotels and Bed and Breakfasts, even the Alexandra on one wedding anniversary, before moving on to holiday apartments, Emily had always seen them retiring to one of the quaint old cottages in the side streets, or maybe an apartment in one of the big, old Georgian houses; but although many of these were rented out for holiday lets, none of them were for sale. For several years running they had rented a lovely old cottage in Sherborne Lane, but it had no parking space. They even asked the letting agents to contact the owner of one rental property they liked the look of to see if they would sell it privately, but the answer was a very definite, 'No'. The houses in town were often noisy in the summer with hordes of holidaymakers passing by all the time, but their money wouldn't stretch to any of the bigger houses further out of town and finally they settled for a tiny, modern terraced house in Mill Green, just off the main tourist area, yet close to the town. Neither of them enjoyed gardening and the garden in Clifton had always been too much for them, but they did like sitting outside in the open air, and this house had a tiny paved yard, big enough for a table and chairs and a rotary washing line and separated from their neighbours by a high fence.

The house was like a doll's house in comparison to their townhouse in Clifton, with an open-plan sitting and dining room downstairs and two bedrooms upstairs, one with an en-suite shower room, and Emily was always telling Peter how easy it was to keep clean. But that was when it was a holiday home and the longest they stayed there was a week. Now they're actually living here, with all their books and possessions crammed into the tiny house, the least thing out of place shows up glaringly, and she's forever picking up Peter's newspapers and books, magazines and odd bits of paper he leaves lying around, to make it look better.

Their holiday visits to Lyme had always been carefully planned in line with the weather forecast and although they didn't expect good weather the whole year round, it's unfortunate that their retirement has coincided with one of the wettest summers on record. There are, however, the odd few days when Peter wakes early to sunshine shafting in through the gaps in the tops of the curtains.

He wakes Emily and they eschew early morning tea, breakfast speedily with the set routine honed from years of going to work, and walk briskly up to the top of town where the MGB is garaged. It's not just the steep climb that makes Peter's heart beat faster. He's in his element. He loves this car with a passion only understandable to someone with the same fervour. He unlocks the garage doors, runs his hand over the bonnet. The engine starts with a low rumble that never fails to send a thrill through him. He reverses it out, parks next to

Emily so she can pack the boot with the walking boots and waterproofs they've brought in case it rains.

If every day could be like this Peter would be happy. This is the life he had pictured for retirement on the rare occasions he ever thought of retirement: cruising along the open road, blue sky above them, the sights and sounds and smells of the countryside all around them. He looks over at Emily: she has a peaked cap pulled low on her head and her sunglasses on, but he can see she's happy, relaxed. She feels his eyes on her, smiles across at him. They revisit the places they've always visited: Beer and Branscombe, Exmouth, Forde Abbey. They stop for morning coffee then head off for a walk. There's something about the steady pace of walking that lends itself to intimacy. Emily hangs on to Peter's arm. They talk and talk, often over and over the same subjects: the house, holidays, Jasmine, the friends they miss from work. Then Peter says, as he always does, how he would like to have worked for longer and she reminds him he had no choice. She asks him if he's getting used to retirement. He says he is, but she knows he's only saying it to keep her happy. "I love this," he says, waving his arm around expansively to take in the swathe of Exmoor, the sweeping hills, the yellow gorse, the low hum of the bees, the birds wheeling overhead in the blue sky, "and the drive over here…" At this point, he starts talking about the car, about how well it's going and the miles per gallon, and how it's well worth keeping it and Emily's mind wanders off. She's wondering how she can bring the subject back around to retirement. This is the perfect time to broach the idea of a hobby, an interest, voluntary work or the Rotary Club. But all too soon Peter's started talking about something else and the moment has passed.

Some afternoons, when it's dreary and wet and there's really no reason to venture out, Peter switches the television on. Emily always feels guilty watching daytime TV. It strikes her as the province of the proverbial bored housewife, or the old or ill or infirm. Watching the lunchtime news is just about acceptable, but sitting down in the afternoons for two hours feels like a waste of time. Peter, however, has no such qualms. "There's a *Poirot* on at three," he says. Or a *Bergerac* or *Lovejoy*.

"I was going to read my book..." she says.

"I've been reading all morning," Peter says. "I can't do any more. Come and watch this with me..." He holds out his hand. "We used to love it..."

Emily gives in. And there's no doubt it's pleasant in their cosy little sitting room. It's a cool summer as well as a wet one and the gas fire is turned on low. It flickers gently, the curtains are drawn and she cuddles up to Peter on the sofa, leaning her head on his shoulder. Presently, however, she begins to feel bored. The programme is hopelessly out of date, badly acted and badly directed. Emily longs to be doing something else. She thinks about getting her book but she can't read while the television is on, and there's nowhere else to go except the kitchen or the bedroom, and anyway, Peter likes her with him so she sits and watches it.

"God, that was awful!" Peter says afterwards. "How did we ever use to watch it?" But Peter's memory is short, he is more tolerant than she is and two days later he's suggesting watching another one. He enjoys sitting there with Emily. It's the only way he can get her attention during the day. If they read together, she sits away from him; he doesn't dare talk for fear of interrupting what she's reading. This sort of mindless pap deserves no real attention; it doesn't matter if they miss a bit while they're talking. There's a closeness that comes from complaining about it together. They can laugh at the ancient computers, the mobile phones the size of house bricks, the baggy trousers and long sideburns of the men, the A-line skirts and big hair of the women. And Emily leans against him; he can smell her hair. He takes her hand; her fingers link with his. Sometimes, if he's lucky, when the programme finishes and he presses the remote off, she doesn't leap up immediately to put the kettle on or take the washing out of the machine, she stays leaning against him. He pulls her closer, kisses her head. He senses her desire. She lifts her face. His mouth finds hers. This is another good thing about Emily. She has no set idea about when and where to have sex. He knew she would be like that the moment he met her. He watched her move. She had the easy fluidity of a cat. He could tell she was comfortable in her body, happy in her sexuality. She's always told him if she needs an orgasm. She keeps a vibrator in her bedside drawer. They often use it together, but if he's ill or worried, or not in the right mood for some reason, she'll happily use it with or without him there. So while he would prefer to have her naked in their super-king-sized bed, or dressed up in some outfit they've chosen together to act out some fantasy, he's not going to let this opportunity pass. He lifts the baggy t-shirt she's wearing and unhooks the white bra so her breasts fall free, slides his hand under the waistband of the shapeless jeans and inside the stripy cotton knickers. She moans, thrusts herself against his hand.

"Wait…" she gasps, standing up and shimmying them off her hips with a laugh and a little pretend half-dance, half-wiggle of her hips. She pulls the knickers off, pushes him back on the sofa, kneels astride him. He grabs her hands. They struggle together. He groans. She grinds herself against his erection. He grabs her breasts, feeling the nipples hard in his fingers. She reaches up, peels off her top, throws it aside, but leaves the bra dangling from her shoulders. Her breasts look bigger like this, leaning above him. She's magnificent, a sexual animal writhing against him. Emily relishes the power. Peter's erection is hard against her. He's trapped under her. She's close to coming, but she wants it to last. She edges down the sofa, unzips Peter's jeans. He tries to get out of them, but she pushes him back, reaches inside, draws him out, takes him in her mouth. "Oh God…" he groans, holding her head. "Not too much. I'll come too soon…" She takes her head away and in one swift moment she's astride him; her tightness enfolds him. He grabs her hips, her breasts that swing above him, watches himself pound into her. It's too much and he comes with a huge bellow, followed almost immediately by her cry as her orgasm spasms around him. "Ssshh…" he says, holding her convulsing body. They giggle as she gets dressed.

"That'll give the neighbours something to talk about," she says, zipping up her jeans.

"You were louder than me," he says.

They haven't even kissed. He reaches for her. She returns his kiss briefly then moves away. "Cup of tea?" she says. He watches her go admiringly, astonished as usual by the swift transformation from whore to dutiful wife. He'd forgive her any amount of nagging, any amount of trying to organise him, any amount of housewifely fastidiousness, just for this. He knows he's lucky. None of his friends have a wife like his. Their wives are staid women in their sixties, with sensible haircuts, sensible clothes, sensible shoes. When she's not in the baggy clothes she wears around the house, Emily dresses like a twenty-year-old: fitted tops, leggings, tight jeans or short skirts with black tights that look far sexier than she realises. With her bobbed hair and tall, slender build, she could pass for ten years younger, fifteen even. Men turn and look, women too, envious of her firm body, slim waist, long legs.

Emily likes to look good. She stopped sunbathing when she found out how bad it was for the skin. Now she has a spray tan at the start of the summer, topping it up with lotion herself when it starts to fade. She looks after herself. She abhors fatness. She weighs herself regularly. Naturally slim anyway, she's still careful about what she eats: homemade flapjacks instead of cakes; no biscuits, half the amount of potatoes or pasta she puts on Peter's plate; one slice less of bread or toast. She likes to keep fit and toned. They've been walking regularly, but she's missed her usual exercise classes and she's looking forward to September and the start of a new term.

"I'm off to bed," she tells Peter one night.

He looks at the clock in surprise. "You got a headache or something?"

"No. I've got to be up early. Zumba. I told you."

The alarm goes off at seven thirty. Peter nudges her, just like he did every morning when they were working.

"Oh God..." she groans. "Why did I decide to do a morning class?"

"Don't go," Peter says. "It's raining. Stay here with me..." He snuggles up to her.

She returns the hug, briefly. "I must," she says, firmly.

"Why?" he laughs, pulling her closer.

"I want to..."

But her voice lacks conviction. It's so tempting to stay here, warm and cosy in bed. Behind the drawn curtains she can see the grey light that signals another dull day, and she can hear the rain pattering on the skylight of the shower room. With a herculean effort she throws back the duvet, ignoring the cold draught on her bare legs and heads for the bathroom.

"You don't have to get up," she says to Peter's humped form in bed. But he does, of course. When they were working he was always better at getting up than she was. Out of bed with the alarm, straight to the bathroom, then down at the breakfast table, kettle on, cereals ready, while she was still struggling around, half-asleep.

And once she's up it's not too bad. It's hardly early anyway and the class doesn't start till nine. It's nothing compared to the tight schedule they used to run to in the old days.

"What time will you be back?" Peter looks up from his book to ask.

"Ten fifteen. Ten thirty…?"

It's a good ten-minute walk to the church hall where the Zumba class is being held. She can hear the pound of the music as she turns the corner. She's nervous. She won't know anyone. The routines will be different. She was used to her other instructor. She may not like this one.

Emily hadn't known what to wear. In her last class people wore anything from exercise kit to dancewear. Emily has come to dance late in life, never having done ballet or any sort of dance at school, her parents believing that drama and singing were more important in her development, but she's always loved the idea of dancing and she's worn the flared dance skirt and leggings she used to wear to her previous classes and brought a belly dance scarf with her. No one else is dressed like her; in fact, everyone else is in baggy t-shirts and loose tracksuit bottoms, some so crumpled it looks like they've been sleeping in them. Emily doesn't mind, though; she's old enough now not to give a damn what anyone else thinks, and she takes out her jangly belly dance scarf from her bag and ties it around her hips. A few people glance curiously at her but no one comes over and speaks. They all know each other, of course, and stand around in knots of twos or threes, chattering non-stop in the way that women do. Snippets of conversation float over to Emily… "I said to him, I don't know what you're moaning about. I'm the one who should be complaining…", "Don't forget that meeting on Thursday…", "I was going to put my washing out this morning before I came but look at it again…". Conversations that cut across each other in that breathless way of women when they're talking together, hardly pausing to wait for a reply, yet knowing afterwards exactly what was said. This is what Emily has missed, that peculiar female friendship that men find so hard to understand.

She's relieved to see that most of the women are her age; a brave few are older like the slightly stooped, silver-haired lady she sees, the only one apart from her who has also tied a scarf around her, though it's round her waist rather than her hips. She's talking to a plump, grey-haired woman. They must both be in their seventies. It was like this in her last class, presumably like this in most daytime classes, the evening classes being the province of the younger working women, and the instructor usually tailors her class accordingly: fewer up tempo numbers, more salsa and jazz dance. There's the inevitable 'YMCA' and Abba songs.

The instructor (Tiffany, she remembers from the website) is up at the front of the room, checking her choreography notes. She speaks briefly to a couple of the women who wander over to her, but although she glances at Emily, she doesn't come over and talk to her. She's a strongly built, muscular girl, around mid-thirties, her peroxide-blonde hair scraped back in a tight ponytail, and wearing a skimpy t-shirt and tracksuit bottoms that cling to her well-sculpted bottom and tight thighs.

"Right, ladies. Let's get started!" she booms, suddenly. She has a strong northern accent. "Single, single, double!" she bellows. "Now, cha, cha, cha!"

Emily struggles with the new routine, going left instead of right, laughing as she bumps into people, and afterwards a couple of women speak to her. "Angela," one of them introduces herself, "and Kathy." She gestures to the almost-identical woman next to her. They're probably not much older than Emily, with bobbed hair like hers, but theirs is perfectly set in place with hairspray and has hardly moved during their half-hearted exertions; whereas Emily's is tousled, damp at the back of her neck and sticking to the top of her forehead with sweat. They have the lined faces of people who have sunbathed too much, and their eyes are blue-eyeshadowed and black-eyelinered in the way of women who were teenagers in the sixties. Emily feels years and years younger. The girls in her office were all younger than her. She didn't realise how much she'd become used to their youth. These women seem old and staid. But at least it's someone to be friendly with, and she waves goodbye cheerily as she sets off down the road, with an exhilaration that hasn't just come from the physical exercise. It's been good going out on her own, getting out of the house for a while, doing something different, something that doesn't involve Peter, she realises guiltily.

She lets herself back in. "I'm home!" she calls out.

Peter is still sitting in the same chair as he was when she left him, reading the same book.

"Haven't you moved since I've been gone?" she laughs.

Of course Peter has. He's been on the computer; he's been out to the car to check the oil; he thought about cleaning the windows but decided against it when it started raining again, but he made damn sure he was back in the same place when Emily came home. He hates her going out without him. If he makes her feel guilty enough, maybe she'll stay in all the time and keep him company.

But two days later she's off again. "Pilates," she says. "I'll be back around eleven."

The Pilates class is at the top of the town in Woodmead Hall, up a steep hill that leaves Emily puffed out and reminds her how unfit she is. Everyone here is older than her too, but a woman called Pam introduces herself in a friendly way. She's a retired schoolteacher. "I hate not feeling useful," she confides quickly in the way women do even when they first meet. "But I've found some voluntary work…"

Emily's interest quickens. She's always wanted to do voluntary work of some kind.

"Where?" she asks.

"At the local school."

Her heart falls again. Of course. Pam was a teacher. But Emily knows nothing about children. "Doesn't your husband mind you going out to things?" she asks.

Pam laughs. "He's never in himself!"

Emily's mind flies to Peter, probably still sitting where she left him, reading a book.

"What does he find to do?"

"Golf. Rotary. Endless committee meetings…"

Peter doesn't even go to the pub. He's never said anything, but she wonders if he's missing male company.

As she walks back down the hill she rehearses a way to bring up the subject to Peter, but in the end she blurts it out, as she often does, scarcely aware she was going to say it at all.

"Pam's husband is in Rotary."

"Really?" he says, mildly.

"They meet on Thursdays at the Pilot Boat Inn. You know. On the front. Six o'clock. It's only once a fortnight."

"Emily…" he sighs.

"I just thought…"

"I know what you thought. I don't like men's clubs. You know I don't."

"I just thought it would give you something to do."

"I don't need you to organise me. I'll sort myself out," he says firmly.

★

Late September brings a week of sunshine: the Indian summer everyone had hoped for. Day after day they wake to blue skies and sunshine, like being on holiday in some foreign clime. Lyme Regis in September is the province of the retired: the silver-haired brigade, slow-moving, easy-going; or young couples with toddlers and babies, pushchairs and prams blocking the narrow pavements. The sunshine brings a rash of last-minute visitors, everyone in a good mood, 'Good Mornings' called out by strangers, smiles as people move out of the way, casual conversations in shops.

Woken by the early morning sunshine, Emily looks at the clock. Half past seven. No need to get up yet, even though it's Pilates today. She doesn't have to look to know that Peter is already up. She can feel the emptiness of the bed next to her, and now she listens carefully she can hear the clink of teacups, the sound of the kettle boiling. She stretches, turns over, listens to the other sounds that drift to her ears: the distant cry of seagulls, the coo of the nearer pigeons on the rooftops, the twittering of smaller birds. A dog barks, once, twice, then stops at the sharp command of a man's voice; a car door opens, then clicks shut, the engine starts, the sound disappears up the road. All so different from the noises she used to hear in the city: the constant swoosh of passing cars, the distant hum of constant traffic, the voices of passers-by, the constant raucous crowing of crows in the tall trees opposite, almost drowning out the cheeping of the sparrows.

The door opens. "I know it's early," Peter says. "But I thought you'd like to go out somewhere…"

"I've got Pilates."

"D'you have to go? It's such a lovely day…"

"I'll be back at eleven. We can go out then…"

"But it's so late by then. The roads will be busy."

"I want to go, Peter. It's a commitment. Anyway, we went

out yesterday. And we can go tomorrow. I've got things to do in the house…" She thinks of the pile of washing she didn't have time to do yesterday because they went out; the kitchen floor that needs cleaning.

"You've always got things to do," he says grumpily. "Can't they wait till another day?"

"They build up. Then it's worse. You don't understand."

"No. I don't."

They drink their tea in silence, have breakfast in silence.

"We can go for a walk later on," she says as she kisses him goodbye. "After lunch maybe, when I've done the washing and things. There's plenty of time."

"It's not the same," he says.

"Come on, Peter," she wheedles, slipping her arm through his. "We used to love walking around the town when we first came here. We didn't spend all our time out in the car. We can walk down the front, out on the Cobb, buy an ice cream…"

"Okay," he concedes.

But she's only buying time. The next day and the next she wakes to blue skies and sunshine, to Peter raring to go out somewhere, until she finds herself longing for dull weather, for rain even, so they can stay at home.

★

September turns to October. The clocks go back. The temperature drops. Blue skies turn to grey. Peter is fed up. He likes the sunshine, the excuse to be out somewhere. He hates being cooped up at home.

"At least it's not raining," says Emily, ever the optimist.

He watches her leave for a class one day: Pilates or Zumba, he can't remember which. It's okay for her. Always something to do. He stays staring out of the window unseeingly, long

31

after she's disappeared down the road. He's restless. He tries to read a book, but loses concentration. Nothing in the paper interests him. He can't bring himself to look at the unfinished painting he's been working on. He can't be bothered to do any work on his photos. He opens the back door, steps out onto the tiny terrace at the back of the house, breathes the air. Always that slightly salty tang in Lyme Regis, the slight breeze and a freshness that comes from being near the sea. Seagulls wheel overhead. He raises his head to look at them. Lowers it again to the ground. Weeds poke up from amongst the paving stones at his feet. That's something he could do.

He's still on his knees, prising out the weeds from between the slabs, when the back door opens and Emily appears.

"Peter!" she says incredulously. "What're you doing?"

"Spot of weeding," he says, smiling up at her.

"In those clothes?"

"For God's sake, Emily!"

"But you'll destroy them! You could've got changed!"

"It's hardly a dirty job!"

"Yes, it is! Look at you! We've only just bought those jeans! You'll wear them out!"

"Don't treat me like a child, Emily!" he snaps. "I'll wear what I bloody like! You must stop bossing me around!"

He throws the trowel down, gets up and stalks past her. He'd been going to clean the windows as well. Emily had been saying for ages that they needed doing. It was going to be a surprise. He's not going to do it now though. Serve her right. Pay her back for nagging him.

They spend the rest of the morning avoiding each other. When Emily goes to hang the washing out, the trowel, Peter's gardening gloves and the pile of weeds is still thrown down where he left them. She picks them up with a sigh, tidies everything away.

At lunchtime she tries to start a conversation, but Peter replies in monosyllables. He's fed up. Fed up with everything. With the house. With life. With Emily. Especially with Emily. When did the balance of power change in their relationship? What makes her feel she can order him around? It can only be because she feels he's no longer the breadwinner. He feels out of control. But he's not going to let her get away with it. He'll show her who's in charge, show her he's as much of a man as he's always been.

For two whole days he scarcely speaks to her. He knows he's hurting her. It shows on her pale face, her tense body, the way she jumps away from him if they get too close in the kitchen or on the sofa or in bed at night. She avoids him as much as possible in the tiny house. Several times she tries to break down the wall of silence. She puts her arm around his shoulders, "Come on, Peter," she says. "Don't be silly." But he pushes her away. He knows he's being childish, but he can't help it.

Emily starts waking up at night again. She goes on to her laptop, searches for *Retirement. Difficulty*. But although Google helpfully tells her that everyone struggles to get used to their new lifestyle, men more than women, it doesn't tell her how to deal with it. *It's important to have a hobby or interest,* it says. *Join a club or society. Take up a sport. Do some voluntary work.*

"I *know* that!" she mutters at the screen. But it doesn't tell her what to do with the recalcitrant husband who won't do anything; the husband unable to face up to the inevitable; the husband in permanent denial.

She starts to get headaches, day after day, culminating one day in a blinding migraine. Leaving her lying in bed, a cold flannel on her forehead, a bowl on the floor next to her in case she's sick, Peter knows it's his fault. Forced into the role of comforter, he berates himself. Where before she irritated him, now he misses her. The house is so quiet without her rushing around the place. He has to get his own lunch. He finds eggs in the cupboard, tins of beans, a hard-as-nails sandwich container of leek and potato soup in the freezer, but all these things require effort, the synchronisation of heat and toaster, microwaves and hobs. It's all too much to think about and he settles for toast and Bovril instead. Even then, he manages to burn the first piece while he's making the tea and the second piece goes cold while he's eating the first. The afternoon is worse than the morning. It's a lovely day but he can't go out, even to the patio, in case she needs him. He turns the television on and moves his chair up close so he doesn't disturb her. He creeps around from room to room, listening at the foot of the stairs for any movement, rushing up when he hears her go to the loo to ask if she'd like a cup of tea.

He knows he should apologise, make it up to her by being extra nice. But it's not easy to come down off his high horse, and the next day, as Emily struggles around with post-migraine listlessness, they're still scarcely speaking.

Emily's the type who looks better with a bit of make-up. Her eyes without mascara and eye shadow are small and piggy, her hair is sticking up all over the place.

"Leave that. I'll do it," he says, seeing her wiping the surfaces.

"I don't know how you manage to get tea on every single surface," she says. Too late, she realises this is just the sort of thing he calls nagging. She waits, but he says nothing.

"I'm sorry, Peter," she says in a small voice. "I know you think I'm nagging all the time. I don't mean to. I don't mean it…" She starts crying. Her head starts to pound again.

"Don't," he says, putting his arms around her. "You'll bring your migraine back."

He's no longer cross. She can hear it in his voice. He could say sorry, should say sorry. But it doesn't matter. Everything's all right again.

Chapter Three

"We bicker all the time," Emily tells Grace.

"You're not used to being together so much," Grace says. "I'm sure it'll get easier."

"And Peter's drinking more. Five bottles of wine in the recycling bin last week. And he has a whisky every night…"

She feels guilty even as she says it. She's always hated women who moan about their men. But she's never really had to before. And Grace is the only one she can tell. Old school friends never mind what they say to each other. Secrets are safe in their hands.

"They say men always find it hard when they first retire," Grace is saying. "But Peter's got plenty of hobbies, hasn't he? His painting, his photography…"

"He scarcely seems to touch them." Then she adds in fairness, "Well, okay, he does sometimes, but mostly he reads."

"Nothing wrong with that. Wish I had more time to read…"

"But it's all so insular. He needs to get out more…" They both laugh at the well-worn cliché, but then, "No. I'm serious," Emily says. "He doesn't see anyone apart from me. He loves people. He needs to do something more sociable. But if I suggest anything he just says I'm nagging…"

She drops her voice as the men walking on ahead slow down to let them catch up. Matt and Grace have come down for the weekend. Matt is Grace's second husband, an optician like her. They met at some sort of optical conference. Grace was already divorced and Matt's marriage was all but over.

Four months later when his wife found out, then walked out, Grace moved in. They married as soon as his divorce came through. They have two children, Kate and Jack. Kate's just left university; Jack is in his first year.

Grace is small and blonde; her hair cut professionally short for work. Always bigger than Emily, she has never lost what she calls her 'baby weight': her thighs bulge in the designer jeans she bought especially for her trip to the country, and she puffs as she tries to keep up with Emily. Matt is tall and slim, broad-shouldered. He has gentle, brown eyes. His hair, jet black when they first knew him, is now iron grey; a crew cut tight to his head.

Weekends with Matt and Grace always follow a set pattern. The men sit and have a drink on the Friday evening while Grace helps Emily with dinner or vice versa, Saturday is always a walk somewhere and Sunday they have lunch in a pub to save more cooking. Grace and Emily chat non-stop in that way that close friends do: conversations that dart backwards and forwards, repeating and overlapping, but never flagging. It's lucky that Matt and Peter get on so well, somehow finding enough common ground to fill their time while the women talk. Unlucky that living in London and working most Saturdays (optics being akin to retail in that respect), they see so little of each other.

Emily feels better when Grace has gone. It's good to have a real friend, someone she can talk to properly. The friends she has made in her classes aren't at all the same thing. Angela and Kathy are too involved with each other to bother much with her, though they do say hello when they see her. There are, however, a couple of other women she quite likes: Andrea, who is probably younger than her, but looks older: a blonde-haired, blue-eyed, plumpish woman, who tells her she works part-time, and whose husband is never in. "I'm a fishing widow!" she jokes. She seems to have plenty of friends, but most of them are working and she invites Emily to coffee, to go out for a walk with her, or "A look around the shops sometime, when your husband's out." Emily doesn't like to say Peter's never out and he would hate it if she went out even more than she already does.

Then there's Felicity, the reserved mousy-looking type of middle-aged woman, with dead-straight hair and no make-up who Emily wouldn't normally have much to do with. But she's new to the Zumba group as well and somehow she and Emily pair up together. She soon realises, however, that she's the type who's stronger than she appears at first knowing. She lived in America and was some sort of research scientist before she gave up work. Her husband, like Peter, is recently retired and is also finding it hard to adapt. "If only there was some sort of freelance work he could do," she says. "He really misses work."

"What did he do?" Emily asks.

"University lecturer."

"Same as Peter!" Emily says. "Maybe we should get them together." But even as she says it she knows it will never work. Men don't like being teamed up with people they don't know. Like children, they like to make their own friends, not be engineered into a friendship someone else has decided will be good for them.

And in Pilates she has Pam and another woman called Kate, a divorcee who gives away very little about her personal life but manages to be friendly nonetheless; always interested in whatever anyone else has been doing. Emily also gets on well with the instructor herself, Sarah, a slim, pretty, well-toned blonde girl in about her thirties, who makes a point of making everyone feel welcome to her class. Not so Tiffany, the Zumba instructor who scarcely speaks to Emily, no matter how hard she tries to make friends with her. Emily suspects her of taking an instant dislike to her, until she notices she's the same with everyone.

Walking back from a class one day she notices how the season has subtly altered again. Autumn is sliding into winter. A few trees still have autumn colours, but many of the leaves have turned from gold to yellow or brown, some have no foliage left at all and fallen leaves litter the ground. She never had time to notice these things before: at this time of year it was dark when she went to work, dark when she came back. And on the days she wasn't working she was always so busy dashing around from one thing to the next, she had no time to notice the passing of the seasons.

As Christmas approaches, Lyme Regis turns into a ghost town. The shops deck their windows with Christmassy things to entice the few holidaymakers who brave a seaside town out of season: the locals from Taunton or Chard, popping down on their days off if it's sunny, who may just be tempted into buying that odd little present for their daughter-in-law or aunt, pleased to tell them they found it, 'in a quaint little shop in a side street in Lyme Regis'.

The season brings the inevitable opening gambit, "What are you doing for Christmas?" from everyone.

"Just the two of us as usual," Emily says lightly to Andrea when she asks.

"Lucky you. I've got an onslaught. The kids and their wives, four grandchildren. Jon's parents to visit. My mum to stay…"

Emily laughs in a semi-sympathetic way, knowing what will come next.

"So when *are* you seeing your family?" Andrea asks.

"Our parents are dead," Emily says. "I've got a brother in Cumbria. But we never see him at Christmas…"

Andrea frowns. "I thought you had a daughter. Jasmine?"

"Step-daughter," Emily corrects her. "Peter's daughter from his first marriage."

"Oh. Sorry," Andrea says, clearly thinking she's put her foot in it.

"No, it's fine. It doesn't matter."

Christmas brings a handful of invitations, to 'drinks' or 'coffee' or 'seasonal nibbles'. Some they can refuse, like the ones from the church and the Lifeboat Association, but Emily feels obliged to accept the ones from Felicity and Andrea.

"Do we have to go?" Peter asks. "I won't know anyone."

"Me neither. But we have to. You know we do."

"What will I wear?"

Peter has a gap in his wardrobe, where casual ends and smart begins. He has nothing that falls into the category of 'Smart Casual'. Not wanting to be underdressed, he decides on smart trousers, an open-necked shirt and a jacket, but feels like he's going to a meeting rather than going out for drinks.

Emily has a similar problem. Most women her age wear long skirts with neat blouses or jumpers. Emily's casual skirts are short to be worn with thick tights and the longer ones, the ones she used to wear to work, make her look like the secretary she was, even worn with a jumper. Jeans look too casual. Leggings too sexy. Finally, she settles on her smartest jeans: black ones, with a long top.

Felicity's party comes first. She and John live in a modern bungalow, suiting the retirement lifestyle they have chosen. It's within walking distance, but it's a cold night and forecast to be icy later and Emily's wearing high-heeled shoes so they decide to drive. "I'll drive home," Emily offers. Peter likes his red wine. He needs it more than she does.

"I'm nervous," she says as they drive over.

"Me too." Peter takes his hand off the wheel to cover hers, and she folds her gloved fingers around his.

They turn into the street. "It must be that one," Emily says. There are lights on in every window and cars line the road outside.

Felicity arrives at the door. They kiss politely. "This is Peter," Emily says. She sees Peter's eyes sweep over Felicity. Although she had told him she was nothing to look at, she can sense his disappointment. He had half-hoped that she was exaggerating and that she might be the sort of attractive, vivacious type he can flirt and have fun with, like Grace and some of Emily's other friends. But he sees nothing in this whey-faced, thin-mouthed woman with her wispy fringe falling over her eyes and her inability to meet his gaze. He scans the room. There are a few women who are quite attractive, nicely made-up with their hair in the ubiquitous bob favoured by women of a certain age. He can only hope Emily knows them. Emily's also looking around. 'Smart Casual' has translated into 'Smart Smart', it seems. The women are all wearing dresses or skirts and tops, some have glittery gold or silver cardigans on; many have dressy jewellery. Emily feels desperately underdressed in her black jeans and plain, long-sleeved jumper, and is glad that at least she wore high heels rather than the flat boots she normally wears with them. Peter fits in better: the men are in blazers and slacks. Most have a tie. One or two are wearing suits.

"You must meet John," Felicity is saying. "Let me find him for you…"

John looks much older than his sixty-five years: balding, slightly stooped. All hopes of him getting on with Peter quickly fade from Emily's mind when she hears him speak. He is slow, hesitant, pedantic, the sort of shy man who picks his words carefully before he says anything. College lecturer he may have been, but it was obviously a role he fell into rather than chose. His speciality turns out to be some sort of obscure science and she sees Peter floundering as they try to find some common ground.

"Oh, there's Pam!" She waves to her. "You must meet her, Peter. Would you excuse us?"

"Of course," John says, looking relieved.

"Pam's husband's in Rotary," she tells Peter as they make their way over.

"So you keep telling me," he says, drily.

David is a bluff military type ("ex-Royal Navy" he tells Peter), equally balding and with a huge stomach that hangs out over the top of the tightly-belted trousers that he has to hoist up frequently. Despite the weekly Pilates, Pam has a similarly over-hanging stomach and Emily finds herself wondering how they ever manage to have sex. His face is rosy and moist. He's wearing a navy jumper under the military-style blazer even though it's stiflingly hot in the room, and Emily sees a smudge of toothpaste on the front. She's surprised Pam hasn't noticed it. Maybe when she does, she'll whisper fiercely into his ear, and then march him off to the kitchen to scrub it off with the corner of a damp tea towel. A similar white smudge lines his bottom lip and bobs up and down as he speaks. Emily stifles a smile and turns to Pam.

David starts off asking Peter about the rugby and whether he plays golf, and when that fails to elicit a response he moves on effortlessly, in that easy way services people do, to safer subjects like the weather and holidays, and what Peter likes to watch on television, steering clear in his practiced way, of controversial subjects like religion and politics.

"You must come along to one of our Rotary meetings," he says.

Peter glances at him swiftly, suspecting Emily and Pam have put him up to it, but David's face shows no sign of it.

"Thank you. I'm a bit busy at present…"

"Of course, of course." David laughs easily. "We're all so busy once we retire. We don't know how we ever found time to work, do we? So what d'you find to do?"

Peter's ready for this. "Oh, I read a fair bit. And we go out in the car, you know. For a drive or a walk. I've got an MGB…"

"Oh yes," David says, vaguely. *Clearly not a car man then*, Peter thinks.

"And I paint. Pictures, I mean." He laughs. "That was what I taught. Art."

"Oh yes. Art. Not something I know much about. But look, we could do with a chap like you in Rotary. There's a lot going on. And the little woman can get involved. We've got an active Inner Wheel Group."

Peter glances quickly at Emily to make sure she hasn't overheard herself being described as 'the little woman'.

★

Andrea's *At Home'* two days later follows a similar pattern. This time Emily has gone prepared in a plain, black knee-length skirt, she used to wear to work, with high-heeled black shoes and a suitably Christmassy bright red jumper with a silk scarf tied round her neck. Many of the same people are there and Peter finds himself agreeing to 'try a round of golf' or 'pop in for a pint' with various men, invitations he knows he will never accept.

"Thank God that's over," he says when they get home.

"Peter…" Emily admonishes him as she unzips her skirt and steps out if it.

"Oh come on, Emily. I know you feel the same."

"But we have to make friends. You know we do. We can't just stay at home like Darby and Joan!"

"I don't see why not…"

Emily has never particularly enjoyed Christmas: a time for children, for families. There must have been a time when it was exciting, enchanting, when there was magic in the air and fun and pleasure, but it's so long ago she can't remember. Her parents made very little of Christmas. There were no parties or get-togethers with cousins and aunts and uncles. No games or charades. No turkey even. "Much too big for the four of us," her mother used to say. Except for the Christmas pudding, crackers and party hats, Christmas lunch was like every other Sunday lunch. Afterwards, the four of them sat down for the annual 'treat' of watching the pantomime and all the usual Christmas shows, which her parents usually dozed through, and that was that for another year.

They gave away the Christmas tree from the house in Clifton when they moved, knowing it would be far too big for the tiny sitting room here, so they go into Taunton one day to buy a small one which Emily decorates minimalistically, with the best of the decorations they brought with them.

They don't bother with big presents. If there's anything they want, like a camera, or a new phone or a laptop, they buy it during the year. There's no point in waiting for Christmas or a birthday. Prompted by copious hints from Emily, Peter buys her a book she wanted and she gives him a DVD. She can remember a time when Peter used to buy her sexy underwear or a new vibrator, a new perfume specially chosen, a silk scarf or a new jumper. She can't remember exactly when he stopped, but she does remember the disappointing feeling she had the first year there was only the one present she had chosen for herself to open on Christmas Day, whereas Peter had a pile of carefully chosen surprises from her. He didn't seem to notice, though, and she waited all day for a surprise present to be produced but it never was.

They ring Jasmine on Christmas Day as usual, calling her mobile as they have no idea where she is.

"Daddy!" she says, delightedly. Peter's heart constricts. He might not see much of her, but she's still his little girl.

"Where are you?" he asks.

"Shaftesbury. Staying with Stasie and Joe. You remember Stasie? Anastasia Lethbridge?"

"Yes, of course," he says. Big girl. Red head. Parents had their own advertising business.

"Ma's here too…"

Peter nearly drops the phone. "I thought she was in the States."

"Daddy!" Jasmine drawls. "She's been back since July. I told you…"

"Yes, of course," he says, hurriedly.

"You're getting senile!" she teases. "How is retirement? Missing all those lovely students of yours?"

Now she even sounds like Anusia, the same hectoring tone, and for a split second it's Anusia's face he sees in his mind, not Jasmine's.

"Not at all," he says, defensively.

"I'm only joking, Daddy," she says more quietly.

"Of course," he says. "What have you been up to then?"

He listens fondly as she reels off a string of events, paying little attention to what she's actually saying. It's just good to hear her happy voice rattling on about this job and that job, the places she's been, people she's met as she's hurtled around. Like her mother in this respect also, Jasmine doesn't believe in a nine-to-five job, a steady lifestyle, a husband or children. The expensive education has led to little more than temping jobs, but she's happy. That's all he cares about.

"Emily would like a word," he says, when she stops talking for long enough.

Emily's heart sinks. She dreads talking to her mercurial step-daughter. She always feels out of her depth. Her life compared to Jasmine's is so parochial. Even when she first knew her as an awkward thirteen-year-old she felt on a different level from her. Poles apart. They will never have anything in common.

"Emmy!" Jasmine enthuses.

Emily feels her insides curling up. She doesn't know why she has to be so gushing. It's hypocritical at best.

"How are you?" she asks, knowing she sounds cold, but not being able to help herself.

"Wonderful!" Jasmine continues in that breathy way she has. "It's fab here. You'd love it…"

Emily knows she wouldn't, but she listens patiently while Jasmine describes the cottage she's staying in, the privations that she finds "so basic, so fundamental": the bathroom with its bare wooden floor, kitchen with its Aga, sitting room with its open fire that has to be lit every day and throws smoke back into the room. "It's hilarious – we have to open all the windows! Then we're freezing again!" Then she starts talking about someone called 'Si'. It's "Si this" and "Si that," until finally Emily feels obliged to ask, "Who's Si?"

"Simon. Simeon Blackwood. The artist, you know. You *must* have heard of him. *Everyone's* talking about him. He's going to paint me." She drops her voice confidentially. "In the nude, of course. He only does nudes. Don't tell Daddy…" she giggles.

"I thought you were seeing someone called Will?"

"Oh, he was a beast!" she exclaims in such a loud voice that Emily has to hold the phone away from her ear. "You'd never believe the things he wanted to do to me!" She lowers her voice to a stage whisper. "I'll tell you when I see you next time. I'll bring Si with me. You'll love him!"

Emily knows instinctively she won't.

45

"Have you heard of him?" she asks Peter when she puts the phone down.

She sees his quick look of concern. "Simeon Blackwood? Yes. But it can't be him. He's my age. Anyway, he…" He stops, his face red.

"He what?" Emily asks.

"Well, he went out with Anusia."

"You mean slept with?"

Of course that's what he means. Emily starts to laugh, then stops when she catches sight of Peter's face. But it's so absurd, and ridiculous, and so typical of the free-and-easy, laissez-faire attitude of mother and daughter.

"Maybe it's not the same one," she says, quickly. But they both know it is. "She'll have to start settling down," she adds, almost to herself. "She's thirty-three. She can't go on living like a teenager forever."

"I don't see why not," Peter observes mildly. "Her mother does."

He hasn't seen Anusia for years, but he knows from the way Jasmine links her name with 'Tony' or 'Geoffrey' or 'Jonathon' that she hasn't changed. Like 'The Bolter' in Nancy Mitford's novels, she's permanently on the lookout for a new man, even when she's just started on the current one.

Luckily, no one has invited them to see in the New Year, and they stay up as usual until midnight, just the two of them: Peter with his red wine and whisky; Emily with just the red wine, waiting for Big Ben on television to chime the hour. Peter just has time to wish her "Happy New Year" and kiss her, when the phone rings.

"Jasmine!" they both say together. No one else ever calls. Peter's parents did, until they became too old and frail. Emily's never had. It wouldn't even occur to Emily's brother who is probably fast asleep in bed.

"Happy New Year!" Jasmine shrieks. In the background Peter can hear loud music, shouting and bursts of laughter.

"I've got some news!" she yells again.

"Oh, yes?" Peter says.

"I'm engaged!"

"What?" he says weakly, glancing quickly at Emily for support, even though she hasn't a clue what Jasmine has said.

"Engaged. To be married. I think you know him. Si. Simeon Blackwood. The artist."

Chapter Four

"It'll never happen," Emily says confidently. "It was just the champagne. The excitement. The heat of the moment. It'll be over in a few weeks. He'll say it was a mistake. Or she will."

Wise Emily. No-nonsense Emily. Practical Emily.

"I wish I could believe you," Peter says, morosely. "You were the one who said it's time she settled down."

Emily laughs. "Hardly 'settling down' though, is it? How old did you say he was?"

Peter shifts uncomfortably in his chair. "Late fifties…?"

"Your age, you said," Emily says in that same no-nonsense tone. "Sixties?"

Peter nods, wordlessly.

"Married before?"

This time he shakes his head. "Women though. Girls," he corrects himself.

"Children?" She laughs at the shocked expression on his face. "I mean, has he got any?"

"Oh, I see. No. Yes. I don't know. Possibly. He's not the family type. If he has got any no one ever hears of them."

"Well, I don't see Jasmine wanting any anyway, do you?"

"Oh God, don't, Emily!" Peter groans. "I don't want to think about it."

He thinks of Simeon, last time he saw him: his lined face; lively, dark eyes; wide smile; bony, artistic fingers; thinks of him kissing Jasmine; touching her. He shudders.

"It won't last," Emily says again, stopping in the middle of clearing the table to put her arm around Peter's shoulder. He leans his head against her.

"You're right. It won't. It can't."

★

Mid-January brings snow. Just for a few days. It seldom lasts long here on the coast. But the temperature remains low. There's a frost every morning for weeks. An icy blast off the sea. They wake each morning to the wind howling around the house, almost drowning out the sound of the seagulls.

"You're not going today, are you?" Peter asks as he sees Emily putting on her jogging bottoms.

"It's only up the road," Emily says.

"But it's icy," he says.

"They'll put grit down, or salt or whatever. I'll be careful. It'll be fine."

It's only Tiffany waiting in the church hall when she gets there.

"Good Christmas?" she asks.

"Yes, thank you," Emily says, politely. "How about you?"

"Good, thanks."

It's the most she's ever said to her and Emily's desperately wondering what else to say when Kathy and Angela appear, their noses and cheeks red, rubbing their hands together and searching for the radiators to put them on.

"God, it's freezing, isn't it?" they say almost simultaneously. "Good Christmas?"

For a while it looks like it may just be the three of them, but then Felicity arrives, then Andrea, rushing in at the last moment. "Sorry. I had to de-ice my car!" she shouts above the loud music.

"There's a talk on jewellery making next Thursday

evening," Felicity says afterwards as they put on their coats and scarves and gloves. "We could go together. You doing anything?"

"I don't think so," Emily says, trying to make it sound as if she and Peter are invited out every evening. "But I'll check with Peter when I get back."

"It's by the girl from the shop in the high street. 'Poppy Fields.' The one with all the jewellery and handbags and vintage stuff in the window. She paints as well…"

Emily knows the shop. She's often stopped to look in the window over the years they've been coming here. She's even been inside a couple of times on the rare occasions Peter's not with her. He hates shops like that, full of bric-a-brac and the sort of eclectic arty stuff they think will appeal to the holidaymakers. Emily thought the paintings quite good actually: watercolours of seascapes. But Peter wasn't interested when she tried to persuade him to have a look at them. "I don't need to see them," he said. "I know exactly what they'll be like. The usual sort of amateurish daubs turned out by some middle-aged woman with nothing else to do, who fancies herself as an artist."

"I think she's quite well known, actually," Emily said. "And her jewellery's beautiful."

All the way home she wonders how she can ask Peter if she can go. She writes it on the calendar and waits for the right moment.

"D'you really want to?" he asks.

"Well, yes. I would like to. You can come with me…"

"No, it'll be all women…"

"I don't see why…"

But he's right. It is. Women 'of a certain age' fill the hall and Emily knows he was right not to come. It's a cold evening and the electric bar heaters on the wall glow red but struggle to take the chill off the air. Emily and Felicity keep their coats on. Felicity unwinds her scarf and takes off her gloves, but Emily keeps hers on.

She picks up the leaflet lying on her chair. *"Poppy James,"* she reads. *"Artist and Bespoke Jewellery Maker."*

Up at the front on the raised dais that passes for a stage, two women fuss around with a laptop and a screen.

"That's her," Felicity says.

It's easy to tell which one. Her hair is dyed dark auburn; it cascades in Pre-Raphaelite waves over her shoulders and down her back. She's wearing a loose, velvet patchwork jacket over a long, black chiffon skirt and heavy, black biking boots. From this distance it's hard to tell her age, but the way she holds herself, thrusting out one hip, throwing back her head and tossing her hair around, makes Emily think she's in her late twenties maybe, old enough to have confidence in herself.

"She's lovely," she says. Immediately, she wishes she hadn't. Felicity's not the sort of woman to say anyone, especially another woman, is lovely. "Who's that with her?" she adds, quickly.

"Suzie Fields. She owns the shop." Felicity lowers her voice. "They say they're... you know..." She reddens and looks away.

Emily looks at them interestedly. What a waste if they are. Poppy could have any man. The other woman though... Wide hips. Short, dark hair. She must be around fifty, but she's wearing the sort of flared floral skirt teamed with a striped jumper that make her look much older. She's not bad-looking actually, with the sort of sharp, spiky face that's striking, might even be called beautiful if only she smiled a bit more. As it is, her face is set; she's the one in charge, the 'man' of the relationship. Poppy the submissive, wifely one. Except she doesn't look particularly submissive. Even as she watches, she sees her snatch a piece of paper away from her, frowning, and the other woman turns away, clearly hurt.

It's Suzie who runs the show, making the introductions. "My colleague Poppy," she booms in a deep, mannish voice that has a strong Kent accent. Poppy, by contrast, has a cultured voice, clear but light. She waves her hands around a lot as she speaks. She has long, delicate fingers. Emily watches, entranced, as she talks about her designs, holds up the materials she uses, explains how she gets her ideas.

People gather around her afterwards. Evidently used to this, she basks in the adulation, smiling and laughing, giving the same undivided attention to each one. Up close, Emily sees she is, in fact, a good ten years older than she thought. Late thirties maybe? Laughter lines crinkle around her pale blue eyes. She wears no foundation and tiny, red, thread veins stand out around her nose. Her skin is pale, almost translucent.

Suddenly, she turns to Emily. "Did you want to ask me something?" she says.

Emily's mind goes blank. She's been so taken up with looking at her, so absolutely fascinated by her, that she hasn't even considered what she might say to her.

"Umm, yes, no…" Her face is burning. She's behaving like a schoolgirl. She pulls herself together. "I just wanted to say how much I enjoyed your talk," she says more levelly.

Poppy laughs, that confident laugh she's been giving all evening, slightly false, slightly theatrical.

"Thank you. Well, you must pop into the shop. Look at all my designs. I'm sure you'll find something you like…"

"Thank you. I have already. Been in, I mean. But I'll come again."

"Do. Please. I'd love to see you. If I'm not there just ask for me." She holds out her hand. Emily takes it. Her long fingers fold around Emily's palm. She feels a gentle squeeze. She looks up. Poppy's eyes hold hers. Far longer than necessary. Emily reddens. Someone else is trying to speak to her. "Poppy," she's saying. "Miss James…" Poppy turns around, but still holds Emily's hand. Embarrassed, Emily draws it away. She's shaking. Hot all over. *What's the matter with me?* she thinks.

★

Peter's watching television when she gets home. The ten o'clock news. She can hear it blaring out as she lets herself in. He scarcely looks up when she puts her head around the door and waves her away vaguely, but with a nod and a "yes" when she says, "Cup of tea?"

The kettle boils to the accompaniment of the background sound of gunfire and a reporter's voice, "… the war here in…" Mechanically, she takes a cloth and wipes the surfaces of the drips of tea Peter has left on each one.

Peter is sitting in the pool of light from the table lamp, his face lit up sporadically by the flashing images on the television. He moves his whisky glass to one side for her to put the teacup down.

Only when the local news has finished and then the weather, does he mute the television and look up and say, "So how was it?"

Emily had been dying to tell him all about Poppy ("You'd love her!"), about the shop, the talk, the women there ("typically middle-aged"), but the moment has gone, the excitement vanished and she finds herself saying instead, "It was good. Very interesting."

Peter seems satisfied though. "Good," he says.

He turns up the volume again. Flicks between television channels in that way Emily finds so exasperating. One moment it's a comedy, the next *Newsnight*, the next some obscure film.

She picks up a magazine. Tries to read. Puts it down again. Goes into the kitchen, switches on her laptop.

Poppy James, she types into the Google Search box. An image of Poppy leaps onto the screen. Not the Poppy she knows now, but a younger version, the face rounder. Her hair is mousy, almost straight, much shorter. No mistaking those eyes though: pale blue; fixing the photographer with an unwavering gaze.

She closes the laptop quickly as she hears the sitting room door open.

"I thought you'd gone to bed," Peter says.

"Just checking my emails," she says quickly, wondering at the same time why she feels she has to lie to him.

Chapter Five

The door opens with the clang of one of those old-fashioned type shop bells that hang on a coiled wire. It's late January. Hardly any visitors. The shop is empty. Not even the ubiquitous shop assistant perched on the stool behind the till. Emily hesitates, wondering whether to turn around and go out again. Then she sees a picture on the wall. It's not much. Just a view of Lyme Regis, looking down on the bay, the silver sea, the curve of the Cobb reaching out. It has the half-finished look of a French Impressionist painting. She turns away. Glances around the shop. It's crammed with stuff in that higgledy-piggledy way of shops like this: things you'll never need, priced at ridiculous prices. Amazing really what people will buy. The jewellery is kept in a glass-fronted cabinet: *Designs by Poppy*, she reads. They're certainly different: twists of gold and silver, bright blue stones, all tagged so the prices aren't visible. If you have to ask you can't afford.

It's the smell of warm pasty that alerts her to the fact she's not alone. From the corner of her eye she sees the twitch of a beaded curtain and the bored-looking assistant she was expecting climbs onto the stool, clutching a greasy paper bag. "Can I help you?" she asks.

"Just looking," Emily says.

"Okay." Relieved, she tears open the bag, reaches for her magazine from under the desk and bites into the pasty.

Feeling obliged to do something, Emily wanders around, stroking objects, picking them up now and then, turning them over and gasping inwardly at the price. The assistant turns the pages of her magazine, glancing up at Emily every so often.

The words buzz around in her brain. *Is Miss James here? When will Miss James be here? Is it Miss James's day off? Can you tell Miss James I've been in?* But she's too scared to ask. She's outstayed her welcome. The assistant is taking more notice of her. Obviously wondering if she's a shoplifter. Growing warm under her scrutiny, Emily mutters, "Thank you," and the bell clangs as she leaves. Peter will be wondering where she is anyway.

She's only gone a few feet when she hears footsteps running up behind her. "I *knew* it was you!" a breathless voice says. "I *knew* you would come! Just *knew* it!"

She turns around, finds herself enveloped in the softness of velvet, the brisk, whiskery feel of fur, a sweet yet musty smell of perfume, strong arms holding her, a cold face against her cheek. Alarmed and embarrassed by the vehemence of the welcome, she draws back. Poppy doesn't seem to notice. "Come back in. *Please!*"

She sounds like Jasmine. Even looks like her suddenly, in her Bohemian clothes, and Emily wonders why she didn't notice the similarity before. In that moment Emily realises her foolishness. In her mind she has built her up into someone quite different. An artist, yes, but a serious artist, not some empty-headed woman, playing at being an artist, pretending still to be a girl even though she must be nearly forty.

"I'm sorry," she hears herself saying. "I must get back. My husband's not well."

"Oh, I'm so sorry!" That same too-effusive voice.

"No, it's okay. I mean, it's only a cold. But you know what men are like…" She breaks off, reddening, remembering suddenly that this woman is rumoured to be a lesbian.

But. "Don't I just!" Poppy laughs. "My father is dreadful

when he's ill. The slightest ache or pain and you'd think he was dying!"

She throws her head back as she laughs, runs her hand through those tumbling curls. Emily finds herself staring in fascination at her parted mouth, her white teeth. Her cheeks and nose are red from the cold air, her eyes moist from the cold wind. She puts her hand on Emily's arm, as if she knows the effect she's having on her. "Give me your number," she says. Her voice seems more normal now, less deliberately arty, less like Jasmine. "I'll give you a ring. Show you round properly. When your husband's better."

The invitation is ambiguously left so she's not sure if Peter's included or not, but even as Emily writes down her mobile number on a piece of paper torn from the bottom of her shopping list, she's decided he isn't. Peter wouldn't want to look at jewellery and he would categorise the paintings as 'amateurish daubs'.

"You were a long time," Peter complains when she gets in.

She ignores the reproach. I bought you some more Lemsip," she says. "How're you feeling?"

Peter's been waiting all the time she's been gone to tell her this. "Still bad. And I've got a pain here." He lifts his jumper, points to his side. "D'you think it's my lungs?"

Emily resists the urge to laugh. "Let me see."

"Don't fuss!" he snaps, but he lets her push and prod him. "Breathe in," she says briskly, like a doctor. She hasn't a clue what she's doing, but twenty years with Peter have taught her she needs to take him seriously. "I think it's just muscular," she says. "From coughing."

He looks relieved. "That's what I thought. Thanks, Emily. I love you." He takes her hand, kisses it. She leans against him. Feels his warm, masculine body against her. His rough cheek under her hand. Remembers Poppy's soft feminine embrace; her cold, cold cheek.

"I popped into that shop. You know. The one with the jewellery. The girl who gave the talk…"

He drops her hand. "While I was home here on my own?" he says in a small, hurt voice.

Oh for God's sake! she thinks irritably. "I was only a moment," she says, quickly.

Too late. She sees the sulky look on his face. "Come on, Peter!" she laughs. "I haven't been out for ages. I didn't go to Zumba yesterday…" He'd kept her awake all night coughing. She'd overslept. He hadn't woken her.

"I haven't been out either," he retorts.

"But you've been ill!"

He says nothing. It's okay for her. He's stuck at home, feeling dreadful, nothing to do.

Emily goes to the kitchen, starts unpacking the shopping, opening doors and drawers, throwing away packaging, rinsing the grapes under the tap, finding space in the fridge for the vegetables. Her phone on the table lights up and buzzes. Her heart leaps. She scarcely needs to look at it to know it's her. Her face floods with colour. Her hand shakes.

Friday 10am, the text reads. *If your husband's better. Let me know. Px*

She looks at the calendar. Friday. MGB MOT. If Peter's better.

And she's lucky. He is. In fact, the thought of the MOT has spurred him on. After a lot of research and driving around the various garages, he's found one in Axminster that specialises in older cars like his.

"You don't want me to come with you, do you?" Emily asks.

He had assumed she would. The MOT would take an hour. They could look around the town, have coffee somewhere.

She sees his face. Says quickly, "Only I've arranged to see a friend."

One of those dreary girls from her classes, Felicity or Andrea or someone.

"Okay," he says. He can stay in the garage instead, look around the cars.

He's gone by nine, even though the MOT is booked for ten and it only takes ten minutes to get there. Peter's always early for everything. They both are. They've got worse as they've got older, often having to sit in a lay-by for ten minutes to avoid arriving too early. "We'll get a bad reputation," Emily always giggles.

She dithers for ages about what to wear: discarding leggings and a top, putting on jeans, then a skirt with thick tights, but it's cold and raining; she goes back to jeans, the smart, black pair she wore to Felicity's party. She doesn't know why she's bothering so much: she'll keep her coat on and Poppy's the sort of woman, like Jasmine, who doesn't notice what anyone is wearing and certainly doesn't make any sort of effort herself. Nonetheless, she takes her time with her make-up, scrutinising her face in the illuminated magnifying make-up mirror, suddenly noticing the lines around her mouth and eyes. She rubs concealer into them before putting on foundation and extra blusher, an extra layer of mascara to accentuate her eyes, which everyone always comments on.

The cold air hits her the moment she steps outside. After the warmth of the house it's like stepping into a refrigerator, and she's glad she wore jeans and not a skirt or leggings. Like Peter, she's far too early and it's still only ten to when she reaches the shop, far too early, far too eager-looking, so she walks smartly past so that if Poppy does happen to see her she'll assume she has shopping to do first. She slows as she gets past the café on the corner, the art gallery on the right, goes down the steps and turns right towards the beach front. A blast of cold air hits her as she rounds the corner, taking her breath away, blowing her hair onto her lips and unwrapping the scarf from round her neck. She strides on. A few hardy people are walking dogs, but it's far too cold for most people. All the shops are closed, the amusement arcades shuttered, the restaurants shut for the season. Nothing as depressing as a seaside town out of season. The fishermen are there, of course, stocky men in heavy jumpers or jackets; the odd speedboat, healthy-looking men wearing fashionably branded weatherproofs. Emily walks to the end of the promenade then turns back.

She stops outside the Bell Cliff Café on the corner, pretending to look at the menu, but using the reflection to smooth down her hair as best as possible then walks up to the shop.

The door opens likes magic. "I thought you weren't coming!" Poppy cries.

"Am I late?" Emily says, casually. "I didn't think it mattered..." Then she realises, of course, it probably does. Poppy is an artist, a working woman, time is important. Maybe she's stopped part-way through an important project to see Emily. She feels suddenly foolish. She should have come in earlier. Waited if necessary. Instead of arriving fashionably late like some sort of guest at a function.

"No, it's fine!" Poppy laughs. "I'm looking after the shop today. It's Kitty's day off. And Suzie's in town."

"Town?"

"London. Seeing our accountant. She deals with all that sort of stuff. Now what can I show you? A ring perhaps? Or a necklace? A painting for your bedroom? I've got a lovely landscape of Lyme..."

Emily's mind goes blank. She hasn't thought of buying anything. She just wanted to see Poppy. Embarrassment washes over her.

Poppy doesn't seem to notice. "Here," she says, taking a

painting off the wall. It's the one Emily had looked at before. About a foot square. A view of Lyme from the gardens at the top of the cliff: the sea glinting in the sunshine, the curved stone arm of the Cobb.

"It's lovely," Emily says. "But I'd like my husband to see it…"

Poppy doesn't seem to be listening. She flits across the shop floor like some exotic bird in her brightly coloured, floaty top and skirt.

"Or some jewellery," she's saying, reaching in her pocket for a key and unlocking a glass cabinet. She takes out a ring, grabs Emily's hand, slides off her glove in one swift moment and slides the ring onto her finger. "Perfectly!" she says triumphantly, holding Emily's hand at arm's length to admire it. "Like Cinderella's slipper! You'll *have* to buy it now!"

Emily stares mesmerised at the ring on her finger: the delicate filigree of gold, the topaz stone. The ring is on the forefinger of her right hand. She would never have thought of wearing a ring on that finger. And never this ring. It makes all her other rings seem so boring, all versions of engagement rings, bands of gold set with sapphires and diamonds or solitary stones. It's totally outré, the sort of ring Jasmine would wear.

"My step-daughter would love it," she says. "But it's not for me."

"Don't be silly!" Poppy says. "It suits you."

She turns back to the cabinet, her hand hovering over the other pieces of jewellery. Then, suddenly, she wheels around.

"How rude of me!" she says. "I haven't offered you a drink. Tea? Coffee?"

She sees Emily's hesitation. "Did you think I just wanted to sell you something? Well, I'd love to, of course. And Suzie would certainly expect me to. But I thought maybe, you know…" She breaks off.

"Yes," Emily says quickly to cover the awkward moment. She feels chosen, special. "Yes. I'd love a cup of tea. Thank you."

"I'll just lock this up. In case someone comes in." She peers out into the empty street, then up to the heavy sky. "Though I doubt anyone will. Not in this weather."

Emily slides the ring off her finger, taking a surreptitious peek at the price tag while Poppy's back is turned. But without her glasses the print is too small to see.

Poppy settles the ring back on its plastic stand then disappears behind the beaded curtain. There's the sound of water running, the metallic clink of a kettle lid.

"Tea or coffee?" she calls.

"Tea, please."

"Camomile? Peppermint? Fennel?"

She laughs again at Emily's silence. "I'm only joking. This is Kitty's stuff, I think. Suzie and I drink coffee. But there's tea here somewhere. I'm sure I've seen some…"

There's the sound of crockery and cutlery being moved around, then a crash and a "Blast!"

"Don't worry, I'll have coffee," Emily tries to say.

"No, it's okay. I've found it."

The smell of strong coffee precedes her entrance. The beaded curtain clings to her shoulders as she shimmies through and plonks the mugs on the counter, next to the till. She disappears again, returning with a low wooden chair.

"Here," she says. "I'll sit on the stool. We can hide the mugs under here if anyone comes in."

Emily wonders if she knows that Kitty eats her lunch and reads her magazine with total disregard to the customers, but decides not to bother her with this information.

"So tell me all about yourself," Poppy says, suddenly.

"Oh, well. There's nothing to tell," Emily says, embarrassed by this sudden onslaught.

"Don't be silly. Everyone's got something to tell. When did you move here?"

"Six months ago. No, longer. Seven maybe. When we retired."

"You're too young to be retired."

"I know. But my husband's older."

"Oh, yes. Second wife. You said. Your step-daughter…"

"Jasmine. You'd like her. She's like you…"

"How do you know?" Poppy says. "You don't know what I'm like."

"No, of course. But…"

"You mustn't judge people by appearances."

"No. I know." Emily feels foolish again. Why does this woman, so much younger than her, make her feel so gauche?

"I like your work," she says to hide her embarrassment.

"Thank you," Poppy says. "What do you, *did* you do, for a living?"

"Secretary. Medical Secretary. Only part-time. Pretty boring, I know."

"Not at all. I'm sure it was very interesting."

"No, it wasn't!" Emily laughs. "But I liked it anyway. Going out to work. The routine. The girls in the office. I miss it."

But Poppy's an artist. She works alone, unstructured, free from routine; she can't possibly understand. They're poles apart. What is she doing, thinking they can possibly be friends? She'd be better off meeting Felicity or Andrea who know about working, who are married, have homes to run, husbands to look after. This woman probably doesn't even do any housework. Artists are notoriously undomesticated.

"It's silly, I know," she hears herself gabbling, the words

falling out one after the other, far too fast in her nervousness. "It's not that I'm bored. I'm always doing something. I don't know how I ever had time to work! The house. The shopping. And I cook more. And we're out all the time. In the car. Going for walks. The theatre. The cinema. And I do classes. Zumba. Pilates."

"Pilates?" Poppy says in a polite, restrained voice. "I'd like to do that. When is it?"

Emily's grateful to her for the interruption, for stopping her rattling on interminably. She knows it's a failing of hers, but she can't seem to help it. She's even more grateful when the shop bell clangs, announcing a customer. They push the mugs under the counter. The customer is interested in a white cotton nightdress she's seen in the window. "My daughter just *loves* that sort of thing!" and while Poppy searches for the right size in the pile of cellophane-wrapped nightdresses in the cupboard underneath, Emily finishes her tea. She wonders whether she should take the mug through to the space that lurks behind the beaded curtain, but decides it would be too intrusive, so leaves it next to Poppy's half-full cup of black coffee instead.

Prompted by Poppy, the customer has moved on to her art work. "It would look perfect in a bedroom," Poppy is saying. Just what she had said to Emily. Part of a practised patter obviously. "And would remind you of your time here. It's the light, isn't it? The way it sparkles off the sea. That's what I love…"

Emily glances at her watch. Peter will be back soon. She moves to the door, catches Poppy's eye, gives her a little wave, doesn't wait to see if she's seen it. She'll hear the bell, know she's gone.

Walking back, she relives every moment. She made a fool of herself, she knows she did. She didn't even buy anything.

Not that she had the chance. But still. She knows they won't meet again. Not like that. Silly of her to think they could be friends.

Peter's back already. She can feel it the moment she opens the door.

"Did it pass?" she asks.

"Of course. No problem. I've been back for ages. Where've you been?"

"I told you. I met a friend."

"Andrea? Or Felicity, wasn't it?"

"No. Poppy. The woman who has the shop. The artist, you know."

"I didn't know she was a friend of yours."

"She's not." Emily winds her scarf from round her neck. Childish tears prick her eyes. "I just thought…" Her voice breaks.

"What's the matter?" Peter asks. "What's happened? Has someone upset you?"

"No, it's silly. It doesn't matter."

He hovers around her, at a loss as usual when she's upset.

"Please, Peter, I'm fine. Honestly." She takes her coat off, hangs it up. "Let me get you a cup of tea or something."

"I've had about a gallon at the garage. I'll get you one if you like."

"No, I'm okay. I'll check my emails. I didn't have time before I went out."

He watches her as she sits at the table and tucks her hair behind one ear. Her face is flushed. From the cold and from being upset. He recognises the telltale mottled red rash that spreads from her cheeks to her neck. She looks different. She's wearing more make-up or something. He puts his arm on her shoulder. He can smell perfume, a smell he realises he hasn't noticed on her for a while. She made all this effort, then someone upset her in that inexplicable way women can be upset. He knows she doesn't want to talk about it. He probably won't understand even if she did. Whatever it was will soon be forgotten. It always is with Emily.

She leans her head briefly against him. "Was it okay? At the garage? Any interesting cars?" she asks as she waits for her laptop to load.

"An Austin Healey. Couple of BMWs. Nothing much else. What would you like to do this afternoon? We can go out if you like."

"Okay. You choose where. I'll just do this then we can have lunch."

Peter's on his way to the study when he hears her phone ringing. He reaches into her coat pocket. Lifts it to his ear. "Hello?" he says. "This is Emily's phone," he explains to the bemused silence.

"Oh…" The giggle sounds so young that for a split second he thinks it's Jasmine. But paternal instinct tells him otherwise.

"You must be Peter," the voice says. "This is Poppy. May I speak to Emily?"

He can tell she's pretty, beautiful even. It's in that throaty giggle, in every perfectly spoken syllable. In the short time it takes him to take the phone to Emily in the kitchen, he has drawn up a mental picture of her: not only pretty but young, vivacious, flirtatious; a million miles away from those other boring friends of Emily's.

Emily jumps up so quickly she almost knocks over her laptop. He sees the colour flood to her face, the light come into her eyes.

She recovers quickly. "Hello?" she says, levelly.

"Your husband sounds gorgeous!" Poppy giggles, conspiratorially. "I forgot to say," she goes on. "We're having some people over. Next Thursday. Private viewing. To look at my work, you know. Suzie's idea. Nine o'clock. Both of you. If you're free."

Emily makes a big fuss of checking the calendar, even though she knows she would cancel anything booked. But there's nothing. "We'd love to," she says.

Chapter Six

"I don't see why she has to come too," Emily grumbles.

"Well, one more won't make any difference. I can't see it'll be a problem. She'll probably be glad. Jasmine might buy something. You know she likes that sort of thing. But ring first if you're that worried. Ask if it's okay."

"No," she says, quickly. "No, you're right."

But she doesn't want Jasmine to come. She'll upstage her. She'll wear some sort of Bohemian getup, like Poppy does. Poppy will love her. She'll love Poppy. She and Peter and Poppy will all talk about art and artists. Emily will be left out. The only saving grace is that 'Si' is too busy preparing for an exhibition to come along too. Peter is especially pleased about this. The thought of one of his contemporaries sharing his daughter's bed, the other side of the bedroom wall, is more than he can bear.

Jasmine arrives on Tuesday evening, climbing out of her 2CV and throwing herself into Peter's arms with a squeal of delight. Peter grimaces over her shoulder, catching Emily's eye sympathetically as she glances around, embarrassed, worried about the neighbours. Jasmine releases him, stands back to look at him. "You're putting on weight, Daddy!" she says, poking him in his stomach. Peter knows it. Emily does too, but she would never dare tell him.

Jasmine turns to Emily, wraps her in a headily-scented hug, before holding her at arm's length in that theatrical way she has and exclaiming, "You look wonderful! Retirement obviously suits you. You're glowing!"

Emily pulls away self-consciously. "Let's have a look at the ring!" she says, her voice to her own ears sounding falsely jovial. Jasmine doesn't seem to notice, though, and holds out one delicate coffee-coloured hand.

The ring is surprisingly conservative. Except for the colour of the stone, an emerald, Emily might have chosen it for herself; the small square-cut stone nestles between two diamonds. It's even gold, not platinum or palladium or any of the fashionable silvery colours that are so popular nowadays.

Jasmine senses her reaction. "It's antique," she says, quickly. "Si chose it."

"A friend of mine is a jewellery designer," Emily says. She regrets it the moment she has said it. She had been going to lead up to the private viewing by degrees, convince Jasmine she would find it dull.

"Hardly a friend!" Peter laughs.

He doesn't mean it unkindly, but Emily is stung. "It *is* a private viewing," she defends herself. But Jasmine is only half-listening. She reaches into the car, takes out cellophane-wrapped flowers for Emily, wine for Peter.

Peter takes her bag in and she disappears upstairs to shower and change. Emily hears the familiar sound of the television being switched on: Peter watching some inane television programme, *Pointless* or something; a more apt title for a programme she can't possibly imagine. He tried to get her to watch it with him once, but she couldn't understand the rules and it seemed such a waste of time. There's the sound of laughter, then applause, then more laughter; Peter joins in. Jasmine comes careering down the stairs. A damp, fragrant cloud hangs around her. Her hair, still wet from the shower, is piled up on top of her head in a blue-black coil; she's wearing a loose, white cotton top and white cotton trousers that set off her olive skin. Emily envies her the easy knack of looking so perfect just out of the shower.

"What's for dinner?" she asks, lifting the lid of the saucepan on the hob.

"Homemade chicken pie in the oven," Emily says. "About twenty minutes. I've just got the veg to do."

"Can I help?"

"No, it's fine."

Which is just as well because she's already disappeared.

"Daddy!" Emily hears her exclaim. "What on earth are you doing watching trash like this?"

"I'm just waiting for the news." She hears Peter's pat reply, but the television falls silent, replaced by the more civilised sound of their voices. She feels a stab of jealousy. It's not fair that Jasmine can get away with everything Emily can't. It's the same at dinner.

"My God, Daddy!" Jasmine says. "Wipe your mouth! You look like an old man!"

The last time Emily tried to tell Peter this he turned on her so angrily that she had never dared say it again. Since then she has kept her eyes fixed firmly on her dinner plate, avoiding looking up as much as possible. She's sure his table manners weren't always like this, maybe it's something that happens to everyone as they get older. She's grateful, in an odd way, to Jasmine for pointing it out, though she doubts if Peter will take any notice, or even remember, once Jasmine has gone home.

All day Thursday she worries about what to wear to Poppy's do. She really can't justify buying something new. But she can't keep wearing the same black jeans to everything. She goes through her clothes in her mind, discarding outfit after outfit, finally deciding on her black 'work' skirt with a purple polo-necked jumper.

Jasmine comes down looking like a model in jeans and a tight white top that accentuates her generous bust. Against

70

her, Emily feels suddenly overdressed, but it's too late to go back up and change.

It's a cold night and her legs, even in thick tights, feel bare and exposed. Her high heels click in time to Jasmine's on the pavement. Peter walks between them. Emily hangs on to one arm, Jasmine the other. He can smell their perfumes, something light and classic on Emily, mingling with a younger, sweeter scent from Jasmine. "Can I go in like this?" he says, jokingly. "I'll be the envy of every man in the room!"

But, of course, the door is too narrow and Jasmine goes in first. It's Kitty who greets them. "May I see your invitation?" she asks.

Jasmine turns to Emily, questioningly.

"I don't have one. I'm…" She was going to say "a friend of Poppy's" but glimpsing the crowded room beyond she says instead, "Poppy invited me. By text. I can probably find it…" She reaches in her bag for her phone, but Kitty laughs. "Don't worry. I'm sure it's fine. Go on in…"

The clothes on racks and the odd knick-knacks have been put away so that people can move more freely around the glass jewellery cabinets. Every wall is hung with Poppy's paintings. It's only just gone nine but already the tiny shop is packed. Emily searches the sea of faces, ostensibly looking for anyone she might know, but in fact, looking for Poppy. But there's no sight of her or even Suzie. Tables of differing heights have been pushed together along one wall and covered in several white tablecloths for bottles of wine, glasses and cartons of orange juice.

"Shall I get you a drink?" Peter says.

Her hands are freezing cold, and the thought of holding a glass of cold wine or orange juice is more than she can bear. A cup of tea is what she'd really like, and she glances subconsciously towards where she knows the kettle and tea bags are stored. She notices the beaded curtain has been looped to one side.

"Emily?" Peter repeats.

"Oh yes, I'd love one," she says vaguely.

"Wine or juice?"

"Oh. Um... Wine, I think."

She expects him to turn to Jasmine next, but she has already disappeared to look at the paintings. It's not hard to see where she is. It's rare to see anyone with her colouring around here, and her dark skin and jet black hair stand out amongst the sea of pale faces, light hair. Emily sees him touch her shoulder and bend close to her ear as he squeezes past her.

Emily feels obliged to do something while she waits for Peter to return, but she doesn't like to move too far away so she examines the paintings on the wall next to her. These, too, are of course of Lyme, but not the usual views of the Cobb, the harbour, the sea. These are more detailed. Watercolour again: obviously, this is Poppy's medium. A cat on the doorstep of a house, a seagull perched on a car roof, the brook babbling over stones.

Peter has returned. "It's awful," he says.

"I thought it wasn't too bad. But then I know I don't know anything about it."

He follows her gaze. "No. The wine. Cheap Spanish as far as I could tell from the label. That's not bad..." He nods at the painting of the brook. "Water's always hard to paint..."

There's no signature at the bottom. Just an artistic scrolled number 7, drawn the French way with a bar across it. He frowns. He's seen it before somewhere. Years ago. An art gallery maybe...?

Suddenly, he's aware Emily is blushing. Her face has lit up with a smile. "Peter." She touches his arm as she says his name. "This is Poppy."

72

He turns. In the time that had intervened since the phone call he had prepared himself to be disappointed by Poppy whatever-her-name-is. The confident voice, the teasing laugh had all been consigned to the back of his mind. She would turn out to be like all the other women he had met here: middle-aged, plain, dull. Worse, in fact, since she considered herself to be artistic. But the woman in front of him is pretty. No. Beautiful. Arresting. The eyes. Clear. Blue. Piercing. She can see into his soul. He drops his gaze, confused. Takes in, instead, with one sweeping look the pale, wide face, the auburn hair, the slim, artistic hand she holds out to him. She's dressed like most artists in an odd mixture of clothes, loose blouse, voluminous jacket, long skirt. Impossible to make out her figure underneath, but she holds herself confidently and he decides she's slim, firm, full-busted.

She pays him scant attention. Turns back to Emily. Emily bends her head to listen to her. The blush he noticed earlier has deepened and spread down her neck. She's smiling, laughing. She looks lovely. He feels proud of her. A sudden image of having them both together comes into his mind: their cool, soft hands on his body; their warm breath in his ear; that long, auburn hair against his chest... He pulls himself together. Tries to listen to what they're saying. But their voices are too light to make out above the hubbub of conversation around them. Emily touches his arm again. He leans in close. "Poppy says there's more work through there..." She points to the doorway where a beaded curtain has been looped back. "And it's a bit quieter..."

He follows them through, the crowds parting magically like the Red Sea as Poppy makes her way through. "Excuse me. Excuse me. Oh, hello. I'll be with you in a mo..."

The room behind the looped curtain is little more than a cupboard: toaster, kettle and sink one side, shelves for mugs, tea bags and coffee the other. The door the other side is open and they pass into a large square room. This must be Poppy's studio. There are paintings everywhere, some hung rather crudely on the walls, others on the floor, leaning against the skirting boards. There's an easel and on a table nearby a pile of rags, a palette, brushes, paints. The walls are whitewashed. There's a bare fluorescent tube light above them.

The people in here are mostly what Emily calls 'the silver-haired brigade': retired like them; the type who like to think they know about art. Amongst the few younger ones Emily recognises the owner of the bookshop down the road, who nods to her vaguely, clearly uncertain where she's seen her before.

"Do you know her?" Poppy asks, catching the exchange.

"Not really. Not to talk to. She runs the bookshop, doesn't she?"

"Yes." She leans closer. Her hair brushes across Emily's lips. She can smell her mint-flavoured breath. "She's a right cow," she says, even while she's giving her a friendly nod. "They all are. All the business people round here. But Suzie says we have to keep in with them. I hate these sort of do's," she shudders with mock disgust.

As if invoked by her name, Suzie appears next to them. Poppy jumps like a child caught out doing something wrong.

"This is Emily," she says, quickly. "Her husband, um…"

"Peter," Emily supplies for her.

"Is an ex-art teacher," she finishes.

Even as Emily wonders how she knows this (she certainly can't remember telling her), she registers first the look of suspicion Suzie gives her, followed swiftly by the quickened interest at the mention of someone who knows about art.

Unfortunately, Peter has disappeared. He's peering closely at one of the paintings. But he hasn't lost track of where they are. Poppy might appear to be totally taken up with Emily, but he knows it's just a front. He hadn't mistaken the spark in her eyes when she saw him. He knows she fancies him. He can feel it. The invisible thread of physical attraction. Even while she's been speaking to Emily he's seen her glance at him, seen the toss of her head, the way she runs her fingers through her hair, slides her tongue over her lips, all the signs he recognises of an earthy, physical woman, the type he likes.

He pretends to be surprised when Emily touches his arm. "Peter…"

Poppy smiles at him. "This is my partner, Suzie. Suzie, Peter…?"

"Stanchester," he supplies.

"Oh, yes. I'd forgotten…" She shakes her head and the ornate silver earrings in her ears dance.

"How do you do?" Peter says, politely.

"And what do you think of Poppy's work?" Suzie asks. "I understand you know about art…"

"It's very good," Peter says. "Interesting use of light here…"

Emily stands like a spare part, while Peter and Poppy discuss light and shade and the use of colour. This was everything she dreaded, the only saving grace that clearly Suzie feels the same. She tries to catch her eye for a bit of mutual sympathy, but Suzie studiously avoids the looks she gives her, standing guard over Poppy like a jealous husband. Emily knows Peter fancies Poppy. She's always known he would. Who wouldn't? She's beautiful, unusual, magnetic, artistic. Everything Peter could possibly want. She watches as he turns on his particular brand of charm, and Poppy laughs and smiles in all the right places. Suzie sees it too. Much as she needs Peter's artistic comments, she needs Poppy more, and any doubts Emily might have had about their relationship are quashed when Suzie puts her arm around her waist, gives her an intimate squeeze, the sort a lover gives, and says, "Poppy, my sweet. We do need to circulate. I'm so sorry…" she turns to Peter, "But Poppy has her duties…"

"Of course. Of course," Peter says, airily. Above her head (she's a good head-height shorter than Poppy and nearly as far round), he catches Poppy's eye. He doesn't need to ask her number, he can get it from Emily's phone. He checks quickly to make sure Emily isn't watching him, but she's already turned to go. He grabs the opportunity, mouths, "I'll call you." And mimes the sign for a telephone. He's rewarded with the briefest inclination of her head, a fleeting secret smile.

"She's lovely, isn't she?" Emily asks.

"Suzie or Poppy?" he teases.

She gives his arm a playful push. "Don't be silly," she says. "I knew you'd fancy her."

"Hardly fancy."

"Oh, come on, Peter. You forget how well I know you…"

He decides to ignore it. "What d'you want to do now?" he asks. "Anything else you want to look at or shall we find Jas and go?"

"I don't mind."

By tacit agreement they make their way back through to the front of the shop. They've just come through the looped curtain when Emily hears someone calling her. Turning round, she sees Pam.

"I thought we might find you here," she says. "David's around somewhere… oh, over there, look, with the artist."

David's stomach almost obscures Poppy. She's pointing out something in one of her paintings. Emily notices a wide gold bracelet slide down her arm. It's engraved with a name: Suzie? Poppy? It's too far away to make out. Suzie's hovering to one side, waiting to move her on, but David won't be hurried. He asks her another question, then Peter notices with astonishment as he takes out his phone and keys in the number she reads out to him. It takes him some time and she laughs as he stops, starts again, shakes his head, all in clear sight of his wife. Peter has a quick mental image of Poppy astride David's huge stomach, trying to find whatever lurks below, but when David makes his way over to them he says, delightedly, "She's agreed to give a talk to Rotary."

"Oh, good. She was excellent at Inner Wheel," Pam says.

Emily loses sight of Poppy for a moment and then the inevitable happens: she sees her talking to Jasmine, sees Jasmine smile and nod, then point over to Peter and Emily. Poppy grasps her hand, brings her across the room.

"I hear this lovely creature is your daughter!" Poppy laughs.

"Yes," says Peter proudly, putting his arm around Jasmine's shoulder.

"Well, aren't you the lucky one?" Poppy teases. "A beautiful wife *and* a beautiful daughter!"

Emily blushes and laughs.

"I was just talking to Poppy about Simeon," Jasmine says.

Emily's heart sinks. Just as she thought, Jasmine's upstaging her. "He's got an exhibition coming up," she goes on. "Give me your card and I'll make sure you get an invite."

"Oh…" Poppy searches in various pockets. "Suzie!" she calls. "Do you have one of my cards?"

The ever-efficient Suzie produces a card, but gives Jasmine the once-over jealously.

"Jasmine's boyfriend is an artist," she starts to explain. "She's inviting us to his exhibition."

The *us* isn't lost on Emily, or on Jasmine. A quick frown crosses her face, but then she brightens as she remembers: "Fiancé, actually." She twirls her left hand in front of Poppy's face.

"*Fiancé.*" Poppy laughs, grabbing hold of the hand to

examine the ring. "Antique, isn't it?" she asks. "I can design you a wedding ring to go with it if you like. And one for your husband."

"Oh, that would be lovely," Jasmine squeals. "I'll have to check with Si of course…"

Not that it will ever come to a wedding, Emily thinks. And even as she's thinking it Poppy catches her eye and Emily knows, just *knows* she's read her mind, that she thinks the same thing, that she has Jasmine absolutely and correctly summed up. And in that moment she sees that Jasmine and Poppy are nothing alike, not at heart. It's as though Poppy is playing a part, dressing and acting like the Bohemian artist, whereas in fact behind that façade is someone as natural, down-to-earth and genuine as Emily herself.

"Have you looked at my jewellery yet?" Poppy says. "Here. Let me show you…"

She takes out the little key from her pocket, unlocks the glass cabinet.

"This is the one I showed your…" She stops, obviously uncertain whether to call Emily her stepmother. "Emily," she says instead.

"Oh, Em, you *have* to have it!" Jasmine enthuses. "It's just *perfect* for you. Daddy, you *have* to buy it for Em. I *insist!*"

Emily reddens and Peter shifts uncomfortably. This is Poppy's moment to slide it on Emily's finger like she did before, to push for the sale. Emily sees her glance towards Suzie, but Suzie is talking earnestly to a large lady in a fur coat.

"Emily was thinking *you* might like it actually," Poppy says casually.

"*Me?* Oh, Em, how sweet! For my birthday, you mean? Oh, I would have it if it weren't for…"

She glances down coyly at her engagement finger again, and Poppy exchanges a small smile with Peter and Emily.

"That was good of her," Emily says while they're waiting for Jasmine to come back from the loo.

"What?" says Peter vaguely. He was looking at Poppy's back, trying to work out what sort of figure she might have under all those clothes, hoping they might hide a firm bottom, slim legs.

"About the ring. She knows I don't really like it."

"I do," he says to her surprise.

"You do? But it's not my sort of thing…"

He shrugs. "Okay," he says, easily. "But if you want it. For your birthday…"

Emily's birthday is the week before Jasmine's.

"No," she says, firmly. "It's too expensive. I don't need another ring. And it's not my style."

"Okay," he says, again.

Jasmine has joined them again. She links one arm through Emily's, one through Peter's. "Ready to go, you two?"

They don't bother to find Poppy and Suzie. As Peter points out, they've said goodbye and thank you twice already. A third time would be ridiculous. With Emily standing next to him, Poppy had studiously avoided looking at Peter the second time but he hasn't forgotten the quick complicit smile, the barely perceptible nod. As he walks back through the ice-cold streets, Emily on one arm again, Jasmine on the other, he sees himself sliding Emily's phone from her coat pocket, jotting down Poppy's number, ringing her when Emily is out at one of her classes, hearing a note of surprised delight in her voice. At this point the scenario vanishes. He's not sure how it will progress. Does he want an affair? His mind darts away from the idea like a sore spot not wanting to be touched, his guilt enhanced by the pressure of Emily's arm through his, the animation in her voice as she chats to Jasmine, something he knows doesn't come easily to her, something he knows she does just for him. But he hasn't done anything yet, he tells himself. He's innocent, and he reruns the scene, sees himself calling her, hears the delight in her voice, her sexy giggle, sees himself meeting her, touching her. The blood zings through his body; he feels alive again, young again, happy, excited, his excitement heightened by the sound of Emily and Jasmine's high heels clicking on the pavement.

Chapter Seven

Emily grips the sheet as she comes, looks Peter straight in the eyes. It's almost enough to make him hard again.

"Shhh…" he whispers, glancing fearfully at the wall that divides their room from Jasmine's, the head of their bed only feet away from the head of hers. Emily gives him the sort of look that says, *There's no way Jasmine could possibly have slept through that.* And he knows it's true. Neither of them could keep their hands off each other when they got back. In the kitchen as Emily went through the mundane motions of filling the kettle, putting it on and taking out mugs, milk and tea bags, Peter found his eyes following her every move. Her bottom jiggled provocatively in her high-heeled boots, the material of the demure black skirt stretched tightly over it as she reached up to take out the tea bags. Jasmine saw him looking, rolled her eyes heavenward, yawned dramatically.

"I'll take my tea up to bed, I think," she said, drily.

The moment she was gone Peter made a grab for Emily, ran his hand over her bottom.

"Peter!" she protested, glancing towards the door. "She might come back!"

"You're my wife, aren't you?" he laughed. "I'm allowed…"

And he'd sensed she was willing, more than willing; she wanted it as much as he did. But not here, not now. They sat at the kitchen table, drank their tea, talked about ordinary things, about Jasmine, what they would do tomorrow, what the weather might be like, whether they needed to buy milk or anything.

They went upstairs as quietly as possible. No light showed under Jasmine's door. Upstairs in the bedroom they went through their usual routines: Peter undressed while Emily cleaned her teeth, then he went and did his. When he came back in she was taking off her make-up. He had never understood why it always took so long for her to get ready for bed. Anusia had been the same. It wasn't just the lengthy make-up removal and moisturising ritual. For some reason they both had to pick up his clothes from the untidy heap he had thrown them down in (both tutting in exactly the same way), shake them out, sort them into clean and dirty piles, then do the same with their own. Worse still, both insisted on spending hours in front of wardrobes and cupboards saying, "I wonder what the weather's going to do tomorrow? What d'you think I should wear?" He'd long since given up suggesting anything. Whatever he suggested they'd act in horror. "Oh no! I think I'll wear jeans (or a skirt, or shorts)."

Tonight, though, Emily was quicker than usual. His clothes had already been dealt with and as soon as she had smoothed on moisturiser, she stood up to unzip her skirt. He hoped she might do a little strip-tease for him, but instead she slipped out of it quickly. He had forgotten she was wearing those awful thick tights but they went quickly too, and the bra and knickers, and instead of hanging everything up she put them on the back of the chair, slipped into bed next to him and slid her hand down to his ready erection.

The necessity to be quiet heightened the excitement. Emily's usual moans, his loud groans, all reduced to breathy gasps, quiet keening sounds in their throats. The lights were still on (they never made love in the dark) and Peter watched as Emily lowered her head. He ran his fingers through her hair, his mind turning again to Poppy's long, auburn tresses, and as he pulled Emily up, slid his hands over her slim, firm, familiar body, it was Poppy's body he thought of, Poppy's hands on his buttocks as she guided him in.

Emily thought of Poppy too. Her face, her smile, the way she stood, the way she spoke. Her body was suffused by her. Every nerve tingled. It was all she could do not to call out her name when she came.

Am I a lesbian? she wonders to herself afterwards. But the memory of Peter's firm cock inside her is enough to convince her she isn't. A woman could never be enough for her. But there's no doubting the effect Poppy has on her: the excitement, the fascination.

She can't sleep. She gets up, goes downstairs, automatically fills the kettle and puts it on. While she's waiting for it to boil she turns on her laptop, then checks her phone. She almost drops it when the name *Poppy* appears as though she's conjured her name onto her phone by thinking about her. She scrolls to the message. *Hi. Sooooooo loved seeing you tonight. I'm free for coffee tomorrow. Eleven at the Bell Cliff. Please say you can come x*

It's Friday tomorrow. No classes. What else can she tell Peter? Then she gives herself a shake. Why should she need an excuse? It's ridiculous. She looks at the time the message was sent. Ten minutes ago. She glances at the kitchen clock. Ten to one. Poppy keeps late hours. Maybe she can't sleep either. She's tempted to text straight back, but something stops her. The thought she's being overly keen. The thought she'll look foolish. The thought Peter will say she should stay in as Jasmine's with them.

But he doesn't. He's in the study when she tells him. She sees his little jolt of surprise.

"Poppy," she repeats, thinking he hadn't heard her properly. He can't possibly have forgotten, already, who she is.

"Just you?" he asks.

She looks at him blankly.

"Not Jasmine as well, I mean," he says, quickly.

"No. Just me," she says, annoyed now.

"Of course," he says quickly. "I didn't mean…"

"No, of course you didn't," she says, brusquely. "That's okay, is it?"

"Yes," he says.

"You'll be okay? You and Jasmine? You'll find something to do? I won't be long…"

"We'll be fine. Maybe we'll walk down with you. Go on for a walk after…"

"Okay," Emily feels obliged to say but her heart sinks. If Poppy sees them she'll feel obliged to invite them to join them. Luckily, Jasmine's late up. At ten thirty she's still sitting at the kitchen table in her dressing gown. Peter's still frantically trying to think of an excuse to go with her when Emily's pulling on her boots.

"The road's pretty icy," he says. "Are you sure you don't want me to walk down with you?"

"I'll be fine, Peter!" she laughs. "You stay in the warm with Jasmine."

She's early, of course, so she's not surprised when she can't see Poppy at any of the tables. She stands uncertainly just inside the door, unwinding her scarf from around her neck and pulling off her gloves, searching in her pocket for a tissue to wipe her nose that's running from the cold.

She's just heading for a table in the corner when the door opens, again, with a blast of cold air and a voice says, "Phew! It's positively glacial out there! Morning, Mrs. S."

Emily sees Poppy plant a kiss on the café owner's cheek, a tall, thin, severe-looking woman, who Emily's done little more than exchange a brief, "Good Morning" with in all the years she and Peter have been coming here.

"Am I late?" Poppy asks, pressing her cold cheek against Emily's face next.

"No, I'm early!" Emily laughs. "Peter and I are always early! We're getting worse…" She stops, determined she's not going to start gabbling again.

"Have you ordered yet?" Poppy asks.

Emily shakes her head.

Poppy summons 'Mrs. S' with a nod of her head. "My usual, please. Oh, and one of your lovely scones. And…" She pauses. "Tea?" she says with a querying smile to Emily, who nods. "Anything else?"

"No, thanks."

"That's how you keep your figure, is it? I'm not strong-willed enough…"

"You look fine to me." Though, as usual, Poppy's wearing far too many layers to be able to distinguish anything at all underneath them.

"How did it go the other night?" Emily goes on.

"Pretty good, I think. Suzie seemed pleased. I don't get involved in the sales side much."

"But you're a good saleslady."

"God, I hope not!" Poppy pulls a face. "Saleslady. How awful!"

Emily's embarrassed. "I meant…"

"I know what you meant. I have to sell my work. But I hope I'm not pushy. I didn't push you, did I? The other night? With the ring? I knew you didn't want it…"

"I love it!" Emily says quickly. "But…"

"Yes, I see," she says, smiling.

The tea and coffee arrive with all the accompanying clattering of cups and saucers, moving around of teapots, plates and coffee pots, until finally they're settled and Poppy says, "Your step-daughter's lovely. Lovely colouring."

"She used to hate it. When she was a teenager. It's so unusual down here. People stare sometimes. And children can be cruel. They teased her at school, I think. But now..." She shrugs. "People are more tolerant."

"You don't have children yourself?"

"No." She wonders if she should explain, waits to see if Poppy will ask why, but instead Poppy says, "Me neither. I never got round to it. Never had the right man at the right time. And it's too late now."

"I thought..." Emily says. Then stops, reddening.

"Thought what?" Poppy says.

"Nothing," she says quickly.

"No, go on. You thought what?" Then she laughs. "I know. You thought me and Suzie..." She bursts out laughing. "Don't worry. You're not the only one. I like to keep people guessing."

Emily doesn't know what to say. She watches while Poppy cuts her scone in half, buttering each side thickly, then biting into it and licking the grease off her fingers.

"Now Mrs. S..." Poppy says suddenly. "*She's* definitely, you know..."

"Really?" Emily looks over at the thin, wiry woman bustling around officiously with tea trays.

"Oh yes. At least that's what they say..."

Emily glances back to Poppy, sees the smile lurking at the corner of her mouth, the sparkle in her eyes.

"You're teasing me," she says.

"Only a little."

"It's not my fault. I didn't think it. I was told. It's Suzie, I suppose. She looks a bit..."

"Butch? Like a dyke?" She frowns. "Yes, I suppose she does. But she isn't. Not really. It's an act. To protect herself. She's had a bad time with men. Haven't we all?" She laughs slightly bitterly, then says, "Not you though. Your husband looks like a nice man."

"He is," Emily says loyally. She thinks about Peter's bad

moods, the way he gets cross with her if she doesn't agree with him on everything, the way he doesn't like her going out without him. But he's not unkind to her; it's not as if he beats her or goes off with other women. Basically, he's a good man. But she doesn't want to get drawn into a conversation about Peter. "How long have you lived here?" she asks.

Poppy counts on her fingers. "Sixteen years, I suppose. *Tempus fugit!* It was Suzie's idea. Move to the coast. Buy a shop. Sell my work. If it wasn't for her I'd probably be dishing out lattes in Costa Coffee."

She picks up the coffee cafetiere, pours herself another cup of coffee. "It wouldn't have made a difference to you then if I *was* a lesbian?"

"No."

"Some people don't like the idea."

"It doesn't bother me one way or the other."

"Good."

Someone calls Poppy's name. A middle-aged woman with short, dark hair. Poppy looks up, smiles and nods. "Claire," she says, though Emily hasn't asked. "Works in that sewing shop place. What're you doing today?" she goes on. "Going out somewhere?"

"Maybe. We haven't decided yet. Jasmine's still here…"

"That's nice. You can take her out somewhere. Show her around the area…"

Emily would like to talk more about Poppy: about how and when she met Suzie; where she learned to draw and paint and make jewellery; what else she liked to do. But every time she tries to steer the conversation back to Poppy, she finds Poppy engineers it carefully back again to her. Poppy's eyes never leave her face. She nods and smiles interestedly. Emily deliberately speaks in a measured tone. She forces herself not to gabble. And yet as she listens to herself talking about the move down here, the house, the way she spends her day, she can see how ordinary it sounds and wonders if she senses boredom lurking in Poppy's eyes.

As Emily lifts the teapot to pour the last half-cup, Poppy glances up at the clock. "My God, I have to fly! I told Suzie I'd only be twenty minutes!" She pulls on her coat, grabs the phone, purse and keys she has left on the table.

"Don't worry about the bill!" she says. "I'll get Mrs. S to put it on my tab! I'll call you. Ciao!"

She pulls on the velvet coat, bends to kiss Emily's cheek. People part magically as she makes her way through the now crowded café. Some turn and stare at this outlandish creature; they look up from their drinks, nudge each other. Poppy, seemingly oblivious, calls a general, "Goodbye!" to anyone and everyone, then she's gone.

A sense of anti-climax descends upon Emily. She gathers her stuff together then stands at the counter uncertainly with her purse in her hand. The plump, young girl at the till consults her slip of paper then says, "No, it's fine. All seen to."

It's still bitterly cold, but a wintry sun is trying to make an appearance and instead of turning right out of the café to go straight home, Emily turns left, down the steps, round the corner and along the seafront. The cold wind hits her with a blast that almost takes her breath away. There's hardly anyone around. The gift shops and ice cream kiosks are closed for the season. There's the usual odd few people walking their dogs, hurrying along with their heads down, hoods pulled up or hats pulled down over their faces, their noses and cheeks red with the cold, scarves wrapped tightly around their necks. They nod and mumble, "Hello" or "Good Morning", but no one is inclined to continue the conversation, not even to say, "Cold morning, isn't it?"

As she struggles on, Emily begins to realise why. She can't

feel her fingers, and her face and mouth are stiff with the cold. She had half thought of walking along the Cobb and standing on the end like the *French Lieutenant's Woman*, but she's scarcely reached the amusement arcade when she turns around and walks back. The wind is at her back now, hurrying her along like an impatient child; her scarf unwraps itself and flaps in her face and she pushes it back irritably, and her hair escapes from under her hat and whips around her face.

"You've been ages!" Peter greets her peevishly when she gets in.

She puts the shopping bag on the table and begins to unpack the milk, bread and eggs she bought on the way back.

"I went for a walk on the front. At least I tried to but it was too cold. Then there was a huge queue in the Co-op. Someone buying lottery tickets…"

But Peter's not listening.

"I thought you'd only be about half an hour. I've been worried. I didn't like to go out in case you'd been hurt or something…"

Oh, for God's sake! Emily thinks impatiently. Aloud, she says lightly, "Oooh, you'd have heard if I was. And I'd have called if I needed you. I'm a big girl now, Peter. I can look after myself." She gives him a brief kiss on the cheek as she squeezes past him to open the fridge, to prove she's teasing him and to jolly him out of his bad mood. *Like dealing with a small boy*, she thinks.

"Have you had lunch?" she asks, noticing for the first time the empty baked beans tin on the draining board, the trail of crumbs and tea stains on the surfaces.

"No, I was waiting for you," he says in the same injured tone.

"Oh, but…?" She holds up the tin.

"Oh, that was Jasmine. She didn't know where you put the recycling…"

She could at least have rinsed it out, Emily thinks, running the cold tap and holding the tin underneath it. "What would you like then?" she asks over her shoulder.

Peter's trying to work out how he can winkle Emily's phone out of her handbag where he can see it nestling on top, and he jumps guiltily when she turns around.

"Oh… we could have beans as well, I suppose."

"Great. Nice and easy. Jasmine's upstairs, is she?"

"No, she went out."

"Oh?"

"To your friend's place. She had a text."

It takes Emily a moment to work out what he means. "My friend? A text?" Confusedly, she thinks of Andrea, of Felicity. Then she realises and colour floods to her face. "*Poppy*?" she asks incredulously. "*Poppy* texted her? When? How? How did she get her number?"

"Dunno," Peter says vaguely. "The other evening, I suppose. Does it matter…?"

"No, of course it doesn't," she says, trying to pull herself together. Ridiculously, she feels like Poppy's being unfaithful to her. She didn't even look at her mobile while she was with Emily. She must have sent the text when she got back to the shop. Jasmine is with her now. They have so much in common. Jasmine won't be gabbling on inanely about the weather, about the walks she's been on, about retirement and exercise classes. Jasmine will be talking knowledgeably about art, about art exhibitions; she'll know what to say to Poppy. They'll laugh about Emily, about how parochial she is.

Peter doesn't seem to notice how preoccupied she is.

"I'll put this away, shall I?" he asks, gesturing to her handbag and the two empty carrier bags scrunched up on the chair.

"What?" she asks, vaguely. "Oh, yes. Please. In the front hallway…"

Peter moves out unhurriedly until he's in the tiny front corridor then grabs her phone from her bag and hurries into the study. There he scrolls through her contacts. James, wasn't it? But there's nothing under *J*. He scrolls down. "P… p…" he mutters to himself. The name *Poppy* suddenly leaps out at him from the screen and he reaches for his own phone and keys in the number.

He has to wait until Jasmine comes back and he hears her talking to Emily in the kitchen before he dares do anything. He's already composed the text in his mind, hoping he's achieved the right balance between flirtatious and casual, just in case he's misread the signals. Though he only has to think of the quick flash of understanding, the widening of the pupils in those clear blue eyes to know he hasn't.

I've been thinking of you a lot, he types. *Fancy meeting up for a drink sometime? Peter x*

He already has his excuse. The email from David Ferguson sits in his inbox. There's a Rotary meeting next Thursday. If Poppy says yes he can meet her afterwards. And if anyone sees them he can say it was purely coincidence she was there. He can already hear himself saying, casually, "You'll never guess who was in the pub tonight? Your friend. Poppy."

The text comes through almost immediately. His heart sinks as he reads it. He reddens as a small wriggle of embarrassment runs through him. *Peter?* it reads. *Peter who?* He comforts himself with the thought that at least she's replied.

Peter Stanchester, he texts back. *Emily's husband*. Here the embarrassment turns to guilt that he swiftly quells. He hesitates, not knowing what else to say, then decides to send it just as it is.

He waits but nothing happens. She's playing it cool, he

decides. He deletes the texts, then slips his phone into his pocket instead of leaving it by his computer as usual. Emily's never looked at it before, but there's a first time for everything. Another ready excuse comes to his mind in case she asks how he got Poppy's number. He can say he asked Jasmine for it in case he needed to get hold of her. She's always moaning about the poor signal she gets on her mobile network down here.

He can hear Emily and Jasmine still talking in the kitchen. He resists the temptation to check his phone again and goes through.

Emily's part-way through a sentence. Her words hang in the air. "…why she should want to talk to you?" She sounds indignant, angry, hurt.

Jasmine laughs. "Em's jealous, Daddy!" she says as she sees Peter. "She thinks I'm stealing her new friend away from her."

Emily's face burns. "Don't be silly!" she says, sharply.

Peter vacillates as usual, not sure whose side to take. He hates it when Emily and Jasmine bicker; comforts himself with the thought it was worse when Jasmine was a teenager and he was stuck in the middle, each one looking to him for support. "She's only a child!" he used to say to Emily. "Can't you just let it go?"

'Letting it go' meant letting Jasmine get her own way in whatever the dispute was and because Jasmine was there so rarely, Emily used to give way for a quiet life. But it didn't stop her resenting it, holding it against Peter in her list of things he did wrong, bringing it up in arguments.

"What did you and the famous Poppy do together then?" he asks, lightly. "Go out somewhere?"

"Don't be silly, Daddy! She's working. She wanted to talk to me about Si *actually*." This last word pointedly at Emily, who's surprised she hasn't stuck her tongue out at the same time like the schoolgirl she sounds like.

Emily ignores the barb, but can't resist saying, "She *knows* him then, does she?" managing to give just the right insinuation to the innocent-sounding question.

"What's that s'posed to mean?" Jasmine snaps.

Peter mentally raises his eyes to the ceiling. Nothing like a couple of women for cattiness. Emily's probably right, of course. These artists think nothing of sleeping together. He's momentarily distracted by the thought of Poppy underneath Simeon Blackwood until he remembers Simeon is engaged to Jasmine. "Emily didn't mean anything, Jas darling," he says soothingly, putting his hand on her shoulder and glaring over her head at Emily.

"*Oh for God's sake*," Emily mutters under her breath. "Of course I didn't," she says.

Jasmine looks up tremulously at Peter, tears swimming in her beautiful eyes. What man could resist? Peter kisses her forehead gently as though she was six years old again. Emily's not going to be distracted by these theatricals though. She still wants to know. "So why did she want to talk about Simeon?" she asks.

"Oh, there's an exhibition or something they're both doing. In Bath. She wanted to know how many paintings he's taking. I told her I haven't a clue. Though he wants to do one of me…"

Here she catches Emily's eye. But she's forgotten Peter knows Simeon. "He only does nudes," he snaps. "You're not going to pose for him nude."

"Oh, Daddy!" She rolls her eyes at him. "Don't be such a prude! It's art!"

"It's pornography!"

Emily almost laughs. If Jasmine only knew Peter like she does. But the look on Peter's face is enough to remind her that no man would want a painting of his naked daughter displayed for everyone to see, even if it was only in some obscure hall in Bath.

"Oh," Jasmine says quickly. "I forgot. She asked me to give you this." She takes a small, crumpled paper bag out of her pocket.

Emily takes it from her. Inside, wrapped in tissue paper, she finds the ring she tried on in the shop.

Chapter Eight

"I wasn't sure you'd come," Peter says, putting the glass of orange juice down in front of her.

"How could I resist?" Poppy smiles up at him.

A thrill shoots through his body, straight to his cock, which twitches.

He's surprisingly nervous. Some of the orange juice has spilt onto the table and Poppy wipes it with the frayed sleeve of her jumper.

"And how was the Rotary meeting?" she asks, teasingly.

"Oh God…" he groans.

"Are you going to join?"

"Hard to get out of it now. And at least it's something to do. To get out of the house."

He doesn't say what they both know he's saying. *A way to get to see you.*

Poppy sips her orange juice. "Does Emily know you're meeting me?"

He almost chokes on his glass of wine. "No," he says, managing to stop himself adding, "Of course not." Doubt seeps into his mind, coupled with guilt at the mention of Emily's name. She had been so pleased he was going to the Rotary meeting. He had felt bad saying goodbye, kissing her, feeling her hold him close, seeing her happy smile. "Have a good time!" and she had stood at the door and waved him off as though he was starting a new job. But he's not being unfaithful to her. *Yet*, a small voice says. He's not even sure he will be. Yet why else is he meeting her? His heart had leapt at the sight of her name on his phone. His fingers had trembled as he tried to get to the message. *Yes. I'd love to. When and where?*

From there it was easy. An email to David to say he'd like to come to the next meeting. A few casual words to Emily: "I thought I'd give Rotary a try…"

"Oh, lovely," she said, casually, but he knew her too well. She was thrilled that at last he was doing something.

"You going to tell her?" Poppy says.

"Of course. Someone might…"

"See us? I doubt it. All the good Rotarians have scuttled off home to their wives…"

His guilt intensifies. Is she doing it deliberately? But it's not enough to put him off.

"I'll still tell her," he says.

"She won't like it."

"Can we stop talking about her?" he says, uncomfortably.

"Guilty already, Peter? Not a good start, is it?"

He puts his wine glass down. He can't look at her. Maybe he should just go…

"I'm only joking," she says, suddenly.

"Bloody poor joke."

"Oh come on, Peter."

He feels her hand on his arm. The grip tightens slightly as he still says nothing. Her fingers slide down to the back of his hand. She strokes it gently.

"I won't say another word," she says, softly. "What shall we talk about then?" in a bright voice now.

His mind goes blank. When he had pictured this scene, as he often had over the last few days, he had seen them sitting together, chatting easily. She would toss that beautiful hair, smile into his eyes. Now, though, he can't think of anything to say.

"Okay," she shrugs easily. "I'll start. What did you think of my work?"

Here, he's on easy territory. "It's good," he says. "Well, I can't say about the jewellery. That's more Jasmine's line. But the paintings. Yes. They're good. Good use of light. The water…"

"It's so easy here. So much to paint. And the visitors like to buy a picture of Lyme to take home with them. Couldn't be better. I like your daughter…"

"I'm lucky," he says, trying to sound modest.

"Lovely colouring. Her mother was Indian?"

"Mixed, I think. I don't think she knows herself. Her parents were… free spirits, easy-going, you know. Anusia's the same. So's Jasmine."

"Yes. Jasmine seems happy with Simeon though. Maybe it'll work out."

He laughs a bitter little laugh. "I doubt it. Knowing Simeon."

She laughs too. "Yes. He does have a bit of a reputation."

"You know him well?"

"Have I slept with him, you mean?"

Peter reddens. "I didn't mean… No…"

She laughs. "Would it shock you if I had?"

He says nothing. He'd love to know. He'd love to know all about her. What she's done. Where she's been. Who she's slept with. But this doesn't seem the right moment.

"What about you?" she asks.

"What?"

"Well, I know you were married to Anusia for…?"

"Ten years."

"And then? You didn't meet Emily straight away, did you?"

He shifts uncomfortably again at the mention of Emily's name, but it's not as if he can pretend she doesn't exist.

"No. There were a couple of casual…"

"Yes," she says, waving them away impatiently.

"Then there was Zena. But it didn't work out. She was... well... highly strung. Emotional." He has a sudden swift memory of Zena careering around the house uncontrollably, screeching hysterically, banging her wrists against the windows, cracking one pane right across. "She had a sort of breakdown..." he says. "It was difficult..."

People thought he should have stayed with her. Helped her through. Her parents certainly thought so. Until she went to live with them. After that, they were more sympathetic to him.

He takes another sip of his wine. Looks at her questioningly. He's told her. She has to tell him.

"Oh, you don't want to hear about me," she laughs. "Way too complicated."

"But..."

"There's been no one. No one special, I mean. Not yet. And I'm getting a bit old for first love."

He laughs. She can't be more than thirty-five. He'd love to know her exact age. But he can't possibly ask her.

"How're you finding retirement?" she asks. "D'you miss teaching?"

"Like crazy." This is what he'd love to say to Emily, but he can't for fear she'll start trying to find him something to do.

"You still paint?"

How does she know he paints? Though maybe it's a natural assumption.

"I've tried, but..."

"You should try again. I can show you all the best places..."

Their eyes meet. Is she thinking the same thing? He sees them high on a cliff top, their easels set up, a cloudless sky, a rug on the ground, a bottle of white wine, strawberries...

"I'd love that," he says.

There's a sudden roar of laughter from the bar. Except for

the occasional holidaymakers (and there are none of them at this time of the year), the Pilot Boat is the sort of pub men go to to escape their wives. He'd been a bit worried some of the Rotarians might stay on for a drink there, but they all left promptly. Nonetheless, he feels self-conscious sitting with Poppy in the corner of the pub.

Poppy's talking about an exhibition she's going into.

"Oh, yes," he says. "Jasmine was saying about it."

"I'd like your opinion on the work I'm entering."

Peter's flattered. It's years since anyone asked his advice. Suddenly, he feels important again. It's a feeling he's missed dreadfully. He tries to keep the eagerness out of his voice. "No problem," he says.

"I don't want to submit all the usual boring scenes of Lyme. But then that's what I'm known for. But I'd like to take some of those smaller ones…"

Peter's feeling more confident. He watches her play with her glass as she talks, sliding her fingers absent-mindedly up and down the outside of it. She has lovely hands, the fingers festooned, of course, with rings. Bracelets clink on her wrist and she pushes them back impatiently as she tucks her hair behind her ears. He doesn't need to say much. She talks about how hard she finds it to work sometimes. The lack of inspiration. The distractions. Having to run the shop, having to paint for business and commercial reasons, rather than for her own pleasure. He listens, nods, agrees.

She's finished her drink. He feels honour-bound to offer her another, but it's she who suggests he ought to get back.

It takes him a while to gather his stuff, shrug himself into his coat, find gloves, scarf, his phone, the sheaf of notes he'd been given at the Rotary meeting. She doesn't get up. He hovers uncertainly, wondering what to do. "Shall I walk back with you?"

"I think I'll hang around for a while," she says.

No woman he's ever known would stay in a pub on her own, especially a pub like this, but then Poppy's not like any other woman he's ever known. Her head is bent over her phone, her thumb scrolling down over it.

"Bye then," he says. He wonders if he should ask when they'll meet again, but decides against it. In this day and age, with phones and emails and texts, it's hardly necessary. Illicit affairs must be so much easier than in his young day.

He wonders whether to bend and kiss her, puts his hand out to touch her shoulder, but she suddenly glances up. "Ciao," she says, dismissively.

He glances around at the door. Her head is still bent over her phone. She's smiling to herself, her lips moving silently as she reads.

Guilt returns as he walks home. It's bitterly cold. No one around. Through the lighted windows he glimpses cosy homes, warm rooms. He won't meet Poppy again, he decides. It's not worth this awful guilt.

He steels himself to open the front door. Emily rushes to greet him, raises her face for his kiss. The burden of guilt, deep in his chest, increases. He's glad now he didn't kiss Poppy. The thought of her face close to his, and then Emily's. What's he been thinking of?

"How was it?" Emily's asking.

He's ready for this, though. "Okay," he says. "Well, a bit dull when you don't know what's going on, but it'll get easier."

Emily forces herself not to ask the obvious question of whether he'll go again. He's pretty much said he will.

"Oh, your friend was in the pub," he says, surprising himself. He had told himself he wouldn't say anything but here he is blurting it out, like a guilty child.

100

"Who? Pam?" Emily assumes she may have gone down to meet David afterwards for a drink.

"No. Your jewellery friend. Poppy." He turns away to avoid her eyes, afraid he may give himself away. But Emily has turned away too, her hand flying subconsciously to the ring that hasn't left her finger, except to do the housework or have a bath.

"I can't keep it," she said to Peter. "It must cost a fortune."

He shrugged vaguely. He had no idea how much things like that cost. "It's only handmade stuff, isn't it?"

"That's the most expensive…"

Jasmine had sworn she had no idea what was in the bag. "I thought it was something you'd asked for."

"But you must've looked."

"I didn't think of it."

But Emily knows her better. She and Poppy must have been in on it together. Impossible to believe Jasmine would have bought it for her as a surprise, even if Poppy put her up to it. No, it must be some sort of joke or a game or something.

Hi Poppy, she had texted. *I'm a bit confused. Jasmine brought home a ring. I think there must be some misunderstanding.*

It's a gift. The reply came instantly.

I can't keep it, Emily texted.

I want you to. Emily could hear her imperious tone.

She picked up the phone, pressed dial. Poppy answered instantly. "I thought you liked it." she said without preamble.

"I do. But I can't… I'll pay for it."

"I told you, it's a gift."

Emily said nothing.

"Okay." With a touch of impatience. "If it bothers you that much, think of it as a marketing tool. Show it to your friends. Tell them where it came from… I'll give you some of my cards next time I see you…"

"Okay," Emily said, relieved.

She suddenly realises she hasn't been paying attention to what Peter is saying. Something about having seen Poppy sitting on her own in the bar. She knows the Pilot Boat. A male province. But although it's something she'd never dream of doing herself, she can see Poppy sitting there having a drink, oblivious to any stares.

Peter hears himself blustering on. *God, he must sound guilty. And he hasn't even done anything*. He stops suddenly. Changes the subject. "What've you been doing?"

He pays no attention to Emily's recital of chores: the washing-up, clearing out a cupboard, writing a long email to Anna who she used to work with. He pats his phone in his pocket, wondering when he can escape to his study to see if Poppy's sent a text. He feels certain she has. Or an email. He takes it out of his pocket the moment he leaves the room. His heart leaps at the 'message' signal, and he's childishly disappointed when it's a text from David, asking him if he's free on Tuesday morning to help with a book sale. "Of course I'm free," he mutters to the screen, before the thought occurs to him this is just the sort of excuse he'll be able to use to Emily when he meets Poppy again.

Every day he expects a message from her. He checks his phone several times a day, clicks onto email while he's scrolling through the day's news on his computer. But there's nothing. He itches to contact her. Several times he types her name for an email, or hits *Poppy* on his phone, but each time he stops. He's not going to chase her. He's made the first move. She must come to him.

He's almost decided not to go to the next Rotary meeting. Only the thought she might somehow be there, waiting for him in the bar afterwards, spurs him on. The meeting is upstairs. Several times he excuses himself to go down to the Gents, passing the bar and glancing in, hoping to see her auburn head bent over her phone. She'd glance up, smile conspiratorially, wave casually. He'd return to the meeting buoyed up, spurred on to cope with the dreary talk of golf matches, book sales, open gardens, Rotary projects. But each time he sees only varying shades of grey heads, the occasional bald pate, broad shoulders, thick jumpers over pot bellies. He returns each time dispirited.

He's put his coat on, stuffed the stack of papers he's been handed, as usual, under his arm, and is heading out of the door when he takes a final glance into the crowded bar. What he sees there sends a surge through his body. He feels young again, alive, exhilarated. She's sitting in exactly the same place as before, head bent over her phone in exactly the same way, her lips moving in that same secret smile as she reads it. Now he has to find a way to extricate himself from David, who's suggesting, in his blustery way, that they meet to discuss the committee they're putting him on. He's so unused to all this sort of thing.

"Hang on, I left those notes behind…" he says.

David is talking to someone else now and he turns at the door, scarcely registering what Peter is saying, and luckily not noticing the papers Peter is holding behind his back.

"Oh, well, I'll email you…"

The door opens with a blast of cold air and he's gone.

"I didn't think —" he starts, but Poppy is speaking at the same time.

"I've got one," she says, lifting a glass of white wine and tipping it slightly.

"I'll just…"

"One for you, too." She nods in the direction of the glass of red wine on the table.

"What if I hadn't come?"

"But you did. I knew you would." She chinks her glass against his. "You told her," she adds.

He reddens. "What? Who?" But of course she means Emily.

"Emily. That you'd met me."

"Well, it just sort of…"

"Yes." She cuts him off in that impatient schoolmistressy way she has. "Are you going to tell her again? Just so I know what to say. Otherwise, it makes it awkward…"

"I didn't know you ever saw her. She didn't say…"

"Well, if she doesn't tell you everything then you don't need to tell her. It can be our secret." She smiles conspiratorially into his eyes. "It's not as if we're doing anything wrong."

He reminds himself of this as he walks home through the ice-cold streets. "Our secret." He hugs the words to himself. This is what he needs. Something to make him feel worthwhile. Something separate from Emily. Something she doesn't know about. Something she can't get her hands on. Something she can't control.

The guilt returns as he nears home, but he stows it away, hearing Poppy's voice in his head. *"It's not as if we're doing anything wrong."*

Chapter Nine

Emily looks around with pride at the clean kitchen. She picks up her cup of tea, grabs her phone and sits down in the sitting room. It's just gone seven. Peter won't be back for another hour or so.

2 messages, her phone informs her. Her heart leaps when she sees Poppy's name. Apart from the texts about the ring she hasn't heard from her. She didn't even drop in the business cards she had promised, and Emily was childishly jealous when Peter said he'd seen her in the pub. She must have been meeting someone. She obviously has loads of friends in Lyme Regis. She doesn't need another one. Silly of Emily to think she might. Every time she checked her phone she hoped to see her name, but as the days passed, then the weeks, she realised it wasn't going to happen.

When can we meet again? the message reads. Emily smiles at its baldness. Typical Poppy. No *Hi, how are you?*

Emily hesitates then decides to tell the truth. *It's difficult,* she taps in. *With Peter around all the time. He likes me to be with him.*

Doesn't he go out ever? the next one says.

Only to Rotary. Every other Thursday. He's there tonight.

Okay. A fortnight today. It's a date.

Emily hesitates again. She used to go out with the girls from work sometimes, but that was to a city bar in Bristol. She can't see herself walking into one of the pubs here in Lyme. Not without Peter. But she doesn't want to look foolish.

That would be lovely, she replies. *Where d'you suggest?*

I'll have a think. Let me know where you live and I'll come around for you. Six fifteen. Okay?

As she taps in *Okay*, and her address, she wonders fleetingly how Poppy knows what time Rotary is. But it's a small town. Maybe it's the sort of thing everyone knows.

She's sitting reading when Peter gets in. "I'm sorry I'm so late," he says. "A couple of the chaps asked me to stay for a drink…"

She glances up at the clock in surprise. "Are you? I didn't notice. Did you have a good time?"

★

The fortnight passes agonisingly slowly. Still uncertain where they are going, Emily hasn't a clue what to wear. Or whether to eat or not. Dinner is supplied at the Rotary meeting and she usually has beans on toast or an omelette. She checks her phone several times but there's no word from Poppy. Finally, in desperation, Emily texts her. *Are we still on for tonight?*

Of course, comes the swift reply. *Six fifteen, like I said.*

"That's not much help," Emily mutters to herself. *So what are our plans?* she texts. *We eating somewhere or what?*

Oh, I hadn't thought of food. I'm a bit skint. Shall we make it a bit later so you can eat first?

Emily thinks quickly. *We don't need to go out at all. We can stay in. I can cook something for us both.*

I don't want to put you to any trouble.

You won't. I have to eat anyway. I can do something easy. You okay with salmon?

Lovely. I'll bring some white wine.

As she prepares everything, Emily has desperate second thoughts. Wrapping the salmon in foil, she wonders if she should have bought fresh fish rather than Tesco's own salmon steaks. The lilies she has arranged in a vase look as though she's trying too hard. The house is pristine and she has a sudden urge to untidy it a bit, make it look a bit more lived-in. Yet even as she thinks it, she knows she won't.

"So what time's this friend of yours coming over?" Peter asks.

"Six fifteen. Don't worry. You don't have to see her."

Peter's uncomfortable about the whole thing. He doesn't know how friendly Emily and Poppy are and he can't possibly ask either of them. Poppy would only laugh, Emily would wonder why he was suddenly so interested in whom she was friends with.

He hasn't heard from Poppy again. He tells himself he's given up bothering about it but he still gets excited when he gets a message, only to be disappointed when it's not her.

"I won't be late tonight," he tells Emily. He's quite sure Poppy won't be there.

"Okay," Emily says. "But it really doesn't matter. I don't mind." She kisses him absently and he feels himself being shooed outside the door.

Poppy is early. She arrives like a whirlwind, pressing her cold cheek against Emily's face, divesting herself of that voluminous fur coat she wears and layers of scarves and an astrakhan hat; shaking out her unlikely-looking auburn hair and talking, talking, talking.

"God, it's freezing out there! Brass monkeys have got nothing on it. The fish smells good. I'm starving! What a sweet little house. I had no idea they were like this inside. Your neighbour gave me a weird look. Don't you get any visitors or something?"

Emily laughs, not knowing which question to answer first, but Poppy doesn't seem to expect any response. She looks out of place in the neat and tidy house, this larger-than-life gypsy girl, examining the paintings, picking up photographs. "This is Jasmine, isn't it? Oh, your wedding photo. How sweet. You didn't wear white?"

She doesn't wait for a reply, moves on to another picture. "Monet. Of course. I knew you'd like the Impressionists…"

The mention of Jasmine and the painting reminds Emily of the ring.

"You didn't give me any business cards."

"What?" Poppy is genuinely confused and Emily reddens.

"The ring." She twists it on her finger. "You said I should use it as a marketing tool…"

Poppy waves her arm theatrically. "Oh, I'll let you have some sometime. I didn't bring any with me tonight. This is a social visit."

"Did Jasmine know?"

Again, Poppy looks at her blankly.

"About the ring," Emily says.

"No. Why would she? Look, you're getting hung up about nothing. I told you. I like you. Why shouldn't I give you a present? It's mine to give."

"But you must have said something. When you gave it to her."

Poppy smiles. "I told her it was from Peter. A surprise."

"Oh. But…" Emily stops, confused. Jasmine didn't say that. And anyway, she would have known Peter didn't do things like that. Alarm bells clang in her head. Here is someone who lies glibly and easily. Someone totally unconcerned about being caught out. Someone who bends the truth to their own advantage.

Poppy is examining another picture. "I don't know this artist," she frowns.

"We bought it on holiday. A pavement artist. The paint was still wet. We had to wait for it to dry. It's nothing special. But it reminds us of Majorca."

"It's lovely."

She keeps up a steady flow of conversation and Emily, who had worried about whether they would find enough to talk about, finds she doesn't have to make much effort. And yet Poppy seems to glean information from her: where she lived, where she was brought up, how she met Peter. Conversely, she gives little away about herself, glancing away when Emily asks about her past, comfortable only when Emily asks about her work.

"Peter says he'll take a look at it. For my next exhibition, you know."

Emily's clearing the plates from the table and she's not sure for a moment if she's heard correctly. "Peter?" she repeats. "*My* Peter? What exhibition?"

At the same time, she wonders how or when or why Peter would be talking to Poppy about an exhibition.

"Oh, sorry," Poppy laughs. "Have I put my foot in it? I thought you knew."

"Knew?" she repeats, knowing she sounds stupid.

"That I'd seen Peter. Oh… weeks ago. It doesn't matter…"

"He said he'd seen you. But not to talk to. At least I don't think so…"

"It doesn't matter," she says again, quickly.

Alone in the kitchen, Emily feels uncomfortable. It's not like Peter not to tell her. Yet what was there to tell? She pictures him stopping to talk to Poppy. Why wouldn't she ask him to look at her work?

"You okay in there?" Poppy calls through. "Can I help with anything?"

"No, I'm fine. I didn't do dessert," she calls back. "I've got yoghurts. Or fruit."

She senses Poppy's hesitation.

"Or there's some sponge puddings in the freezer," she says.

"Yummy!" Poppy calls. "Got any ice cream?"

Poppy's scraping the last scrap of treacle pudding from the bowl with childlike gusto when she suddenly glances at her watch. "My God! Is that the time? I have to go!"

"What about coffee?" Emily thinks of the coffee tray laid with the best cups, the antique silver coffee spoons left to her by her mother and the box of After Eight mints.

"No, I'm sorry. I've got to get back. I promised Suzie…"

She leaves in the same flurry of excitement she arrived with. The house falls silent when she's gone. Emily clears up mechanically, thinking over the evening, cringing at some things she said, smiling at others.

"I'll text you," Poppy said when she left. "We can do this again. My place next time…"

Remembering Suzie's possessive arm around Poppy's shoulder, Emily doubts this will ever happen. She sees her waiting impatiently for Poppy to return. Does Poppy tell her where she's going, who she's meeting? Probably not. But you can't tie someone like Poppy down. Suzie must be used to it by now, used to those easy lies.

Peter's late back. Nine o'clock comes, then half past. She checks her phone. Nothing. Then, just as she's wondering if she should go out and look for him she hears the click of the latch.

"Sorry," he says before she can say anything. "I didn't realise it was so late…"

"It doesn't matter," Emily says. "Cup of tea?" She heads for the kitchen.

"No, I'll have a whisky. I'll take it in the study. I want to go over this stuff…" He gestures to the folder in his hand.

"How did it go?" Emily asks, dutifully.

"Oh, same old stuff. I just want to get my head around it…"

"You don't have to do it now. Don't you want to watch the news?"

"No," he says, testily. "I just said I want to do this."

"But you've got all day tomorrow," Emily persists. "Why d'you have to do it now?"

"Why d'you always have to organise me? I'll do it when I like."

"Okay, okay," Emily says, soothingly.

"And don't patronise me. I'm not a child."

In his study Peter listens to the ice cracking gently in his glass while his computer gradually comes to life.

"*Poppy*," he says to himself. "*Poppy. Poppy. Poppy.*"

She had arrived in a flustered rush just as he was leaving the pub. "Oh, Peter, I thought I'd missed you!" she gushed, grasping his arm.

Peter had reddened, conscious of David next to him, other Rotarians milling around.

But he should have realised Poppy was an expert at this sort of thing. "I was wondering if you could pop in and take a look at those sketches. I need to know which you think will be best for the exhibition..."

He had made a big thing of looking at his watch, muttering something about Emily expecting him back, but she was ready for this too.

"Oh, it's fine. She's not expecting you back for hours. We had a lovely dinner. She's a marvellous cook..."

No one seemed to notice them go. Rounding the corner and out of sight of anyone, she linked her arm through his.

"Suzie's out," she said.

Electricity shot through him. His cock stiffened, straining uncomfortably against his pants and trousers, and he wished he could reach inside and rearrange himself.

The shop bell tinkled as Poppy opened it. He followed

her through as she switched on lights, switched off the alarm, switched off lights again.

"This way," she said.

For a brief heart-stopping moment he thought she was inviting him up to the flat. It was only then that he realised that wasn't what he wanted.

She followed his gaze to the stairs. If she knew what he was thinking she said nothing. This was what was so frustrating about her. He never knew where he stood with her. He was out of his depth.

He only stayed half an hour. They looked through the paintings. He told her which he thought were best. She was no great artist, certainly, little better than many of his students. But her work was selling. And he couldn't deny it had appeal.

His initial sexual response to her invitation had waned. Standing next to her like this, it felt like she was one of his students and all his professional instincts came to the fore.

He turned down her offer of a drink. Suddenly, he wanted to get home to Emily. But as soon as he stepped outside, into the icy air, he found he dreaded going back. What could he say to her? He couldn't tell her he'd been to see Poppy's work. She'd wonder how he knew her well enough to be asked in and why he was going in the evening. So he wouldn't tell her. But David saw them going off together. What if he told Pam and she said something? Or what if Poppy told Emily? Maybe she already has. She almost said as much. *Emily won't mind.* But they had made a pact, hadn't they? *"Our little secret. It's not as if we're doing anything wrong."* He walked past the turning to their road, on towards the Alexandra Hotel, up the hill, down again, along the front, past the silent, darkened, closed shops and lighted, noisy pubs. He sat down on one of the benches that overlooked the sea. The streetlight above him illuminated only his immediate surroundings. He could see the path, the low wall next to it, beyond that nothing; though he could hear the waves washing onto the beach and the sucking sound of the pebbles being drawn back and forth. He had no idea how long he sat there. When he got up to go he still hadn't decided what to say to Emily. It all seemed so complicated. He had no idea what he was doing, where it was going. He was scared and exhilarated all at the same time. It was the most alive he had felt for years and whatever the cost, he wasn't going to stop.

Chapter Ten

The cold winter turns into a cold spring, the temperature struggling to reach much above zero even as Easter approaches.

"We've still got the heating on at home," Pam says as they warm their hands on the radiator at the back of the Pilates hall.

Emily's only half-listening. She fingers her phone in her pocket, wondering if Poppy's texted yet. Nine o'clock. Still a bit early for her.

She checks again after the class. *1 message.* Her heart leaps. She knows it's Poppy even before she sees her name appear.

How are you? she asks.

They text every day. Sometimes just a brief exchange, other times long messages. Poppy tells her about her work. *I've been asked to design a wedding ring.* Or, *I've been working all day on a painting and I just can't get the lighting right.* Emily's flattered by these confidences. By comparison, her own messages, *Just back from Zumba* or *Going for a drive* seem mundane and dull, but Poppy doesn't seem to mind.

The fortnightly dinners have become a fixed event. At first, Poppy would send a text, *Can I come round tonight?* but now she just turns up, ten past six, regular as clockwork. She's gone just as promptly, back home, Emily assumes, to the patiently-waiting Suzie. She's never repeated the invitation for Emily to go there, and Emily wonders sometimes where she tells Suzie she's going every other week.

"How's Peter?" Poppy always asks.

"Fine," Emily lies loyally.

In fact, he's not. He's been in a foul mood for weeks. Just occasionally he comes out of it, and she has a glimpse of the Peter she used to know, but then he slips back into it again. She can't seem to do anything right. If she asks how he is, he snaps at her. If she doesn't ask, he accuses her of not talking to him.

But she can't tell Poppy this. She can't even tell Grace. It's not fair to Peter. She knows the answer. Or thinks she does. He needs to get out more, just like she told Grace. She laughs to herself even as she thinks it. But it's true. He needs to see people other than her. The fortnightly Rotary evenings haven't helped as much as she hoped. He's always in a bad mood when he gets back, and he never wants to talk about what they do.

"Are you going to help with that book sale?" she asks.

"Why're you always organising me?"

"I'm not. I just wondered, that's all. Pam says David's been talking about it for ages. Shame we gave all those books to charity before we came here."

"And you made me throw loads out."

"Only the text books, Peter. They were no good to anyone. And there's no room here. I told you there wouldn't be."

"I could've kept them in the garage."

"And what would be the point of that? You'd never be able to look at them there."

This is an old argument, one that dragged on for weeks when they were packing up to move. Peter is a hoarder. Emily is the practical one. "We can't keep all this," she kept saying.

"But those are all my old steering wheels," Peter said, aghast. "I've had them for years. I can't throw them away."

"They've been in the shed for years. You've never even looked at them. What're you going to do with them? We'll have nowhere to put them..."

"In the garage. I'll hang them on the wall."

"You said you'd do that before and you never did."

But Peter was adamant and they're still packed in a box at the back of the garage.

When they were working these sorts of arguments had soon blown over. A day apart, talking to other people, the distraction, the inevitable problems at work and they had fallen into perspective. Now, day after day together, the arguments drag on. Peter's moods become worse. He can't bear to be crossed. He's always right. She can't even express an opinion on a news or TV programme without him getting angry. "I'm right," he says. "You know I am." And in the end it's easier to agree than to antagonise him.

She longs to be on her own for a while, to be her own person like she used to be when she was working. Apart from her exercise classes her only escape is the fortnightly Thursday evenings with Poppy.

She's just taken two chicken breasts out of the freezer one Thursday lunchtime when her phone rings. "Hi, it's me! Look, Suzie's away. Why don't you come over here tonight?"

Emily throws the chicken pieces back in the freezer.

She's ready to go at six o'clock. "I'll walk down with you," she tells Peter.

"It's a bit early," he says, glancing at his watch. "You go on if you like…"

"Don't be silly. I'll wait for you. You're right. It's far too early."

She picks up her book and tries to read, but the words don't make sense.

"We could watch the headlines," she says, even though she's never very interested in what's going on in the world.

Finally, it's six fifteen.

She hangs on Peter's arm as they walk down the road. "I'm dying to see Poppy's flat," she says.

Peter says nothing. He'd love to see it too. It's not fair that Poppy's invited Emily before him.

Poppy's waiting on the step. "Hello, you two!" she smiles. She hugs Emily and pecks Peter politely on the cheek.

"I'll look after her for you!" she laughs as he walks off.

The staircase is hidden behind a wooden door. It's steep and dark. There's another door at the top. The flat is as she expected and worse. Tiny, cramped. Bright colours everywhere. Stuff on every surface. A huge sofa dominates the room, a coffee table in front; a tiny, round dining table pushed against one wall below the casement window. The roof is gabled. They're under the eaves. It's fine for Poppy, but Emily is tall and she needs to bend slightly so she doesn't knock her head on the ceiling.

"Sit down, sit down," Poppy says, moving books, papers, newspapers to one side on the sofa. "What can I get you? Wine? Elderflower? Tea?"

"Tea," Emily says, suddenly overcome with shyness.

They eat at the tiny table-for-two by the window that overlooks the main street. The meal is surprisingly good: quiche from the delicatessen, salad, new potatoes ("The only thing I can cook!" Poppy laughs.) and blackberry cheesecake from the cake shop for dessert. "Deee-licious!" Poppy says in her childlike way, licking the spoon.

"More tea?" she asks.

"Yes, please."

"You're quiet tonight."

Emily laughs. She's always quiet nowadays. It's Poppy who talks, yet afterwards she can never remember exactly what she says, just the sound of her voice, her hands waving around, her throaty laugh. It's either about her work, or her travels, or people Emily has never heard of, different ones every time. The stories are sometimes the same, though, or at least similar.

Different settings maybe. A slightly different slant. And Emily has come to realise, although there may be an element of truth lurking somewhere, they are, in fact, more like stories Poppy has fabricated to make a fantastical tale. It doesn't make them any less appealing and as she listens she inhabits, just for a while, Poppy's world of fiction and fantasy, a world so different from her own practical life of housework and Peter and classes and shopping that it might be on a different planet and Poppy from a different race.

At half past eight Poppy's hand predictably flies to the watch on her wrist. "My God!" she says as usual. "Look at the time!"

At Emily's house this is her cue to gather up her bag, her coat or shawl or cloak or whatever she's brought with her, press her cheek to Emily's and fly out of the door. Here in Poppy's house it is Emily who rises, hovers uncertainly, wondering where Poppy's put her coat.

"Oh, it's in the bedroom..." Poppy says, seeing Emily searching amongst the wraps, shawls and blankets heaped up on the sofa.

"Can I just go to the loo?"

"Of course. Through here... Oh damn!" A loud burst of song explodes from her mobile. "Hello? Yes. Hang on..."

Emily follows her out into the tiny landing and Poppy points to a door at the end, disappearing herself behind another door. Emily opens the creaky door, reaches for the light cord. A naked bulb overhead emits a feeble, yellow glow. The room is tiny. Cracked yellow lino on the floor, rimed with dirt. Cracked white tiles on the walls. The loo seat sits at an odd angle, the sort you know will swivel uncomfortably under you when you sit down. Not that Emily has any intention of sitting on it. It looks like it hasn't been washed for years. A curly, black hair clings to the edge of the rim. The toilet bowl is rimmed brown, a yellowy tinge to the water. Emily hovers uncomfortably above it, washes her hands afterwards in the grimy bowl, wipes them briefly on the damp, frayed grubby-looking towel hanging underneath. There's no bath, just a shower. A collection of bottles lines the floor alongside. Amongst them she sees a bottle of auburn hair dye. The shower curtain's half closed, but she can't help herself hooking the edge back with the tip of her little finger. Brown stains run down the sides of the white tiles, a rusty-looking shower head lies at the bottom of the shower tray, along with a tangle of auburn hair that has obviously been pulled out of the drain hole and left on the side, and greenish grey mould has formed around the edges. She lets the curtain drop, rinses her fingers again, dabbing them against her jeans rather than risking the damp towel again.

Poppy is still on the phone in the bedroom. The door's closed but she can hear her voice, low, secretive; she doesn't want Emily to hear what she's saying. The only other door must lead to the kitchen. Emily hesitates. She doesn't want Poppy to think she's snooping. But she can always say she wanted a drink of water. She edges the door open. The room beyond is worse than she possibly could have imagined. Like every other room, it's tiny. Every surface is laden with stuff: the kettle next to the toaster next to a coffee percolator next to a bread bin next to a vegetable steamer... The china is all on open shelves, higgledy-piggledy, saucepans next to teacups. But nothing can excuse the filth. Even in a quick glance she can see crumbs, smears and bits of food amongst the spoons, plates, dishes and mugs lying around. The draining board is piled high with crockery; saucepans precariously balanced on top. A greasy tea towel and oven glove hang on the back of the chair. The oven door is open. Emily can't bear to think what it's like inside. She closes the door quickly, feeling suddenly queasy. She won't come again. Not to eat anyway, not even to drink, judging by the grubby-looking mugs and the filthy sink.

She's safely back on the sofa when Poppy reappears. She's wearing her coat, carrying Emily's over her arm. "I'm going the opposite way," she says as she hands it to her. "But I'll come out with you... oh, unless you're coming to meet Peter?"

"*Coming?*" Emily's puzzled. But maybe she's misunderstood. "No!" she says aloud, with a little laugh. "He'd hate it! And I couldn't! Not walk into a pub on my own like that..."

"But I'm going."

"What?" So she hadn't misunderstood.

"To the Pilot Boat."

The inference is impossible. But it can't be. Poppy says nothing. Her head's bent. She's searching in her bag, checking keys, phone...

Emily feels foolish, but she has to say it. "You're meeting Peter?"

"What would you say if I was?" Poppy laughs. "If we had some sort of clandestine arrangement?"

"I... but you haven't... you can't... don't be silly..."

Poppy's darting around, in and out, turning off lights, closing doors.

"Poppy," Emily says, suddenly cross.

"What?" Poppy stands on the threshold, holding the door open for Emily to leave.

"You're not meeting Peter," Emily says in a decisive voice. "Are you? Why would you?"

"Why indeed?" Poppy laughs. "Come on. I'm going to be late..."

Emily scarcely feels the peck on her cheek, the brief, warm hug, and as she turns to watch Poppy's figure hurrying down the street, she wonders if she even said goodbye and thank you. Maybe she should rush after her to make sure. But Poppy's far too far away now, and anyway she must have done it. She always does. Even when Poppy's coming to see her she says, "Thank you."

"For what?" Poppy always laughs. "*You* were the one doing the cooking!"

"For coming to see me!" she laughs back.

She can't bear to think of losing this. This friendship. This warmth. Poppy's the only one here she can count as her friend. Yet it's a strange friendship: no confidences, no common interests. Even Emily can see it for what it is: a sort of hero worship on her part. And Poppy needs to be hero-worshipped. But if Poppy was seeing Peter. If they were meeting secretly behind Emily's back, talking about her maybe. Laughing at her. But the idea's preposterous. Why would Peter see Poppy? To advise her about her work? But then he'd tell her. And yet. And yet. He's always in such a bad mood when he gets back. And Poppy rushes off so promptly each time. "Gotta go!" She had always assumed this was for the waiting Suzie.

She's so wrapped up in her thoughts she can scarcely remember walking home and she's at the door before she realises. She lets herself in, switches on lights, puts the kettle on. She's just sat down with a cup of tea when she hears the front door opening. She's so relieved she nearly jumps up and throws her arms around Peter, but one look at his face and she's glad she didn't. The black mood is still with him, she sees. But she has to try. "Good meeting?" she asks.

"Tedious," he says. "I don't know why I keep going." But of course he does. If he didn't, how could he go on seeing Poppy? The fact that she didn't turn up tonight won't change anything. He'd forgotten what it felt like to be stood up. Over and over again he checked his phone. Humiliation washed over him. *"I'm not doing this again,"* he told himself. Yet even as he walked home he found himself making excuses for her. Some sort of emergency maybe. Yes, that was it. And she couldn't let him know. No signal on her phone maybe. The coverage around here is hopeless. He's rehearsed this next bit carefully. "Just get myself a drink," he says, casually.

"Okay," Emily nods, turning back to her book.

He turns around at the door. "Oh. How was Poppy?"

"Fine. We had a great time. Thanks."

Emily hesitates. Then. "You didn't see her then? At the pub?"

All Peter's composure vanishes but somehow he manages a strangled, "What?"

"She said she was going there. To meet someone. I thought it was you!"

Emily is laughing. She doesn't seem to have noticed anything wrong. Peter laughs too, though he doesn't know how he manages it.

"No," he manages to say. "No, I didn't see her. No, I wasn't meeting her. Why on earth would I?"

"That's what she said."

Alone in the kitchen, Peter finds his hand is shaking as he pours whisky into the glass. He stops. Pours a bit more. Adds ice.

He's just about to go back in when he feels his phone vibrate. He doesn't need to look at it to know who it is.

Chapter Eleven

Suddenly it's summer and Lyme Regis bursts into life. Holidaymakers swarm in the streets. They fill the pavements, the shops. The main street blocks with cars queuing for car parks. Children trail down to the beach with buckets and spades. Boats appear in the harbour. The seafront smells of fish and chips. After months of cold weather they wake day after day to blue skies and sunshine, and when Peter brings Emily her morning tea she drinks it quickly so they can be up and out of the house before the traffic builds up. They go for long drives, taking a packed lunch and a flask of tea. Sometimes they find a nice pub and the sandwiches stay in the boot of the car, thrown away with a guilty pang when they get home. Classes stop for the summer holidays but now, conversely, they go out less. The roads are busier in the school holidays. Instead they sit on their tiny terrace, reading books and magazines, waiting until the holidaymakers have gone back to their hotels in the evening before venturing out for their favourite walks in the town, the ones known only to the locals.

Peter's in a better mood now. "He seems to have settled into retirement," Emily tells Grace on the phone. "Thank God for this Rotary Club. He's always off to something nowadays. He's on one of the committees. He's gone to a meeting tonight. Heaven alone knows what it's all about. He never says…"

She was hoping Poppy might have come over, but she said she was busy. "I've got an exhibition coming up," she told Emily. "I don't really want to do it but Suzie says I must. It's such a drag." She paused. "Emily…" she began.

Emily recognised the tone. "Yes?" she said, tentatively.

"You wouldn't. I mean…"

"Help with posters? Hand out leaflets? Type something out for you?"

"No," she laughed. "At least, that would be great. I just wondered… I'd love to paint you."

"What? Don't be silly. You don't mean…" Her mind flew, ridiculously, to Simeon Blackwood painting only nudes.

In that uncanny way she has, Poppy seemed to have read her mind. "Your face, silly!" she laughed. "I'm sure you have a lovely body," she went on, pausing as if picturing it and Emily's flush deepened. "But your face is so interesting."

"I don't know…"

"Peter would like it. You could give it to him as a birthday present. I could have it finished by October."

"How d'you know when Peter's birthday is?"

But there's a scuffling sound on the end of the phone as if Poppy's covered the mouthpiece and is talking to someone else. "I've got to go," she says in a low voice. "Someone's just come in."

This is the problem with Poppy. She's hopeless at any real sort of conversation. You never get a straight answer to a straight question. She's an expert at avoiding things she doesn't want to talk about.

Not like Grace, who's happy to talk about anything. "Oh, and Peter's started painting again," Emily says now. "He's been going out with the camera to get some shots. On his own. You've got no idea how good it is to have time to myself again…"

She couldn't believe it the first time. "I thought I'd go out for a walk," he said.

She had just sat down with a book and her heart sank, but she put it down dutifully. "Okay," she said.

"You don't have to come."

"What? But you want me to, don't you?"

"Not necessarily."

"Oh. Are you sure?"

"Well, I'm going to take the camera. See if I can find something to paint. You can come if you like. But it won't be very interesting for you…"

"No, it's fine. I'll stay here. Thanks."

Guilt settled on Peter the moment he left her. And it hasn't gone away. *We're not doing anything wrong*, he reminds himself each time he sees Poppy. *It's purely professional.* And it is. They talk. They walk. She shows him where she paints. They both take photos. Sometimes they go back to her studio and he looks at her work.

"Why d'you sign like that?" he asks her one day.

She's crouched down, rifling through a pile of canvasses.

"What?" she says, abstractedly.

"The number 7. Why don't you sign your name?"

"It *is* my name," she says.

He laughs. "Don't be silly. No one's called Seven."

"You'd be surprised!" she laughs. "But I'm not Poppy either. It's a joke. You know it is. The shop. We needed a name to go with Suzie's surname. Fields. 'Poppy Fields'. It worked. So I became Poppy."

"But your surname is James, isn't it?" he asks. "I Googled you…"

"Oh, I bet you did!" she laughs. "And I bet Emily did too! That's the trouble with your age group. You believe everything you read online. Oh, here it is!" She holds up a canvas and he takes it from her. "The same view. A year ago maybe. What d'you think?"

He takes it from her. Puts it next to the other. He can see his influence on her, knows he's doing her good. It makes him feel important again.

He's stopped asking where Suzie is whenever he goes.

"She's out," she always says, vaguely.

He wonders if Suzie knows where Poppy goes and what she does, or if, like him, she's so bamboozled with half-made plans and half-baked excuses that she's given up trying to pin her down and just accepts her for what she is.

"I've asked Emily," Poppy greets him with one day.

"What?" Peter's often confused by Poppy's abrupt announcements.

"About the portrait. For your birthday. Once I'm done with this exhibition."

"Portrait?" he repeats, knowing he sounds stupid.

"Of Emily. I thought you'd like it."

"You said it was for my birthday."

"Yes."

"Didn't she wonder how you knew when my birthday was?"

"You worry too much, Petey."

"My God, you sound like my ex-wife!"

"Don't tell me that! Here." She thrusts a painting at him. "What about this one? Or is it too twee?"

It's one of her many views of the Cobb, that he'd seen hanging in the shop on his first visit.

"I'd put it in anyway," he says. "It'll probably sell."

"Okay."

"Poppy. Emily. You're not going to paint her...?" He hesitates.

"Nude? My God, you're as bad as she is! What's wrong with you two?"

"It's just. Simeon. Jasmine's... fiancé..." He stumbles over the last word.

"Si Blackwood! He only does nudes. Has he done Jasmine yet?" She bursts into laughter at her own *double entendre*.

"No. She wouldn't…"

"I don't see why not. He did mine…"

"What?" His mind flies to an image of Poppy spreadeagled on a tousled bed.

"He paints all his lovers."

Now it's Anusia he sees instead, her dark skin, heavy, nippled breasts, legs slightly open. He can almost smell her musky smell. He clears his throat, pretends to look through the other paintings she's laid out for him.

"Now I've embarrassed you," she says. "Sorry. Jasmine's still with him then?"

"Yes. But I don't want to talk about it."

"Okay." She shrugs her shoulders easily.

Peter's always surprised Emily doesn't notice anything unusual about him whenever he gets home. But she's there as usual with a kiss, an offer of a drink, a brief question about where he's been, who he's seen. He always has a ready answer, but she seldom shows more than a passing interest.

The summer comes to an end suddenly at the end of August with a week of heavy rain. Holidaymakers huddle in shops, hoping the rain will stop. By early September with the schools back, they have all but gone; only the parents with pre-school children and the retired haunt the beaches and the seafront in the late summer sunshine.

"I can't believe we've been retired a year," Emily tells Pam as they stand waiting for Pilates to begin. "I'm so pleased he's got involved with Rotary. It's been really good for him. And he's painting again. Did I tell you? He says he might even exhibit some of his stuff. With Poppy, you know. My friend Poppy James, the artist."

She loves talking about Poppy like this. It makes her feel special and important to have a friend who's an artist and well known in the town.

"Lovely," Pam's saying politely, though she doesn't seem that interested.

Emily's on her way back after the class when she sees a removal van edging into the road. By the time she's reached the house the van has parked outside, boxes are being unpacked, men shouting to each other. An unfamiliar red car is parked behind the lorry. Emily's just fitting her key into the lock when she hears the voice.

"Hi. Hello. I'm Dan. Your new neighbour."

He's tall, slim, dark, good-looking in a boyish way, a bit too much of a girly face to be Emily's type. Extremely pale face. Deep blue eyes. Dark hair which flops over his forehead in a Hugh Grant style that emphasises his boyishness.

"Emily." She hears herself saying, taking his proffered hand. It's firm, confident. She smiles into his eyes. She can tell he fancies her. She reddens, drops her eyes quickly from his.

He leans into the car. "This is Rose."

There's no reply and he calls again. "Rose…"

The girl is twisted around in her seat. She turns around with a distracted look on her face, smiles politely. "Won't be a sec…" she says.

Now Emily sees what she's doing. In the back seat, in a baby seat, sits a baby. No, a child. Toddler maybe. The prettiest child Emily has ever seen. Fair hair curling around her face. Blue eyes. Beautiful eyes. Beautiful child. Emily is captivated.

"Oh, and this is Alicia," Dan is saying.

He pronounces it 'Aleesha' not 'Aliss-y-a' like Emily would.

"Leesha," The little girl repeats. Her voice is perfect too. Sweet. Gentle. She smiles at Emily, revealing tiny, white teeth; plump, rosy cheeks.

Rose is getting out of the seat, and she and Dan are laughing.

"She has this effect on everyone," Dan says. "Once seen. Never forgotten."

Emily laughs too, tearing her eyes away from Alicia to shake hands with Rose. Easy to see where the little girl gets her looks: Rose has the same pale, clear skin; same wavy, fair hair; except hers is long and loose, curling around her face, cascading over her shoulders. She's lovely. Peter will adore her.

"You must meet my husband," Emily says. "Let me find him…"

But Peter's at the door already, attracted by the unusual noises. Emily sees Rose blush under his gaze. He shakes hands with Dan, peeks in at Alicia, instantly smitten like Emily was.

"I remember when Jasmine was that age…" he says.

"Oh, you've got children too?" Rose asks, interestedly.

"My step-daughter," Emily says quickly to avoid any misunderstandings. "She's thirty-three now."

Rose colours. "Yes of course, silly of me. Well, I'm sure I'll meet people with children. A playgroup or something. I haven't had time to look into anything yet…"

Examining them more closely as they talk, Emily sees she's been mistaken in thinking of them as a young couple. Like most mothers with young children, Rose wears no make-up and her eyes crinkle at the corners as she smiles. Tiny thread veins stand out either side of her nose. Her face has lost the bloom of youth. She could be as much as forty. Dan, too, is older than at first sight. He, too, has lines on his forehead and his hair is just beginning to go grey at the temples.

Trapped in her car seat, the little girl starts to make impatient little grizzling noises.

"I'd better get her in," Rose says. "We've got such a lot to do, but you'll have to come around when we're a bit more sorted."

"No, you must come to us," Emily says.

"Thanks. Daytime is best obviously with Leesha. Just a cup of tea or something. That would be lovely."

"And let us know if we can help with anything," Peter says. "Bread, milk, tea, a cup of sugar…?"

"Thanks, but I think I've got everything," Rose laughs. "But I'll shout if I've forgotten anything."

She reaches in to unstrap the little girl, hoists her onto her hip and they disappear into the house.

"They seem lovely," Emily says. "It'll be great to have young people next door."

"As long as we don't get dragged into babysitting."

"But you liked the little girl," Emily says. "She's beautiful…"

"Yes, but that doesn't mean to say I want to look after her. And I hope we don't hear her crying…"

"We've never heard a sound before."

"The Edwards weren't the sort to make a noise."

"No. Of course." The Edwards were in their late seventies. They put the house on the market when Mrs. Edwards began to find the stairs too much, and they've moved to a bungalow in Axminster.

"But at least it's someone living here properly. Not a holiday let."

It's another week before she sees Rose again. She's hurrying out with the little girl in the pushchair. She gives Emily a harassed look and a wave, but doesn't stop. Disappointment sweeps over Emily. Foolishly, she thought they might be friends. She had never had the 'stay-at-home wife' lifestyle, and she'd pictured Rose popping in for coffee or tea, bringing the little girl with her. Peter would stay for a while, just long enough to be polite, until, bored with conversations of washing powder or shopping, he'd disappear to his study. True, there was an age difference: Rose can't be much older than Jasmine, but she's married with a child, she's sure to be infinitely more mature than her. And Emily could do with someone more ordinary to be friendly with, someone to balance out Poppy's wild ways. Of course, she could invite Felicity over or Pam or someone, but she never seems to get around to it.

She's just come back from town one day when she hears a tap at the kitchen window. It's such an unusual sound that she nearly drops the loaf of bread in her hands. Dan's pale face smiles at her through the glass. She opens the back door.

"Look, I'm so sorry," he bursts out without preamble. "Rose isn't well. I just wondered. I know it's an imposition. But if you'd look after Alicia for an hour or so…"

Now she sees the frown between his eyebrows, the worry in his eyes, despite the broad smile.

"Well, I'm not…" *used to children* she was going to say. But it's more than that. Her mind darts to Peter. This is exactly what he said would happen. They're being used.

"No, of course. Silly of me," he says. "You're busy. I shouldn't have asked. It's just I've got to get some stuff off for work and I can't concentrate and Rose's head is so bad…"

"Migraine?" Emily says. "Oh, poor thing. I know what it's like. Look. Wait. Bring her over. It's only… I'm not used to children…"

But he scarcely seems to have heard her. He's gone and two minutes later he's back, holding the little girl by the hand.

"Leesha," he says carefully. "This is Emily."

"Emmy," Alicia replies.

"She's going to look after you just for a little while. While Mummy has a rest."

"Mummy sick," Alicia says, screwing up her face in disgust.

"She's been sick?" Emily says. "Oh, poor thing. Has she got stuff to take?"

"Yes, thanks," Dan says. "I've got some things here. Nappy. Beaker. Lego. But you can stick children's television on if you like. That'll keep her quiet."

Nappy. She's never changed a nappy in her life. Maybe she won't need to. Peter might know what to do...

"Twelve okay for you?" Dan asks. "That's when she has lunch."

Emily glances at the clock. Just gone eleven. *An hour.*

"Yes, fine," she says.

"Thank you so much. You've saved my life."

He throws her a beaming smile which reaches his eyes this time. Blue, blue eyes. She senses his attraction. Blushes. He holds the gaze a moment longer then he's gone.

Emily holds out her hand. "Shall we go and find Peter?" She hears her voice take on the tone she used to use to her friends' children when they were little.

"Peter," the little girl says. She puts her hand into Emily's. The instant trust is disarming. Emily feels her heart fill in her chest.

"You're mad," Peter says.

"Shhh..."

"She can't understand."

"She can tell from your tone, Peter."

"What're you going to do with her?"

"What channel's children's TV on?"

The hour flies by. Emily's only experience of looking after small children has been weekend visits with Grace and Matt, and Peter is thirty years out of date. They follow Alicia around, removing breakable objects, making sure she doesn't knock her head, telling her the names of everything. "Table." "Picture frame." "Lamp." And she repeats them like a parrot. The television stays on but she hardly bothers with it. Peter tips the bucket of Lego onto the floor and builds her tower after tower which she knocks down with glee. His initial annoyance has vanished under the onslaught of Alicia's charm, and a pang goes through Emily as she watches him sprawled on the floor playing with the little girl. A dark-haired, dark-eyed Jasmine takes Alicia's place in her mind. Anusia looks on proudly. A whole episode of Peter's life unknown to Emily.

The knock on the back door comes as a surprise.

"Any time, any time!" Peter says to Dan, waving goodbye to Alicia like a fond grandfather.

"You soon changed your tune!" Emily laughs.

"But she's so sweet," he says. "I'd forgotten what it's like to have a child around. And she's so good…"

"I'm sure she has her moments…"

Emily finds herself looking out for Rose and Alicia, making excuses to go out to the bin or the garden if she sees or hears them. Alicia's face lights up. "Play with Emmy and Peter?" she asks and soon she's coming in almost daily, either in the morning before her nap or after her four o'clock tea. Rose, who looks increasingly pale and worn, is always grateful. "She's an IVF baby," she confides. "I'm too old for all this."

"How old are you?" Emily asks.

"Forty-two."

"That's not old!" Emily laughs. "Most of my friends waited till then to have their babies. Except for the odd ones who started at the other end of the scale."

"The teenage mothers, yes. We had a few of those at my school too. But at least they've got the energy when they're young. And they're adaptable. We'd got used to doing whatever we want, whenever we wanted. Weekends away. Holidays. Now there's always Alicia to see to. And there's no money. I can't work with her to look after."

Emily stays tactfully silent, but she thinks of all the women she's known over the years paying for childcare or relying on parents to babysit so they could work to pay the bills. Or working at weekends while their husband looked after the children. There's always a way. And Dan works from home anyway, some sort of IT or website stuff or something. Rose could easily get a job if she wanted, part-time if necessary. But maybe it's the principal of the thing. Maybe having gone through IVF she feels she should be home to look after the baby.

These conversations with Rose are from necessity, fleeting; seldom intimate or detailed. Alicia's always hanging around, wanting attention, wanting to get home, needing feeding and their friendship doesn't progress as much as Emily had hoped.

She finds herself talking about Alicia all the time, to Pam, to Felicity, to anyone who'll listen to her.

"I didn't know you liked children," Poppy says.

"I didn't either," Emily laughs. "Oh, there's my friends' children. Especially Kate and Jack. But I've never been very good with them. But Alicia's different. She's lovely. You'll have to come and see her…"

"I'm not into children!" Poppy laughs.

"You don't know this one!"

"How come you never had any?"

Emily freezes. It's the question she dreads. "Oh… you know…" She shrugs.

Poppy waits.

"Well, Peter already had Jasmine. I didn't think he wanted any more."

"Didn't think," Poppy repeats.

"And I wasn't too fussed," Emily adds quickly. "I enjoyed working. We had a good lifestyle. Children would have cramped us…"

"But you regret it," Poppy says. It's a statement of fact, not a question, and she says it so caringly, so sympathetically, so lovingly. It's so unlike Poppy, usually so caught up with her own concerns, that Emily feels tears prick her eyes.

"I didn't know," she says. She starts crying. "I thought…" She breaks off. Then. "Years ago," she says, knowing she's not making any real sense, but knowing also that Poppy will work it out. "We were coming back from staying with Grace and Matt. I saw Peter glance in the rear view mirror. I turned around. Saw what he was seeing. They made a nice little nuclear family, Grace and Matt, their arms around each other, both waving, eleven-year-old Kate and nine-year-old Jack either side of them. 'Shame we never had children,' Peter said."

Emily can remember now the rush of blood to her face, the physical hurt in her chest. "But I thought…" she had said. She couldn't go on…

"What?" he said.

"It doesn't matter," she forced herself to say.

"Yes, it does. Tell me."

"I thought you didn't want any more. That's what you said."

"No, I didn't."

"You did. I'm sure you did."

He was quiet for a moment then he said, "I thought you didn't. You always said children were a tie. You liked your work, you said."

"That was because I thought…"

They both fell silent.

"Too late, too late," Emily sobs now. "I was forty-seven at the time. I'd had a hysterectomy five years before. All those years of being careful, of condoms, the pill, diaphragms, all wasted as it turned out. I should have taken more risks, gone with the flow, seen what happened. But that's not me. My life was planned out. Organised. A good life. A safe life. Good job.

Steady income. A husband who loved me. Holidays abroad. Freedom. Why complicate things?"

"And Peter?"

"What?"

"What did he think?"

"I don't know. I didn't ask. We never talk about it."

Chapter Twelve

"I often wonder what our daughter would have looked like." Peter says. "Nothing like Jasmine, of course. More like Kate, I suppose. Emily's quite like Grace. Fair hair. Blue eyes. Except Grace is bigger. Kate was a strong little girl. Strong-willed. Knew how to get her own way. She used to climb on my lap, smile at me."

He remembers her wheedling voice: *"Peter, Peter, come and play outside…"*

"Our little girl would have been like that," he says, "except slim, dainty, a fairy child. Like Alicia. Or maybe we'd have had a boy…" He warms to the idea. "A boy like Jack to play football or cricket with, to have a train set, a scalextric track. I never had any of that with Jasmine."

Peter's never told anyone before. But then nobody's ever asked. Men don't talk about things like this. He's not sure how they got on to the subject even. Maybe they were talking about Alicia. He knows he talks about her a lot. He and Emily scarcely talk of anything else nowadays: what she says, what she does, when she's coming over. They mimic her voice, the silly things she says by mistake. "D'you want to get down?" he asked her the other day, holding his arms out to lift her from the kitchen chair.

"Not yet," she said, solemnly. "Not today."

She couldn't understand why he and Emily laughed so much, but she joined in anyway, clapping her hands and laughing with them. He's never been fond of a little girl like this, one who isn't his own flesh and blood.

"What about Emily?" Poppy is asking.

"What?"

"Didn't she want children?"

"She never said so."

"I've finished the portrait."

"Can I see?"

"No!" she laughs. "It's your birthday present. A surprise!"

Emily's told him about it, of course. She tells him everything, piling more guilt on to his already over-burdened conscience.

"I'm pleased with it," Poppy says. "I was wondering if I could put it in my next exhibition. If you two don't mind. 'Not For Sale', you know…"

"It's up to Emily."

They invite Rose and Dan over on Peter's birthday: tea and birthday cake with Alicia sitting at the head of the table in her party frock. She gets confused, thinks it's her own birthday. "She's been going to so many birthday parties lately," Rose excuses her.

Peter lets her blow out the single candle and she jumps up and down on the chair, laughing and clapping.

Poppy comes over later with the picture, wrapped up in red tissue paper.

Emily watches Peter's face. He's impressed, she can see he is. Personally, she has no idea whether it's good or not. She can see it's her. She recognises the look in her own eyes. The slight uncertainty behind the confident façade. But Poppy has made her far too beautiful. And mysterious, as though she has a secret to hide. She wouldn't let her smile. She looks slightly haughty, turning away slightly, looking back at the viewer. Head and shoulders. On Poppy's instructions she wore a plain black, round-necked top for the sittings, but this has been left out of the finished picture. It could be a low-necked top of course, but somehow there's a suggestion she's naked. She's been worried about this, but it's far too late to do anything about it now. The painting is signed with Poppy's characteristic '7'. It's not their first original, but it is their first commission.

"Why don't you sign your name?" Emily had asked her.

"Oh, it's just a gimmick," Poppy shrugged. "To keep people guessing. Add to the mystery. Get me known. That sort of thing."

Peter knows they're waiting for his reaction. "It's lovely," he says, hoping he's injected the right sort of appreciation into it. Artistically, it is good. But it's not the Emily he knows. This Emily is much prettier, her nose straighter, her cheekbones higher, her mouth smaller. "Really lovely," he goes on quickly, "Thank you, Poppy. Emily."

He turns to Emily first, holds her, kisses her. Then Poppy. It was only going to be an air kiss, a hand on each shoulder, but she moves in, envelops him in a hug, presses her lips to his face, holds her cheek against his. She's bigger than he expected. Warm, soft flesh presses against him. Emily is firm and hard in his arms. He can feel every bone in her body, her ribs under his fingers, her shoulder blades against his chest. Poppy feels like a downy pillow, her body melts into his. He has a sudden vision of her generous breasts, her round hips, her ample bottom. He springs away from her like he's been stung. Emily and Poppy both laugh.

The exhibition is in Taunton. "Somerset Arts Week," Poppy says. "I think Si Blackwood is exhibiting too."

"Bit parochial for him, isn't it?" Peter asks.

"I thought so too. But apparently his agent thinks he should broaden his appeal or something…"

Jasmine rings up the week before. "Si said he'd book the Castle Hotel!" she wails. "But he forgot! He's so useless! And I'm not going to some downmarket dump! Can we stay with you?"

They arrive on the Friday evening in a battered old VW camper van, two hours later than expected. "It took ages to unload the paintings," Jasmine explains. "Then we had to stay for a drink…"

"Are you hungry?" Emily asks. "I did a casserole. There's enough left over…"

"No, it's fine, thanks. We grabbed something just now."

Jasmine has thrown herself out first, enfolding first Peter then Emily in a perfume and wine and silk-scarved embrace, chattering non-stop at the top of her voice. Emily glances nervously to the blinded upstairs window of the next-door house, where she knows Alicia will have just got settled for the night. She peeks curiously over Jasmine's shoulder to get a look at Simeon as he clambers carefully out. He conforms exactly to her mental image of him: bigger built maybe, towering over Peter, at least six foot, and strongly built with it, wide shoulders, broad arms that grip her strongly as he kisses her theatrically on both cheeks, flicking back the long, grey, straggly hair that falls over his shoulders. There's a long, grey beard to match and an old, lined face, and he's scruffily dressed in a frayed checked shirt and grimy jeans.

Jasmine steps back, grabs his arm. "Si. My step-mum Emily. Emily, Simon. Simeon Blackwood. "

Emily reels inwardly at being called 'Step-mum'. She's only ever been 'Dad's wife'. It must be the current expression to use.

"Simon, please," Simeon is saying. "Or Si. Everyone calls me Si. Simeon's just an affectation my agent dreamed up and now I'm stuck with it."

Emily feels him examining her face in the streetlight. In the glare of the kitchen she feels his eyes on her again.

"Poppy," he says. "Poppy Jamieson. She's done a portrait of you."

"James," Emily corrects him. He can't know Poppy very well if he doesn't even know her right name. "How did you...?"

"Yeh, yeh, whatever she calls herself nowadays," Simeon is saying, but Jasmine speaks over him. "We've just seen it!" she laughs. "At the exhibition."

"I didn't know it was up already." Emily's suddenly uncomfortable at the thought of other people, strangers, seeing her picture. But she did agree to it. And Poppy was so pleased.

"They don't open till tomorrow," Jasmine is saying. "We can go first thing if you like. Si always likes to get there early. Don't you, darling?"

She cuddles up to him, and he kisses her long and full on the lips. Peter reddens and Emily can almost feel him shudder. "Cup of tea? Coffee? Something stronger?" Peter asks to cover his embarrassment.

Coffee for Jasmine. Tea for Emily. Whisky for Simeon and Peter. The kettle boils. Teacups. The smell of coffee brewing. Peter getting in Emily's way with the best cut-glass whisky tumblers and ice. Jasmine flits around, chattering madly. She's uncomfortable, Emily realises, unsure whether to be Daddy's girl or Simeon's woman. There's the usual little girly voice she reserves for Peter, modified into something with more adult overtones for Simeon. It's not the first boyfriend she's brought home, of course. From when she was fourteen a succession of boys has been in tow, all older, all with either cars or motorbikes to bring her down to see Daddy and ferry her around. From acned teenagers to bearded university students to short-haired aspiring bankers, Jasmine has brought them home. But this is the first man. How old is he? Sixty-four, sixty-five? The lines on his face stand out sharply in the harsh fluorescent light of the kitchen. He looks years older than Peter. Jasmine, conversely, looks like a teenager: her olive skin smooth and unlined; her shiny, dark hair falling down her back; her young, firm body pressed against his.

Simeon is as interested in Emily as she is in him. "You have a wonderful profile," he says, suddenly. "I can see why Poppy wanted to paint you."

The remark falls right into the middle of a conversation about Jasmine's work and Emily's thrown, also embarrassed, unused to being talked about like this. Oh, there's no denying it's flattering, but she's not used to such overt compliments.

"You're embarrassing Emily," Jasmine says, the use of her full name betraying her jealousy more clearly than the swift black look that crosses her face.

"Have you known Poppy long?" Emily says quickly to cover the awkward moment. Peter cringes inwardly. Poppy and Simeon. They're bound to have slept together. These Bohemian types think nothing of jumping in and out of each other's beds as the carnal whim takes them. He jumps up, grabs Simeon's half-empty glass.

"Another one?" he says.

"Oh. Yes. Great, thanks. Poppy. Known her years."

Too late, Emily has seen Jasmine falling into one of her sulks. But Simeon has seen it too. "You were saying about your job, darling. We interrupted you."

"Oh, it's nothing," Jasmine says, peevishly. "It doesn't matter…"

"So what time d'you need to be there tomorrow?" Emily says, brightly.

"Oh, around nine, I should think. You can come with us if you like. There's plenty of room now we've unloaded…"

Emily, who noticed the state of the inside of the camper van when the door slid open, says quickly, "Thanks. I'll check with Peter but we'll probably pop over later."

"Would you like anything more, Jasmine? Tea? Coffee? Hot chocolate?"

Jasmine shakes her head. "I'll go up in a mo. I'm whacked."

"I won't be long either," Emily says.

In the silence that follows it seems to Emily that Peter has been gone an age, and she's just about to jump up and go and find him when he comes in.

Jasmine stands up, gathers her bag, cardigan, magazine and kisses everyone goodnight. Emily's about to follow when she catches Peter's eye. *Don't leave me alone with him*, the look says, so she waits patiently, making desultory conversation until finally even Simeon runs out of things to say. "I'll take this on up," he says, tipping the last of the whisky to one side in his glass. "Early start. See you in the morning."

Peter can't sleep. The thought of Jasmine and Simeon just the other side of the thin wall is more than he can bear. That man's hands on his daughter's perfect body. The little girl he bathed and washed, dressed and bottle-fed. Her mouth on his. Her lovely hands on that pervert's dirty, old body. For ages after he'd kissed Emily goodnight, he listened to them moving around next door: their murmured voices, the sounds of them unpacking their stuff, arguing gently about where things were, just like any other couple. The door opened and closed a few times. There's no en-suite for the spare room and the light on the landing clicked on and off as they both went to the bathroom, doors opened and closed, whispered, furtive exchanges of conversation and then all fell silent. He waited for the sounds of bedsprings, a muffled moan, deep breathing maybe. But all was quiet. *Is Si still up to it?* he wonders. He's a few years older than Peter. Married to a woman his own age, he probably wouldn't bother. But a young woman, that's a different story, as he knows only too well. Emily's firm body, her flat stomach, tiny firm breasts, like a schoolgirl. Or Poppy, younger still, that soft yielding flesh he'd felt against his body fleetingly. He feels himself harden, stirs impatiently in bed, considers for one mad moment waking Emily up for a quickie. She seldom refuses, even if to give him relief if she doesn't feel like it herself. But equally as quickly he rejects the idea, his erection waning as he remembers Jasmine and Simeon next door.

★

They're all up early the next morning. Emily squints at the clock beside the bed in disbelief as she hears the shower.

"What time is it?" Peter groans as he feels her moving.

"Six. My God. She could've waited a bit longer, couldn't she?"

"It might be Simeon."

"God. Don't. Simeon naked." She shudders. "I can't bear to think of it."

Peter can't help laughing with her.

"He doesn't look like he's ever seen hot water anyway," she goes on. "It's Jasmine. She'll want to look her best. 'The artist's muse'."

Breakfast is hectic. Used to just the two of them and their leisurely routine, Emily dodges Jasmine as she opens the fridge and cupboards, groaning at whatever she finds: "Don't you have any honey? God, only brown bread... isn't there any butter?"

"You know we only have marg," Emily says as politely as she can. *This isn't a hotel, for God's sake!* she mutters inwardly. No point in saying anything though: Jasmine's been the same since she was thirteen years old and basically she's in a good mood, brimming over with excitement at the thought of the day ahead; the attention she will undoubtedly get on the arm of the famous London artist.

Simeon appears wearing the same filthy clothes he wore yesterday, greeting Peter with the same hearty bonhomie that irks him beyond reason.

"How's the old lady?" he asks, his mouth full of toast.

Peter glances across at Emily, confused. Then reddens. "Anusia, you mean? We've been divorced for years, you know that."

"Sorry, old chap. No offence, Em."

Emily only just stops herself saying, "Emily". She hates her name shortened. Jasmine's the only one who does it and she's never corrected her for fear of spoiling their fragile relationship.

"So, Anusia," he goes on. "How is the old thing?"

"I haven't a clue," Peter says, tersely. "You've seen her more recently than I have. Wasn't she there last Christmas, Jasmine said."

"Yeh, yeh. I just thought…"

"Si, don't!" Jasmine hits him playfully. "He's doing it on purpose, Em. Ignore him. He loves stirring things up."

"Oh, it doesn't matter to me," Emily says as lightly as possible. "Peter was already divorced when I met him. It wasn't as if…"

But Simeon seems to have lost interest anyway. He and Jasmine are having a mock fight over the last piece of toast. Emily sees the flash of the gold cap in his teeth as he laughs and tussles with her. How can Jasmine bear to kiss him? Peter stares steadfastly at his bowl of cereal, longing for them to be gone.

Suddenly, Jasmine leaps up. "My God, look at the time!"

She grabs the coffee she had made such a fuss about making, ("Si likes it really strong!") and thunders upstairs. In the small house they can hear every footstep overhead as she patters from bedroom to bathroom and back again, slamming each door as she goes. An awkward silence seems to have fallen, though Simeon seems totally unconcerned by it, finishing his coffee unhurriedly and in silence. When the cup is empty he stands up, looming large in the tiny kitchen behind Peter, who moves his chair in slightly to let him by. He stands by the sink rinsing his cup.

"Don't worry about that," Emily says. "I'll put it in the dishwasher."

He carries on rinsing it anyway, craning his neck to read the paper over Peter's shoulder, until Peter, annoyed, passes the paper back to him.

"Oh, it doesn't matter!" He waves it away, laughing. "I s'pose I'd better go and…"

"We don't need to go yet, do we?" Emily whispers the moment he's gone.

"God, no. It'll be deadly dull. We can go later…"

Emily clears the table and stacks the dishwasher to the accompaniment of doors opening and closing as Jasmine dashes up and downstairs again several times, shouting, "Oh God, I've forgotten my…"

Finally, they leave and the house falls silent.

Peter has disappeared to the study. Emily sticks her head around the door. "What time d'you want to go over?"

"Don't mind."

"Poppy says no one turns up till mid-morning."

"Okay. Around ten then?"

The exhibition is in the theatre in the centre of Taunton. The car park is also used for shoppers, and the queue this Saturday morning stretches into the next street.

"No point in even trying, is there?" Peter says, driving past the turning.

"Where d'you think's best?"

Every car park is the same and they edge nose to tail through the streets.

"Maybe there's some sense in going in early," Peter grumbles.

"Yes…" Emily agrees mechanically, though privately she knows there would have been no point in hanging around with no one else there. Part of the reason to go is to see other people there, hear them admire Poppy's work.

"We don't need to rush," Emily reminds Peter as he runs his fingers through his hair, swears at another driver who stops to let a pedestrian cross the road.

"I hate being late."

"It doesn't matter what time we get there. No one's expecting us."

But Peter hates traffic, hates queues, hates being held up.

It's raining hard by the time they find somewhere, and Peter, searching for an umbrella in the boot of the car, raindrops trickling down the back of his neck, has fallen into a foul mood and Emily's beginning to wish they'd never agreed to go.

The foyer of the Brewhouse is crowded: people shaking wet umbrellas, taking off coats and raincoats, flicking raindrops from their hair, wives searching for the Ladies so they can sort out their dampened hair, men searching their pockets for combs to do the same. There's a smell of damp coats.

"I'll just go and find the loo," Emily says, falling in with the rest of the crowd. "D'you want to go on in?"

"No, I'll go too. Meet you here."

There's the usual long queue and reappearing much, much later she half-expects him not to be there, but he's waiting dutifully, his face lighting up expectantly as the door opens.

In the first crush to see the paintings she doesn't see Poppy, but then suddenly, there she is, talking earnestly to a wispily balding man. She catches sight of Emily at the same time. "Here she is!" she carols gaily.

Emily reddens. Behind Poppy's head she suddenly sees her portrait, neatly labelled 'NFS'.

"This gentleman…"

"Richard Broom," he supplies.

"Mr Broom," Poppy says, deferentially, "was enquiring who the mystery lady was. And here she is. Emily Stanchester. Richard Broom."

Emily shakes hands mechanically, thanks Richard Broom for his compliments, tries to ignore the crowd that begins to gather around her, people nudging as they recognise her.

Peter swells with pride: his lovely wife, the beautiful and successful artist: both his women. Then with a whoop of pleasure Jasmine is there as well. "Daddy!" People turn and stare. Jasmine, used to the attention, basking in it, clings on to his arm. "Can I drag him away in a mo, Poppy, my love? He *must* come and see Si's work!"

"Be my guest!" Poppy laughs. "As long as you leave Emily with me! She's my star turn!"

Peter follows Jasmine through the crowds. Then suddenly she stops. "Oh, Daddy, I forgot. There's a picture of me…"

Peter freezes. "What?" he says, peremptorily.

"Don't be silly, Daddy," she says, but there's an edge of fear in her voice.

"Where are these pictures?" Peter knows he's sounding like a cross old man but he can't help it.

She gestures to a separate room. "In here."

Of course, they've put Simeon's pictures in a separate room. Some people consider them pornographic. Peter hesitates. He's just about to go in when Emily appears like magic by his side. "I managed to escape!" she says. "Oh my God!"

The room is full of pictures of nudes. Not just women, but men. Painted in fleshy tones, they're as real as photographs.

148

Some of the men are old, some young and muscular. The women are all young, all beautiful. Peter doesn't see it at first. In fact, he's looking around relieved. If *he* doesn't recognise Jasmine then no one will. He won't even have to tell Emily. She and Jasmine are chatting together, heads bent. There's too much noise to hear what they're saying, but Emily's laughing and smiling. Clearly, she doesn't know about the portrait. Then, suddenly, she stops, glances quickly at Peter, and he knows this is it. He follows her gaze. It's a small painting. Arresting. Powerful. Jasmine sits on a chair facing the viewer. Her eyes look straight ahead. Challenging. Proud. Her coffee-coloured skin glows. She's leaning forward slightly. Her breasts hang down. Dark, big, erect nipples. Her legs are slightly open, her vulva clearly visible. She's shaved. Like the little girl he remembers bathing and dressing. Peter feels sick. Below the waist, she's his little girl. Above it, a woman he could take to bed.

"Peter!" Vaguely, he hears Emily's voice and, "Daddy" from Jasmine. He feels hands on his arm: Emily? Jasmine? He's not sure which. He shakes them off, pushes through the crowds. Everyone's looking. He's sure they are. He sees the back of Simeon's head. He's standing talking to a group of people. His long, straggly hair is tied back in a ponytail, and Peter has the sudden urge to grab hold of it and batter his head right into one of those bloody nude pictures.

Outside, it's still raining. And it's cold. He left his coat and umbrella on the rail in the foyer. Heavy drops of rain fall on his head from the guttering overhead. He watches them forming perfect semi-circular globes on the sleeve of his jumper before they sink in and begin to feel damp. He sees a roofed-off paved area, presumably used for interval drinks in the summer and dashes over to it. Cigarette stubs litter the ground, and suddenly he realises that's what he wants. A cigarette. He hasn't smoked for years. Not since

Jasmine was born. *Oh God, Jasmine.* Girl-woman. Woman-girl. There for all the world to see. Shameless. Proud. *What have you done to her, Simeon bloody Blackwood? What have you done to my little girl?*

A man comes out. Peter feels rather than sees the instinctive familiar way he reaches in his pocket for his cigarettes and lighter. He feels Peter's eyes on him. He looks. Looks again.

"Peter Stanchester, isn't it?"

Peter groans inwardly. He doesn't recognise the man. Must be one of Emily's endless friends' husbands. Or someone from Rotary. Years of in-bred politeness force him to put out his hand automatically.

"John Heywood," the man is saying. "Old friend of Anusia's."

Ah. That explains it. One of Anusia's conquests. From her artistic period, obviously.

Peter waits until they've covered the formalities of how many years it's been, what they're both doing now, and how good the exhibition is, and then asks, "I don't suppose I could cadge a cigarette, could I? Seem to have left mine inside…"

"Yeh, of course."

The first drag makes him cough and he turns away embarrassed, but John doesn't seem to notice and they puff away in a companionable enough silence. People pass them coming in and out of the exhibition. Amongst them, Peter suddenly sees Emily. His heart sinks as she hurries over to him, her face set and white.

"I've been looking everywhere for you, Peter! Why didn't you say you were coming out here?"

She stops, amazed at the sight of the cigarette in his hand, embarrassed to see him with someone else.

"Oh, John. This is my wife, Emily. Emily, John Heywood. An old friend."

If John's surprised at being termed an old friend he doesn't show it. Maybe he thinks Peter doesn't want to say anything about Anusia. Whatever the reason, with one of those strange male bonding instincts, he recognises Peter's in trouble with 'the wife' for some reason and he's going to stick by him. He shakes hands affably, asks Emily what she does, where they live, whether she likes the paintings, and Peter sees Emily relax, smile, laugh, as if she's forgotten what it was that brought her out here. Eventually, though, John has to go. He stubs his cigarette out on the ground and jerks his head in their direction, "Coming back in?"

"In a minute," they both say together. Peter knows he can't just pretend nothing's happened. If he doesn't deal with it now it'll just drag on and on. He may as well let Emily have her say.

"It's only a painting," she says.

"I know."

"Well then."

Peter waits. There's bound to be more. But there isn't. So he says into the silence, "She's my daughter."

"She's a grown-up."

"It's... oh, I don't know... indecent..." he ends, lamely.

"You wouldn't say that if it was..." He sees her searching for a name. "Poppy," she ends up.

He knows it was the first name she came up with, but she couldn't have chosen worse and the shock makes him angrier still. "Of course I would!" he explodes. "You'll be telling me you'd do it next!"

"Don't be silly!" she snaps.

They're both silent, then she puts her hand on his arm. "It's okay," she says. Like he's a child. He hates it when she treats him like this. Patronising him.

He shakes her hand away. "You don't understand," he says.

"No. I don't!" She's angry now, angry and upset. He can

hear the tears in her voice. He can't stand a scene. Not here. She walks away. He hurries after her. "Where are you going?"

"Back in."

"What? I thought we'd go home."

"You go." She's crying now.

"Don't be silly. Look, let's just go. You can't go in like that…"

"Okay," she sniffs, wiping her nose. "I'll find our coats. You staying here?"

"Yes."

Every time someone comes out he thinks it'll be her. Then the door opens and it's Poppy. His heart gives the usual little lurch of pleasure he's grown to expect when he sees her. Today she's dressed more flamboyantly than usual in peacock blue and green.

"Emily said you were out here," she says.

"Don't tell me she sent you to find me."

Poppy shakes her head and laughs, setting a long strand of silver, gold and turquoise beads dancing from her ears.

"Don't be silly. She doesn't know I'm here. I snuck out while she was deep in conversation with Jasmine. About you, I presume. You are silly, Peter. You might have guessed he'd paint her. He paints all his women."

"I s'pose I'll come across one of you one day," he says.

She laughs again. "Did I actually *say* I'd slept with him?"

Peter reddens. "I just thought…"

"Look, it doesn't matter. Jasmine didn't do anything she didn't want. It's only a picture."

"That's what Emily said." Then he realises. "That's what you *told* her to say."

"We're not ganging up on you, Peter. It's what anyone would say. It's a picture. Art. Good art. You know it is. Men have been painting nudes for years."

"But it's so real. And…"

"Erotic?"

He looks away. "Yes."

"Ah, now we come to it. Your nude daughter turns you on."

"Don't be silly," he snaps.

"She's not your daughter. In the picture, I mean. She's a woman. Any woman. An interpretation. Not Jasmine."

"And she's…" He hesitates.

"What?"

"Shaven."

"What?"

"Her…" He gestures downwards.

He sees the light of understanding in her eyes. She starts to speak, then breaks off as she sees Emily coming, Peter's coat draped over her arm. She doesn't seem surprised to see Poppy there, reinforcing Peter's original impression she sent her out to talk to him. She manages a watery smile but avoids both their eyes as she hands Peter his coat. Her face is red and blotchy, a mottled rash running down the side of her neck like a weal. Peter finds himself talking too loudly, too quickly to cover up for her. "Sorry about this," he hears himself saying. "But we have to get back…"

Poppy plays along with it, embraces Emily, then Peter. "I'll text you," she whispers into his ear and he responds by the firm pressure of his cheek against hers.

Even before they get back to the car he feels his phone buzz against his chest. The thought that it's Poppy sustains him as Emily marches silently next to him through the busy shoppers, sits silently next to him all the way home. That, and the look of understanding in Poppy's eyes, the look that saw into his very soul.

Chapter Thirteen

"I don't know why you had to make such a fuss," Jasmine says.

"Can we just drop it?" Peter snaps. "I've apologised, haven't I? Why d'you have to go on and on?"

Emily and Simeon can hear every word above the sound of the television that Emily switched on to cover their mutual embarrassment, even though neither of them wanted to watch it. Actually, Emily's not sure Simeon's embarrassed. She has a sneaking feeling he's enjoying every moment of it, though even he must be finding it a bit tiresome now.

"I'm not a little girl any more! I can do what I like!" Jasmine rails for the umpteenth time.

"It's demeaning!" Peter retaliates.

Of course, they've argued many times before: about money, about clothes, how late she stayed out, whether she'd done her homework, but this is different. Emily should be feeling smug. This is what she's always wanted to hear, but instead she just feels sorry for Peter.

Finally, Jasmine runs out of steam and storms off upstairs. Peter appears a moment later, a glass of whisky in his hand. "Fancy one?" he asks Simeon.

"No, thanks, mate."

Emily cringes. It must be the first time anyone has ever called Peter 'mate'. He doesn't seem to have noticed though and sits down heavily next to Emily, reaching for the remote control. "You watching this?"

"No. Switch it off. I'll go on up if that's okay?" she says.

Simeon has made no move to go and she's not sure how Peter will feel about being left alone with him. Maybe he might like a bit of male bonding after what he's been through. But Simeon gets up and stretches lazily. "I'd better go too. See to the little woman." He winks. "Night, mate."

Simeon follows her, far too closely, up the stairs. She can feel his eyes on her bottom, knows he's watching her hips and thighs as she moves; wishes she was wearing a longer top, or her jogging bottoms or something loose rather than the tight black jeans she put on for the exhibition. At the top of the stairs, the hand that's been only millimetres away from hers on the hand rail all the way up, deliberately covers hers. She pulls away sharply as though she's been burnt.

"Come on," he laughs. "I don't bite, whatever you've heard!"

Emily doesn't know what to say. Her face is burning. She can't look at him. "Goodnight," she says, firmly.

He laughs again, as though at some sort of private joke.

He must have woken Jasmine up, or maybe she hadn't actually got to sleep yet. Emily hears her surprised voice, then a murmured conversation, mostly Jasmine, clearly justifying herself for the argument, and Simeon's deep voice, acquiescing, agreeing, reassuring. Before long there's silence.

She's not sure what time Peter comes up, but he wakes the next morning with a hangover and in a foul mood. Jasmine conversely is in a surprisingly good mood, desperately trying to make things better. And gradually, as the day progresses, Emily sees Peter warm to it until by the evening they're right back where they started: Jasmine with her little girly voice and Peter catering to her every whim. Emily sighs inwardly. She's lost patience with Peter. He'll forgive Jasmine anything, in a way he would never do with her. And he's scarcely speaking to Emily. She's not exactly sure why, but she traces it back to the exhibition and the painting, and the fact that she didn't give him the sympathy he wanted. But what did he expect? It's not *her* fault Jasmine posed in the nude, in that provocative girl-woman way.

Peter can't think about the painting. He's pushed it to the back of his mind, along with all those other painful things he keeps hidden away, like Anusia's infidelity, the painful divorce, losing Jasmine, Jasmine growing up and being a woman, Jasmine getting engaged to Simeon Blackwood.

"It's not good for you to bottle up your feelings," Poppy says.

"It's never done me any harm before," Peter says, tersely.

"It's probably done you untold harm," she persists. "All those resentments and jealousies, the hurt pride…"

"Men don't go in for things like that!" he laughs. "We're not like you women, storing up things to fling at us when you're angry, then say you didn't really mean them when you know full well you did, you've just been waiting for the right moment to throw them in our face."

They've been on this new intimate footing ever since the exhibition, when Peter saw that light of understanding in Poppy's eyes. He no longer feels guilty. Well, maybe just a little, but not much. He can see now that Emily has never really understood about Jasmine. She's always been jealous of his relationship with her. Poppy's different. Different from anyone he's ever known. She doesn't judge. She just listens. And cares. He knows she cares.

"She didn't realise how it would come over," he says, suddenly.

"Jasmine? The painting? I thought you didn't want to talk about it," Poppy says.

"She was misled. *He* misled her. You know he tried it on with Emily?"

An exaggeration probably. But Emily did say he'd 'come on to her'. And it doesn't surprise him. Nor Poppy either, it seems.

"He does that with everyone!" she laughs.

Peter hesitates. Then says, "Have you…?"

"You've asked me twice already."

"Not twice. Surely."

"Well, you've asked me. I'm not telling you. I don't talk about things like that. It's not right."

"I'd like to know," he persists. "I want to know you. I want to know everything."

They're walking in the gardens on the headland overlooking the beach. He stops, puts his hand on her arm. She doesn't pull away. But she's not looking at him. She's looking out to sea.

"Poppy," he says, quietly. He leads her to a bench. She acquiesces like a child. He faces her, wills her to look up at him. "I want to know all about you," he repeats.

"You'd be shocked, Peter. And none of it means anything. I just want to have fun. Without getting hurt. And without hurting anyone else. Is that what *you* want?"

"Yes."

He glances around, but she's read his mind.

"Not here," she says quickly, laughing. "Someone is sure to see us. I'll work something out. Text you."

An electric thrill races through him. His cock stiffens and he shifts uncomfortably, colour flooding to his face.

"Come on!" she laughs suddenly, jumping up and pulling him to his feet. "Race you to the top!"

"Oh, Poppy, I'm too old for that!" he groans, but she hasn't even heard and he watches her as she races up the path in a flurry of long, black skirts and scarves. She stops way before she gets there, out of breath and panting, waits for him to join her.

"It's lovely, isn't it?" She turns around to view the beach

below, the curve of the Cobb, the blue sea, the distant coastline. "I never get fed up with it. Think I'll stay here forever."

"Have you moved around a lot?"

"We lived in France when I was little. My mother's French, you know."

"No, I didn't know," he laughs. "You never tell anyone anything."

"My mother's French." She laughs, linking her arm through his. Strange how she doesn't worry about these outward signs of affection. But then she's an artist, she's like this with everyone. He remembers seeing her hanging on to David's arm at the Rotary talk.

"My father's English," she's saying. "What else d'you want to know, Mr Nosey Parker?"

"When did you come to England?"

"When I was five. My parents split up. Daddy brought me here. To live with Grandma and Gramps. In Wimbledon."

"Why didn't you stay with your mother?"

"I don't know really. No one's ever said. Someone has to have custody. I think they thought I'd do better in England. Schooling and things…"

"Which art college did you go to?"

"Oh, please, Peter…" she groans. "That's enough for one day!"

★

Emily's in the kitchen doing the ironing when he gets in. Peter sighs inwardly at the sight. She's always doing something. Something totally unnecessary. Never free just to go out whenever he wants. Then he remembers he wouldn't have been able to see Poppy today if she had wanted to come with him.

"Did you have a good time?" she says, automatically.

"Yes, thanks. Oh, I bumped into Poppy."

Sometimes he says this. Sometimes he doesn't. It's insurance: if someone *has* seen them together she'll think nothing of it. Usually, Emily says vaguely, "Oh yes?" but this time she says, archly: "Again? I'm beginning to think there's something going on!"

She laughs and he manages to join in, but makes a mental note to stop saying it. "No Leesha today?" he asks quickly.

"No. They've gone out."

"Together?"

"Yes and no. Dan had to go up to London for a meeting. She's taken Leesha to see her parents while they're there."

"Do them good," he says.

"Yes..." she says, vaguely.

They often talk about it. Things are bad with Rose and Dan. Rose's migraines are getting worse. Dan's always asking if they can look after Alicia to 'give her a break'. The walls of the house are thin. They hear the arguments, see the lines of stress in both their faces. Rose has stopped confiding in Emily. Conversely, Dan has opened up to her. "She finds it hard," he said when he came over last time, handing over the selection of toys Alicia had insisted on bringing with her. His hand brushed against Emily's. She could feel him willing her to look at him and when she did she saw the look in his eyes, the unmistakeable sexual attraction. She looked away quickly.

"It must be," she said. "Not everyone takes to motherhood. I never had to try." Instantly, she regrets the confidence. He's bound to see it as a come on.

"But you're so good with Leesha," he said. "You obviously love children."

No embarrassment, no questioning about why she never had them herself. Men don't consider these things like women do. They accept there's a reason, but they don't need to know.

"But I can give her back any time!" Emily laughs. "Rose has her all the time. It's quite different."

She decides not to tell Peter about Dan. He hasn't quite got over the business with Simeon, though it's hard to work out whether it was her or Jasmine he was most concerned about.

"How dare he?" he said. "He's supposed to be engaged to Jasmine." Then, illogically, "You don't fancy him, do you?"

"Don't be silly!"

She had told him as a joke, dressing it up to sound funny. Poppy had burst out laughing when she told her. But Emily had forgotten how jealous Peter could be, and his mood, already soured by her lack of sympathy over Jasmine's portrait, only worsened. For over a week they scarcely spoke. He began taking solitary walks every day, even in the coldest of weathers, and she'd watch him go with a pang, relieved to be on her own and away from his bad mood, but guilty she wasn't going with him, and wishing they were getting on well enough that she could. He was always in a better mood for a while when he came back, but it only needed one wrong word from her and they were back were they started. She began to wonder if they would ever get back on an even keel.

It's Alicia who brings them back together again. It's hard for Peter to stay cross with the little girl around. She cuddles up to him, wheedles her way around him, laughs at him until he's more like his usual self. Is this what keeps parents together, Emily wonders: the children? Yet it doesn't seem to be working for Dan and Rose. The last time she took Alicia back Rose was up in bed. She'd had a bad night with Alicia the night before, and Emily had offered to look after her so she could grab some sleep.

"Is that you, Emily?" she called, weakly. "Come on up. I'm just getting up…"

The curtains were drawn, but in the dim room Emily noticed that Alicia's cot had been moved in next to the double bed, and on the way back down she glimpsed the crumpled sheets on the single bed in the room next door. It seemed unlikely that Dan would be sleeping in there just while Rose was ill. From the clothes piled on the chair and strewn on the floor and the shirt hanging on a hanger on the front of Alicia's white bookshelves, it looked far more like a permanent arrangement.

★

Christmas approaches, their second in Lyme Regis, bringing the same round of invitations as last year, coupled with the Rotary Christmas Dinner. Emily drives to Taunton to look for a new dress. Peter offers to come with her but looks relieved when she says she'd rather go on her own. The thought of Peter trailing around from shop to shop telling her everything she puts on looks fine is more than she can bear.

She buys new decorations for the tree while she's there, taking ages to choose things she thinks Alicia would like best. Not since Jasmine was young has she taken so much trouble, but Jasmine had such definite tastes that differed so wildly from Emily's that Emily soon gave up and let her choose her own and decorate the tree herself; whereas Alicia is a little girl who'll be pleased with anything she sees.

"You could've let me help choose," Peter says, petulantly when she takes them out to show him.

She sighs, inwardly. "You'd have been bored," she says.

"No, I wouldn't. Why did you have to go and get them on your own? It should be a joint decision."

"Oh for heavens' sake, Peter!" she snaps. "I don't know any man who'd want to be dragged around the shops choosing Christmas decorations!"

She doesn't usually decorate the tree until just before Christmas but this year she does it early, especially for Alicia. She didn't know what to get her for Christmas. She has so many toys already. But one of her favourite games is playing shop, so she buys her a shopping basket full of plastic fruit and vegetables. She wraps it up and puts it under the tree together with the few presents she's bought Peter, and the bottle of perfume she bought for herself which he wrapped up for her. They make a big ceremony of bringing Alicia in, dimming the lights so the Christmas tree lights show up better and telling her there's a special surprise. Her eyes widen when she sees it. "Christmas tree!" she says. "Oooh!"

Emily leads her around it, pointing out the golden angels, the silver stars, the wooden nativity scene.

Two weeks before Christmas, Jasmine telephones. "What're you doing for Christmas?" she asks.

"What we always do!" Emily laughs, her heart sinking. Surely Jasmine's not going to suggest they get together? Ever since she's known Peter, Christmas has been a traumatic time with Jasmine. At ten years old he naturally wanted to see his daughter open her presents on Christmas Day. The court ordered alternate Christmases, but Anusia never kept to it, sometimes flying off somewhere exotic with some new man or a group of friends, taking Jasmine with her; other times ringing up at the last minute on some flimsy pretext to say Jasmine would *have* to come and stay with them. "I have a terrible cold," she'd croak. Or "A stomach bug." Or "The hot water tank has broken." Jasmine was surprisingly loyal on these occasions, never letting on what they all knew: that Anusia's latest boyfriend wouldn't tolerate a difficult teenager around the place. Because by then Jasmine had certainly become difficult: self-willed and precocious, not helped by Peter feeling he had to overcompensate for the divorce and the ad-hoc custody arrangements. Showered with presents and money, allowed to wear what she liked, do what she liked, stay up late, watch TV in her room, get up at midday, eat and drink whatever and whenever she liked, having her to stay, even for a few days, was a nightmare for Emily.

"We have to have some ground rules," she had said over and over again.

"Emily, please!" he'd say. "I scarcely see her. She won't want to come at all if you nag her all the time!"

It's not improved much since Jasmine has reached adulthood, but at least now she can make up her own mind about when she comes or whether she comes at all.

"Hang on a moment," Emily says now. "I'll get your father."

"Oh, you know how hopeless he is about arrangements. He'll only ask you anyway. We're going to Shaz and Roo's on Christmas Day but we thought we'd come and see you next week if that's okay? Have lunch, bring your prezzies…"

"You'll do a Christmas lunch, of course," Peter says afterwards.

"I wasn't going to. It's such a hassle."

"But Jas will want it."

"She won't mind what she has, Peter. She's not a child."

But she gives in, of course, and they drive to Taunton at the busiest time of the year to buy turkey and crackers, and all the extra things she hadn't planned to get.

Jasmine is suitably appreciative though, "Wow! Christmas lunch! You didn't have to bother! We'd have been fine with soup or something."

But they've brought a Chateauneuf du Pape with them so they obviously expected a proper lunch. Simeon hands it to Emily with the same accidental brush of the hand that Dan gives her, and a confidential wink that makes her blush.

Jasmine dashes around as she always has done, admiring the Christmas tree, excitedly shaking the presents underneath, getting in Emily's way, not offering to help at all, pulling the crackers at the table with the expected childish glee and clapping her hands at the sight of the Christmas pudding. Alone in the tiny kitchen, which isn't geared up for cooking Christmas lunch for four, Emily gets more and more fraught, snapping at Peter whenever he appears, which he does infrequently and always at the last moment. "Can I help with anything?" when she's already done whatever needed doing. Yet whenever she calls him to help he takes so long to appear she has to call again and then he accuses her of nagging.

Making the coffee is always Peter's task and she sits down gratefully at the table while he disappears to the kitchen.

"Emily!" he calls almost instantly.

In the kitchen she finds him opening every cupboard, leaving the doors swinging so she nearly bangs her head on one when she goes in. She closes them one by one. "What're you looking for?"

"That jar of Harrods coffee Jasmine gave us."

"That was two years ago!" she laughs. "Here." She takes out a storage jar.

"But it had a Harrods label on," he says.

"Yes. I took it off."

"Why? I liked it. Harrods. It was special. And Jasmine gave it to us. She'll expect to see it."

"She never comes in here! She wouldn't *dream* of looking at a coffee jar. She won't even remember!"

"She gave it to us," he persists, stubbornly. "Specially. To keep. You should've asked me first."

She's so flabbergasted she can't think of a reply. It's one of those small incidents that typify the gulf between them. The sort of small incident that leads to resentment. Peter's cross with her the rest of the day and she finds herself apologising again just before they go to sleep. "It doesn't matter," he says tersely, but she knows it does. Lying awake while he snores loudly next to her, she tries to justify it to herself. What other husband would worry about a Harrods coffee jar? What other wife would have to ask her husband before she removes a label? Peter has always been domineering, but he's getting worse. Only two days ago he was cross when she changed the sheets on the bed. He never used to interfere with her household routine. But then he was never home to see it. Now she's begun to feel she has to do her chores when he's not around to see them. She tells herself it's ridiculous to allow herself to be cowed by him, but she can feel it happening all the same. She hates conflict. Easier to do what he wants and agree with him than have him cross with her all the time.

It's the Rotary Dinner the next evening. The dress Emily chose is black velvet, full length, high-necked, close-fitted, with a side slit to show off her legs. She loved it when she tried it on in the shop, but now she has desperate second thoughts about it. Is it too smart? Too dressed up? Too sexy? But the invitation said 'Black tie', so surely it will be fine.

She's relieved when they get there. Most of the ladies are in ball gowns, full length, plunging necklines, showing off ample bosoms and rounded arms.

The seating plan has put them with Pam and David, of course, and three other couples who Emily doesn't know. The conversation skims discreetly over children and grandchildren once they know Emily doesn't have any, hovers over sport and music, then settles for a while on looking after ageing parents, another subject Emily and Peter have no experience of, Emily's having died early and Peter's long before she knew him. Pam and David turn out to be the sort of couple who score points off each other. Clearly, their parents are fair play to each other.

"Our daughter gave us a set of plastic wine glasses for Christmas," Pam trills. "For the patio, you know. I'm thinking of using them when David's parents come over next. His mother breaks one nearly every time she comes!"

"At least she helps with the washing-up," David retaliates. "Pam's mother just sits in a chair and moans about her arthritis."

Peter catches Emily's eye. They exchange a small knowing smile. He's proud of her tonight. He has the best-looking wife here; streets ahead of any of the other women. Her fair hair shines in the candlelight. Her face is smooth and unlined. Her slim arm reaches out to pick up her wine glass. The black dress tightens across her body. He has a sudden image of Poppy here instead, dressed in an assortment of outrageous colours, laughing unnecessarily loudly, making sure she's the centre of attention, telling all sorts of inappropriate and wildly exaggerated stories. Women like Poppy aren't meant to be partners in life, the sort of women you bring out and show off to your friends. He thinks of her the last time he saw her: in bed; naked; her plump, white breasts; her rounded thighs; her dimpled bottom. He remembers turning her over, smoothing his hand over its roundness; amazing himself at how exciting he finds her. He has always liked his women slim and firm, women who look after themselves, make sure they look good for him. But Poppy doesn't give a damn about that. Her love for food matches her lust for life. She lies there unashamed in her unwashed sheets, un-cleaned, untidy house. She's like no other woman he's ever known, more caring than Anusia, more level-headed than Zena who followed her, but most of all so very, very different from Emily with her neat, tidy, organised life; her never-ending nagging; her bossiness; her oh-so-apparent lack of appreciation of everything he does. Poppy makes no demands on him, expects nothing from him.

She's not looking for love, for commitment, for a future. She knows he loves Emily. Emily, sitting across from him, looking so lovely. He raises his glass to her. She lifts her eyebrows in slight surprise, but leans across the table to chink her glass against his. "Merry Christmas," he mouths.

"Merry Christmas," she mouths back, smiling at him.

Chapter Fourteen

Rose and Dan go away for Christmas. "Dan's Mum and Dad's this year." Rose pulls a face. "I hate it. Dan's dad's in the Navy. They drink non-stop. Dan's mum makes me feel like I'm hopeless. She's got four boys. She knows nothing about girls. She thinks Alicia is spoilt."

Emily says nothing. Alicia *is* spoilt. Emily spoils her too. It's hard not to. She's such a lovely child.

"What are you doing for Christmas?" Emily asks Poppy.

"God, I hate hearing that!" Poppy groans.

"Me too," Emily laughs. "But what *are* you doing?"

"Oh, I don't know. I hate Christmas."

"Me too," Emily says. "It's always such a hassle. The shopping, the presents, the pressure of trying to make sure everyone has a good time. It's for kids really, isn't it? And if you don't have any it's just something to be got out of the way."

It's only afterwards, walking home, that she realises Poppy didn't actually tell her what she was doing.

"Going to Suzie's parents as usual," she tells Peter when he asks her the same question.

"Where? When? When will I see you again?" he asks.

"Oh, I don't know. We'll be back in the New Year."

"But I've got a present for you."

"*Have* you?"

This is what he loves about Poppy: her childish delight for presents, for food, for excitement, for anything remotely out of the ordinary.

"Yes," he says now, running his hand through her hair. "But you have to open it with me."

"Have you got it here?" She leans over the back seat of the car, rummages around amongst Peter's coat.

"No!" He grabs her arm to stop her and they tussle playfully. Instantly, he feels himself grow hard again. He thought he'd gone past having sex in the car years ago, but they can't always go to the flat. *Suzie's here*, she'd text at the last minute and the car is the only other place. Exciting though it is, he longs for more than these hasty sex sessions, after Rotary or while Emily's at a class. "Maybe we can go away for a weekend somewhere," he suggested once.

"What would you tell Emily?" she asked.

"Oh, I don't know. Rotary do. Men only."

"She knows all the other wives. She'd find out."

"College reunion then. God, it can't be that difficult. Other people do it…"

"Let's not get too complicated, Peter. Suzie'll keep out of the way when we want her to."

"She doesn't know, does she?" He's often wondered this.

"Don't be silly. No, I just tell her I 'need to be alone'. The artistic temperament, you know. She understands…"

"You're not…?" He hesitates.

"Lovers?" she laughs. "Why? D'you want to watch?"

He shudders inwardly: Suzie with her hard, masculine face, thickset body. "No, thanks," he says. Now if it was Poppy and Emily… he grabs Poppy's hand, grinds himself against it. She reaches inside his trousers, his cock springs out. She lowers her head… She's like a drug. He can't get enough of her. Emily doesn't seem to have noticed any difference in him. They've been distant for a while anyway. Ever since the business over Jasmine's portrait. She's never understood how he feels about Jasmine. But he couldn't put off having sex with her forever, and when he did finally make the first move she responded with such passion that he felt guilty for the first time in ages. It was strange to feel Emily's familiar, firm, hard body grinding needily against him again; strange but comfortingly familiar, and as she climbed astride him he tried to dispel the recent image of Poppy's large breasts hanging over him, her soft, heavy thighs rubbing against his hips. Luckily, after weeks without sex (though he knows she must have used the vibrator), Emily came quickly and he managed a reasonable climax soon after, nothing like the earth-shattering ones Poppy always brings him to, but enough to make Emily feel all was okay again.

★

Christmas Day passes with the minimum of fuss. They go to church as usual, though they never go at any other time, and Emily cooks turkey steaks followed by two individual Tesco Christmas puddings. Peter checks his phone a dozen times, when Emily's not looking, for a text from Poppy but there's nothing. He tells himself it's probably because she can't get a signal wherever she is (she was typically vague about where Suzie's parents lived: "the Lake District somewhere"), but he's still disappointed, and only the memory of her sitting in bed surrounded by wrapping paper and tissue paper, wearing the red basque and black stockings he bought her for Christmas, keeps him going throughout the day.

"You didn't tell me there was a firework display on New Year's Eve," Emily says, suddenly.

Peter's mind is still on Poppy and what he'll do to her in the red basque when she comes back, and he jumps guiltily.

"What?"

Emily gestures to her phone. "Pam says there's fireworks. On the front. On New Year's Eve. It's Rotary. You want to go, don't you?"

Peter doesn't. But he can see Emily does. And he feels suddenly guilty. "Okay," he says.

★

New Year's Eve is cold and rainy, with a strong wind blowing. All day long Peter hopes she'll change her mind but Emily's set on it. "It'll be fun," she keeps saying.

She hangs on to his arm, chattering happily all the way down the road. A blast of biting wind hits them as they round the corner. Crowds of jostling people line the narrow path. Emily moves in a bit, then stops.

"You'll never see anything from here," Peter says.

"The fireworks are above us," she laughs. "It'll be fine."

But Peter forges on, pushing almost roughly through the crowds to get to the front, leaving Emily to follow after as best she can. He's partly right, she concedes, as some of the display is low on the skyline to make the best of the harbour wall. They're just nearing the front when a heavy, stinging hail starts to fall.

"This is hopeless," Peter says. "I didn't want to come anyway."

Hurt cuts through Emily's chest like ice. Her face floods with heat and tears rush to her eyes. She turns round, starts to push her way back through the crowd.

"What're you doing?" Peter asks, grabbing her arm.

"Going," she manages to say in a strangled voice.

"Why? Look, there's another one." He gestures skywards, but she doesn't look. "Don't you want to watch now?" he asks.

"It's rather spoilt now."

Her voice wobbles, he hears the tears, feels bad immediately. He's spoilt the evening she was looking forward to.

"Come on, Emily." he says, taking her arm. "Look, that's a good one…"

She knows he's doing his best, allows herself to be placated, but she can't help thinking that at one time he would have done anything she wanted if it made her happy.

The fireworks reach a crescendo at midnight with the inevitable 'Auld Lang Syne', and kisses all around. Some people have brought champagne, others beer or wine. The atmosphere is electric, yet Emily can't shrug off the unhappiness welling inside her. On the way home, through the crowded, wet, black streets, Peter takes her hand, threads her arm through his. She knows he's trying to make up for it, knows she shouldn't allow resentments to build up. These are the things that kill the love: unkind words and deeds that lodge in your mind, hardening your heart, distancing you so that you don't get hurt again.

In the blackness of the bedroom, the tears that she's been holding back all evening fall easily. As usual, Peter has fallen instantly asleep, un-tuned to her sadness. *How things have changed*, she thinks, as she wipes away the tears that slide down her face and into her ears. At one time she would have told Peter how she was feeling. He would have comforted her. *I'm sorry. It was me... No, it was me. I didn't mean it. It was my fault... No, mine...* They would have made love probably, like they used to, not the hurried lustful sessions they have now, both of them fantasising about something, but long, unhurried lovemaking, sensuous and slow. Peter could last for ages in those days, he'd turn her on her side, move in and out oh-so-gently, just the tip of his cock sliding inside her, tantalising her. He was such a good lover, so considerate. And the kisses, long, slow, passionate, his lips hard on hers, his tongue in her mouth. When did those kisses stop? Now it's never more than a brief, dry touch of the lips when they say goodbye, and they scarcely ever kiss when they have sex. "Kiss me," she says sometimes, but they're forced, clumsy kisses, with no real beginning or end. Peter doesn't like her much any more. They're no longer the best friends they used to be. Is she partly to blame? She sees herself pushing him away sometimes when he puts his arm around her when she's cooking or putting her make-up on. She's sharp with him. He's right. She treats him like a child, tells him his shirt needs changing or his eyebrows trimming. This is what happens after twenty years of living together.

"Peter…" she says, touching his arm.

He stirs, groans slightly, then he's awake. "What's the matter?" he asks, groggily.

"Nothing," she says. "I love you."

"What?"

"I love you."

"I was asleep, Emily." he grumbles, but she can tell he doesn't mind.

"I know. Sorry. I just…"

"Yes…" he says, reaching for her hand. "I love you too…"

And he goes back to sleep.

*

Spring bursts on them suddenly in March, with blue skies and daffodils, warm winds and warm sunshine. Emily picks up the post from the mat one morning, recognises with a start Jasmine's distinctive childish handwriting, feels the thickness of the crisp cream envelope, knows with a sinking heart what it is. Her first instinct is to hide it. Peter's in such a good mood. He watched the weather forecast the night before. "Fine and dry all day!" he said. "Let's drive down to Beer. We can walk over to Branscombe. Have lunch in the pub." They set the alarm for seven o'clock. She can hear him upstairs shaving. He's been so much better lately, the bad mood that infected him since Christmas seems to have lifted. Their relationship, while not completely back to normal, is on more of an even keel. One wrong word, though, and they're arguing again. No point risking anything. She stuffs the envelope quickly into a drawer. All day long she tries to put it out of her mind, but it keeps popping back in again. Several times she nearly lets it slip. *"Jasmine will be setting a date soon,"* she could say. But he'd wonder why she'd brought it up.

Next morning she puts the envelope on top of the pile of post. Peter picks it up, looks at it. "From Jasmine," he says. "Why's she writing to us?" He feels the weight of the envelope. "Not an invitation to some other exhibition, is it?"

He reaches for the letter opener, slices the envelope neatly open.

"Oh God..." he groans. "No. I don't believe it..." He throws the crisp cream card over to Emily, leafs unseeingly through the sheets of paper underneath. Emily vaguely sees: 'Wedding list, Itinerary, Places to stay...'

She looks at the card in her hand: *Simeon Blackwood and Jasmine Stanchester invite you to their wedding on Saturday 14th July...*

"Well, you knew she was engaged..." she starts tentatively.

"I didn't think she'd go through with it! And what's all this?" He grabs the card from Emily's hand. "I thought *I* was supposed to invite the guests. Anusia and I. Mr and Mrs..." he breaks off, embarrassed, suddenly realising what he's saying. "Or you and me. I don't know how these things are done nowadays."

"But we're not paying," Emily says.

"I'm surprised she hasn't asked me to."

So is Emily, but she says nothing. "It looks pretty low key," she says, taking the invitation back. "The Orangery... Sounds very romantic." Hopefully, Peter will realise it's not the conventional sort of service. Obviously, Jasmine should have asked him to give her away. It must be a civil ceremony.

"Has Simeon been married before?" she asks, casually.

Peter frowns. "No. At least I don't think so. Anusia would know."

"Or Poppy," Emily says, quickly. "I'll ask her." She reaches for her phone.

"She'll think you're mad asking her out of the blue like that, won't she?" Peter says, surprised.

Emily laughs. "Of course she won't! She's my friend! We text nearly every day."

Peter feels uncomfortable. Bad enough to be having an affair (he still can't believe it), without the two women being friends.

"It's not the first time though, is it, Peter?" Poppy asks one day.

It's tempting to tell her it's none of her business, like she told him, but he doesn't. "No. Yes. Well, not really…"

"Which?" Poppy laughs.

"Not like this," he says.

"One-night stands."

"That sounds so cheap," he groans.

"Students?" she asks.

"They weren't children!" he says. "They were grown women. They knew what they were doing. It meant nothing. It just sort of happened, you know…"

"Does Emily know?"

"God, no!"

He's silent for a while, thinking. Then, "When I first met her she was such fun." He pictures her across the table at the dinner party: her slim arms, her sparkling eyes, the way her mouth opened in that ready smile. He could tell she knew he was watching her. When she got up she allowed her dress to stay hitched up slightly before she smoothed it down. Instant sexual attraction.

"She was so down to earth, practical, no nonsense. It was such a change from Zena, who was so…" He searches for the right word. "On edge. Volatile. God, practically suicidal in the end. We were in the car once. On the motorway somewhere. In the days before central locking and things. She tried to open the car door and throw herself out. I was doing about seventy. I nearly drove off the road trying to stop her. God, it was awful…"

Poppy reaches out, cradles his head in her arms. He feels the hard nudge of her bracelet against his neck, wriggles away slightly, squints at the engraving. "Who gave you this?" he asks, though he doesn't really want to know.

"No one," she laughs. "I made it. One of the first pieces of jewellery I made."

He traces his fingers over the letters. 'Poppy'.

"When we lived in France, Grand-mère used to call me 'Ma petite poupée'," she says.

The sudden burst of French sounds exotic, exciting. He has a sudden image of the teenage Poppy in Paris (though she hasn't said that's where it was), wearing a short skirt and high-heeled boots; red, lipsticked lips blowing the smoke out in a long stream, lounging on a street corner surrounded by a group of boys… He forces himself to concentrate on what she's saying.

"Her little doll," she translates. "When we came to England Daddy changed it to Poppy…"

"I thought you said…"

"What?"

"That you made it up to go with Fields. Poppy Fields."

"Well, I did. But it's what Daddy calls me. Does it matter?"

"No, of course not. But…"

"But what?"

"I never know what to believe with you. You're always making things up."

176

"Oh, Peter, does it matter? Everyone makes things up. Never let the truth get in the way of a good story…"

These are the times he appreciates Emily more. Emily with her down-to-earth, practical, no-nonsense attitude. She's never made up a story in her life, never lied to him, or at least not about anything really important, never prevaricated. He knows her, trusts her, loves her. He puts his arm around Emily when he goes in, nuzzles her neck with his nose, tells her he loves her. He can tell she's surprised. It's important not to overcompensate, he reminds himself. This is what gives people away.

Emily's trying hard with Peter. She knows he's upset about the wedding. Jasmine phoned a few days after the invitation arrived. "I've got the most beautiful dress!" she told Emily. "Ivory silk. A long train. Antique lace. So tight I can hardly breathe in it. I'll have to lose weight."

Jasmine is as thin as a rake and Emily said nothing. "I'll get your dad for you," she said as soon as Jasmine paused long enough. Listening to Peter's monosyllabic replies, she knew Jasmine was repeating the details of the wedding: the old house and garden, the romantic Orangery where the service would be held, the Rolls Royce they would arrive in.

"Should we offer to pay for anything?" Peter asked afterwards.

"I don't see why we should. She hasn't asked. It's not as if they're young newly-weds. Simeon's *your* age, for God's sake…"

"You don't need to remind me!"

"Sorry. But it's true."

"I just wondered. The dress, you know. She's my daughter…"

"Yes, of course," Emily said, quickly. "Ring her back. Say you'll pay for it…" She can only hope it wasn't too expensive.

"She should've involved us from the start," she tells Poppy later.

"Who? What?" Poppy asks.

"Jasmine. About the wedding. Told us about it. Asked Peter to give her away. Every father wants that, don't they?"

"Yes, of course," Poppy says, idly. She wanders over to the mantelpiece, picks up the invitation. "But it's not that sort of wedding, is it? More an informal do."

"I don't understand that either. I thought she'd want the full works. Church, bridesmaids, you know... you're quite sure he hasn't been married before?"

Poppy's answer to her text – *No. Why?* – had taken so long to come through Emily couldn't even remember what it was she'd asked her.

"Quite sure," Poppy says now. "Maybe she's just not into all this white wedding stuff. Not everyone wants it. I didn't."

"What? You've been married?"

"Don't be silly!" Poppy laughs. "I mean, I've never wanted to get married."

"You may change your mind."

"Not at my age."

"How old are you?" She's never dared ask before.

"Thirty-nine."

"You certainly don't look it."

"You don't look your age either. Listen to us two!" she laughs. Then, "Oh no..."

Emily follows her gaze. Rose has appeared at the window. She taps, holds Alicia up in her arms. Emily nods, waves, jumps up to open the door.

"You let her take advantage of you," Poppy says.

"I love having her," Emily says.

"You're just an unpaid babysitter," she continues, unabated.

Emily blushes. Rose has appeared. She must have heard. She looks uncomfortable.

"I'm sorry," she says, flustered. "I didn't know Poppy was here…"

As Alicia struggles to get out of Rose's grip, Rose and Poppy eye each other, each waiting for the other to make the move to leave.

"Emmy, Emmy!" Alicia calls, holding out her arms.

"No, come on, Leesha," Rose says firmly. "Emily is busy."

"No, honestly," Emily says. "Please, I'd love to have her…"

"If you're sure. Only I've got such a headache. I didn't sleep well. Just for an hour…"

Emily glances at the clock. "I'll bring her back at five. For her tea…" It's only just gone three and she pretends not to see Poppy roll her eyes heavenwards.

"You don't have to go," she tells her when Rose has gone. "She's no trouble." Alicia is sitting cross-legged on the floor, piecing together the wooden jigsaw she has brought with her.

"I'm not very good with children," Poppy says.

"Neither am I!" Emily laughs.

"She's very pretty though, I'll give you that…"

Emily sees her running an artist's eye over Alicia's blonde curls; soft, rosy cheeks; dark eyes.

"We could take her for a walk," Emily says, looking out of the window.

"Okay. Oh, what time did you say Peter would be back?"

"God knows. He's gone to get new tyres for the car. Why?"

"I wanted to ask him something, that's all."

"What?"

"Nothing."

"Don't be silly, Poppy."

"No, it's nothing. About a painting, you know…"

Poppy often says things like this. Emily knows she should be pleased that she values his opinion, but it makes her feel… jealous? No, left out, the way she feels when Peter and Jasmine laugh at something she doesn't find funny, or when Jasmine hangs on to Peter's arm, leaving Emily trailing behind like a spare part.

"Come on, Leesha," she says absentmindedly, threading her arms through the sleeves of her coat, "we're going for a lovely walk," in that special jaunty voice she uses for Alicia.

"Lovely walk," Alicia repeats.

They head for the stream. "It's too far to the beach," Emily says. "Without the pushchair. And I don't want to disturb Rose again."

Poppy says nothing, but she knows what she's thinking.

It's slow progress, with Alicia crouching down every so often to examine a stone or a tuft of grass, or stopping to point at various things.

"So, this painting," Emily says when they're finally sitting on the bench with Alicia tottering around their feet, a safe distance from the bank.

"What?"

"The one you want to ask Peter about."

"Oh, yes. Bit of a departure for me. I want him to tell me if it's too avant-garde. D'you think he could come over tonight?"

"I don't see why not. We both could. I'd love to see it."

"I don't want anyone else seeing it," Poppy says, quickly. "Not yet. Peter's different…"

"Okay." But a quick pang of hurt goes through her and foolish tears prick her eyes.

Alicia's soon bored and they walk back leisurely, holding a hand each, pausing every so often for her to rest. They're at the top of the road when Emily sees Peter. "Peter!" she calls. He turns, hesitates squinting into the sunshine, waves, waits for them at the door. His heart leaps when he sees Poppy, but anger quickly replaces the pleasure. He texted her several days ago when he arranged to take the car in. *I'm not sure*, she replied. *I may have to guard the shop. Kitty's ill.* Yet here she is with Emily. Kitty's obviously better, so why couldn't she have contacted him? He hates seeing Poppy and Emily together like this. Luckily, Alicia is so thrilled to see him, holding out her arms to be picked up and laughing and chattering, that he can get away with the briefest of nods and a peck on the cheek for Poppy. He tries to inject a meaningful look into it, but Poppy skilfully avoids it.

"How did you get on?" Emily is asking.

"Fine, fine," he says vaguely, forgetting for a moment that he's been on a legitimate mission to get tyres. He's so used to trying not to sound guilty.

"They were the right ones this time then?" Emily persists.

"Yes. Here, I've got the receipt somewhere. Emily has a filing system…" he tells Poppy. "She goes through my pockets if I don't let her have it straight away."

"I shall have to remember that!" Poppy laughs, catching his eye.

The next day, when Emily comes back from Pilates, Peter's not there. This often happens nowadays and while she knows she should be pleased he's going out more she finds herself illogically irked by it. She was so used to finding him sitting there reading. The first time it happened she'd picked up some shopping on her way back, and she struggled in with two heavy shopping bags that she had to unpack herself. "I went for a drive," he said when he came back in. "It seemed a shame to stay inside…"

This time she's pretty sure she knows where he is. "I might go and see Poppy," he said when she kissed him goodbye this morning. "About that painting." He likes it when he has a legitimate reason to see her, even if he knows he'll end up fucking her anyway.

"Emily's worried about you," Poppy greets him.

"I do wish you wouldn't talk about her like this."

"She *is* your wife."

"It doesn't seem right…" He gestures to the rumpled bed, their naked bodies. She laughs.

"She thinks you're upset about Jasmine," she says.

He sits up, pulls a sheet around him. "I am. It's ridiculous. Simeon's *my* age. Older maybe. Why the hell does she have to marry him?"

"Maybe they're in love. Maybe she wants kids…"

"No, don't…" he groans.

"You should talk to her…"

"She won't listen to me. Kids never do."

"No. I meant Emily."

"I can't. I mean… it's not just Jasmine, is it?" He strokes the bare white thigh that lies next to his.

"Don't be silly, Peter. Emily's more important."

A cold chill runs through him. "You're not saying…?"

"No!" She laughs. "I haven't finished with you yet. Unless *you're* getting tired of *me*?"

"Never, never, never!" he laughs, rolling over and pinning her to the bed.

"No, wait!" she says, breathlessly. "I'm serious, Peter. I don't want to hurt Emily. I love her."

His erection wanes instantly. He sits up, throws the sheet to one side, reaches for his clothes. On the way home he vows not to see her again. She's a bitch, a witch. When he gets in, Emily is cramming clothes into the washing machine. She scarcely stops long enough to give him a kiss and ask where he's been before she's crouching down again. '*She's worried about you,*' Poppy had said. If only she knew. Emily doesn't worry about anything except her household routine.

In his study he reaches for his phone. He's just wondering what to say when the text comes through: *Come back to me. I need you.*

I need you too, he types, instantly.

The warm spring turns into a warm summer. Visitors flock to Lyme Regis. The roads in and out of town become gridlocked, the pavements thronged with slow-moving families meandering along.

It's early July when Jasmine calls. Emily knows it's her even before she speaks. There's the distinctive sound of her sobbing, the sound she's heard so many times. Usually, it was an argument with Anusia, sometimes one of her friends, occasionally a problem at school, more latterly a boyfriend issue. She waits for Jasmine to pull herself together. "It's off," she says, finally.

"What?" Emily says.

"The wedding. Off, off, off!" she's shouting now, hysterically. Emily can hear her voice strangled in her throat.

"Hang on," she says. "I'll get Dad."

"No. I can't…" Jasmine gasps. "Please, Em, just tell him…" And she's gone.

For once Emily is as worried as Peter. "We'll have to go there," she says.

It's mid-morning, a Saturday.

"Oh, God. Do we have to?" Peter says. "Think of the traffic. Anyway, Simeon will be there."

"Well, presumably not, since they've split up."

"But it's *his* place."

"I'll text her. Ask her where she is. We'll go and pick her up…" Even as she says it she feels a knot of dread in her stomach at the thought of Jasmine mooching around in a depressed state down here with them.

"I just don't think it's a good idea," Peter says. "It'll blow over. You know it will. It's just a lover's tiff. Pre-wedding nerves. You know what she's like…"

He gets the text the next morning. *Can I come down, Daddy? I've got nowhere else to go.*

Emily makes up the spare bed, the knot in her stomach tightening further. Jasmine is surprisingly upbeat when she arrives, beautifully dressed as usual, make-up intact, the slight shadows under her eyes the only sign of any strain. "I don't want to talk about it," she says. The next day, however, when Peter has disappeared into his study after breakfast, she suddenly says to Emily, "Can I tell you something?"

Despite herself, Emily's flattered. Jasmine has never confided in her before.

"It's Si," she says, her voice breaking on the name. She reaches for her tissue. Emily knows she should go to her, put her arm around her, but she can't. She's never been like that with Jasmine and it's too late to start now. Jasmine is crying. She waits. "Anusia…" she makes out among the sobs.

"What?" Emily asks, though she's pretty sure she knows what's going on now.

"Ma…" Jasmine repeats. "Hang on. Come upstairs. I'll show you…"

Hearing them passing and Jasmine crying, Peter comes out of his study. Emily waves him away with a quick frown and he disappears quickly again. In her room Jasmine rummages in her bag. "Here…" she says.

It's a roll of old black and white film, the sort you develop yourself, and as Emily unrolls it she can see why. The pictures could almost be of Jasmine, except that they're clearly taken in the '60s. Anusia stands fully clothed at first, before predictably first her cardigan, then her blouse, then the huge, lacy, white 1960s' bra come off, one frame at a time. Interestingly, her smile doesn't quite reach her eyes. Even at this distance in time you can see she's uncomfortable with what she's doing. It doesn't square with the image Emily has of Anusia. She lets the roll drop back into Jasmine's hand. "But you knew what he was like," she says.

"Yes, but he *told* me…" she sobs. "He *swore…*"

"It doesn't necessarily mean…"

"Of *course* it does! Don't be silly, Em!"

"Yes… but it's years ago. It doesn't mean he doesn't love you now." She doesn't know why she's saying it really. The man's impossible. He's not going to make Jasmine happy. She just can't stand all this fuss. Jasmine has collapsed onto the bed, sobbing again. Emily sits down next to her, pats her shoulder awkwardly. Eventually, the sobs stop and Jasmine falls asleep. She looks like a child lying there and Emily knows she should feel some maternal pull, but she doesn't.

"So?" Peter says when she comes back down.

"It's about Anusia," she says.

"I thought it might be."

"You knew?"

"I told you, didn't I?"

"Sort of. I don't see it makes much difference really. The man's a born womaniser." She shudders at the thought of his hand on hers. "She knew that before."

"Yes," he says.

She wonders whether to tell him about the photos, but decides against it. "How long d'you think she'll stay?" she asks instead.

"It's her home," Peter says. "She can stay as long as she likes."

"But it's not!" Emily says. "She's got a home!"

"Simeon threw her out."

"She left," she corrects. "But she can find somewhere else. She has before."

"It's just till she's feeling better."

But days go by, then weeks. Though he can't admit it to

185

Emily, Peter agrees with her. Jasmine has sharp eyes and ears; she has a way of seeing everything that's going on. "Where are you going, Daddy?"

"For a walk."

"D'you always go out when Em's out?"

And another time. "Poppy's very attractive, isn't she? Shame she's so big. You've never gone for that type, have you?"

"She knows," he tells Poppy.

"Don't be silly. It's just your guilty conscience."

"I thought we were going to keep off that subject."

"Sorry, I forgot," she laughs. "What about her job?"

"She's jacked it in."

"We need someone to work in the shop. To cover Kitty's holiday."

"Are you crazy? She'd find out about us!"

"Not if we're careful…"

Emily's heart sank when she found Jasmine looking for a job in the local paper. Her face must have given her away. "Just for the summer," Jasmine had said, quickly. "I can't go back to London yet…" and the ready tears started to fall.

"I suppose then at least she might pay some rent," Emily said drily, when she told Peter.

"This is her *home,*" Peter said.

"So you keep saying. But it's costing a fortune having her here. She's so damn fussy. You don't know how easy you are, Peter, eating the same meal two nights running. I can't do that with her. She doesn't like half the stuff we have anyway. God, I should know by now. She's always been the same. A vegetarian one moment, vegan the next… then there's the washing. Two lots of sheets and towels. All those damn jeans and tops. 'Leave it. I'll do it myself,' she says, but she never does…"

"She won't be here long, Emily. Can't you just try and get on while she is?"

Peter hates all this friction. Jasmine's his daughter, he reasons; she's only young, she's going through a hard time. It's up to Emily to make things easy for her.

Emily does her best to keep out of Jasmine's way. Her Pilates classes have stopped for the summer (Sarah has two school-age children to look after in the holidays), but there's still Zumba, and the extra shopping needed to cater for Jasmine gives her an excuse to go out almost every day. She always peeps into the shop as she passes by and sometimes Poppy runs out to see her. Once or twice she even manages to slip out for coffee at the Bell Cliff Café.

"Any idea when Jasmine's going back?" Poppy asks one day.

"I can't ask her," Emily sighs. "And Peter won't talk about it."

"He must want her gone as much as you do, though."

"Yes… no… I don't know. He always takes her side."

"It must be cramping your style, though!" Poppy laughs. "With her and you two, in that tiny little house, with the thin walls…"

Emily reddens, remembering the furtive lovemaking session of the night before.

"I offered her a job," Poppy says, casually.

Emily feels a stab of hurt. "What? Why? I told you I don't want her here any longer than necessary."

"Oh, don't worry. She said no. And it was only for a couple of weeks. While Kitty's away."

"You could've asked me first," Emily says, still hurt.

"I thought I was helping you. You and Peter. Get her out of your way for a while…"

Emily's not convinced, but "She'd never work in a shop anyway," she says, thinking out loud. "Oh, I don't mean…" She suddenly realises what she's said.

"It doesn't matter," Poppy says easily. "I know what you mean. Obviously, she thought the same."

She links her arm through Emily's as they walk back. The streets are crowded. They thread their way past a middle-aged couple who stop suddenly to look in a shop window, then overtake a family with a pushchair and two young children. The child in the pushchair is bawling, and one of the other children throws his spade onto the pavement and refuses to pick it up. Poppy tuts loudly and drags Emily past. "I haven't got to get back yet," she says, looking at her watch. "Let's go into the Gardens."

Jubilee Gardens, the park on the cliff above Lyme Regis, is always quieter than the beach in the summer and they find a shady bench and sit down. On the stretch of grass beyond them a young couple lie entwined in each other's arms.

"Love's young dream," Poppy says.

"Everyone has their summer of love," Emily says. "Mine was when I was fifteen. Mike Gray. He was my first love. Everyone fancied him. But I got him. We were inseparable. He used to meet me from school. We'd walk back through the fields, flatten down the long grass to make a nest. It was…" She gestures towards the young couple. "You know…"

Of course, Poppy knows. "Yes," she says.

"We stayed out one night. All night. A party at a friend's house. My parents would've killed me if they'd known. Nothing happened. Not like that. We got drunk, messed around. We all slept in one room. I woke at dawn. Bodies everywhere. Mike was still asleep. He'd rolled away from me in the night. It was cold. First light. Grey. I desperately needed a wee. When I got back there was another girl getting up. She was naked to the waist. Tight hipster jeans. Long, untidy hair. She came over to me. Slowly. Put her arms around me. Kissed me. Really kissed me. Her tongue in my mouth. Her soft body pressed against me, so different from Mike's hard male one. I never knew who she was. By the time I got up later she'd gone. I wondered if I'd dreamt it. But I don't think I did." She stops. Her face is burning. She can't look at Poppy. "I've never told anyone else," she goes on. "I don't know why I'm telling you now…"

Poppy says nothing. She puts out her hand, takes hold of Emily's, curls her fingers around it tightly.

Chapter Fifteen

It's late September. Jasmine has gone back with, it turns out, the minimum of fuss. One of her girlfriends (Anastasia? Elfrida? Some weird name that Emily can't remember) has offered to take her on holiday with her. "Italy!" Jasmine enthuses. "Her father has a villa on Lake Garda. And they've got friends on Lake Como. Bellagio. She's staying a month. But I might stay longer…" Emily doesn't ask where the money's coming from. Jasmine hasn't worked for two months. But she's the sort who can always find the money for something she wants to do. And Emily doesn't want to find out Peter has stepped in. She'd rather not know. There's no mention of Simeon. Emily wonders sometimes how Jasmine must feel about the painting of her: her naked self revealed to strangers' eyes in the most intimate erotic fashion; men revelling in it, the girl-woman they know they shouldn't fancy but do; women embarrassed yet fascinated by it: themselves, their daughters, mirrored in this one painting.

Emily and Peter are going away too. They always try to go somewhere in late summer, after the school holidays, before the winter sets in. Last year was the first time in years they hadn't gone, but that was because of the move, and settling into the new house.

It takes ages for Emily to get organised. They haven't been away for over a year. Peter has to haul the suitcases down from the attic, and she can't find where she packed the sun cream, sponge bags and insect repellent. "Can't you just buy more?" Peter asks when he finds her rummaging around in a cupboard.

"You don't understand!" she says, impatiently. "I put them all together, ready for the holiday. It's ridiculous to buy more when we've already got it."

They always go to Majorca in September, to an apartment on the south-east coast of the island, on the edge of the Mondrago Natural Park, away from the touristy areas. Although it's nearly October it's still hot. Neither Peter nor Emily sunbathe any more. Emily has a spray tan done before she goes and tops it up with lotion every day while they're away. Peter doesn't worry about being pale any more. The archetypal Englishman abroad, he wears long trousers, a long-sleeved, loose-fitting shirt; a hat.

They get on better while they're away, a team spirit enforced on them by coping with the airport, the hire car and dealing with the natives. The apartment block is managed by Carlos Fernanda, a slim, good-looking man in his thirties, whose almost-perfect English is only marred by his insistence on referring to the 'island' as the 'ice-land'. Every year Emily wishes she had the courage to correct him. "Everyone else probably thinks the same!" Peter laughs with her. He notices how Carlos' eyes sweep, as usual, over Emily's slim, brown body in her tight t-shirt and short skirt. He's proud of her.

Upstairs, he runs his hand over her bottom as she bends to unpack the groceries they bought in the town. "Stop it, Peter!" she laughs, but he feels her respond and later on they make love voraciously in the cool, air-conditioned bedroom.

In this romantic holiday mood he feels guilty checking his phone daily for messages from Poppy, but he can't help himself. He texted the moment they arrived. *Arrived safely. Miss you so much.* Poppy's reply took a whole day to come through. "Have you got a signal?" he kept asking Emily.

"Yes. I've had two texts, one from Grace, one from Poppy."

He cursed Poppy inwardly, but his heart leapt the next time he looked and found, *Miss you too.*

This has to suffice for the next three days, and he has to force himself not to text again to find out if she's okay.

"I miss Leesha," Emily says.

"Me too," he admits.

"And Poppy," she adds.

He only just stops himself agreeing. He misses her more than he ever thought possible: he thinks about her constantly, calls her name in his mind, checks his phone every few minutes for a message from her. When the blank screen faces him day after day he begins to wonder how important he actually is to her. But he's not going to chase after her. And he can't let Emily see how concerned he is. So he buries his hurt behind a façade of happiness, and strangely finds it works after a fashion. Emily responds to his happy mood: she's loving and caring, hangs on his arm when they're out shopping, cuddles up to him in bed at night. Freed from all those chores that seem to take up all her time at home, she's more like the Emily he used to know. If she could be like this all the time maybe he wouldn't need Poppy. But then when they're out one day he glimpses a girl who looks like Poppy: the same wavy, auburn hair, same flamboyant clothes, same confident swaying walk. For one mad moment he thinks she's followed him here. He wouldn't put it past her to turn up, screeching "Surprise!" at the top of her voice and wowing tourists and locals alike. His heart beats faster, his whole being floods with excitement, followed swiftly by sweeping disappointment when she turns around and he sees it's not her. In that one moment he knows he can never do without her. So he forgives her the days of torture, believes her when she texts, *I'm sorry. I've been so busy. I miss you. Hope you're having lovely time xx.*

The two weeks that had stretched out before them finally comes to an end. They have their final dinner in the restaurant on the seafront and walk back along the road to their apartment, a full moon shining over the sea. The familiar nostalgic end-of-holiday mood sweeps over Emily. She squeezes Peter's hand, knows he feels the same.

Woken that night by Peter's snoring and the uncomfortable fullness of too much paella, she stares out of the apartment window in the kitchen while she waits for the kettle to boil. The fishing boat lights in the harbour wink and bob. The lighthouse flashes rhythmically on and off. It's been a wonderful holiday, one of their best, but she's ready to go home. And there are things to go home for: Alicia, who she misses so much; Poppy; Rose even. She yawns and stretches. They have an early flight. She should really go straight back to bed, but Peter's still snoring and she reaches for her book instead.

The next day she's tired and grumpy. She snaps at Peter as he wanders around the apartment, getting in her way as she's trying to pack things up, leaving his toothpaste and toothbrush still in the bathroom instead of putting it in the suitcase.

"It's like looking after a child!" she says, half under her breath.

"What?"

"Nothing. It doesn't matter."

"Well, why did you say it then?"

The familiar bickering returning. Emily sighs.

Home seems an interminable journey, though in fact it's only an hour's drive to Palma Airport, a two-hour flight and an hour and a half drive back to Lyme Regis. Emily's dying to see Alicia, but there's unpacking to do, washing to put on, and it's the next day before Rose knocks on the window and Alicia comes flying into her arms. Tears come into her eyes as she holds the warm, little body tightly in her arms until Alicia squirms, impatiently, free.

"Did you have a good time?" Rose is asking.

"Yes, wonderful, but we missed you…"

Alicia is fussing around Peter now and Emily has a chance to look at Rose properly: she's paler than usual, her polite smile of welcome doesn't meet her eyes. She looks stressed.

"All okay with you?" Emily asks.

"Yes, fine," Rose says lightly, but her eyes slide away from Emily's knowing look.

The next day, when Emily's hanging out the first lot of washing on the line, she feels herself being watched. She turns and finds Dan looking over the garden fence. "Good holiday?" he asks.

"Lovely, thanks."

"You look good," he says.

She looks away, embarrassed, though flattered. "Thanks," she says, lightly.

"No, you look *really* good."

The inference is unavoidable. She looks him straight in the face this time. "I'm a one-man woman, Dan," she says.

He reddens, inclines his head slightly in acknowledgement, shrugs slightly. "See you later," he says, casually, and goes back inside.

Peter has easily found an excuse to see Poppy. "I need to check the tyre pressures. That front one looks slightly down…"

And Emily, rushing around unpacking cases and throwing piles of clothes into the washing machine, seems only too relieved to have him out of her way.

His first sight of Poppy catches him by surprise: he's forgotten how big she is. She even looks like she's put on weight, or is it just that he's got used to Emily's firm little body, and her tanned face and arms? Poppy's face looks pale and puffy. She hurls herself into his arms, holds him close, but he finds himself less excited than he expected to be. She feels different, smells different. She hasn't forgotten what he likes though, and afterwards as he runs his hand through her long, auburn hair he knows he'll be back again and again.

Back home, Emily is still unpacking and sorting out. He nearly falls over the empty suitcases at the top of the stairs. Sponge bags are strewn around the bathroom, toiletries on almost every surface. Piles of washing stand in front of the washing machine.

"Oh good, I'm glad you're back," Emily says. "Can you put the suitcases back up in the loft?"

"I'll do it later."

"Why can't you do it now?"

"I've only just got in, Emily!" he says, testily.

"I haven't stopped all day, Peter. I don't see why you can't do it now. What else are you doing?"

Peter was going to sit down and read his book. Or the motor magazine he bought at the airport.

"For God's sake, stop trying to organise me, Emily. It doesn't have to be done now. I'll do it sometime, don't worry."

"But they're in the way..."

"No one's coming to stay. They're fine where they are!"

Emily knows there's no point arguing with Peter when he's like this. The more she goes on at him, the less likely he is to do it. She wishes she could go up in the roof herself. Maybe if Peter goes out tomorrow she could try to do it on her own. But then there'll only be trouble when he gets back and finds she has.

She takes another lot of washing out of the tumble dryer and folds it, then finds some mince in the freezer and puts it in the microwave to defrost.

"Peter!" she calls. "Can you peel some potatoes for me?"

"What, now?" he asks. He's only just found the motor magazine and is in the middle of an article on the new BMW.

"Well, if you want dinner tonight!" Emily snaps.

"It's only five o'clock."

"It has to be cooked!"

"Okay, okay!" He throws the magazine down, impatiently, then picks it up and smoothes it out carefully. He hates his magazines creased.

Emily scoops up the pile of washing to take upstairs. Right in the middle of the freshly-made bed she finds the flight bag tipped upside down: books, passports, wet wipes, an empty bottle of water, all strewn everywhere.

"Peter!" she yells.

"What?" he calls from the foot of the stairs.

"You could've asked me to find whatever it was you were looking for! And why the hell didn't you put it back afterwards?"

"I thought you needed it unpacked."

"Not like that! God, what a mess!"

Peter sighs. He can never do anything right. He thinks of Poppy in her untidy flat: every surface, every chair, even the floor, strewn with clothes and various other paraphernalia. He remembers seeing her rummaging through the pile of junk on a chest of drawers to find her hairbrush. He couldn't live like that of course, but if only Emily could be a bit more relaxed about things.

But Emily hates chaos. She begins to wonder when she'll get straight again. The moment she put the washing on the line it started to rain. Torn between leaving it to dry between showers and bringing it in to put in the tumble dryer, she chose the former, but it's been raining solidly ever since, coupled with a strong wind that's pulled half the clothes off the line, leaving them scrunched up together in a way that means they'll take ages to dry even when the rain stops. She's just put the final lot on to wash, and is trying to unpack and put away the toiletries and sun creams, somewhere she may remember where they are for the next time, when Rose turns up with Alicia. Emily's heart sinks: usually, she'd love to have her, but there's so much still to do. Rose reads her face. "It doesn't matter," she says, quickly. "I know you're busy."

But Rose looks a mess. She never makes an effort at the best of times, She could look really good if she tried, Peter commented once, but today she's wearing a stained, crumpled top that looks like it hasn't been washed for days and equally creased and stained jeans. Her fair hair looks grubby, her face is strained, and the smile she gives Emily is forced.

"Don't be silly," Emily says. "You know I'd love to have her."

"It's just... I've got so much to do..."

"Yes, of course..." Emily says, vaguely, thinking of all the things she had wanted to do this afternoon.

"Leesha and I are going away next week."

"To London?" Emily asks. Rose's visits to see her parents have become more frequent.

"Yes."

"How long will you be gone?"

Rose looks away, shrugs, bends down to tie the bow on the front of Alicia's dress, her hair hiding her face. Alarm bells sound in Emily's mind but she dismisses them: it'll be good for Rose to get away, her mother will help with Alicia, and Dan will miss her and appreciate her better when she comes home.

England in mid-October feels cold, drab and damp after the high sunshine of Majorca. They drove back from the airport in pouring rain, and the odd few hours' sunshine soon disappeared under grey, stormy skies. The already-turning leaves are falling and lie damp and squelchy on the pavements. They picked up the essentials on the way home, but Emily has to go out two days later for milk and vegetables. She looks into the shop on her way by. Her heart leaps when she catches sight of Poppy. It's scarcely more than a glimpse, just from the back. Fondness wells up in her at the familiar sight of Poppy's long, auburn hair, the way she waves her arms around and tosses her head as she talks, the usual voluminous clothes hanging from her shoulders. Emily hopes she'll feel she's being watched, turn and see her. She even thinks of tapping on the windows, visualises Poppy's face light up with pleasure, sees her excusing herself and rushing out to hug her. But in reality she knows none of this would happen. Poppy's with a customer. She would frown, shake her head. Emily would feel foolish. So she goes down to the Co-op, but all the time she's wandering around the aisles, choosing vegetables, queuing at the till, her mind is on Poppy.

The shop is empty when she goes back. The bell tinkles. No one appears. Emily puts her heavy shopping bags down, rubs her wrists, looks around vaguely at the stuff she has looked at so many times before: the frilly starched 'vintage' nightgowns; the useless fragments of slate, shaped into hearts and diamonds, threaded with silk; the painted wooden egg cups; the tea trays lined with paper doilies. Amongst these useless oddities, Poppy's jewellery and paintings stand out like a shining beacon. Even Emily with her limited knowledge of art can see they're the only thing worth buying.

Her kagoul drips onto the floor. Still no one appears. She can picture Poppy in the tiny kitchen area making her coffee, hoping and praying that she'll hear the shop bell tinkle again, the unknown customer having given up and left. Maybe she *should* go. Maybe Poppy *will* see her as a nuisance, an interruption to her coffee break. She reaches back to pull up her hood, reaches for each shopping bag, grips the handle of the door awkwardly with the first two fingers of her right hand, manoeuvres out of the door.

"Emily! Wait!"

Then everything happens all at once: Poppy's hugging her. "My God, you're soaked!" Taking Emily's shopping bags, peeling off her wet kagoul, holding her at arm's length. "You look fantastic!" Hugging her again. Emily has never felt so welcome. The feel of Poppy's soft arms around her, her soft, warm body enveloping her, the smell of her, the smell she realises she has missed so much, it's all too much, and she finds herself almost crying even as she laughs and smiles.

"You had a good time?" Poppy is asking. "Of course you did. I can see you did! Tell me all about it. Oh, I've missed you so much!" She holds both Emily's hands in hers. Poppy's hands are small, the skin quite rough.

"There's nothing to tell. We walked, read, went out for drives. All the usual…"

She walks home in a haze of happiness.

Peter is at the back door the moment it opens. "You were gone ages! Where've you been?"

"Shopping. I told you." She was looking forward to telling him she'd seen Poppy, but she's not going to now.

"You were hours," he says, accusingly.

"No, I wasn't."

She passes the shopping bags to him, the bags she had carried through the town, the ones Poppy had taken easily from her. He grimaces as he takes them, nearly drops one. "You could've warned me they were heavy!"

She sighs, impatiently, reaches out to take back the heavier one.

"No! Leave it!" he snaps. "I can manage! I'm not infirm!"

"You just said it was heavy!" she snaps back.

"I didn't say I couldn't do it!"

Emily hangs up her wet coat, follows Peter into the kitchen. He's unpacking the bags onto the surfaces. Emily scurries around him, putting the milk and cheese into the fridge, bread into the freezer, vegetables into the cupboard, stepping around Peter until finally he says, "I'll get out of your way."

"Yes, please," she says, coldly.

"Next you'll be accusing me of not helping!"

"But you're not!"

"And if I try you say I'm in the way!"

"You could put those suitcases away if you want something to do."

"Why are you always nagging me? I've *said* I'll do it and I'll do it!"

"But *when,* Peter? They've been sitting there for a week."

"Don't be silly. We only got back the other day."

"Wednesday. Five days ago. You *said* you'd do it!"

"And I will. But not now. I don't feel like it."

Emily throws the bag of potatoes into the cupboard and slams the door. "I didn't *feel* like doing the shopping! Carrying it all through town in the rain! How would it be if I didn't *feel* like ironing your shirts, cooking your meals, washing your clothes?"

"I would've come with you if you'd asked."

"What? In the rain? You'd spend the entire time grumbling!"

"And you don't grumble, I suppose!"

"I'm sick of this, Peter!" she yells. "You do bugger all! You sit around and read or play with your computer, wait for me to provide meals and tea. And if I ask you to help you say I'm nagging you!" Her voice has risen to a hysterical shriek and Peter glances around nervously. "Shhh!" he says.

"I don't give a damn who hears!" She picks up a bag of carrots and hurls it across the room.

"Emily!" Peter says. "What's wrong with you?"

"*Me?*" She's started sobbing now. "It's *you!* You're the one…" She can't finish. Her voice has become strangled. She sobs uncontrollably.

She waits for Peter to come to her, put his arms around her, comfort her, tell her it's all going to be okay, but she hears the door open and close and realises she's on her own. Crying and sniffing, wiping her nose on a tissue, she picks up the carrots from the floor, puts them in the fridge, mechanically unpacks the rest of the shopping, folds the carrier bags up, puts them away. She's calmer now. She goes into the study. Peter is sitting staring at a blank computer screen. He scarcely glances up. "Where did you put my book?" he asks.

"In the sitting room."

"I wish you wouldn't keep moving it."

She says nothing, goes out, fetches it, puts it down in front of him, wordlessly. Then she goes out again, returns with the pile of motor magazines she's found strewn around the house, plonks them down on top. He looks up at her strangely. "Emily, I'm worried about you."

"What? Why?"

"You're acting in an odd way."

Just for a moment she believes him. A small moment of doubt in herself. Then she sees what he's doing. "You can't try that with me, Peter. I'm not Zena. I'm as sane as you are." She gives a bitter little laugh.

★

Emily can't sleep that night. She thinks, nostalgically, of the happy holiday mood in Majorca. Tears of tiredness and self-pity run down her face and she wipes them impatiently away. When she eventually gets to sleep she dreams she's shouting at Peter, telling him all the things she hates about him, all the things she'd never say to his face, the words that would do too much damage: "You're lazy!" she yells at him. "You don't even try! You just sit around like a lazy lump reading all day!"

She wakes with a jolt. Something's woken her. The sound of a heavy lorry pulling into the road, the hiss of brakes. It stops outside. Doors slam. She hears voices: men asking each other if this is the right house. Then Rose's voice. Emily gets out of bed, pulls back the curtain carefully so as not to wake Peter.

BENNETT REMOVALS, she sees on the lorry. NO MOVE TOO BIG OR TOO SMALL.

She dresses quickly, runs downstairs. At the front door she hesitates. It's none of her business. And Rose won't be able to talk with the men there. She's standing by the open lorry doors, directing them as they stack the boxes.

"Maybe they're just going for an extended stay," Peter says when she takes him up a cup of tea.

Emily shakes her head. "Not with all that stuff. Why didn't she tell me? I thought she was my friend."

"Well, *I* wouldn't go round telling everyone if it was me."

"You're a *man,* Peter. Men don't."

They talk about it again over breakfast. "I knew they weren't getting on," Emily says. "They bicker."

Peter shrugs. "What's a bit of bickering? Doesn't mean a thing."

"No..." she says. She peers out of the window. The lorry has gone. "When d'you think I can go round?"

"You can't. It's not our business, Emily. She'll tell you when she wants to. *If* she wants to."

Emily hates it when Peter says things like that. It makes her want to do exactly the opposite. But he's probably right. She can't just barge in and demand to know what's going on. "I don't understand," she says, sadly. "I thought she was my friend."

"She *is* your friend."

"I mean, she could have told me. *Should* have told me."

"Maybe it's nothing then. Maybe they're just going for an extended stay. A trial run or something."

"I couldn't bear not to see Leesha."

"I know."

Peter feels sorry for Emily. He'll miss the little girl too, but not like Emily will. With his pity comes a rekindling of love, a desire to make things right for her. He goes upstairs after breakfast, takes the suitcases from the spare bedroom, takes them up to the loft. Then he goes into his study and tidies his desk, putting away CDs and DVDs, piling his magazines and the travel books and maps of Majorca in the corner of the room.

It's the first fine day for nearly a week. "Let's go out for a walk," Peter says.

"I've got a huge pile of ironing," Emily says. Then she looks out of the window. "You're right. I can do it tomorrow. I'll get my jacket."

They're just rounding the corner when they see Dan backing the car out. Alicia's sitting in her car seat in the back. She waves excitedly. Dan stops, winds down the window. "D'you want to open the back door?" he asks. "So you can see her properly?"

"Hello, sweetie," Emily says, reaching out to her, touching her soft, little cheek.

"Peter?" Alicia asks, reaching her arms out to him. He takes her chubby hand, smiles in at her.

Rose comes out, waits for the car to draw away. "We're going today," she says.

Peter says nothing. It's Emily who says, "Leaving? For good?"

Rose nods, tears rolling down her face. She reaches for a tissue. Emily puts her arms around her. "Rose, I'm so sorry. I wish…"

"Don't say anything." She pulls away, wiping her nose and face. "You'll make me worse. Please. It's the only way…"

"Leesha?" Emily manages somehow.

"I'll bring her round later. To say goodbye. She doesn't understand. She doesn't know."

Emily nods, wordlessly. Peter puts his arm around her shoulders, guides her inside. As the door closes she gives way to huge, heavy, body-wrenching sobs. "It'll be all right," Peter is saying. "We can go and see her."

Emily shakes her head. "No, no. It'll never be the same. You know it won't."

She waits impatiently for the last goodbye, but when it comes at three o'clock, when Alicia wakes up from her nap, it's an anti-climax. Alicia's excited about going in the car. "Granma. Granma," she keeps saying. She wriggles out of Emily's arms, holds her hands out to go back to Rose. Emily manages a swift kiss on her cheek, Peter scarcely that, then they're waving goodbye as the car drives off.

"I can't imagine what Dan's going through," Emily says, watching them drive away. "Driving her up like that. Knowing it's the last time they'll be together."

Peter shakes his head. "It's hard…" he says. "But then there's something of a relief once the decision's been made and you know there's no going back. And it's not as if he won't see her again."

"But it'll never be the same."

"No."

"He'll miss her terribly."

"Yes."

Too late, Emily wonders if she's bringing back memories of Anusia and Jasmine, but Peter looks unperturbed. He's never spoken about their break-up and she knows him well enough to know not to ask about it.

She's not sure what time Dan gets back that night but the car is outside the next morning. All the curtains are drawn and it's nearly midday before she sees the kitchen blind pulled up.

"What do we say to him?" she asks Peter.

"Nothing. Leave him to it," Peter says. "He knows where we are if he wants us."

Over the next few days bin liners appear outside. Dan comes and goes in the car, the passenger and back seat piled high with boxes and bags.

"He's moving out," Emily says.

"It's not our business," Peter replies.

"I know. But…"

She's dying to know what his plans are. She feels sorry for him, in there on his own, suffering in silence, no one to talk to. Peter's right. It's not their business. And if she saw him she wouldn't know what to say. Then suddenly she walks right into him. She's putting out some rubbish and he's on his way in. They stand awkwardly opposite each other. Emily can't look into his eyes. She notices, almost subliminally, his deathly white face, the drawn look of it. He looks terrible, like he hasn't slept in days. Above the neck of the torn jumper he's wearing she can see that his shirt has been buttoned wrongly. His jeans are crumpled at the knees.

"Hi," she says.

"Hello."

"Umm. Are you okay?" Stupid, stupid question.

His face hardens. He says nothing.

"Sorry," she says. "If there's anything…"

"Thanks. Nothing. Thanks."

She feels a stab of hurt and tears come to her eyes. He doesn't need to be so rude. Hard to excuse him, despite what he's going through.

She misses Alicia terribly. "At least you'll have more time now," Peter says. "You were always saying she took up so much time."

"I didn't mind. Not really. I'd have it all back if I could."

She can't bear to look at the photos she took, looks away when she sees children in the town. Her eyes fill with tears whenever she thinks of her.

It's another week before they see Dan again. He knocks on the back door. "I'm sorry. I've been so busy…"

"Come in, come in," Peter says.

Emily can see he's being too effusive to hide his embarrassment, but Dan doesn't seem to notice. Or maybe he's used to it.

"I'm leaving at the end of the week," he says.

"Where are you going?"

"I'd rather not say."

Emily can see Peter thinking the same thing: Dan's been having an affair. He's moving in with someone else.

"We'll be sorry to see you go." Emily says, carefully, still smarting from his previous rudeness.

"I'll miss you too. We haven't been very good neighbours."

"Yes, you have."

"We kept meaning to invite you round. Properly, I mean. For a drink. For a meal. But it was difficult…"

"Yes," Emily says. "Never mind. New beginnings," she says, brightly.

"I'm just trying to concentrate on the practical at the moment," he says. "It's the only way I can get through."

Emboldened suddenly, Emily says, "Is there someone else?" She senses Peter shift uncomfortably next to her.

"What?" Dan seems genuinely surprised. "Another female, you mean?"

"Yes."

"No. No." He shakes his head emphatically. "Oh, I see. You thought... no, no. I'm just not sure what I'm doing, that's all. A bit of travelling, maybe. But I don't want people contacting me. I need to be alone. Take stock, you know."

"Yes," Emily says. That's what she could do with. A break. A break from everything. From Peter, from the house, from her friends. Well, all except Poppy. She's the only one she would miss.

After his initial sympathy over Alicia, Peter has lost patience with Emily.

"I don't know why you keep talking about her when it upsets you so much," he says when she dissolves into tears again remembering how she used to call the fridge magnets 'Mag-er-nets'.

Like all men, Peter has the ability to put to the back of his mind things that upset him. "I never knew she was so fond of children," he tells Poppy. "She was never like it with any others."

"She *was* a lovely little girl," Poppy says. "I would've loved to have painted her."

★

On Dan's last day Emily wakes to the sound of the howling wind. Peter is still asleep. He can sleep through anything. She goes downstairs, puts the kettle on. Rain lashes against the window. Depression sinks on Emily. This is it now until the spring: cold, grey weather; endless rain; snow and ice maybe. Nothing to look forward to, not even Christmas this year with Alicia gone. She sees Dan run out to the car, open the boot, shove a few bags inside. Feeling himself being watched, he looks up, waves, runs over. Emily unlocks the back door. He steps inside, shaking drips of water from his hair. Emily looks up at him, mesmerised. With all that's been going on, she's forgotten how good-looking he is. She feels drawn to him.

"I'm on my way," he's saying. "Thought I'd make an early start. No point in staying."

"Peter's still in bed," she says.

"Don't disturb him. I hate goodbyes anyway."

"Okay."

She senses his awkwardness, reaches forward to peck his cheek. He puts his arms round her. She feels his slim, hard body against hers, his strong arms and shoulders under her hands. "Take me with you," she hears herself saying.

He draws back, laughs. "What?"

"Everything's so…" She waves her arm as if to sum it all up.

"I thought you were a one-man woman."

"I am. I didn't mean…" She blushes scarlet. "I'm just so unhappy… I want to get away…" Her voice breaks and she starts crying.

"I can't take anyone else's problems on as well as my own," he says.

Foolishness overwhelms her. She's not sure what they say to each other, then he's gone. She watches him drive away. She replays the moment time and again, cringing with embarrassment. Thank God she'll never see him again.

With no classes and no point in going out in the rain, she and Peter spend the morning trying to keep out of each other's way. Peter would like to see Poppy, but can't think of an excuse. He sits in front of his computer, staring at the screen, willing Poppy to contact him. He looks at his phone, but there's no text either. He goes into the sitting room, picks up a motor magazine, but he's read it several times already. He picks up his book. Emily appears, dragging the Hoover behind her. He looks around in exasperation. "For God's sake, Emily! You only did it yesterday! It doesn't need doing!"

"I don't go on at you about how often you clean the car!" she snaps.

"That's different! I clean it when it's dirty! This place is pristine. You're becoming so house-proud!"

"I've told you a million times, Peter! I'm not doing it any more often than I used to! Just because I don't like sitting around doing nothing!"

"I'm not staying here to be criticised!" Peter snaps, jumping up and throwing down his book. Emily hears him grab his keys from the hall table and the slam of the front door. Tears roll down her face as she runs the Hoover round. Is she becoming house-proud? What a dreadful indictment! She's always hated women who clean their house day after day, get lost in their little routine.

She's just switched the Hoover off when she hears a knock at the kitchen window. Just for a moment she thinks it's Rose with Alicia before memory returns with a sharp pang. Poppy's the only other person to come the back way and she rushes out to greet her.

"Did I see Peter driving past earlier?" Poppy asks.

"Yes. He's gone out to get…" She can't think of anything. "Something or other," she goes on vaguely.

"Awful day to go out. I'd have stayed in if I'd been him. In here in the warm with you." She gives Emily's arm a friendly squeeze. At her touch, her warm, friendly, sympathetic voice, Emily feels her eyes fill with tears again. She blinks them back, looks away, but Poppy has noticed.

"Hey, what's the matter?" she asks.

Now the tears well up in Emily's throat. She can't speak. She shakes her head, wordlessly. Poppy puts her arm around her. A huge sob rises in Emily's throat, then another, then she's crying uncontrollably. Poppy pulls Emily's head onto her warm, soft shoulder; holds her, rocking her gently until eventually she calms down.

"D'you want to talk about it?" Poppy asks as Emily wipes her eyes and nose.

"Just a silly argument," Emily says.

Poppy says nothing.

"No, it's more than that. Oh, it's everything." And suddenly Emily finds herself telling Poppy about Alicia, about Rose, oh God, even about Dan.

"But why?" Poppy seems confused. "Not just because Alicia's gone?"

"No, it's Peter. Me and Peter. Ever since we've been here. He drives me mad. He's changed. I feel like I'm married to an old man." The words tumble out of her. "He's so lazy. When he was working he had an excuse not to do anything. Now he hasn't, but he just sits in a chair and reads. He says he'll do something but doesn't, so I end up doing it. But if I ask him to help he says I'm nagging him. He leaves things lying around everywhere then can't find them. He gets cross if I don't agree with everything he says. And I can't do anything I want..."

"You go to your classes," Poppy says, surprised.

"He hates me going," Emily says. Then, in fairness, "Well, he's been better lately. But the rest of the time we always do what Peter wants. If we don't, he sulks like a child. It's easier to give in. Oh, you're not married. You wouldn't understand."

"You'd be surprised!" Poppy laughs. "Working in a shop you see it all. The bored, disgruntled husbands telling their wives, 'You don't need that. You've got plenty already.' The wives, remembering how they used to exhort her to 'have whatever she wanted'. And resolving to bring a girlfriend instead next time. One more small resentment. One step nearer the divorce court. How easy it is to light the fire, how hard it is to keep it burning."

The expression sounds borrowed, something someone has said to her at some time, but Emily doesn't mind.

"Poor old Dan!" Poppy says, laughing again. "He must've wondered what hit him, you coming on to him like that!"

"I feel so foolish," Emily groans. "He must think I'm mad."

"He's got other things to think about."

"Yes…" says Emily. "I just feel…" She searches for the word. "Rejected."

She doesn't know why she looks into Poppy's eyes when she says it. Poppy holds her gaze. She moves closer, takes Emily's face between her two hands. "Don't," she says.

"Don't what?" Emily whispers.

"Don't feel rejected. There's no need." She leans forward. Emily pulls back, but Poppy holds her face firmly. She feels Poppy's soft lips press against hers. Emily hears herself moan deep in her throat. She opens her mouth, Poppy's tongue writhes against hers. She tastes of coffee. Her hands move down to her shoulders, her breasts. Emily moans again, gasps, opens her legs to Poppy's exploring hands, runs her own hands over the alien, soft body squirming against her. Suddenly, she springs away, looks towards the door. "Peter…" she says, warningly.

"He won't be back for ages," Poppy says. Her face is flushed, her eyes alight with desire. She reaches for Emily again, but Emily shakes her head.

"I can't. Not here. Not now…"

"Okay," Poppy says. "We'll work something out." She gets up, pulls Emily towards her, kisses her again, her tongue deep in her mouth. Emily clings to her, moaning, weak with desire, runs her hands through Poppy's long, thick hair.

"I'll text you," Poppy says.

Emily sinks on the sofa. Feelings overwhelm her: happiness, disbelief, guilt, shame, embarrassment, but happiness wins. She has something to look forward to, something to hold on to, something all Peter's bad moods can't diminish.

Chapter Sixteen

Poppy's breasts are huge. Peter forgets each time how big they are. She's astride him. They're dangling in his face, the nipple aureole nearly as big as Emily's entire breast. She's heavy. Vast rolls of fat cascade either side of him. He can roll the dimpled flesh in his fingers. Emily is firm, tight, every rib is visible; she throws back her head, rides him like a horse. That's far too energetic for Poppy: she lolls lazily on top of him, lets him do all the work. Afterwards, he lies in her arms, his head cradled on top of those downy, pillowy breasts.

"What're you thinking about?" she asks, suddenly.

"Nothing," he replies quickly, too quickly.

"You were thinking of Emily," she says, perceptively.

"Don't be silly."

She shifts him away from her, turns so she's looking in his face. "Yes, you were. You're not getting on."

"Of course we are. Anyway, it's…"

"None of my business?"

A small trickle of suspicion runs through Peter. "Did she tell you we're not getting on?"

"Of course not. She's far too loyal," Poppy says. "I guessed."

"How?"

"Well, for one thing, *you're* here."

"That doesn't mean a thing. Lots of happily married men have affairs. It's… well… it's time off."

"For good behaviour?" she laughs. "But I don't think you *are* well behaved."

"I don't want to talk about this," he says, irritably.

"Okay," she shrugs. "What *do* you want to do? Fuck me again?"

He feels himself hardening.

"Do you still fuck Emily?" she asks, suddenly.

His erection wanes. "Yes, of course. She's my wife."

"Not as often though. Not since you've been screwing me."

He says nothing.

"You're not afraid she'll find someone else?"

He laughs. "Emily? She's far too caught up with her cooking and her cleaning and her endless exercise classes to have an affair."

Yet even as he says it, he knows it's not true. Emily with her lithe, sexy body; her healthy, open attitude to sex; her vibrator in the bedside drawer. He remembers the last time they had sex. He struggled to stay firm, came very quickly. He sensed her disappointment. Is this why they're not getting on? Or is it the other way round? His mind darts away from the intricacies of it.

Poppy is watching him.

"You okay?" she asks.

"Yes, fine," he says, testily. "I told you I don't want to talk about it."

"There's a lot you don't want to talk about."

"Don't go on, Poppy. It's not like you."

"How do you know what I'm like?"

Peter sighs, inwardly. Poppy's beginning to sound like Emily. This is the problem with women. They always have to complicate things, look too deeply. He hates this sort of 'relationship talk'. Maybe it's time to finish it. Now, before she starts making any demands on him.

When he gets home Emily's not in. He glances at the clock. Twenty to five. She's usually back by now. Or is that

Thursdays? He gets so confused about the classes and he knows it drives her mad when he asks each time.

"Half past four, Peter," she says, testily. Or "Eleven thirty. You should know by now."

"Zumba, isn't it?" he'll guess wildly.

"No. That's Thursdays. It's Tuesday. Pilates," she sighs.

He'd like a cup of tea but Emily always wants one when she comes in, and he'd far rather she made it for him so he sits down with his book to wait for her.

Another ten minutes goes by, and he's just wondering if he should go and look for her when the door opens.

"You're late!" he exclaims. "I was getting worried…"

"I'm sorry. I didn't realise what time it was. Dan emailed this morning. Asked me to pop next door. Put the heating on. Make sure everything's okay."

"I thought he had an agent or something to do that."

"He changed his mind. Too expensive."

Dan's plans seem to change daily. First, the house went on the market, then the sign came down and a To Let sign went up. That, too, has gone and in his last email it sounded like he might be back. *In the spring*, he said vaguely, but Emily's not convinced.

"He'll meet someone else," she said, confidently.

"Maybe he's hoping Rose will come back," Peter said.

The email today came like an answer to her prayers. Ever since Poppy went, she's been trying to work out how they can see each other.

You can't come here, Poppy texted. *There's Suzie…*

Emily's relieved actually. The thought of Poppy's filthy flat, her no-doubt unwashed sheets, is off-putting.

"And Peter's here," Emily texted back.

"Not all the time."

"Most of it."

"We'll think of something. We can go out in the car…"

But it's the middle of winter. Freezing cold. And while the idea of furtive fumblings in the car makes Emily squirm inside, it isn't quite what she had in mind. Which brings her to another thought: what exactly will they do? What *do* lesbians do? She has a vague idea about strap-ons, but the idea seems absurd.

Then there's her body. She looks down at herself in the bath. She's so flat-chested. It's always bothered her, though it never seems to have concerned Peter or any of her other lovers. But she's felt Poppy's breasts. They're large, bountiful, beautiful. Her body is soft and feminine. In comparison, the slim body Emily is so proud of will look scrawny. Out of the bath, she examines her legs as she dries them with the towel. Once her best feature, they're now so ugly: pale, thin skin showing clumps of blue and purple veins and spidery, red, thready veins.

These are the moments she tells herself she's crazy. Bad enough to think of taking a lover at all at this stage in her life, let alone embarking on something she's never remotely considered before. Strangely, she doesn't feel guilty. It's not another man. It doesn't count. And if she's found out? Well, two women, what could be more natural? Women are always cuddling and touching. At the very worst, even if Peter found Poppy in bed with her she could think of something. She could say she was comforting her. It's risky being next door, but in the unlikely event Peter leaves his study, looks out of the window, sees Poppy going in, Emily can say she asked her to check on the house.

Poppy's thrilled with the idea. "We can pretend we're living together."

"It'll only be for the odd hour or so," Emily warns her.

"I know, but it's so exciting. Our own little place. No one will know…"

Emily's nervous. Terrified. She washes herself with extra care, sprays on intimate deodorant, then perfume, puts on the new padded bra and g-string carefully hidden at the back of the drawer. If only she didn't have to put jogging bottoms and a t-shirt on top.

"I'm off!" she calls to Peter.

"What time will you be back?"

"Eleven thirty. No, twelve. Pam asked me to coffee after…"

"Okay."

She walks down the road, turns to wave as usual, though she's never sure whether Peter actually waits and watches. At the corner she stops, turns straight round, walks briskly and deliberately back towards the house as though she's forgotten something. She's rehearsed this over and over again, in the bath, in bed at night, while she's cooking dinner, watched herself as though she's on television, seen herself skirt around the row of terrace houses, round the back, past her kitchen window, not looking to see if Peter's in the kitchen. If she looks, he'll be there. He'll see her. In her rehearsals he's in the study. She sees him sitting at his computer. Or in the sitting room maybe, watching television or reading. She can't consider the alternative scenario: that he's standing at the kitchen sink filling the kettle or that he chooses just today to go out of the back door to his car. She has her excuse ready. "I suddenly thought I'd left the tap on in Dan's house."

He wouldn't think to ask why she might have put a tap on and if he said, "You should've called me. I'd have done it," she'd say, "But I've got the key."

But it doesn't happen and her hand shakes so much she can hardly fit the key in the lock. The house strikes cold despite the twice-daily central heating Dan asked her to put on, and it has that unlived-in feeling of any house that's been unoccupied for even a short length of time. She had wanted to open the windows to air it, but she didn't dare spend too much time there. She would have liked to give it a good clean and tidy too. Dan left it in a typically man-type way: a peremptory tidy, a brief wipe of the surfaces, the floors unswept and unwashed. Still uncertain whether he was moving out or coming back, boxes stand stacked in the front hallway. Emily turns the heating on to constant (Dan will never know, she surmises, he'll just pay the bill); takes out the small bottle of milk she smuggled into her kit bag this morning, and puts it next to the kettle with the tea bags and things she brought in the other day. Upstairs, she switches on the electric blanket and lights the scented candles she's carefully arranged around the room. She'd like to draw the curtains but someone might notice.

Her phone buzzes and she jumps as though she's been stung. *Nearly there*, Poppy says.

Emily runs down, almost falling in her haste, opens the front door. Her face is burning. Her legs feel like jelly. She sees Poppy hurrying towards her. Their eyes meet. Neither of them speak. She's scarcely closed the door and they're in each other's arms. Poppy's soft lips on hers. A strand of her long hair entwined with their tongues. Soft, feminine hands on her body. They're both panting, both moaning. Poppy slides her hand down the back of Emily's jogging bottoms, gasps as her fingers find Emily's bare buttocks. She eases aside the g-string, her small fingers slide inside.

"Let's go upstairs," Emily groans.

But halfway up, they collapse on the stairs, stripping aside clothes. Poppy isn't wearing a bra. Her full breasts spill into Emily's face. Emily rolls one of the hard nipples between her fingers. The harsh stair carpet rubs against her back. Her legs are wide open, Poppy's fingers working rhythmically against her. "Don't stop," Emily gasps. "Don't stop…"

She comes with a shuddering force, stifling her cry in case sound carries through to next door.

Poppy cradles her head. "There, there, that's better..." she whispers and Emily realises she's crying and laughing at the same time.

Poppy takes her hand, guides it down. "My turn..." she smiles.

Emily shifts down on the stairs, spreads Poppy's legs wide, stares in fascination at the reddened, moist flesh; the thick, dark pubic hair. Except in magazines and films, she's never seen a woman exposed like this. She lowers her head, the tip of her tongue burying deep into Poppy's erect clitoris. Poppy moans deep in her throat, arches her back, grabs Emily's head, grinds it into her. Emily moves back, opens Poppy up, slides two fingers into the wet slit. Poppy smells musky, fishy, the scent increasing as Emily's fingers slide in and out. She takes out her fingers, holds them to her nose, breathing deeply. "Please..." Poppy moans. Emily lowers her head again, her tongue circling round and round the nib of hard flesh until the rhythmic thrusting of Poppy's hips reach a climax. "Ssssh, ssssh," she warns her.

Their bodies are sticky with sweat. Emily tries to move her arm but Poppy holds her closer. "My arm's gone to sleep," Emily giggles. As she extricates it she has a swift glance at her watch, amazed to see that only ten minutes has gone by.

"And I'm bloody uncomfortable here now you mention it," Poppy says, getting up. "And cold..." she says, pulling Emily towards her again.

"I did suggest we go to bed," Emily laughs. "Come on. The electric blanket's on."

They race upstairs naked, giggling ridiculously and fall into bed. Poppy opens her arms, pulls Emily's head onto her shoulder. Instantly, Emily's aroused again. "You're insatiable!"

Poppy giggles, as Emily grinds her hips against her. They both come quickly again and collapse exhausted. Poppy falls asleep but Emily lies awake, too scared of losing track of time, though she's desperately tired. She's scarcely slept since she first kissed Poppy, since she realised what was happening to her.

"I love you," she wants to say, but she knows Poppy will laugh. For Poppy this is just a bit of fun. Everything's fun for Poppy. Nothing lasts. Emily mustn't frighten her off. She watches the bedside clock that she brought in especially, along with the sheets and towels, candles and shower gel, biscuits and clean knickers. She'd so enjoyed setting it all up. All for Poppy. Their own little hideaway. Where no one can bother them.

"What time is it?" Poppy says, suddenly.

Emily jumps, picks up the alarm clock. "Time to go," she says.

She looks down at Poppy. Mascara speckles are peppered under her eyes. "I don't want to get up…" she groans, stretching her arms above her head.

"You don't have to," Emily says. "You can let yourself out. Have a shower. A cup of coffee. Just don't make too much noise…"

She's pretty sure Peter won't hear a thing. They never heard Rose and Dan, except maybe the odd raised voice, a slammed door, Alicia crying, a sneeze maybe. But she and Poppy must have made far more noise and she worries about it the whole time she's letting herself out, sneaking past the kitchen window, round the front and in through the front door.

"*There were some strange sounds from next door,*" she can hear Peter saying.

"*Oh, the estate agents were going round, I think,*" she would answer vaguely.

But surely she must look different: flustered, that post-sex glow. And she must smell of sex and sweat.

Peter is in his study. Sometimes he comes out when she comes back, sometimes he rushes out to greet her, eager to tell her something he's found online or an email he's had or a letter that's arrived. This morning he doesn't come out. "I'm back!" she calls. "Desperate for the loo!" This isn't true but it gives her an excuse to run straight upstairs, wash herself quickly, compose herself as much as possible.

"You didn't go out today then?" she asks when she comes back down.

"It was raining."

Peter was hoping to see Poppy, but her replies were evasive in that annoying way she has.

I think Suzie will be here, she texted.

We can go out in the car, he replied.

Too cold, came back.

She's right, of course. It's freezing.

He waited all evening for another text from her. Sometimes she did this, left him on tenterhooks all night, then texted the next morning, *I'm waiting for you*. It's all part of the game, he knows that. And there's no doubt it increases the anticipation. But it's beginning to pall just a little and he tells himself it's time to put an end to it. But on his own this morning, while Emily's out, he feels at a loose end. Of course, he could find things to do. He hears Emily's voice in his head: *"You could've tidied up in here, run the Hoover round, made the bed, emptied the bins."* But he sits down with a book and before he knows it Emily is back. He hears her now, busying around, the kettle predictably on for the cup of tea she always has when she comes in, the dishwasher, the washing machine. She plonks a cup of tea down next to him. "Good class?" he asks, as he always does.

"Yes, thanks."

"Aren't you going to sit down with me?"

"A thousand things to do, Peter!"

"Oh, come on. I've been on my own all morning…"

"An hour and a half, Peter. Not all morning!" she laughs.

"Well, it felt like all morning. And you've got all day to do your 'thousand and one things'. Come and sit down with me…" He takes her hand, pulls her down next to him, grabs her bottom playfully. It feels firm, springy and suddenly he's aroused. She pulls away.

"Don't be silly, Peter!"

Her face is flushed, a sheen of sweat on it. He grabs her again, slides his hand down her jogging bottoms, encounters damp, bare buttocks. She's wearing a g-string, he realises with surprise. He's instantly erect. He pulls at the silky fabric, pictures it sliding against her wet slit.

"Peter!" she pulls away. "Don't!"

He stops, surprised. It's unlike Emily to refuse him, at any time of day.

"I don't feel like it," she says. "I'm worn out."

"Well, maybe you shouldn't go to these classes then!" he snaps.

"I *like* going to my classes."

"More than you like being with me."

"Don't be childish. I'm not a doll, to be picked up and played with when it suits you!"

Peter nurses his cup of tea to the background accompaniment of Emily banging pots and pans in the kitchen. Thank God he has Poppy. He takes out his phone even though there's no buzz to tell him she's been in touch, scrolls down to her name just to see the picture of her on his 'Contacts'. He wishes he could comfort himself by reading through her messages, but he's always careful to delete each one.

I miss you, he taps out, then deletes it before he's tempted to send it. *I miss you* is only one step away from *I love you*. And he doesn't. But he does need her: far, far more than she needs him.

Emily has left the kitchen now. He hears her run upstairs, hears her moving around above, drawers opening and closing. She must be getting changed. Then the back door opens and he hears her drag out bin liners and bags, the clank of bottles, the sound of the wheelie bin being wheeled around the front. He knows he should go and help her. In fact, he should do it for her. It's a man's job. But then so is cleaning the shoes and Emily does this along with most of the other dirty chores. He keeps his head firmly bent over his book, pretends to himself that he hasn't heard her, like he does each time. If Emily wants to do everything herself then let her. Why should he bother? On the rare occasions he *has* offered to help she's always refused. "Don't worry. I'll do it. I know where it all goes."

Emily's mind is far away while she does the mundane chores. All day long she replays the hour and a half with Poppy: the long, slow, sensual kisses (she's forgotten what it's like to be kissed like that); the small, soft, feminine hands, the gentle yet urgent exploring fingers, the gasps and moans, the soft pillowy breasts, the musky smell. Each memory evokes such spasms in her innards she's almost tempted to throw herself at Peter. Except it wouldn't be the same. It wouldn't be enough. Peter's hard, masculine body; his hard thrusting cock, it's not enough. Not now. Hard to believe what she's been missing out on all these years.

I can't stop thinking about you, she texts to Poppy.

Poppy's reply is instant. *Me neither. When can I see you again?*

But Emily can't always miss Pilates or Zumba; can't always say she's meeting Pam or Andrea or someone. And Poppy can't always get away when Emily's free. Sometimes they meet for coffee. These meetings now have an added spice. Emily watches Poppy come in. Their eyes meet with a secret shared. She sees her talking to Mrs. Symonds, the café owner, sees her throw her head back and laugh, remembers kissing that open mouth, touching the soft skin on her face, hearing Poppy pant with pleasure. When Poppy sits down she slides her hand up Emily's thigh. Emily squirms. She grabs the hand, squeezes it, their eyes meet. Poppy's face is flushed.

She hasn't needed to tell Poppy this is her first time with a woman. Poppy knows, like she knows so many other things about Emily: that she's never late, that she likes to be stroked ever-so-gently like a cat, even her fastidiousness: except for that first time she's always washed herself afterwards. Sometimes, on the rare occasions they have a whole afternoon together, they shower together, wrapped soapily in each other's arms, and Poppy blow-dries her hair for her.

Emily enjoys picking out special underwear to wear for Poppy: matching satin bras and skimpy knickers, g-strings, even stockings once that she smuggled into her sports bag along with the bottle of perfume she keeps there now. Poppy, on the other hand, doesn't seem to make any effort. There was one memorable occasion when she wore a red basque that thrust her breasts into an amazing cleavage and sculpted her waist in tightly. "I can hardly breathe!" she laughed, but otherwise it's clearly anything she's thrown on: plain white bra with black lacy knickers, flowery bra with stripey cotton ones. One pair even had a rip at the edge where the seam had come adrift. Emily worked her fingers into it, feeling the material rip even more, yanking it down so it bit into Poppy's soft flesh. "Little bitch!" she moaned, gripping Emily's hand.

In bed, on those long-but-all-too-short afternoons, they talk in that special intimate post-coital way, new lover way, that Emily has completely forgotten about.

"When did you first have sex?" Poppy asks.

"When I was seventeen."

"Oh yes. I remember. Your 'first love'. Mike, wasn't it?"

"Yes. No. I'd finished with him by then. No, this was Steve. It was different with him. Not like Mike. He was older. Experienced. I was…" She searches for the right word.

"Curious?" Poppy asks.

"Yes. And overwhelmed by him. He was so sure of himself. Sure of me. I was in awe of him. I'd do anything for him. But he realised that. He treated me like a doormat yet each time I went back for more."

"Sex is about power," Poppy says.

Emily says nothing.

"It *is*," Poppy insists. "How many times have you said no to sex to get your own back on Peter for something he's said or done? How many times have you gone along with it even when you're not in the mood just for a quiet life?"

Emily still says nothing.

"It's a power struggle," Poppy says. "We like to be the one in charge."

"Peter says I boss him around," Emily says.

"That's what all men say about their wives. But they have their way of getting their own back. Sex is one way. They're on top. Literally." She laughs.

"You seem to know a lot about men. About husbands."

"I've heard it all. Believe me."

The thought of Poppy with anyone else is unbearable, but she needs to know. "Tell me. About you. Everything."

Even as she says it, she knows she won't believe whatever Poppy says. Poppy tells the most fantastical tales that Emily loves to listen to, treating them as fairy stories as she lies with her head resting on Poppy's ample stomach. Her head rises and falls as Poppy speaks, bobs around uncomfortably when

Poppy laughs. She can feel her breathing, hear the occasional rumble of her tummy. She marvels at her own reaction to this intimacy. Was she ever like this with Peter?

"How did you meet him?" Poppy asks.

"A blind date," Emily laughs. "Well, sort of. A friend of mine knew a friend of his. She knew we were both single. I'd just split up from someone. We'd been together for years but it was going nowhere. I wanted marriage. He didn't. I became needy, clingy, an albatross around his neck." She stops, clears her throat. "Peter, well, Peter was playing the field a bit. He'd just split up from someone too. Zena her name was. Bit of a nightmare actually. She tried to kill herself. Several times, apparently. Anyway, this friend of mine sat us together at a dinner party. We clicked. He was…" She stops, remembering. "So different from anyone else I knew. Artistic. Clever. He knew so many things I didn't. Important too. Someone used to being in charge. I wasn't even put off when he told me he'd been married and had a child. And about Zena. And the others. A man with a past. A touch of the 'bad boy' about him. I loved it. I loved him." She gives a bitter little laugh. "I fell in love with the handsome prince and woke up with a frog …"

Back home, she finds Peter annoys her more than ever. The difference between Poppy's strong, happy, carefree ways and Peter's carping, morose, old mannish attitude is more than she can bear. Now that the weather's turned he goes out less. She always finds him in the study or the sitting room, crouched over the computer or a book. He's looking older since he's retired. His hair is greying and he's getting round-shouldered.

"You should get out more," she says, only half-jokingly.

"There's nothing to do."

His self-pity irks her nowadays. "You could *find* something," she snaps. "Other people's husbands do."

"I don't like golf."

"It doesn't have to be golf. I don't know. Voluntary work of some kind."

"You know that's not my sort of thing."

Well, what is? she thinks, but says nothing.

"I didn't want to give up work," he goes on.

"No one can go on forever. You have to find a life outside work."

"Don't go on. I'm quite happy."

But she knows he isn't. "He's so reliant on me," she tells Poppy. "He won't *go* anywhere, won't *do* anything unless I'm with him."

Poppy says nothing, just strokes Emily's arm gently.

★

As Christmas approaches with lights and Christmas trees outside the shops, Emily tries not to think back to last year, of little Alicia gazing in wonder at the tree, of watching her unwrap her present, trembling with excitement.

She can't think what to buy Poppy. Last year she didn't bother. She's never bought presents unnecessarily. Too much money is frittered away at Christmastime. But this year is different. Jewellery is no good, since Poppy makes her own. She knows what perfume she wears, but perfume seems too easy a choice: as though she hasn't made any effort. Poppy seldom reads, so a book is no good and she never watches television so she can't buy a DVD. A scarf maybe? Poppy loves scarves. There's a shop in Lyme Regis, the sort she can never get Peter into: stinking of joss sticks and crammed with scarves and shawls and heavy woven clothes, along with ethnic jewellery and useless little wooden carved boxes. But Poppy probably buys stuff there anyway so Emily goes round all the shops in Taunton, even Debenhams and Jaeger, fingering silk scarves and running her hands through rails of shawls. She's nearly given up and settled on perfume instead when, in a tiny shop in Bath Place, she finds just the one: a wonderfully soft fringed pashmina in shades of pink and purple. She wraps it carefully in layers of pink and purple tissue paper, and puts it in a ridiculously expensive cardboard carrier bag in the same colours. She's never taken such trouble with a present before.

Poppy is thrilled with it. She wraps it round her bare shoulders. Her pendulous breasts hang down between the fringes. Emily reaches out, holds one nipple between her fingers, feels it harden. Poppy moans softly. Then she moves away. "Wait," she says. "I've got something for you."

She hands Emily a small package. Emily unwraps it, opens the box inside. It's a gold bangle, exactly the same as the one Poppy always wears, engraved 'Emily'.

"My grand-mère made mine," Poppy says, rolling the r in *grand-mère* in a throaty French way. "When we were living in Paris." She pronounces it *Parree*.

Emily can distinctly remember her saying they lived in Lyon, but she doesn't contradict her.

"She was a jewellery maker too?" she asks instead.

Poppy nods, "That's where I learned it from. She was very famous in France. She made jewellery for film stars. Some of her stuff went recently at an auction for thousands."

Emily doesn't ask who got the money. Clearly not Poppy since she lives so frugally.

"When I was little she called me Poupée," Poppy goes on. "Ma petite Poupée," she croons in a French way. "My little doll."

Emily could point out that the bracelet says Poppy, not Poupée but she doesn't. She knows it's all made up. Like Poppy's litany of lovers, male, female, sometimes both together. In one rendition Poppy has only had 'one great love', her first boyfriend Philippe. "We made love under a full moon in a cherry orchard," she says, dreamily. "I remember how it hurt. How I cried to think I'd lost my virginity. I was fourteen."

In another rendition it was an actress who seduced her. "She lifted up my skirt, spread my legs wide... I remember looking down, in surprise, at her peroxide blonde head buried into my black pubic hair, and feeling her ringed fingers digging into my thighs..."

Emily suffers agonies of jealousy listening to these stories. She reminds herself it's pointless to be jealous of things that happened before she knew Poppy. Pointless being jealous at all with someone like Poppy.

"What about Suzie?" she asks, as casually as possible.

Poppy shrugs, her breasts lifting infinitesimally with the movement. "What about her?" She's been talking about France and there's a slight French accent to accompany the gallic shrug.

"Are you lovers? *Were* you lovers?"

Poppy laughs. "You asked me that before, I remember!"

"Tell me..." Emily pleads.

"Oooh, Miss Jealousy. I don't like jealousy. You don't *own* me, you know. No one does..."

"I know, but..."

"Don't, Emily," she says, suddenly serious. "Don't." She strokes Emily's shoulder gently. "Don't spoil it."

"Okay," Emily says, meekly.

"What're you buying Peter for Christmas?" Poppy says, suddenly.

"A book. He asked for a book."

"And what's he buying you?"

"A book," she laughs.

"Not very romantic, you two, are you?"

"Not after twenty-odd years!"

"D'you want me to ask him to buy you a surprise of some sort?"

"It wouldn't be a surprise if you'd asked him! Anyway, he wouldn't do it."

Peter has looked around all the shops in Taunton for a present for Poppy. As he absent-mindedly fingers the g-strings in Ann Summers he realises it's an effort to choose something this year, whereas last year it had been so thrilling.

"Can I help you, sir?"

Peter jumps guiltily, looking around quickly to make sure there's no one he knows in the shop, though the thought of any Rotarians being in there is ludicrous. "What size are you looking for?" she continues in that same cheerful no-nonsense way. Why are all the girls in these shops so big and boisterous?

"About your size," Peter says, just to keep her quiet really.

"Sixteen," she supplies, rifling through the rack.

"Yes. That should be fine."

The basque he bought last year had been a fourteen, but by her own admission Poppy's put on weight since then. If it were Emily she would have been devastated and embarked immediately on a strict diet, but Poppy doesn't give a damn.

"Here we are," the sales assistant says, triumphantly. "Shall I gift wrap it for you?"

Peter finds himself nodding meekly even though he's not sure he even wants it. It's an absurd price for such a tiny scrap of fabric, he realises, as he finds his glasses to check the label. But it's red and it's Christmassy and he has to give her something. In the card shop searching for a card for her and one for Emily it suddenly strikes him how ridiculous he's being. What exactly is he getting from Poppy? Sex, of course. But he can get that from Emily. Companionship? Love? Sympathy? He's not getting any of those.

In the car on the way home he practises how he's going to

tell her. It's been years since he's had to finish a relationship. This hardly counts as a relationship, he reminds himself. They're seeing less and less of each other. Either Poppy's 'busy' or Suzie's there or something. And he can't always find an excuse to go out.

He hides Poppy's present and card in the garage and lets himself in. The house feels empty. Surprised, he glances at the clock. He's sure Emily said she'd be back by four. Or maybe that was yesterday. She's out more and more nowadays. "It's Christmas," she keeps saying. "There's loads to do."

Jasmine's coming to them this year. Back from Italy after ten weeks, where she predictably fell in love. This time it's the nineteen-year-old gardener Micheli. "He's only doing gardening to get some money together," she explained on the phone. "He wants to get into finance. He's coming over here to live as soon as he's got enough."

"How long is she staying?" Emily asked.

Peter hates it when she's like this. "She can stay as long as she likes," he says, tersely.

"*I'm* the one with all the work to do."

"You're such a martyr."

When did they stop being nice to each other, Peter wonders as he hides the 'To My Lovely Wife' Christmas card in the bottom drawer of his desk. Carping at each other has become a habit.

He sits down at his computer, scrolls through the news headlines, glances idly at the weather then goes to his email inbox. Poppy's name lights up in front of his eyes. Instantly, his resolution to finish with her vanishes. Poppy doesn't nag, she doesn't treat him like a child. He opens up the email. The words *finish, good idea, before we get involved* swim disjointedly in front of his eyes before they start to make any sense. *The bitch, the downright, whoring little bitch*. She's finished with him, before he had the chance to do it himself. Grown tired of him obviously, found someone else. He's speechless with rage. His first instinct is to write back telling her precisely that. He even starts the email, *So you've found someone else to take up with? Well, I hope he's more long-suffering than I am.* But he deletes it. Thinks for a while. Starts again. *It was fun*, he types. His finger hovers over 'send' but he saves it to 'Drafts' instead. You never know, she might change her mind.

A Christmas card arrives from Rose and Alicia. Emily emails to thank her. *I couldn't send you one*, she explains. *I didn't know your address.*

Still with my parents, Rose replies. *Why don't you come up in the New Year?* She attaches a photo of Alicia that tears at Emily's heart.

"We could go up," Emily says to Peter.

"It's a long way to go just to see someone we hardly know."

"I could go on my own then."

"Don't be silly. You'd never drive all that way on your own."

"There's the train. Or the coach…"

But even as she says it she knows she won't do it. Peter will make such a fuss it's not worth it.

No Christmas card from Dan, but an email a few days into the New Year. *I may come down in the spring*, he says. Emily feels a stab of alarm. Where will she and Poppy go if they can't go next door?

"Don't worry so," Poppy says when she tells her. "It's a long way away. We'll work something out."

With Jasmine staying on long after Christmas, Emily and Poppy are back to meeting for tea and coffee and the frustration is almost unbearable. They can hug when they meet, like the two female friends they are, Poppy's hand sometimes sliding inside Emily's coat and around her waist, but any other physical contact is almost impossible. One day Poppy leans closer, pretends to flick something off Emily's shoulder. Her other hand reaches under the table, nudges Emily's knees apart, reaches up between Emily's thighs. Emily almost groans aloud.

"I wish Jasmine would go back," she says.

"She can't stay much longer," Poppy says, "What about work?"

"She's between jobs again. The new one starts on the 23rd. I don't know how she does it…"

"I can invite her over if you like. Get her out of your way for a while."

The thought of Jasmine on her own with Poppy is agony. "You never invite *me* over," she says.

"Don't be silly, Emily. I was only thinking of you."

"Will Suzie be there?"

Poppy slams her coffee cup down with a crash. Heads turn in their direction. Emily blushes.

"I've told you before," Poppy says, angrily. "I don't do jealousy. I won't have it. Understand?"

Tears blinding her eyes, Emily nods.

Peter has always hated January: that dull, cold time after Christmas and before spring, the short, dark days, nothing to look forward to until Easter. This year seems worse than most. He has nothing to do. No Poppy to see. Jasmine is hanging around the house, but he's run out of things to talk to her about and she spends most of her time on her phone, texting, talking or emailing. Emily seems to find some reason to go out every day. "Shopping," she tells him, or "Meeting Felicity," or Poppy or someone. He knows it's just an excuse to avoid Jasmine, but he can't be bothered to say anything. It'll only provoke another argument. Anyway, Jasmine will be gone soon. He heard her on the phone to Micheli the other day.

"Friday," she said. "Definitely. I can't stand it down here much longer…"

He got the impression Micheli was coming over, but he didn't tell Emily. She would only ask where he would get the money for the flight and he'd lent Jasmine £500 the other day.

"I'll pay you back, Daddy," she promised as she always did. Lucky he kept one bank account separate from Emily, though she'd find out in due course; she always did.

The day before Jasmine's due to go back she asks him to drive her into Taunton. "I must have some new clothes," she says. "I've got nothing to wear for this new job."

Peter thought Emily might like to come too. In fact, it might do them good: her and Jasmine, the two girls going around the clothes shops together.

"God, no!" Emily groans when he suggests it.

"I thought you'd want to," he says. "You used to love going shopping together."

Back in the days when Emily was trying to impress Peter by trying to get on with Jasmine. But she'd hated every moment. Jasmine never liked the shops she liked, or the clothes she liked. The whole thing was a hassle for both of them.

"I meant the shops will be busy with the sales. Anyway, it'd be nice for you and Jasmine to be on your own together. For the drive, I mean." Of course, Peter won't go into town. He'll look around the car showrooms. "You can take the MGB. Jasmine will love it."

A whole day with Poppy. She can hardly wait. She watches Peter and Jasmine leave, Jasmine waving one arm cheerily out of the top of the open car, her dark hair billowing around her, then hurries next door. The house has been closed for two weeks and it smells musty. She puts the bag of shopping on the kitchen floor: smoked salmon, white wine, cupcakes for Poppy. Smears of dust lie on the work surfaces and she reaches under the kitchen sink for the bleach. She's only just started when she hears Poppy come in.

"In the kitchen!" she calls.

Poppy comes up behind her, puts her arms around her waist. The rubber gloves Emily's wearing are too big (they're a brand new pair she found in the drawer that Dan must have bought and never used) and water has trickled down the cuff and dampened Emily's hands. If it had been Peter she'd have pushed him away, pulled off the clammy rubber gloves and dried her hands, but it's Poppy. She leans back into the warm, soft body, turns around, buries her face into Poppy's neck. She can taste perfume, smell freshly applied deodorant. Poppy lifts her face, kisses her hard, her tongue sliding into Emily's mouth. "Come on, bitch!" she says, laughing. "Upstairs!"

"My God, I've missed you," Emily says in bed later.

"Me too. You're amazing. Fantastic."

"It's you," Emily says. "You do it to me. I've never felt like this before."

"Yes, you have. You've just forgotten."

The words are like a bucket of cold water. Emily's throat closes. Tears well up in her eyes. *Stupid, stupid,* she tells herself.

"Hey," Poppy says, gently. "You okay?"

Emily can't trust herself to speak. She nods, her head kneading against Poppy's shoulder.

"What time d'you have to be back?" Poppy asks, lightly.

"Oh, I don't know. Four maybe? Peter's meeting Jasmine for lunch at The Castle."

"And she's going back tomorrow."

"Yes, thank God."

Jasmine comes back from town loaded down with carrier bags. Peter has the slightly harassed look of a man who's been subjected to a tirade of girl talk. He heads straight for the wine bottle, waves it in Emily's direction. She shakes her head.

Peter's been looking forward to seeing Emily. He'd forgotten how tiring it is being with Jasmine, the constant chatter about herself and unconcern about anyone else, and how irritatingly unreliable she is, late for lunch with no attempt at an apology.

"What have you been doing all day?" he asks Emily, putting his arm around her shoulders.

Although she's expecting this question, although she should be used by now to prevaricating, Emily feels herself reddening guiltily. "Oh, nothing," she says quickly, darting away from Peter's arm. "Housework, you know. Bit of ironing…"

Luckily, Jasmine is too taken up with her shopping trip to notice Emily's blush.

"I bought *such* a fab top," she says, rummaging around amongst the carrier bags. "Here." She shakes it out, holds it up for Emily to see. "It looks better on. Hang on. I'll go up and put it on…"

She runs upstairs, leaving the other bags in an untidy heap on the chair. Somehow Emily resists the urge to tidy them.

Jasmine comes careering back down the stairs.

"Ta-dah!" she says, striking a pose. The top looks terrific: sleeveless, low-necked, midnight blue. The colour against Jasmine's brown skin is amazing.

"I thought it was for work." Emily can't keep the acid tone from her voice.

"Under a jacket?" Jasmine says, unaffected by Emily's disapproval. "It'll be fine, I'm sure. Don't you just love it?" She pirouettes around the room, waving her arms above her head.

"Did you buy the bracelet today too?" Emily asks, her eyes drawn to the gold bangle.

"No." Jasmine's hand flies to the bangle. "Poppy gave it to me," she says, smiling at the bangle fondly. "She was going to engrave it with my name but there wasn't time. She said she'll do it next time I come down."

Emily feels her whole body suffuse with heat. Sweat breaks out on her brow and under her arms. Then just as quickly she feels icy cold. Her legs are shaking yet somehow she leaves the room. In the kitchen she hangs on to the edge of the kitchen sink for support. Distantly, she can hear Jasmine and Peter still talking. Neither of them seems to have noticed she's gone out. She looks down in the sink. Part of her mind registers that it needs a good clean, while the other part swarms with visions of Poppy and Jasmine together, their heads bent close, their voices softly murmuring, Poppy's white hand on Jasmine's perfect brown wrist, holding it gently while she slides the bangle on, just like she slid it on Emily's wrist. Did she kiss her afterwards? Take her in her arms? Run her hands down her body? *Don't be so ridiculous*, she tells herself. Jasmine's not a lesbian. *Neither were you*, a little voice replies.

Everything Jasmine says or does all evening irks her. She hears her own sharp voice, sees herself looking heavenward inwardly, knows she's being unfair, but can't help herself.

"What's the matter with you tonight?" Peter whispers fiercely to her in the kitchen. "You could make a bit of an effort. She's going tomorrow."

It only makes things worse and she goes to bed early, saying she has a headache. She's still awake when she hears Peter come up and she hastily hides the book she's reading and switches out the light. Peter's a man, of course, and doesn't sense she's still wide awake; though even if she had been asleep he would have woken her as he stumbles about the room, trying to find the bed, slides in beside her, moves around restlessly, until finally he starts snoring. Emily's convinced she's not sleeping but when she looks at the clock she sees it's just gone two, so she must have slept a bit. She's wide awake, her mind buzzing: jealous thoughts of Poppy and Jasmine alternating with reassuring memories of

Poppy's arms around her, Poppy's lips on hers, Poppy's soft body pressed against her in bed. She gets up, pulls on her dressing gown. Peter stirs slightly as she opens the bedroom door and she freezes for a moment. She doesn't want him coming down with her. She wants to be alone.

Downstairs she blinks in the sudden glare of the flickering fluorescent light, waits for her eyes to get accustomed to it. Teacups and Peter's wine glass stand next to the sink. Neither Peter nor Jasmine has thought to rinse them out and leave them to drain, and there are drips of tea and rings of wine on every surface. She hears herself tutting and sighing at the sight, sees herself as Peter and Jasmine see her: as a fussy housewife; but it doesn't stop her reaching for a cloth and the bleach and standing back proudly when it's done and everything's neatly put away.

Jasmine leaves with the usual fuss the next day. Peter paces impatiently around the tiny front hallway, casting anxious glances every so often up the stairs.

"She'll miss the train," he says to Emily.

"Well, go and tell her," she says.

But, of course, he doesn't and is all smiles and no recriminations when eventually Jasmine appears. Her suitcase and various bulging carrier bags are stuffed in the boot and they leave, as they did the day before, with the top down and Jasmine's cheery wave.

Emily revels in the silence, runs upstairs to strip Jasmine's bed, then down again with Jasmine's sheets and towels.

The first lot of washing on, she grabs her phone to text Poppy, her heart leaping when she sees she's beaten her to it. She has to read the message twice and even then she can't believe it's from Poppy.

Going up to London for a break, it reads. *Be in touch when I get back.*

238

It has the sound of a message sent to other people as well. Emily stares at it blankly, hoping another message might appear: a personal one, with Poppy's usual teasing intimate tone. She opens her emails, but her phone is frustratingly slow, so she turns on her laptop, waits for it to come to life, launches Facebook and Twitter as well as her email account. The same message appears everywhere.

It's too much of a coincidence, yet she doesn't want to believe it. Jasmine blocked her on Facebook years ago, but she's on Twitter. *On my way back to town*, the tweet reads. Emily laughs with relief. Of course Poppy wouldn't be with Jasmine.

But the hurt stays with her, a great feeling of loss and disappointment, a pain heavy in her chest. Her throat closes, tears well in her eyes, trickle down her face. She searches for a tissue, tries to force herself not to cry. If she starts now she'll never stop. But the tears continue and she puts her face in her hands and gives way to the sobs.

After a while she stops, exhausted, gets up from the kitchen table and looks out of the window. It's a dull morning. She watches a flock of pigeons wheel against the lumpy, grey clouds. Peter will be gone at least two hours. Two hours she'd visualised with Poppy. Now they stretch emptily in front of her. Her eyes feel heavy and puffy. She's suddenly overwhelmed with tiredness. She thinks of her bed, sees herself creeping upstairs, curling up under the duvet, hiding from the world, waiting only for Poppy to bring the colour back into her life. For a moment she almost gives way to the temptation, but instead she throws herself into a frenzy of activity: bleaching all the surfaces and cleaning the sinks, the bath, the loos, even though none of them need doing. Only when she finds herself disinfecting the inside of the kitchen bin does she realise she's going too far. She glances at the kitchen clock: Peter will be back soon. She flies upstairs, sits on the bed to repair her make-up; her eyes look small and piggy, there are smudges of mascara under her eyes and down her face, and her foundation has rubbed off. She's just finished when she hears Peter's key in the lock.

"All okay?" she asks.

"Yes, fine," he says, tersely.

"You got there in time?"

"Only just."

"You should tell her, Peter…"

"She's not going to change, is she? She's always been the same…"

"Yes. It's just…"

"Just what? I wish you wouldn't keep finding fault with her all the time! It's no wonder she doesn't want to come here!"

"That's not true, Peter!"

"How d'you know?"

"She's here all the time, that's why!"

"She comes to see *me*!"

"To get your money!"

"How *dare* you!" He takes a step towards her, raises his hand and Emily flinches. But his hand drops, he turns away, goes into his study.

Peter sits down at the desk, puts his head in his hands. Why do they always end up arguing like this? When he's away from her he looks forward to seeing her, yet the moment he comes in they're at it again.

All the way driving home he'd been wondering how to tell her. "*Poppy was there,*" he would say as casually as possible. "*She's going to stay with Jasmine for a few days…*"

Of course, it's possible Emily knows, but somehow he doubts it. Emily likes to think Poppy is her special friend. She hasn't realised yet that Poppy doesn't have any special friends. Not even him.

240

He'd been bowled over when he saw her. She looked so young, so beautiful, so full of life, so Bohemian. He'd quite forgotten how magnetic she was, and despite the fact that Jasmine was hanging on to his arm, he expected her to acknowledge him in some special way. He tried to catch her eye but all her attention was on Jasmine.

"You're *so* late!" she gushed, enveloping her in a huge hug and kissing both her cheeks. "I was worried you weren't coming! I've *so* been looking forward to seeing you! I'm *so* excited. You smell *divine*! Let me look at you! God, you're beautiful! I'm *so* excited..."

Jasmine laughed, threw back her head. Everyone was looking at them: the beautiful, slim, dark girl; the exuberant redhead. Peter hung back, feeling in the way. Scarcely looking at him, Jasmine took her suitcase, her bags.

"Thank you, Daddy," she said, absently.

Poppy glanced over Jasmine's shoulder. "Oh, hi, Peter," she said, vaguely.

Even now, Peter hoped for something more. He willed her to look at him, but she turned back to Jasmine.

"...I thought we could go to the Tate one evening..." she was saying.

The train had emptied. Doors were slamming. Peter was worried they wouldn't get on but they ambled frustratingly slowly towards it, still chatting excitedly, taking their time to load bags and suitcases on board. Jasmine turned at the last moment. "Bye, Daddy. Thank you *so* much for *everything,* you know..." She emphasises the last words with a wink.

For the money, she means. She hugged him briefly. He felt her warm body, her soft cheek against his, the smell of some expensive perfume. He watched her make her way down the train, walked along the station until he saw her find a seat, watched as Poppy swapped places with her so she could be by the window, waved until the train was out of sight.

He'd thought of Emily all the way home. He'd have her to himself now. No Jasmine. No Poppy. Just the two of them. But the Emily he had in mind then, the sweet, kind, caring Emily, the one he couldn't bear to be hurt by Poppy's thoughtlessness, bears no resemblance to the Emily here, the catty Emily with her snide remarks about Jasmine. He's almost tempted to go and tell her now about Poppy. But he thinks better of it. Far better for her to find out for herself.

Chapter Seventeen

Emily tries to check her phone surreptitiously. But Pam has seen the swift movement. "Are you waiting to hear from someone?" she asks.

Emily reddens. She hates people who constantly check their phone. It's so rude. "No," she says, quickly. "At least. Yes. A friend of mine's away in London. I was wondering when she's coming back…"

Her point made, however, Pam has turned back to the knot of women around her. "…so I decided to have lemon for the walls…" she says. "With the end one in ochre, just for a bit of accent, you know."

"I *love* the curtains," the woman next to Emily says.

"Laura Ashley," Pam confides. "Cost an *absolute* fortune. Just don't tell David!"

They all laugh the conspiratorial laugh of women of a certain age and income, confident in their husbands and the power they hold over them. A feeling totally alien to Emily. She can't imagine re-decorating the entire sitting room without consulting Peter. He'd have a fit. It's not just the cost (though there's that as well) but Peter likes to be involved in every aspect of the house. He'd never allow her free rein. She's got to the stage now that she scarcely dare voice her opinion on a colour or a design. "Oh no!" he'll say. "You don't like that! This is what we need…" So she waits to see what he goes for and agrees with his choice, whatever it is. It's just not worth the hassle of arguing. She reminds herself he's an artist; he knows better than she does, but just occasionally she finds herself gazing longingly at something she'd like and telling herself that one day, one day, she'll be able to choose for herself.

"More coffee?" Pam asks, hovering the silver percolator above Emily's cup.

"Oh, tea please. I can make it myself if you like…"

"Oh no. No trouble. I always forget you like tea…"

She swishes off to the kitchen in her flat shoes, long, flouncy skirt and neat, high-necked top. Emily hears her giving instructions to the Romanian cleaning lady who comes three times a week to clean the four bedroom, three bathroom house, but has been drafted in today for "an extra couple of hours," Pam told them, "so I can spend more time with you all."

Pam's 'At Home's' are marvellously synchronised: bone china coffee cups and plates for the homemade biscuits, brought in on the sort of wheeled tea trolley that Emily hasn't seen since her mother's in the 1950s. Emily's request for tea every time she comes always meets with disapproval, mostly, Emily suspects, because the teacup and saucer doesn't match the coffee set.

"Where d'you get your hair done?" the woman next to her asks.

Emily puts her hand up to her head. "Oh, there's a girl who comes to the house. She used to do my neighbour's hair…"

"It's lovely. It suits you. I used to go to Emma Louise. But then the girl left…"

Emily tries to remember the woman's name, as she launches into a long story about going to a hairdresser in Taunton who didn't listen to how she liked her hair done. Anne is it, or Susan? Susan probably, most women of Emily's age are called Susan. The woman leans in closer and Emily can smell the sweet, powdery scent of Chanel Number Five. She has a fine moustache along her upper lip and spiky, little hairs sprouting on her chin, that stand out in the sunshine pouring in through Pam's conservatory windows. Emily finds herself staring in fascination at the downy, golden hairs. Why doesn't someone tell her to use a depilatory cream, or her husband's razor or something? Her best friend or her daughter or her husband? Emily can't be the only one to have noticed.

"...so I ended up back here in Lyme after all that!" the woman ends up triumphantly. "Do you have a garden?" she goes on. "We've been trying to find someone to cut our hedge..."

The tedious conversation of middle-aged women. All around her she can hear discussions about shopping and cleaning, new outfits, the best place to buy coffee or how to clean their conservatory windows. This is all Emily has to look forward to now Poppy has disappeared from her life.

It's been three weeks now. Emily has sent text after text, email after email. She's left plaintive voicemails, upbeat voicemails, silent voicemails. Poppy's replies have been brief, vague, with none of the teasing intimacy Emily has been used to.

I'll be back soon, she says. Or *I miss you too xx*

She ignores all Emily's questions of where she is or who she's staying with. She's obviously found someone new, Emily tells herself, or maybe just something new. Something to amuse and excite her, take her mind completely off Emily. And yet when she thinks of those hours together, Poppy's lingering kisses, her explosive orgasms, she finds it hard to believe she'd give up on her just like that.

Emily's route back from Pam's house takes her past Poppy's shop; the usual feeling of special intimate pride swelling in her chest at the sight of the name, 'Poppy Fields', above the window and one of Poppy's pictures centre stage of the window display. It's the familiar view of the Cobb and she stops to look at it, then darts back quickly as she sees Suzie reaching into the window to place a price ticket carefully in front of a necklace on a plastic stand. But Suzie has seen her. She beckons her in. Emily has no choice.

She pastes a bright smile onto her face. The bell on the door clangs. They both speak at the same time. Emily catches something about Poppy. "Sorry," she says. "You go first."

"No, you."

"I only asked how you were."

"I thought you might know when she's coming back."

Emily reddens. "Me? Why?"

"Don't be silly," she says, tersely.

Emily's whole body is on fire, her armpits wet with sweat. "No," she says, shaking her head. She can't say more. She thinks she's going to cry.

"Come through," Suzie says, quickly. Her voice is surprisingly gentle. Emily feels the tears well in her eyes, trickle down her face. She reaches in her pocket for a tissue. She's vaguely aware of Suzie closing the door behind her, turning the sign around to 'Closed'.

"It's nearly lunchtime," she says, briskly. "Come upstairs. We can talk."

"No. Please…" Emily manages to say, her voice strangled in her throat.

"Don't be silly," Suzie says again, in that masculine no-nonsense voice. "Come on." She puts an arm around Emily's shoulders and Emily allows herself to be led through the shop; Suzie switching off lights as she goes, through the beaded curtain, the narrow cupboard-cum-tea room and up the steep stairs. Part of Emily smiles in amusement at seeing herself go upstairs with this woman, so obviously a dyke. Knowing what she obviously knows of her and Poppy, will she leap on Emily when they get up to the flat, drag her into the bedroom, shove her hard, masculine hand between her legs, her hard, masculine tongue in her mouth? Emily sees herself fighting her off, hears Suzie saying, "But you did it with Poppy…"

"Poppy's different," Emily would sob, beating her away. "I love her."

"Oh, so do I…" Suzie would say.

But of course none of this happens, and upstairs in the flat Suzie gestures her to the sofa and goes into the kitchen.

"Tea or coffee?" she calls.

Emily tries to answer but her throat seems to have closed up.

"Of course, it's tea, isn't it?" Suzie says. "I remember Poppy told me. She talked a lot about you."

The flat seems different. Still messy, but tidier. Books have been stacked in one corner. Magazines next to them. Poppy's scarves, coats and jumpers, usually trailed on the backs and arms of every chair, are nowhere to be seen. There are still dirty mugs lying around though and the remains of Suzie's breakfast – a cereal bowl and a plate with half a slice of toast on – sit on the coffee table in front of Emily. Suzie moves them out of the way to put Emily's tea down.

"I've put some toast on," she says. "Would you like some?"

Emily nods vacantly. Suzie disappears again. She hears her moving around in the kitchen, the sound of crockery and cutlery. She puts plates, mugs, knives on the table.

"Peanut butter? Marmite?" she asks.

"I don't mind," Emily says, politely.

"I just wondered if you knew when she's coming back," she says when they're settled with toast and mugs of tea.

The peanut butter squeaks between Emily's teeth, sticks drily in her throat when she swallows it.

"I don't know," she says.

"I need her here, you see," Suzie goes on. "For the shop.

And... well, I need her. You know..." She runs her hands through her short, spiky hair, leaving it standing up on end almost comically.

"Yes," Emily says. Stupid of her ever to have thought Poppy and Suzie weren't lovers.

"I knew," Suzie says. "I always know. Men. Women. She tells me. We have what you would call an understanding."

"Yes," Emily says again, mechanically. What else can she say?

"She always comes back. Eventually."

Emily can't say anything more. The tears have started again, only worse now. Suddenly, a huge sob rises in her throat, escapes loudly. She puts her face in her hands, sways from side to side, sobs uncontrollably.

Suzie does nothing. Then she gets up, goes out, returns with a roll of loo paper.

"I couldn't find tissues," she says, handing it to Emily. Emily unrolls a long piece, tears it off, wraps it round her hand, blows her nose, wipes her face. Eventually, she stops.

"I love her," she says, like she saw herself saying just now. Her hands are still shaking. "I love her so much it hurts," she says.

"Yes," says Suzie. "She has that effect. On everyone. Even when you hate her you love her. Whatever she does to you. However cruel and unkind. It doesn't matter. You just want her back."

"I want to know," Emily says. "About Poppy. Everything. I need to know." She glances at her watch. "Oh God, Peter'll be wondering where I am!" She reaches for her phone.

"Yes. Peter," Suzie says. "Another one under her spell."

"What?" Emily says, vaguely. She's scrolling down to Peter's name, trying to think what to say.

"Nothing," Suzie says, quickly.

Emily taps out, *Took longer than I expected. Back soon x* Then she looks up deliberately into Suzie's eyes.

"What about Peter and Poppy?"

"Nothing. Honestly. I'm sure it was nothing. He used to come here, that's all."

"I know. To look at Poppy's work. He told me."

"Yes," Suzie says.

"Can I come back?" Emily asks. "Tomorrow? Soon? Please."

"Thursday afternoon. Kitty's covering the shop. Two-ish?"

Chapter Eighteen

"Thursday?" Peter says, peevishly. "It's going to be a nice day. I thought we'd go out somewhere."

"We can go out any time."

"But the forecast says…"

"It's never right. You know it isn't."

"There's high pressure on its way. Wall-to-wall sunshine."

Peter's obsessed with the weather. He never misses the forecast on television, shushes Emily if she speaks while it's on, spends hours on Google examining fronts, wind speeds and depressions. It's all he ever does. That and sit and read. But she hates it when he sulks.

"I've said I'll go now," she says. "There'll be other nice days. We'll go out tomorrow instead. You wanted to look at new curtains for the bathroom. We can go into Taunton."

Even as she says it she has a mental image of Pam and her friends laughing at the thought of their husbands wanting to look at curtain material.

"She's not even a friend of yours," Peter continues, stubbornly. "I don't know why you want to go."

"She *invited* me, Peter. It'd be rude not to."

He's been like this for ages now: clingy, demanding. It's suffocating. It makes her want to go out more, not less.

"David's helping out with that new magazine," she says, lightly. "They're looking for people to distribute it."

"I don't know how he's got time," Peter says. "With everything else he does."

"Maybe he's not ready yet to sit in a chair and read," Emily says.

Peter doesn't notice the barb, or if he does, he ignores it.

The next day he's up at eight. Emily hears him shower, shave, then crash around in the kitchen. He plonks a cup of tea on the bedside table. "We'd better make an early start," he says.

"The traffic's worse early," she says. "With the schools and offices. It'd be much better to go a bit later."

"It'll be impossible to park," Peter insists. "Much better to get in early."

It's good to have an aim for the day. It reminds Peter of when he used to go to work: up early, dressed and out of the door before he scarcely had time to think.

Downstairs in the kitchen he waits an age for Emily to appear, then watches her wander around the kitchen in a half-daze.

"We ought to get going," he says.

"There's no rush, Peter."

He's up from the table the moment he's finished, cleaning his teeth, pulling on his jacket. He waits in the front hallway. "Emily!" he calls up. "Are you coming?"

"I won't be long!" her voice floats down.

They're just on the way out when she stops. "Damn! Forgot my glasses. Two ticks!"

"Oh, let's not bother," Peter snaps.

"What?" She turns in the doorway.

"It's not worth it. There'll be nowhere to park..."

"Don't be childish, Peter. I won't be a mo. Anyway, I told you, it's better later."

"No, it isn't. All the spaces will have gone."

She's so tempted to go back in, slam the door, leave him to it, but she flies upstairs, grabs her glasses, flies back down and he's still waiting by the door.

"So we're going?" she asks.

"Nothing else to do," he says, shrugging.

The journey in is tense. Neither of them speak for a while. Then Peter says, "You're quiet."

"What d'you want me to talk about, Peter?" she says, heavily.

"It's just that normally you don't stop talking."

"I've got a headache," she lies.

"Oh, I see."

But the intimacy of the car and the monotony of the journey have a calming effect, and as they near Taunton she finds herself saying, "Suzie wondered if I knew when Poppy was coming back."

Poppy's name has a strange effect on Peter but he manages to answer lightly. "Why would *you* know?"

"That's what I said!" Emily laughs. "Why would she tell *me* and not *her*? I mean *she's* her business partner after all."

"Is that *all* she is?" Peter asks.

He's negotiating a roundabout and Emily's glad he can't look at her face. "How would I know?" she says, trying to keep her voice neutral.

"Well, she'd tell you, wouldn't she? She's your friend."

"It's not like that with Poppy. You know it isn't. Even if she said it, I wouldn't believe it. You can't believe anything she says."

"No," he says. "Shall we try the Crescent Car Park?" he goes on, hoping she'll change the subject.

But once Emily's got something on her mind it's hard to sidetrack her. "You know her as well as I do," she says. "Suzie says you spent a lot of time with her."

"You know I did," he says, quickly. "To look at her work."

"That's what I said," Emily says. "Suzie thought you might be having an affair!" She laughs and Peter manages to laugh with her.

"Anyway," he says, desperate to steer her away from the thought. "Jasmine says she's fed up with her there. You can tell Suzie she'll be back soon."

"What?" Emily says, confused.

"Poppy," he says. "She's staying with Jas. I thought you knew."

The shocked silence next to him tells him she didn't know. He can feel her hurt, wishes he could take the words back. "I thought you knew," he says again.

There's a snuffling sound next to him. "Emily?" he says. They're in town now. He can't take his eyes off the road to look at her. She's reaching in her pocket, searching her bag, finds a tissue, wipes her nose, sniffs.

"Emily!" he says, more sharply now. He knows he's upset her, but oddly he finds he's angry with her. "For God's sake, what does it matter?" he says, impatiently. "If she's s'posed to be your friend she would've told you!"

"I know," Emily sniffs, trying to pull herself together. Peter will wonder what she's making such a fuss about. "You're right. It's just she *could've* told me." Fresh tears start at the injustice, the duplicity, the sheer thoughtlessness. Jasmine of all people! She knows how she feels about her!

By the time they've reached the car park she's calmed down, mostly because she has to hide what she's feeling from Peter. Left alone, she would have been uncontrollable. Peter, feeling guilty now, is solicitous, and keeps asking her which material she likes best, although they end up as usual buying what he likes.

They stop for lunch in a new café in the high street. Peter orders coffee. "With hot milk," he says as usual.

The young girl serving looks at him confused. "Latte? Cappucino?" she asks.

"Black," Emily says quickly, embarrassed. "With a jug of hot milk separately, please."

Peter waits until the girl has left. "You *are* infuriating!" he hisses.

"What?" she says, colour rushing to her face.

"You *have* to take over. Makes me look stupid."

"I just…" Her voice trails off. "*I just wanted to help,*" she wants to say but the words choke in her throat. Hurt surges through her chest and tears rush to her eyes. Peter never used to find her infuriating. She hasn't changed. It's him. He's turning into a grumpy old man. "*Oh, Poppy.*" she moans inwardly. Poppy always sees the best in her, not the worst. She doesn't find her infuriating. She likes her just the way she is, with all her faults and foibles. She doesn't want to subdue her, to make her have to think before she speaks, to turn her into someone she isn't.

★

The next day dawns, as promised, bright and sunny. "You still want to go?" Peter asks Emily.

"I made an arrangement," she says.

"But look at it, Emily. We don't get many days like this. Text her. Say you've got a headache or something."

"Peter, don't. I said I'd go."

"But there's no need. Look, I can phone Jasmine. Find out exactly when that woman's coming back. You can text her. That's all she wants to know. You don't need to go and see her."

"I *want* to go."

"Rather than going out with me."

"Don't make it sound like that, Peter. I can go out with you any time."

"You can see *her* any time. It's not like she's a friend."

"You don't understand."

254

"No. I don't."

"Why can't you just go out on your own?"

"It's not the same. I like you with me."

This should be a compliment, of course, but it just makes her feel trapped.

She makes sandwiches for lunch. "Is it warm enough to sit outside?" she asks Peter. It's only mid-February but amazingly mild, the sun shining as Peter and the weather forecast foretold, and the patio is sheltered from any cool wind. At half past one she stacks the plates in the dishwasher and leaves Peter still sitting in the shade of the parasol reading a book. It's far too early to go, but she grabs her bag anyway, and her sunglasses, and walks down the road. There's a feeling of spring in the air, birds are singing. Emily lifts her head to the blue sky above her, the white seagulls wheeling overhead. It's almost a crime to think of sitting in that dingy flat on a day like this. Luckily, Suzie agrees.

"Let's go down to the front," she says.

Emily waits while she gives some last-minute instructions to Kitty and they fall into step together.

"Did you know Poppy is staying with my step-daughter?" Emily asks.

"Uh-huh," Suzie nods. "Didn't you?"

"No. She didn't say. She didn't say anything. She could've told me."

"Maybe she thought you'd be hurt."

"I don't think she cares."

"Yes, she does. Just not as much as you do."

The benches along the front are mostly taken: old people with newspapers; middle-aged couples talking to each other; young families with prams or pushchairs, babies and toddlers crying or moaning. They walk on until they find a free one.

"I thought she was a homeless person when I first saw her," Suzie says. "It was in London. I moved there when my marriage broke up. To get away. Start afresh, sort of thing. Anyway, there she was. Scruffy. Two carrier bags at her feet. Turning out all the stuff from her shoulder bag. 'I've lost my key,' she said, looking at me hopefully. Of course, I didn't believe her. And I certainly wasn't about to let her in. 'I'm Seven,' she added. The woman's mad, I thought, and I turned my back on her. 'Seven Jamieson,' she said with a smile, reaching out her hand to me: long, artistic fingers, a ring on each one: a skull's head, a gold Celtic love knot. Short fingernails, a grubby frayed cuff. I didn't take her hand and she let it drop by her side, but the smile stayed in place. 'Séverine actually,' she was saying, rolling the 'r's in the proper French way. 'My mother was French. My father...' She paused for effect. 'Wasn't.' It was obviously a well-rehearsed joke and I found myself laughing politely."

"Hang on a minute," Emily interrupts, confused. "Seven?"

"That's another thing about her. She changes her name to suit her mood. She was Seven when I knew her first. It was only later she changed to Poppy."

"Her petname," Emily says, knowledgeably. "From her French grandmother."

Suzie shakes her head, laughing. "She's not French. It's all made up. Her mother's as English as you and me. Surbiton, or Woking or somewhere. A secretary. Her Dad was an accountant. All too middle-class and boring for her."

"No French grandmother?"

"No!" she laughs again.

"But Séverine...?"

"Made up too. Hang on. Let me tell you properly."

Chapter Nineteen

"I can't just let you in," I said, coldly.

"No, of course." She smiled again, holding my gaze with her clear blue eyes. "Now let me see. What've I got...?"

Her grubby-looking fair hair fell over her face as she fumbled in her pockets. "Only my train ticket..." she laughed, "That's not much help, is it?"

I shouldered my bag. Went inside. Closed the door behind me. I don't know what made me open it again, but immediately I wished I hadn't.

"Thanks." She was in like a shot, the carrier bags by her feet manoeuvred expertly with her. I glanced up the stairwell wondering if Mr Harris would hear my screams if she drew a knife. She marched confidently past me to the ground floor flat and I waited to see how she intended tackling the next locked door. But just as she got there the door magically opened. A female voice exclaimed excitedly. And she disappeared inside, leaving me with a host of unanswered questions: Why hadn't she rung the bell? Was she really who she said she was? Who was the mysterious female already in the flat? But it was none of my business and I carried on up the stairs.

It was three days later that the noises began. Music like a wailing banshee. Rhythmic drums. And strangest of all, a high-pitched 'drrrrrr' ending with a shrill 'yip' like a cowboy brandishing a lasso. I banged on the floor. The music stopped. Started again, this time more quietly. One day it was so bad I went down and hammered on the door. The music stopped abruptly. Voices. Male and female. Scuffling. A stifled laugh.

Then the door opened. I scarcely recognised her at first, she looked so different. Wearing some sort of Eastern costume, all jangling beads and sequins, heavy make-up ringing her eyes. Equally, she didn't recognise me. Then she broke into a smile, gripped my wrist and said, "Oh, it's you. Come on in!"

They were sitting on the floor. Well, most of them anyway. In a circle. There was a girl standing in the middle. Dark. Dark skin, dark hair, dark eyes. Wearing a belly dancing costume: sequin bra top, long skirt, jangly coin belt, bare feet. She smiled at me, confidently.

"Come and sit down," Seven was saying. "Here." She nudged a space with her feet between the knees of two girls and they moved apart wordlessly, staring at me. I hesitated.

"Oh, come on!" she said. "We're just getting going." She nodded to one of the boys and the music started again. Turkish or Egyptian maybe. A slow, steady drumbeat. The girl began to move, raising her arms like a snake charmer, her hips began to sway. She smiled at me. Only at me. As though I was the only person in the room. Embarrassed, I looked away, but when I looked back her eyes were still on mine. Her hips swayed. Her arms reached out to me. The girls either side of me began to sway too, rocking back and forth in time to the beat. The music quickened. My heart beat faster. I could feel the excitement growing. People began to clap in time to the music. Then there was that sound, the sound I recognised, a long 'drrrrr' with their rolled tongues, culminating in 'yip'.

"Bellydance," Seven told me. "One of the oldest forms of dance. Come on…"

She took my hand, pulled me to my feet. The girl in the centre took my other hand. I was wooden. Like a wooden doll. But the music took over. I felt my hips sway in time. And that was it. My introduction to Seven's world.

It was over a week before I saw her next. I was working

every day. I had taken a transfer with the bank. I left at eight and it was gone seven by the time I got back. Sometimes I heard the sound of music, the same I heard before, Turkish or Egyptian or something, but played quietly, people talking and laughing maybe, the chink of cups and cutlery, but mostly it was quiet as the grave. It was the weekend when it started again. Saturday night late. This time I didn't hesitate. I knocked. The door was opened. I went in, sat down in the charmed circle.

I quickly realised that everything revolved around Seven. She was the main dancer, the one who decided what music should be played, when it began, when it stopped, who should dance and when. The walls of the flat were covered in her paintings. It wasn't even her flat. "I doss down here," she said.

"You don't have your own place?"

She shook her head. "Still looking. Melanie lets me stay here. Most of the time anyway. Sometimes I stay with Jules." She nods to a slim, good-looking, dark-haired boy. "My brother," she says.

"What do you do?" I asked.

I half-expected her to say "Nothing" but "Art," she said. As far as I was concerned it amounted to the same thing, but I said politely. "You're an artist?"

"Art student," she explained. "At the Slade."

She said the words as though they were in capitals and obviously I was supposed to be impressed, but, of course, I'd never heard of it. I knew nothing about art. But her work looked good. Original. Each one signed with an elaborate number 7, written in the French way with a bar across it.

"Have it," she said of one I stood looking at.

I hung it above the fireplace in my flat. A watercolour of a girl sitting on a park bench, springtime, blossom on the trees. I could almost hear the birds singing.

Like everyone else I was in thrall to Seven. I lived for those evenings, waited each night for the sound of the music, the rhythmic drums, the excited 'drrr' and 'yip' that signalled the fun had begun.

I needed a distraction. I was going through a bad time. I had just found out that my husband of ten years had been having an affair for nine of those. Of course, I was the last to know. The moment I found out I applied for a transfer. The bank was very understanding. I didn't care where I went and the anonymity of London appealed. They even helped me find a flat. They did that sort of thing in those days.

Seven and her crowd were years younger than me, some only late teens, most in their early twenties, all students. Melanie, the girl who rented the flat, was tall and slim, waist length, jet black hair, really, really pretty. Seven had blonde hair in those days, though it was obviously dyed. She's mousy naturally, I think. Even then she wasn't slim. Big, curvy, buxom, the right build for a belly dancer. She loved dressing up, cramming her breasts into a low, tight bra top, her stomach and hips hanging over the top of the low-waisted skirts. She was an amazing dancer: all from the heart, no inhibitions.

She had… oh, you know, charisma I suppose you'd call it; people gathered around her. She was our sun, we were her acolytes. Everything she did, everything she said, we applauded. Jules was the only one who ever dared to criticise her.

"No, I don't think so," he'd say when she expressed an opinion as though it was fact in that authoritative way she had. We'd all hold our breath, wait for her to throw scorn on him, but she never did. She'd just laugh and say, "Well, that's what *I* think anyway."

He was quiet, studious. He never danced. I don't know why he came actually. Sometimes he didn't say more than a dozen words all evening. Seven made up for it. When she wasn't dancing she talked non-stop. Like everyone else I could have listened all night.

I was leading a double life: conservative office worker by day, Bohemian by night. I never knew why the others tolerated me. I must've been at least ten years older than most of them. I didn't agree with any of their radical, idealised views on life. I'd never been to college or university. I left school at sixteen to work in the bank. I didn't even make an effort to fit in. The most I did was to change into jeans after work, often keeping on the same shirt I'd worn to work. I've never cared about what I wear, and washing and drying clothes was enough of a problem without adding to it. Seven got hold of me one night, dressed me up in one of her long skirts and floaty tops, made up my eyes with mascara and turquoise eyeshadow. I had my hair long in those days. She looped it up, threaded ribbons through it. I looked ridiculous. I only went along with it to get close to her, to feel her hands on my face and running through my hair, to get her undivided attention.

I never got the hang of belly dancing either. I just used to move my hips and wave my arms around a bit and hope for the best. Seven said it was a good start and it would come in time. I just needed to 'let go'. It was a phrase she used about me a lot.

After a while she started coming up to my flat on her own. I was surprised the first time it happened. Something about the knock on the door told me it was her. No one ever came to see me, and I jumped out of my skin at the sound of the loud rap. I was just getting over the shock when she called, "Hallo-oo! It's *me-eee!*" in a voice loud enough to wake the dead, and, afraid of the effect on the other neighbours, I rushed to let her in.

"So *this* is where you hide yourself when you're not with us!" she said, taking it all in in one sweep of her eyes. I'd done nothing to the room since I'd moved in. I've never been one for home decorating of any sort and I wasn't sure how long I was going to stay. Her eyes fell on the photographs on the mantelpiece: one of me with my sister as bridesmaids at my cousin's wedding, and one of my parents taken on a family holiday.

"Family?" she asked.

"My sister and my parents," I said.

"No boyfriend?" she asked.

I blushed. "I was…" I had no idea why I was being so ridiculous about it. I'd told everyone at work straight off I was divorced.

"*Married?*" she guesses quickly, her surprise genuine. "*Really?*"

Divorce wasn't so openly talked about in those days and most people changed the subject quickly, embarrassed for me and themselves. But not Seven. "How long?" she gabbled. "What was he like? My parents were divorced," she went on without waiting for an answer. She'd told me this before, but I was relieved to be talking about her not me.

"Oh," she said just before she left. "We wondered if Jules could doss down here tonight."

"*What?* No. No, he can't."

"He won't get in your way. He's got a sleeping bag. You'll scarcely know he's here."

"He's got his own flat."

"Bit of a problem with the rent," she giggled.

"No, Seven." I said firmly. "Absolutely not."

"Okay," she shrugged. "I just thought maybe you and him…"

"*What?*" I said again, blushing furiously.

"He likes you. I thought you knew."

I turned the words over in bed that night, thought about Jules with his long, dark hair; deep, dark eyes; slim hips and long expressive fingers. I didn't fancy him. We'd scarcely exchanged more than a few words. But I'd seen him looking at me. And I was flattered to think he found me attractive.

My work began to suffer. I got up late, arrived at the bank in a state, rushing to the Ladies' to try and do something about my hair and run my hands over my crumpled blouse and skirt. Soon I began making mistakes. I was called in to see the manager.

"I expected more from you," he said.

"I've not been well," I excused myself. "I've been sleeping badly."

I don't know what he was thinking. He knew, of course, I was recently divorced. Perhaps he thought I was sleeping my way through the entire neighbourhood. Or maybe crying myself to sleep heartbrokenly each night. But all he said was, "You can't bring your personal problems to work. I'll give you a month to prove yourself in. Otherwise, I'm afraid…"

I told myself I wouldn't go that night. After I'd cooked myself a meal, I ran a bath. I was in my dressing gown, ironing my work skirt, a towel wrapped around my damp hair, when the doorbell rang. I knew who it was. I ignored it. With any luck she'd think I was out. The ring was followed by a knock, then a low wheedling voice. "Come on, Suzie, I know you're in there. What's the matter? Are you ill?"

I hesitated. Then, "Yes," I said, managing to put a slight croak in my voice.

"Let me in," she wheedled, again.

"No. I'm going to bed. I'll be fine."

"Aww, come on… it's only me. I want to see you."

I knew it was crazy. I just couldn't stop myself.

"You don't look too bad," she said immediately, taking in the towel, the damp smell of freshly washed hair.

My hand flew to my towelled head. "I thought it'd make me feel better," I said, unwinding the towel.

She reached up, ran her hand through my damp hair. Her touch was electric. I stepped back as though I'd been burnt, my face on fire.

"Hey…" she said gently. "Hey…" Her hand moved from my hair, onto my shoulder. She leaned towards me and in one swift movement cradled me in her arms. "Let me help you," she said.

Nothing happened. She towel-dried my hair, combed it out, standing behind me at the dressing table like a maid, watching my face in the mirror, chattering constantly.

"We wondered where you were. Everyone's downstairs. Jules has been asking for you…"

"I can't…" I protested, but weakly, so weakly. And half an hour later I was down there, my still damp hair clammy against my neck and moistening the collar of my one clean blouse.

It was midnight when someone made the suggestion.

"Let's go for a drive."

It was rare for anyone to have a car, but one of the boys had borrowed his mother's mini to help someone move some stuff into their flat.

I was the only one who thought it was crazy. No one was particularly drunk, but most of them had been smoking weed and the boy who had the car seemed pretty far gone.

"I'm going to bed," I said as the gaggle of five, headed by Jules and Seven, staggered to the door.

"Don't be a spoilsport!" Seven said, linking her arm through mine.

And, of course, I went.

To my relief the boy whose car it was didn't drive. He handed the keys unquestioningly to one of the girls. Maybe she was his sister, I don't know, but she slid easily into the seat and drove surprisingly well. We sped through London streets, headed I had no idea where. I scarcely knew the area we lived in, let alone anywhere else. I had promised myself to explore London when I first moved up there, visit the art galleries and theatres, but that was before I met Seven and my every waking moment was taken up with her. Bright lights and glittering shop windows sped past us, there was no car radio, but we didn't need one. One of the boys started singing some pop song and everyone except me joined in, stopping every so often to laugh hilariously when they got the words or the tune wrong. Their mood was infectious and I laughed with them, as drunk or as high as them, without having touched a thing. It was crowded in the back. Jules was one side of me, Seven the other and a blonde girl, whose name I knew at one time but had instantly forgotten, the other side of Jules. Every time we rounded a corner I was thrown either against Seven or Jules, the heat from their bodies in the crowded interior radiating against my sides. It was late summer and warm. My bare arm was jammed against Jules'. Suddenly, without warning, without looking at me at all, he hooked his fingers inside the crook of my elbow. The touch sent a dart of excitement straight to my crotch. My face was on fire. I didn't look at him. I couldn't. I pulled the fingers closer. Now his thigh pressed against mine. Still I didn't look, relishing the thrill in my loins.

The car rounded another corner and I saw we had entered some sort of park: long, green stretches of grass either side in place of the streets. The mood in the car had changed. Everyone fell silent as the car headlights lit the road and dark trees loomed either side.

"Left here," someone said.

"No, it's right," Seven's voice came from next to me. "Then bear left."

"Where're we going?" I asked.

"You'll see," she said, laughing. There was something mildly disquieting about the laughter that followed from everyone else and I began to feel nervous, my grip on Jules' arm slackening.

"It's okay." He and Seven spoke almost simultaneously, making me even more nervous.

"Honestly," Seven added. "You'll see. Just a bit of fun, that's all."

The car stopped and the girl switched off the lights. Instinctively, I fell silent. Long minutes seemed to pass. I couldn't stand it. "What're we waiting for?" I whispered into Seven's ear.

"Shhh. You'll see."

"Over there," someone whispered.

"Yeh." Jules leant forward, pointing, his voice sharp with excitement, an excitement I could feel and taste. I peered through the fugged-up window. Headlights flashing. Then others. There must have been about half a dozen cars around us. Car doors opened and closed. Shadows flickered silently in front of the headlights. Suddenly, an interior light went on in one of the cars.

"Come on." Jules opened the car door, took my hand, "Careful…"

Blindly, I stumbled after him. Some of the cars now had side lights on, engines purred, I could hear odd snatches of voices and laughter and another sound, the unmistakeable, breathy sound of people having sex. Suddenly, I realised what was going on. In the dim light I could make out the moon of a man's bottom against an open car window, see the muscles straining back and forth as he thrust, hear his grunts and a few minutes later as he stepped back, I saw the back of a girl's hand sweep across her mouth, before just as quickly another man took his place.

Other cars rocked gently. Through the misted up windows, in the dim internal lights, I could see pale limbs, half-naked bodies, hear soft moans, loud groans.

We weren't the only ones watching. I could feel, even if I couldn't actually see, other people around me. I felt weak at the knees, overcome with a strange mixture of emotions: sexual excitement, curiosity, fear even – was I expected to join in? The tension was electric. Jules' grip tightened on my hand. Instinctively, I knew he was hard. I reached for him. He pushed against my hand, reached for my crotch. I don't know how long we stood there. I think Jules came. I was very close, but I couldn't really settle, knowing Seven and the others were so close by, even though I was aware they were doing the same, either together or on their own. Impossible not to.

We drifted back to the car. It was a strange atmosphere on the way home. Jules lit a cigarette, draped an arm proprietorially around my shoulder. If anyone was surprised to see him follow me up to my flat, they didn't say so.

We tore at each other on the way up the stairs, pausing only to turn and gnaw hungrily at each other's mouths. As I closed the door of the flat, he pushed me onto all fours. Clumsily, I kicked off my shoes and he dragged my jeans and knickers from my legs, landing in a ridiculous sprawl on the floor from the effort. But we were beyond laughter. He thrust into me so hard I yelled out, careless of any sound carrying through the thin walls. We were animal, primal, desperate for release.

The smell of cigarettes and joss sticks clung to my clothes the next day. I was late for work again. Jules hadn't stayed. I hadn't expected him to. It meant nothing, I knew. But during the day I found my mind drifting to him. He was everything my ex-husband hadn't been: slim, slightly feminine-looking, artistic, shy, and I began to think there could be more to him: the start of a new and meaningful relationship. A flutter of excitement went through me at the thought of seeing him again and I dressed with more care than usual that evening, even spraying on some perfume my sister had given me for Christmas and I had never used. I was disappointed when I saw him again: the mental image I had built up (a Lord Byron sort of figure, with hidden, deeper depths I could plunder) didn't correspond at all with the fey youth I saw sitting cross-legged on the floor. Disappointment turned quickly to hurt when he scarcely looked at me and when he did I saw nothing in his eyes, not even a flicker of a shared secret. In my mind I had seen him gazing at me shyly (like he used to before, only this time with added meaning), making room for me on the floor next to him where he always sat, putting his arm around me, acknowledging me openly as his chosen lover. I was surprised, therefore, when there was a knock on the door just after I got to my room. My heart leapt and I quickly quelled the feeling. It would be Poppy surely. But it was him. I had half a mind to send him away, but of course I didn't. The memory of last night was too strong, the need for someone to show me I was attractive too powerful to resist.

We never talked, either before or after, alone or with a crowd. I was being used, I knew that. I would sit at my office desk cringing inwardly as I looked back at the night before, promising myself it wouldn't happen again, but it always did. After that first time we scarcely even kissed, but Jules was an adventurous lover and he introduced me to things I had only ever read about. I surprised myself with my readiness to acquiesce in his bold games. My ex-husband had had pretty basic sexual tastes in comparison, but I was acutely aware I was older than Jules and I didn't want him to think I was staid and dull. We went out a couple of times again to the park, but it was rare for someone to have a car. I was doubly nervous each time. I wondered if Jules might expect us to join in, but he never suggested it and I had the impression he just liked to watch.

I wasn't sure at first if Seven knew about us. Even at the time, I knew part of Jules' appeal was that he was her brother. Sleeping with him was another connection with her. I can't believe, now, how naïve I was. One night I went downstairs earlier than usual. The sitting room was empty but I could hear voices in the kitchen. "Seven?" I called out.

"In the bedroom," someone called out.

I hesitated, then knocked gently. No reply. "Seven?" I called again, knocking at the same time.

I could hear scuffling; giggling, low voices, the sort of sounds that can only mean one thing. I turned away. Then I suddenly realised it was Jules' voice I could hear. Laughing inwardly at my misinterpretation of an innocent brother and sister meeting, I pushed the door open. It took me a moment to realise what I was seeing: Jules' bare chest, Seven's head appearing almost comically as she emerged from under the sheet, Jules' hands in her hair. She'd been giving him head. Her brother. I froze, dumbstruck, and she laughed. They both laughed. I ran out, ran to my flat, slammed the door behind me. I couldn't move. I kept seeing them there, laughing at me.

I expected Seven to come up. I moved around my flat like an automaton. I ran a bath, then couldn't be bothered to get into it, made a cup of tea and let it go cold. All evening I waited, but she didn't come. It was Seven I was waiting for. I knew Jules wouldn't come now. It was over, not that there was much to be over. Yet I missed it. The meagre 'relationship' had at least given me something to think about as I sat at my dreary office desk or behind the counter in the bank, serving one grumpy, bored customer after another. Now I had nothing, not even Seven. How could I be her friend now, knowing what I knew of her? My mind kept going back to the scene, like a sore place you constantly have to touch. There was no innocent explanation. She was having sex with her brother. My mind and my body recoiled at the thought.

I walked home more slowly than usual: nothing to look forward to, no point in hurrying. Childish disappointment flooded through me. Slow tears trickled down my face and I licked them, saltily, away.

She was standing outside, just like before, carrier bags at her feet; limp, blonde hair falling around her shoulders. She watched me walking towards her, shrugged that carefully rehearsed Gallic shrug of hers and said with a laugh, "I've lost my key."

"Don't be silly, Seven!" I snapped.

"Come on, Suzie," she wheedled, "be friends with me."

"I can't." It was all I could say. I could feel myself weakening. "You…" I couldn't say it.

"What? Jules, you mean? Hey…" She looked into my face, caught my arm, "I didn't realise you cared for him. He said it was just casual."

"Your brother," I spat out.

"Oh, that…" As she shrugged again I felt like grabbing hold of her and shaking her.

"Come on," she said, "we can't talk here. Let me in. Then I can explain…"

So there we were again, back where we started, the carrier bags at her feet swiftly manoeuvred past me. Only this time she followed me up to my flat. I gestured to the sofa. She sat down, looked at me.

"I'm waiting," I said.

"What?" All innocence and guileless.

"For the explanation."

"You must know," she said, baldly. "I'm not *that* kinky."

The penny dropped and I started laughing, a small giggle

that rose in my throat then burst into a sort of hysterical sob, and suddenly I was laughing and crying at the same time and I couldn't stop. Helplessly, I waved my arm in the air. Seven disappeared from beside me, reappeared with a glass of water that I took from her and sipped shakily until, finally, I calmed down.

"Step-brother," she said.

I let the news sink in. Did that make it any better?

"My father re-married. Jules is *her* son."

I had to ask. "You were brought up together?"

"Yes and no. I mean, he came to live with us."

Vaguely, I remembered her telling me she lived with her mother in France when her parents divorced, but I was beginning to realise the truth meant nothing to Seven.

"I loved him from the start," she went on. "He was my hero, always there for me, looking after me, protecting me. Then suddenly, they went. Jules and his mother." I noticed she never said, 'My step-mother'. Clearly, she hated her. "I was eighteen. I came back from school one day and they were gone. My father never said why. I hated him for that."

The father she had previously told me she idolised, but I let it go. The story was so fascinating. I was hooked. "Then when I came here, to the Slade, there he was." She shrugged. "What could I do? We're meant for each other. No one, nothing, can change that."

She turned to me suddenly, all compassion, "I didn't realise though. You and Jules. I'm sorry. He said it was just…"

"It was," I said, tersely. "Nothing."

"You sure?" She put her hand on my arm, squeezed it gently.

"Sure," I said.

So, as I said, there we were, back where we started. I went down that evening, as before. Jules ignored me, as before.

He and Seven were the same as usual. They didn't act like a couple. Nothing seemed to have changed. And yet it had. Seven treated me differently, with a diffidence, a kindness even that I didn't think she was capable of. She came up to my flat more, we talked, or rather, she did, spinning me more of those fantastic tales that I and everyone else loved to hear. Like a fairy-tale princess she wove magic. I was completely hooked.

Then I began to hear about a new professor at the college. "He's *gorgeous*," she oozed. "He says I have real talent." And although I knew nothing about art I could see her pictures were changing. She was trying different styles, experimenting, working harder, partying less. Then that changed too. And I soon found out why. The new college professor, that everyone fancied, was having an affair with another student. Seven, who expected everyone, male or female, to fall in love with her, was incensed.

"I can't stay there," she told me.

"Don't be silly," I said.

"It's just so *humiliating*."

I loved it when she confided in me like this. It made me feel important. Singled out from all her other friends, who were young, who were busy carving their careers and coping with their own relationships, who had problems of their own, who hadn't experienced '*life*' like I had. Or at least like Seven thought I had. In actual fact I was in no position to advise her. I'd never been in love with a married man (I assumed the enigmatic professor was married), I'd never even been to college; I knew nothing about art, about trying to prove myself better than my peers, about trying to earn a living as an artist. I had left school at sixteen, gone straight into the bank, married the first man who showed an interest in me. If he'd been nicer to me I would have had children, waited until they were at school and gone back to work; maybe not in the bank, but in a shop or an office or something. I never expected much from life. I'm very, very ordinary. Maybe that's what she likes about me, what keeps her coming back to me again and again.

Jules fell out of her life. So much for being 'meant for each other'. The new professor eclipsed all that, an obsession so dangerous he almost lost his job over it.

Seven wasn't the type to accept rejection. I'm not sure how she did it but somehow word got around that he was sleeping with one of his students. There was uproar at the college. Seven gave me daily updates, her eyes shining with malice. I felt sorry for the chap.

Ultimately, though, Seven was the loser. I could have told her it wasn't going to work. She did everything she could to get his attention. Nowadays, we would call her a stalker. She hung around for him after lectures, left bottles of wine and food parcels in his office (she'd heard his wife had thrown him out), wrote him cryptic little notes, signed with her hallmarked '7' crossed the French way. She was sure he would turn to her now his sordid little affair had been revealed to the world. But far from falling into her arms he went out of his way to avoid her. Of course he did. He would have been crazy to take up with another student so soon after the one that nearly lost him his job. I don't know whether he ever guessed she was the one who spilled the beans. By then I had my own problems and I didn't listen closely to all the details.

My ex-husband had filed for divorce. Up until then we had only been legally separated. It suited both of us. I hadn't asked for anything. I didn't want anything. Just that elusive thing called my 'freedom'. The thought of divorce, with all that legal wrangling, was more than I could bear. But now he wanted it. He'd met someone new. She wanted marriage. So there had to be a divorce. On top of this the bank was going through a round of redundancies. I knew, even before it happened, that

I would be top of the list. I had hardly covered myself in glory since I'd been there: I was consistently late, my appearance far from professional, unable to concentrate when I was there, and unpopular with my colleagues.

So suddenly there we were, Seven and I, she unhappy at the Slade, I with a generous divorce settlement and no job. That summer we went on holiday. Seven was always saying she loved Lyme Regis.

"Ever since I read *The French Lieutenant's Woman*," she enthused. "Daddy took me down there once. For a weekend. Just the two of us. I loved it so much…"

So we went. And it was just as she described it: the Cobb, the beach, the winding streets and little shops. We stayed at the Alexandra. I really pushed the boat out. Two seaview rooms, four-course dinner every night. I had no one else to spend the money on.

I was a bit nervous. How would she be, this Bohemian wild child in this old-fashioned hotel, in this old-fashioned watering hole? But I needn't have worried. Seven could turn any situation to her advantage. It was like taking a well-behaved child for a special treat. She turned up in her most conservative clothes, clothes I'd never set eyes on before and must surely have been borrowed from someone, and set about charming everyone she met from fellow guest to reception staff to waiters to cleaning ladies, with her own particular brand of personal charm, and soon they were all under her spell. I *was* a little annoyed one night when I overheard her confiding to someone that she had brought me here because my marriage had broken up and I needed a change of scene, generously giving the impression she was the one footing the bill. But by then I knew she'd never change. And if I wanted her I had to accept it. And I did want her.

We saw the shop two days before we had to leave. It had

been run as an antique shop before but the owner wanted to retire. I don't know which one of us made the decision. It just sort of happened. Seven didn't go back to college in the autumn. "I can't face him," she said simply. I saw the solicitors, sorted out the lease and there we were, setting up shop.

'Poppy Fields' was the perfect name for the shop: her first name, my surname. I was the one who called her 'Poppy'. It started as Poppet then changed; you know how nicknames do. She liked it. A new identity. She loves playing games, inventing a life for herself. I'm not sure she knows now what is true and what's made up. And she doesn't care.

The truth is far too parochial. She was rushed into hospital one day. Appendicitis. I had to have her next of kin. Plain old Julie Benson appeared out of nowhere. Father an accountant, mother a secretary or something. Born 7.7.77. The only bit of poetry in the whole mundane scene. No French mother. No French grandmother. No brother of any description. No wicked step-mother. For someone like Poppy it was insupportable. No wonder she makes everything up.

Chapter Twenty

Emily's mind reels as she walks back from Suzie's each time. Each new revelation makes her realise how little she knows the real Poppy. Oh, she'd never believed half the fantastic tales she'd told her, but she had no idea how far from the truth she really was.

"She said she went to art college in Brighton," Emily says, remembering Poppy's words, *'I grew up by the sea. I always wanted to go back. That's why we came to Lyme.'*

"Oh, she did for a while," Suzie replies. "There's always a germ of truth somewhere in what she tells you. Jules *was* her step-brother. But they never lived together. Her parents divorced just before she went to art college. Pure coincidence she met him there. I think she saw sleeping with him as a way of getting her own back on her father. He was the one with French connections. Jules, I mean. His mother's French, he was brought up there. Poppy thought it was so romantic. She borrowed his story. Changed it to suit her. Borrowed his surname too. Jamieson. It gave her a connection with him. She started shortening it to James because it went better with Poppy, and I preferred it for marketing her work. It was easier than having to keep spelling out Jamieson."

Emily longs to talk to someone about it. Someone other than Suzie, who always takes Poppy's side. But no one knows Poppy except Peter and she can't talk to him. He's already suspicious about her visits to Suzie.

"But you only went the other day," he keeps saying. "She's not even a friend of yours…"

"She is now." Emily reddens as she says it. "And anyway, she invited me."

"Can't you just say no?"

"It's not as easy as that. And I want to go."

"I don't see why."

"Why do I have to justify myself, Peter?" she snaps. "She asked me. I'm going. Okay?"

He disappears into his study. She knows he's sulking. *Oh, for God's sake*, she thinks impatiently. *It's like dealing with a child.* She knows he wants her to follow him, wheedle him out of his bad mood. And usually she would, just to keep the peace, but she just can't be bothered. Her mind's too taken up with Poppy.

"She'll come back, won't she?" she asks Suzie.

Suzie shrugs. "I don't know. She always has before. But maybe this time... I don't know. Where else can she go? She needs me."

But it sounds like she's trying to convince herself.

A deep unhappiness settles in Emily's heart, a heavy weight she carries everywhere with her as though someone or something has died. She has no appetite and the weight falls off her. Ironically, after years of taking such care about what she eats, she now finds her skirts swivelling around her waist, her jeans bagging at the hips. In bed she lies awake for hours, chasing thoughts and worries round her mind. *Poppy, Poppy, Poppy*, she calls inwardly. How could she give up on what they had? Surely she must miss Emily as much as she misses her?

Fuelled by wine and whisky, Peter lies next to her in a comatose state, breathing loudly, making odd little snorting noises or snoring deafeningly until she prods him and he grumbles and turns over. Night after night she wakes up: two o'clock, four o'clock, five thirty. She creeps out, goes downstairs, tries to read, checks her phone, searches Facebook and Twitter for signs of Poppy, goes back to bed, wakes again, goes through the same routine. In the shadowy bedroom she finally falls into an exhausted sleep, only to be woken a couple of hours later when Peter gets up.

In the day she performs her chores like an automaton, unable to sit still for a moment, sometimes doing things twice without realising. She avoids Peter as much as possible. They're back to circling past each other in the little house. When he's in the study she goes to the kitchen. If he comes in, she darts past him upstairs. If she's in the sitting room and he sits down to read, she jumps up to put the kettle on or empty the washing machine.

Mealtimes are the only time they meet and conversation is desultory. They're always at odds with each other over some tiny thing or another. "You didn't get the salt out," she complains.

"Well, you can lay the table yourself next time!" he snaps.

After dinner she sits as far away as possible from him on the two-seater sofa, leaning against the arm of it, her legs curled uncomfortably underneath her like a student. If she accidentally knocks against him while changing position when her feet have gone to sleep or she has cramp, she apologises like he was a stranger. Sometimes she finds herself staring in fascination at her hand on the sofa, right next to Peter's hand. She sees herself curling her fingers around it like she used to, cuddling up against him, leaning against his chest. When she got up she'd lean over him and kiss his forehead, touch his face, run her fingers through his hair. All those little things have stopped. Has Peter noticed? She glances across at his face. He's staring fixedly at the television screen. She moves her hand away, hugs it close around herself.

Peter can't be bothered to try any more. If he speaks he says the wrong thing, so he says nothing. Everything he does is wrong. He's always in the way. He can almost hear Emily tutting impatiently as she squeezes past him. He can sense her irritation when he sits in his chair or at his computer while she bustles around the place. She makes him feel idle.

He starts looking for reasons to go out, offers to buy milk or groceries, drives to Taunton to look around the car salesrooms even though they're not looking for a new car. At one time Emily would have wanted to go with him, or would at least have asked how long he'd be, but now she doesn't seem to care whether he's there or not.

Coming back from one of these expeditions one day, he finds her crying in the kitchen. She turns away quickly. "I didn't hear you come in," she sniffs, her voice strangely tight in her throat. He stops himself saying he's not surprised with the washing machine and dishwasher both on. He knows she'll only say, '*It has to be done, Peter,*' in that sarcastic way she has.

"What's the matter?" he asks instead, though he dreads the answer. The guilty thought she might have found out about Poppy springs into his mind, but even if it's nothing to do with that, the question will still lead to the inevitable dragging up of old resentments, opening of wounds, airing of problems.

"I'm just so unhappy," she sobs, leaning her head against his shoulder. He has no choice but to hold her, patting her back absent-mindedly as the sobs shake through her.

"Why?" He knows he has to ask, though he doesn't want to know. The whole thing is beginning to remind him of the sort of 'relationship' talks he had with Anusia just before they split up. But Emily isn't Anusia. Neither is she Zena who'd start yelling and throwing things around.

"I don't know," she sniffs. "It's just… everything…"

"Yes," he says.

An idea strikes Emily, something she's been turning over in her mind for a while now but not had the courage to say. "I thought I might go away for a while."

"Away? What d'you mean? Where? You've never wanted to before."

"Rose has asked me up," she says. "Her parents are away. She'd like a hand with Alicia…"

It's not strictly true. Rose's parents *are* away, but she has no idea that Emily is inviting herself up.

"It's the middle of winter," Peter says. "Cold. Icy. It might snow. Why don't you wait till spring?"

Trust Peter to be talking about the weather.

"But her parents have gone now!" Emily says. "She needs me."

"She's got other friends, hasn't she?"

Emily shrugs, vaguely.

"We could both go," he says suddenly, though instantly he knows he doesn't want to.

She shakes her head. "Don't be silly. You'd hate it. Just us girls. Anyway, it's not the point, you know that."

"Yes. No. Okay. If that's what you want…"

Emily chooses to ignore the sulkiness in his voice. She's amazed by Peter's confidence in himself, in their relationship. If it had been the other way round she would have pleaded with him to stay, told him they could work things out.

She emails Rose, asks if she can come up. If Rose is surprised she doesn't say so, though it's always hard to tell someone's thoughts in an email. *That would be lovely*, the reply says. *My p's are away for a week. How long would you like to stay?*

Emily hesitates. It depends how long it takes her to track Poppy down. And what Poppy will say when she does find her. She may not even be with Jasmine any more, though that's where she'll try first.

"*A couple of days,*" she replies vaguely. "*If that's okay with you.*"

Emily's nervous. She hasn't stayed away from Peter for years, not since she used to go away on courses, back in the days when she was trying to make some sort of career for herself. She'll be lost in London without him. Peter lived in London for years and she's always relied on him to get her around. She's like a little country mouse when she goes up there, dodging the crowds in the streets, completely unable to fathom the tube, trailing behind Peter as he forges ahead confidently, jumping on and off the right train, hailing cabs, asking for places she's only ever read about in books (Angel, Tottenham Court Road, St Pancras) and amazingly knowing where they are and asking to be dropped nearby when the traffic is gridlocked.

I'll meet you at the coach station if you like, Rose emails but Emily doesn't want to be too dependent.

Don't worry. I'll get a taxi, she emails back.

Part of her nurses a forlorn hope that Poppy will turn up to meet her. It's the sort of thing she'd do. Not that she's even contacted her yet. She thought she'd text her on the way up, make it sound like a spur-of-the-moment thing rather than something she's had in mind for ages, just waiting for the courage and the opportunity to put it into action.

Peter keeps thinking she'll change her mind. Emily's never gone away without him. She needs him. She'll hate it when she gets there. She won't know what to do. Part of him longs to tell her not to go, but his pride won't let him. Her suitcase is open on the spare bed in the room he thinks of as Jasmine's room, and it gradually fills with jeans, tops and the various creams and hair things she always takes with her.

"What time does the train go?" he asks the night before.

Emily sighs, theatrically. "I've told you a million times. It's not the train, it's the coach, and seven."

"Okay, okay. You know what I meant. I'll set the alarm for four thirty then, shall I?"

"How long will it take to get in?"

"You know very well. An hour."

"I won't need that long then, will I? Five's fine."

"You want to allow enough time. For the traffic."

"There won't be any. Not that early."

"Hold-ups then. Tractors. Slow cars. And it might be icy," though he's checked the forecast and it's unusually mild for February. "A flat tyre. Lorries, tractors…"

"Okay, okay. Make it four thirty then. Why ask me if you've worked it out already?"

Emily doesn't think she'll ever go to sleep. She's checked and double-checked her case, her tickets, her handbag, but even so, she's back in the spare room bending over the suitcase when Peter goes to clean his teeth.

"You won't let me forget my charger, will you?" she asks Peter just as he's drifting off to sleep.

"You've asked me a dozen times," he snaps. "I've said I won't. Now for God's sake go to sleep."

But she slips out of the room again, as silently as possible, and writes a big note with the pad and pen she always keeps in her handbag: *CHARGER*, and puts it on top of the case.

Surprisingly, she falls asleep easily after that and is awake just before the alarm goes off, throwing back the duvet and jumping out and instantly into the shower before Peter has scarcely woken up.

There's plenty of time, of course. Breakfast is done, her make-up on and the washing-up put away (she doesn't trust Peter to put the dishwasher on – she'd probably come back and find the breakfast things still in there and the sink full of dirty stuff), and by five Peter's pacing the front hallway, calling up to Emily who's checking her case for the umpteenth time.

"It's too early!" she calls back down, but she closes the case anyway and checks her handbag again instead.

"I'll do that!" Peter says as he sees her carrying the case downstairs.

"I'll have to do it myself when I get there," she says.

"Yes, but I can do it now."

So she gives in and passes it over to him, her hand brushing his lightly. The touch feels oddly intimate and with a shock Emily realises it's the most contact they've had in ages. Oh, they still kiss goodnight and goodbye: a swift, dry touch of the lips. They've even had sex, but it's more and more rare, and hardly contact; just a need to be satisfied. Afterwards, she lies awake, wondering why they're bothering at all. Maybe like everything else it's a habit.

It's pitch black outside. Peter switches the outside light on and they feel their way quietly to the car, whispering so they don't wake any neighbours. The car feels icy and Emily huddles shivering in her seat, willing the heating to come on. The black lanes slip silently by, followed by the wide dual carriageway and the white street lights of towns like Axminster and Chard until they reach the orange neons of Taunton. There's an intimacy about being cocooned together in the car like this and Emily racks her brain for something ordinary to say, but nothing comes to mind and she's grateful when Peter switches the radio on.

They're far too early, of course. Six thirty and no one else in sight, the coach station empty and closed-looking. This is usually the time when they turn to each other and joke about their habit of being way too early. *We must have such a bad reputation for sitting around in cars,'* Emily usually says. *'Fancy a quick blow job?'* Peter's always loved it when she talks like this. But, of course, today is different.

"It's only a couple of days," Emily says suddenly, as though reading his mind.

"You might want to stay longer," Peter says, lightly. "I don't mind…"

"No, no. I won't want to get in the way. It's fine. It'll be fine."

Gradually, other cars arrive, pulling up in ones and twos, their engines idling so they can keep the car heating on. Then the coach appears and stops with a hiss of brakes, the headlights still on. Emily feels a rush of nerves; her heart is pounding, her hands shaking. For a moment she forgets her sole reason for going is to see Poppy. She has a sudden urge to tell Peter she's changed her mind. But at the first sight of the bus he's leapt out of his seat and is unloading her suitcase from the boot, pulling up the handle, wheeling it round to her side of the car.

She trails behind him, obediently, as he strides towards the coach. Peter hates anyone beating him to anything, regardless of whether a seat is booked or not. He loathes standing behind people, shuffling to get on. He wants to be first.

"Ring when you get there, won't you?" he's saying. He turns to kiss her. She feels his dry lips, the light pressure of his hand on her arm then he's urging her on to the coach. Like an automaton she follows the others, sits down, searches for the book she's brought with her and her phone, then puts her handbag on the floor and stares out of the window so she doesn't have to look at the woman next to her doing exactly the same things. The woman's elbow hits Emily's arm. "Sorry," she says, briefly, then looks away. Emily's pleased she doesn't exchange pleasantries of any sort. The last thing she wants is to have to make conversation the entire journey up. Peter is waiting in the crowd. She sees him search the lighted windows for her face. She wipes the misted up window, waves briefly.

It seems like an age. Peter's hand predictably goes to his wrist several times as he checks his watch irritably. Then finally, with another hiss the coach takes off.

Emily tries to quell the range of feelings swirling inside her. She should be sad to be leaving Peter but instead it's relief she's feeling, a great weight off her shoulders. No more having to pussyfoot around him, to search for every word she utters to make sure she's not upsetting him in some way or provoking an argument. Yet with a nostalgic pang she remembers what it was like in the past to be parted from him. She feels envious of the ones at the coach station who were hugging and kissing, hardly daring to let go for the last time. And she's still so nervous: she sees herself unable to find a taxi driver, giving him the wrong address maybe, though she's checked it over and over again and Peter has Googled it to make sure it's right. She pictures herself wandering around unknown streets in London with no signal on her phone, and no idea where she's going.

But none of this happens, of course. There's a line of taxis at the terminus, the driver recognises the address immediately, eases through the busy streets. The house is in a row of three-storeyed terraced houses in Wimbledon. Rose answers the door. She hugs her warmly, takes her case. Alicia hangs back, shyly. Four months is a long time for a two-year-old, and Emily does her best to hide her disappointment when the little girl shrinks back from her open arms.

"Look, Leesha, it's Emmy. You remember?" Rose coaxes her, but she runs away.

"She'll come round," Rose says.

Emily follows through to the kitchen. A middle-aged, blonde lady is standing washing up at the sink. Rose notices Emily's surprised face. "Oh, Olga," she says. "This is my friend Emily. Olga helps out for us," she explains.

A cleaning lady. Emily's impressed. No wonder Rose prefers it up here. The house is large, high-ceilinged, beautifully furnished with wooden floors, pale carpets and cream walls. She thinks of the cramped house in Lyme Regis, their big sofa squashed in next to the bookcase, the tiny kitchen with the dining table pushed against the wall.

Alicia trails through, dragging a doll's pram. "Not in here with that!" Rose says, but Alicia ignores her and Rose does nothing about it.

As they sit drinking tea, Rose dodging past the long-suffering Olga to make it, Emily wonders how soon she can send her text to Poppy. It's been saved to 'Drafts' for days now; she's been reading it through again all the way up, even though she knows it by heart now, wondering if she's struck the right balance between eagerness and casualness. *Up in London for a few days*, it reads. *Would love to see you if you're around.*

She fingers the phone in her pocket, longing for another chance to read it, but Rose has waited for the cleaning lady to finish at the sink and she lowers her voice and asks, "Have you heard from Dan at all?"

Emily glances over to where Alicia is ramming the doll's pram into one leg of the kitchen table.

"Oh, don't worry about her," Rose says. "She hasn't even asked about him."

Emily tells her about the emails, about the house, but Rose ventures little about her own plans.

"I like it here," she says, simply.

Emily can see why. The next morning a different smiling, but largely silent, cleaning lady turns up and sets about restoring the house into some sort of order. Alicia's damp bath towel from the night before and her dirty clothes miraculously disappear from the landing, the dishwasher that Emily had helped her stack with their dinner things is emptied of the clean stuff, and their breakfast dishes that Rose had left on top are stacked in for the next wash. The washing machine hums and the cleaning lady ("Rosa", Rose laughs. "Bit confusing!") is doing the ironing. Later on, Emily finds the spare room she was assigned has been tidied, her suitcase closed and stowed under the dressing table; the toiletries she had left in a cluttered pile neatly stacked on the shelf in the en-suite shower room; the bed made, the clothes on the back of the chair hung on hangers on the wardrobe door. The room is square, impersonal, magnolia and cream with a modern seascape print over the bed, a variation of the others she's peeped into, even Rose's parents': all like rooms in a five-star hotel with matching cream curtains, billowing white voiles and thick, beige carpets.

It's years since she slept separately from Peter. It seemed strange last night, slipping between the crisp, white cotton sheets, the bed yawning emptily next to her. She reached for the extra pillows next to her so she could prop herself up to read, but clearly she was more tired than she realised and the words blurred beneath her eyes until finally she gave up and lay down. She pumped the pillow under her head, pulled the duvet cover up around her neck just like she liked and tucked her hair under her left ear. This was usually the point where Peter turned over and took the duvet with him, necessitating starting the whole procedure over again, and it was bliss instead to fall into an instant and dreamless sleep.

She woke several times to the unfamiliar city sounds: the wail of a siren, the swoosh of a passing car; the more distant white noise of constant traffic; voices below in the street, the slam of a car door. Each time she remembered with a jolt where she was, why she was here; but rather than keeping her awake, the thought she might, just might, see Poppy, held a strange comfort, whatever might happen, and she drifted back to sleep, no snores or snorts to keep her awake, no one to disturb her getting out of bed to go to the loo.

The same strange feeling hit her when she woke to an

empty bed, but there was no familiar sense of dread when she opened her eyes, no fear of the day ahead.

"I thought I might pop out later," she says to Rose, casually, as they have lunch. She's had no reply from Poppy, but she's determined not to let this opportunity pass. Her only reason for coming up was to see her. But she has to be careful not to let Rose think that. "An old friend of mine's up here," she goes on, keeping her voice deliberately light. "I thought we might meet up."

"A friend?" Rose says, raising her eyebrows.

Emily realises what she thinks. "A girlfriend," she says, but even as she says it she blushes guiltily, and she can tell Rose doesn't believe her.

It's the most interest Rose has shown in her since she's been there. She has soon realised she and Rose don't really know each other. The odd snatches of conversation they had in Lyme Regis above Alicia's constant clamour for attention hardly amount to a friendship and beyond a cursory, "How's Peter?" Rose hasn't asked anything about what they've been doing since she left Lyme. She's completely wrapped up in herself, and her life here with her parents, the only child with an only child of her own, has only exacerbated this. Maybe that's what Dan found hard, the constant self-interest. But Emily knows better than to blame one person for the breakdown of a relationship.

She decides it would be best to go when Alicia has been settled down for the afternoon nap that Rose still insists she has every afternoon, although it's obvious she doesn't actually need it. Emily may not know much about bringing up children, but it takes Rose ages to get her to sleep and she's sure Alicia wouldn't wake so early in the morning if she didn't have the daytime rest. But Rose likes time to herself during the day, time she spends with her face buried in her phone or laptop, shopping online, messaging her friends and posting photos of Alicia on Facebook.

The rest of Rose's day is devoted to Alicia, who, spoilt before, is worse than ever here. With no housework to do and only the meals to cook, Rose can give her undivided attention from the moment she wakes up to the moment she goes to sleep. The proud grandparents have lined the walls of the house with photographs of Alicia. There are more on every surface and every room is full of toys, ready to occupy her. Although she had longed to see her, Emily finds herself disappointed: Alicia is so used to everything being 'hers' that if Emily picks up a toy she snatches it out of her hand. Emily tries hard to re-establish the relationship they had before. She cuddles up to her on the sofa, but Alicia pulls away. She kneels down to play with her, but Alicia ignores her; offers to read her a story but Alicia shakes her head or wanders off part way through.

"I don't know what time I'll be back," she says to Rose. "Don't worry about cooking for me. D'you want me to pick up anything while I'm out?" She has no idea how or where she would possibly do this, but she feels obliged to ask.

"No, it's fine," Rose says. "There's loads in the freezer. I'll grab a pizza or something. Or I can do bolognese if you're back in time."

Emily has the feeling Rose's mother does all the cooking. Last night they had Marks and Spencer lasagne and the fridge and cupboards are stacked full of easy-to-prepare convenience foods.

It's a relief to escape from the overheated house and the child-orientated atmosphere, and Emily takes a deep breath of the cool, fresh air and looks up at the watery winter sky as she walks along.

The address she has for Jasmine is in Putney. "You can get a taxi from the tube station," Rose said when she asked how she could get there. She didn't tell her it was Jasmine's flat. Rose knows they don't get on, she'd wonder why she was going to see her.

Jasmine is working, *But I can leave early*, she texts. She didn't seem too surprised to hear from Emily. Maybe Peter told her Emily was coming up.

The flat turns out to belong to a friend, but that doesn't stop Jasmine showing Emily around as though it were her own. They too must have a cleaning lady. Hard to imagine Jasmine or any of her friends doing any cleaning, but a strong smell of polish and floor cleaner hangs in the air, mingled with the scent of the white lilies that stand in a vase in the front hallway. "Micheli sent them," Jasmine says, proudly. The flat is like a miniaturised version of Rose's house with wooden floors, pale carpets and white walls, the bathroom equally beige and the kitchen all cream units and black granite. There's no sign of Poppy here in this perfect, neat and tidy place: no cerise or purple scarves lying around, no fringed shawls, discarded bracelets or beads, tapestry bags with half the contents spilling out, not even in Jasmine's untidy bedroom. She knows the answer even before she asks the carefully rehearsed casual question.

"Poppy?" Jasmine asks, surprised. "She left weeks ago. She drove me mad. I don't know how you can stand her."

And she launches into a typically-Jasmine bitchy tirade, the type Emily's heard many times before, usually about one of her best friends. The story involves a trip they'd planned to the theatre that Poppy failed to turn up for – "The tickets cost me a *fortune!*" – then used some flimsy excuse afterwards. "She was with a man, I'm sure of it," Jasmine says. "Anyway, it didn't matter. She couldn't've stayed here any longer. Becca was due back."

Becca's name has peppered the conversation already; it's

her flat, or more precisely her father's that he rents out to her.

Emily doesn't know how she manages to hide her disappointment. All this way, all this effort, for nothing. She checks her phone surreptitiously while Jasmine's clearing up the tea things. Still nothing.

"You and Dad okay?" Jasmine's voice floats out from the kitchen.

Emily jumps guiltily, colour rushing to her face until she realises Jasmine's just asking after their health, not suggesting they're not getting on.

"Yes, fine," she says, lightly.

"Do him good not having you around for a while," Jasmine goes on.

Emily realises with another flood of guilt that she hasn't missed Peter at all. Oh, at first it felt a bit odd not having him around, like there was a part of herself missing. But the relief from the strain and the effort and the worry outweighed that feeling.

She thinks about it as the taxi makes its way back through the busy, unfamiliar streets to Rose. Rose, who has made the brave move with a small child in tow, a child she was tearing away from her father. How much easier to put up with Dan in the hope it might get better again. But Rose had her parents to come to, an easy escape route. If Emily leaves Peter she has nothing and no one. Where would she go? What would she do? She tries to picture herself in a one-bedroom flat. The idea holds appeal. Back in Clifton where she still has friends. One of those Victorian villas with a balcony. She could have it decorated just the way she wanted: choose her own colours, her own furniture and curtains. She could have a cat. Peter hates cats. She could eat what she liked when she liked, shop wherever, whenever she fancied, go to as many classes as she liked or stay at home all day and read a book. No Peter to bother her, to tell her off when she cleaned the house, to ask her the same questions again and again; to sit around waiting like a hungry bird with its beak open for her to provide the next meal. No one to talk to in the evening, no one to go for a walk with or to the theatre, no one in bed at night, no sex for God's sake, no one to share her thoughts and worries. Whichever way she looks at it, there's no escape.

Alicia hurls herself at her when she walks through the door, the few hours away having obviously made all the difference. The contrariness of a two-year-old. Emily relishes the feel of the warm little body close to her. This is what she misses most, she realises; this is what we all look for: unconditional love, close physical contact; the innocent, unchanging intimacy of being held by someone. All too soon Alicia struggles free.

"How was your *friend*?" Rose asks, meaningfully.

Emily has her answer ready. "She couldn't make it after all. I went to see Jasmine. She lives in the same area."

Rose goes to bed straight after dinner, leaving the plates and saucepans that won't fit in the dishwasher for Olga or Rosa to deal with the next day. "Oh, just leave that," she says to Emily when she picks up a cloth to wipe the smattering of pasta sauce from the tiles at the back of the hob. Emily's pleased she doesn't have to try and make conversation for hours after dinner. This was one of the things she'd been dreading. But even through dinner Rose is constantly on her phone, scrolling through messages, tapping away with one finger, her forehead furrowed with concentration.

Emily follows her upstairs. They creep past Alicia's room, whispering goodnights outside the bathroom.

Emily checks her phone. A message from Peter, thanking her for a photo she sent of Alicia. *Hope you're having a good time,* he adds. It doesn't seem to need a reply.

She checks her phone again just before she goes to sleep, almost dropping it when Poppy's name lights up.

Sorry, been busy, the text reads in that infuriating way Poppy has of picking up on a conversation as though there's been no delay at all since she last messaged. *Be home soon. See you then xx*

Disappointment sweeps through Emily, bringing with it childish tears to her eyes. The text has that same feel as the previous ones: that it's been sent to others: Suzie probably; other friends, male or female, lovers, old and new; Facebook, Twitter. God, she may as well put it in the paper. Emily feels as small and insignificant as a squashed insect. She means nothing to Poppy. That much is obvious. She may as well go back to Peter, patch things up, make the most of a bad job. She's not Rose. She doesn't have the courage to break free now. It's far too late.

Chapter Twenty-One

At first, it's relief that Peter feels; a huge sense of liberating freedom, as though a weight has been lifted from his shoulders. He drives home faster than usual, faster than he probably should, certainly faster than he needs to; it's still early and there's nothing to get back for. Exhilaration rushes through him as the black roads speed by.

It's too early for school traffic and there's not much work traffic around either and he gets home in record time. He looks at the milometer, calculates his approximate miles per gallon. Not good. But then he did have his foot down all the way. He throws his car keys onto the kitchen table, hearing Emily's voice in his head, *'Not there, for God's sake! You'll scratch the table!'*

The day stretches before him. No Emily to make him feel guilty when he sits down with a book. He switches the television on. This is another thing she hates. *'D'you have to watch it now? I need to Hoover in here.'* After half an hour of the news and a current affairs programme he feels suddenly weary. He could always go back to bed. No one to tell him not to. No one to disapprove. No one would even know. But he doesn't. He picks up a motor magazine instead and finds an article he hasn't read before, or if he has he's forgotten all about it.

He knows there are tins of soup and baked beans in the cupboard for lunch; bacon and eggs in the fridge, but he resorts to his usual toast and Bovril, which he eats standing next to the toaster waiting for the next slice of toast to pop up. It's the same in the evening: Emily has left a supply of meals in the freezer for him for dinner, and a list of instructions. 'DEFROST FIRST', she has written. 'In the microwave. Setting 2. Do this while the oven warms up. 180 for half an hour'. He rummages through them: shepherd's pie, lasagne, the remains of a casserole, then he throws them back in the freezer, puts his coat on and walks down to the Pilot Boat.

He can't help thinking of Poppy while he's waiting for his steak and kidney pie and chips to arrive. How she'd sit and wait here on her own in this oh-so-masculine place, totally impervious to the stares of the locals with their pints. Life seems dull without her. Well, not so much her, as the excitement, the fun, the daring. Nothing to look forward to now. Except Emily coming back. And he's not sure how much he's looking forward to that.

After three days, however, he's beginning to change his mind. The house is so quiet without her. It's not just the hoovering and the constant cleaning, the sound of the washing machine or dishwasher, or the back door opening and closing as she rushes in and out to her various classes; it's the constant background chatter that he scarcely notices when she's there, but misses now she isn't. She mutters constantly to herself, "Now where did I put that?" or "What was I going to do next?" or "This blasted Hoover!" He even misses the disapproving glances she throws him when he's reading his book and her impatient voice from the kitchen, "Peter, I've told you twice. Dinner'll be spoilt if you don't come now!" even though he knows it's nowhere near ready, and won't be served out for another five minutes after he's sat down at the table.

Except for the pictures of Alicia and a phone call when she arrived, he hasn't heard from her. He didn't really expect to, but nonetheless he checks his phone every day just in case. Finally, he texts her on the last evening, even though he knows full well the answer to his question: the time of the coach is written in capital letters on the kitchen calendar. He can hear her impatience in her terse reply. This is what they've done to each other after years of familiarity. Just recently they were out in the open car, and he was telling Emily how as a teenage boy he had daydreamed of times like this: driving an open top sports car down a sweeping road, blue skies above, the sweep of the sea below. "And the girl of your dreams next to you?" Emily had smiled over at him.

She had annoyed him for something or other that morning and the reply was out of his mouth before he could help it. "Well, things change..." he said. He knew he was being spiteful. Emily said nothing, but her silence spoke for itself. One more point to him. One more resentment to add to Emily's list.

He finds himself looking around the house the next morning, seeing it suddenly with Emily's eyes. He knows he can't get it up to her standard, but he goes round anyway picking up newspapers and magazines, stacking the dishwasher with mugs, plates and knives, putting away the Bovril and wiping work surfaces.

He's just about to leave to pick up Emily when his phone buzzes. It'll be her, of course, reminding him of the time or telling him the coach is running late. But to his surprise Poppy's name appears on the screen. *I need to see you.*

He deletes the message quickly and shoves the phone in his pocket, but the words burn in his mind all the way over in the car.

He sees Emily getting off the coach well before she spots him. She looks tired, worn, pale. Her face breaks into a smile when she sees him but the smile doesn't quite meet her eyes. "Hell of a journey," she says. "I've got a dreadful headache." He hurries to find her suitcase from the pile being unloaded from the coach.

"You had a good time though?" he asks. "Rose was okay? And Leesha? You've got some more pictures for me?"

"Yes, they're both fine. I'll show you the pictures later," she replies. "Oh, and I went to see Jasmine."

Peter's touched. She can only have done it for him. "Thank you, Em."

"You don't need to thank me."

"It means a lot to me," he says, genuinely. "How was she?"

"Fine. She sends her love. It's a lovely flat... I'm sorry, Peter. Talking. It's making my head worse. I'll tell you tomorrow..."

"Yes, of course." He knows Emily. She'll be sick if she doesn't settle down.

In the passenger seat she leans her head against the window, closes her eyes. Peter's alone with his thoughts again. *I need to see you*, hammers again and again through his mind. Of course it's nothing. Nothing more than advice on a painting or exhibition probably. Poppy loves a bit of drama. She knows he'll try and read more into it. He tries to put it out of his mind. He won't reply. Not yet anyway. Maybe not at all. Whatever it is she wants, she can get from someone else. *She* was the one who finished with him. She can get on with it. Yet, faced with the disappointment of Emily's homecoming, it's hard to resist being drawn back in. He sees himself meeting Poppy, hears her saying, *'I made a mistake. I need you, Peter. Let's start again.'*

Back home there's none of the usual rush of unpacking, no complaints, no comments at all, to his surprise, from Emily on the state of the house. Drinking a cup of tea at the same time she rummages in the freezer for something easy to reheat for dinner.

"Can't I do that for you?" Peter asks, seeing her clutch her forehead as she straightens up.

"No, it's okay," she says.

She goes to bed straight after dinner, accepting, for once, Peter's offer to clear up and put the dishwasher on.

He doesn't know quite what he expected when Emily came back, but it's not this. He missed her. He looked forward to her coming back. But was that just because he didn't like being on his own? Because the 'her' he missed, the one he looked forward to seeing again, isn't the one he has now.

Emily is quiet. Oh, she speaks when he talks to her, manages a smile even, but it's all so distant.

"I've still got a headache," she said the first day. "I'm a bit tired," followed that but she can't keep making excuses.

She knows she should try harder. In the coach on the way home she promised herself she would be better to Peter. She pictured them going back to where they used to be. But it's like a huge mountain she has to scale, and she just doesn't have the energy.

The further she pulls away from Peter, the further he pulls from her, retreating into his own world. She knows, deep inside, it's because he doesn't want to face what they're going through, that he's afraid of being hurt, afraid of the consequences of any sort of discussion, but seeing him sitting there day after day in the same position reading or hunched over his computer makes her want to go and shake him.

She finds herself crying at the most unlikely times: tears fall down her face as she washes up, or folds clothes and puts them away or walks to one of her classes. She doesn't know how she manages to put on a brave face in front of Pam and Andrea and the others, but at least here she can be free from thinking about things for a while. A sense of dread pervades her as she walks back home each time.

Then one afternoon it finally happens. There's a crash from the kitchen. Peter swears. She goes out. One of their best whisky glasses lies shattered on the floor.

"Peter, for God's sake, that's one of the ones my parents gave us! What the hell were you doing with it anyway?"

"Putting it away for you."

"Why didn't you leave it to me?" She drops to her feet, begins to pick up pieces of glass. He's beside her in a moment, jostling her out of the way.

"Don't do that. You'll cut your fingers. Wait, I'll put some gloves on…"

"No, I'll do it…" She reaches for the rubber gloves by the sink.

"Why d'you always think I'm so useless?" Peter explodes. "Why d'you always take over everything?"

She throws the rubber gloves back in the sink. "Okay, you bloody do it! I'm so fed up with you, Peter! Fed up with everything, you, this bloody house, my bloody life!"

She starts to sob. He puts his arms around her, mechanically, and she leans her head against his shoulder. "What can we do?" he says.

"I don't know, Peter, I don't know… Maybe I should go away for a while."

"We've just tried that, haven't we?"

"Maybe we should split up." She's shocked to hear the words come out of her mouth. Here it is then, the moment she's been dreading, the moment she knew would have to come.

"Where will you go?" he asks.

"Why should *I* go anywhere?" she says, indignantly, stepping back. "This is my home."

"And mine."

"Oh God, this is awful…" She leans her head against his shoulder and he pats her back again, through habit more than anything else. Suddenly, his phone vibrates in his pocket. He jumps slightly in surprise but doesn't reach for it.

"Aren't you going to answer it?" she asks, moving back.

"No, they can call back."

But there's something about the way he says it. A suspicion darts into her mind. She hears Suzie's voice in her head, *'Ah yes, Peter. There's another one.'*

She makes a grab for Peter's phone. He catches her wrist. "Emily!"

"Who is it, Peter?"

"Leave it!" He bends her wrist back.

"Ow! You're hurting me!" Emily says, pulling her arm away and rubbing her wrist.

"I said leave it, didn't I?" Peter snaps. "I don't go snooping at *your* phone!"

"I've got nothing to hide!" The irony of it strikes her even as she says it.

"Oh, for God's sake, I'm fed up with all this!" he says.

He rushes out. She hears him grab his coat and keys, the slam of the door. She sits down shakily. Is Peter having an affair? Impossible. And Poppy would be the last person he'd choose. And she'd never want him. Not like she wanted Emily. The past tense in her mind brings a rush of fresh pain. It'll never be the same. Not with Peter, not with anyone.

Chapter Twenty-Two

Peter has no idea where he's going. He checked his phone. It wasn't Poppy who called after all. He shouldn't have overreacted. Yet illogically he blames her for everything. She's been texting every day. Variations of the same thing. *I need to see you… When can we meet?* He hasn't replied. He's tired of her games. If it weren't for her, he and Emily would be okay. Well, that might not be strictly true, but there's some truth in it. And Emily's still hung up on her for some weird reason. Jasmine told him she'd been asking about her.

His first thought is to go for a drive, but he knows it's a crazy thing to do when he's so pent up and angry. He strides towards the seafront. Maybe a walk on the Cobb will brace him up.

He can't help glancing into Poppy's shop on his way by. Suzie is in the window, rearranging a display of some sort of lacy stuff. He looks away quickly but he knows she's seen him. He quickens his pace but he hears someone running behind him, panting breath. She grabs his coat sleeve. "Peter, wait!" she gasps. "Wait!"

He wants to shake her off but people are looking. He turns around impatiently. "I'm late!" he lies, quickly.

He can see she doesn't believe him. "Come in. Please. Just for a moment."

She sees him glance back at the shop. "She's not here," she says. "Please. It's important. It won't take long."

"Okay," he says, following her back.

The bell clangs on the door. She turns the sign to 'Closed'.

He follows her through to the back. Poppy's studio is in darkness. She clicks the light on. There's a canvas on an easel. A new painting. Barely started. A sketched outline, partly painted in. A woman sitting on a chair, full length, facing sideways, staring unsmilingly into the blank space beyond. The flowing hair, the generous body, it's clearly Poppy. A self-portrait. Quite different from anything she's done before. It's arresting. Even in its infancy very, very good.

"She's just started it," Suzie says, unnecessarily. "Good, isn't it? I can see it is."

"Yes, very. This isn't what you wanted to talk about?"

"No. She wants to see you."

"I know," he says, carefully. He has no idea how much Suzie knows.

"It's important."

"I can't see what can be so important."

Suzie raises her eyebrows and he finds himself reddening. There's a small pause as though she's making her mind up about whether to say something or not.

"Poppy was at the Slade when I met her," she says, suddenly.

Peter shakes his head. "She went to Brighton," he says firmly. "She told me. John Anderson was her tutor. Old friend of mine." She can't have made it up. Her description of him, his looks, his mannerisms, was just too accurate.

"She was there for a while," Suzie says. "But she was at the Slade when I met her. You taught there, didn't you?"

Peter feels suddenly uncomfortable. "Yes," he says.

His eyes are suddenly drawn to the canvasses stacked on the floor; the flourishing number 7 crossed the French way. He has a sudden swift memory of a blonde student looking up at him challengingly. "Not Julie. *Juillet,*" she's saying with a French accent. "I was born on the 7th of July '77. Maman called me Juillet. Papa changed it to Julie when he brought me to England…"

302

She was dangerous, that girl, with her beautiful, wild eyes. Always spinning tales. Tales about him. Tales about anyone. Anything to get her own way.

"Okay," Peter says, sighing. "I'll see her."

"She's upstairs," Suzie says.

"You said…"

"I know. I'm sorry. I knew you wouldn't come in otherwise…"

He follows Suzie like a sleepwalker up the narrow stairs. The feeling of discomfort, of nemesis even, has increased.

Poppy is sitting in an armchair reading a book. She starts up when she sees him, glances at Suzie as though for reassurance.

"D'you want me to stay?" Suzie asks.

"No, it's okay," Poppy says.

She looks different. At first, he can't work out why then he realises it's because she has no make-up on. Her face looks puffy, blotchy. She looks tired.

"Well?" he says. "I'm here."

"I'm pregnant," she says.

It's so unexpected Peter doesn't know what to say. Then he laughs, relief overcoming the shock. "You're not pinning that one on me. You know as well as I do it can't possibly be mine."

She nods gravely. "Yes, it is."

"It can't be. You know that." She'd always insisted on Durex. He hated them. "Anyway, I'm too…"

"Old?" she says. "I thought I was too. But clearly not. Nothing's a hundred per cent safe, Peter. You should know that."

"Yes. No. I can't believe it."

"There's been no one else, Peter," she says. "I don't know what you take me for…"

"No… I didn't say… I just can't believe it."

"I didn't either. But it's true."

"I don't know what to say. What d'you want me to do?"

"Nothing. I just thought you should know."

He shrugs. "Okay." He waits. "That all?" he says.

She nods.

He turns to go. Then stops. "You won't tell Emily?"

She gives a bitter little laugh. "She'll need to know." She sees his shock. "That I'm pregnant, I mean."

"You're not keeping it, are you?" The thought of Poppy with a baby, a small child, a difficult teenager. The idea is preposterous.

"Suzie thinks I should. And maybe she's right. Maybe a child is what I need, what I've been looking for all this time."

Another thought strikes him. "D'you need money?" he says.

She gives that same bitter little laugh. "That would help. But I'm not blackmailing you, Peter. I won't tell anyone. About us."

"What about Suzie?"

"She won't."

He says nothing. Then. "It was you, wasn't it?" he says. "Julie. Seven. Juillet. Whatever you called yourself. You…"

"Told on you? You deserved it. How old were we? Nineteen? Twenty?"

"Old enough."

"She was a slut anyway."

"And you're not?" It's a cheap jibe and he regrets it the moment the words are out of his mouth. "I'm sorry," he says, quickly.

She gives a dismissive little shake of her head.

"Well…" he says. "You'll let me know. About the money, I mean."

She doesn't look up.

His feet sound heavily on the uncarpeted stairs. Suzie is waiting in the studio. He can't meet her eyes. "Thank you," he says, though it's a ridiculous thing to say. She doesn't reply. He follows her through the dim security-lit shop, past the crowded display stands.

He can't face Emily, not yet. His first thought is to walk down the front, but it's getting dark and the cold wind hits him as he walks down the street. Shops are closing, the slam of doors, voices calling goodnight to each other, people hurrying past him to get to their cars. He feels in his coat pockets, cursing when his car keys aren't there, picturing them in another coat pocket or tidied away somewhere by the over-zealous Emily. A solitary table in the pub, nursing a drink, doesn't hold much appeal but it's the only option.

He doesn't believe her, he realises, by the second whisky. It's another one of her fantastic tales. Women like her aren't faithful. Chances are she's not even pregnant. But if she is, it's definitely not his.

Chapter Twenty-Three

Peter's been gone ages. Emily's worried. It's dark. Maybe he's been run over, fallen down, mugged or something. Well, maybe not mugged, not in Lyme Regis, but any of the others. She thought she'd gone past worrying about him. He's an adult, after all. But it's *her* fault he rushed out. She'd feel bad if something had happened to him. His phone goes straight to answerphone when she calls it. She puts her coat on, finds gloves and a scarf.

Outside, she almost changes her mind. Where on earth will she start? And it's cold out here after the warm house, with a thin drizzle blowing in the air. She shivers and pushes her gloved hands into her coat pocket.

She glances into the shops on her way by, though it's hard to imagine Peter going into any of them. One of the pubs is her most likely bet, though he might just be sitting on a bench somewhere. She remembers years ago when they had a row she found him on a bench outside the station. He'd looked so small and lost and her heart had contracted at the sight of him on his own, staring into space.

She slows down as she reaches Poppy's shop, the same proud proprietorial feeling mixed nowadays with hurt and nostalgia. The shop window is lit but the shop beyond is in gloom, the displays covered, the door sign turned to 'Closed'.

She peers in anyway then her heart leaps. There's a dark figure moving amongst the displays. It's Poppy. Her face burns. Her heart pounds painfully. She bangs on the door glass, rattles the door. Poppy looks up. Even from here, she can tell she doesn't want to let her in. Emily reaches in her pocket for her phone, scrolls to the shop number, but Poppy is already on her way.

"When did you get back? Why didn't you tell me?" Emily bursts out, but Poppy seems to be saying something about Peter.

"What?" Emily says.

"He left about ten minutes ago. I asked him to look at my new picture."

"Oh good." Part of her registers that Peter's fine. He's probably on his way back now. But she can only really think about Poppy. "Where've you been? Why didn't you tell me? I've been trying to contact you. I've missed you so much…" The words fall out in an incoherent gush. She realises she's crying and laughing. The relief is unbearable. The solid presence of Poppy in front of her, after all these weeks, is so incredibly amazing. She knows she's making a fool of herself. She's clutching at Poppy's arm, but Poppy ignores it.

"You'd better come through," she says.

Suzie's worried face appears at the top of the stairs. She takes it all in at a glance, throws a quick warning look to Emily, a look that says, "Don't say we were talking about her." The look she gives Poppy is harder to read, a sort of wry amusement, accompanied by raised eyebrows. "I'll be in my room," she says.

Poppy pats the sofa cushion, but sits down in the chair opposite while Emily searches for a tissue, blows her nose, wipes her eyes. "God, I must look a mess," she says. "Poppy." She leans forward, grabs her arm again.

"Don't," Poppy says, recoiling.

"Why? What've I done? Why're you being like this? I thought you…"

"Emily, don't." She pushes her back gently. "I do," she says. "I do care for you, Emily. That's why I went. It was getting too much. I can't, you see. I can't give myself to anyone like I gave myself to you."

Emily so wants to believe her. But it has the sound of a performance, one she's given before.

"You don't have to believe me," Poppy says into the silence. "But it's true."

Emily looks at her: she's never seen her without make-up, she realises. She looks older, strained, tired. Maybe she hasn't been sleeping either.

"There's something else," Poppy says, suddenly.

"Not Jasmine," Emily says quickly, shocked.

"No!" Poppy laughs. "Jasmine and I are two of a kind. Selfish, self-centred, I mean. We couldn't put up with each other for long. Nothing like you and me. No, it's…" She starts to cry. "I'm sorry, it's just been such a shock…"

"What? What?" Emily says, alarmed. "Are you ill?"

"No," she snuffles. "Well, yes, in a way, but not that way. I'm pregnant."

The shock runs through Emily like a knife. She's on her feet before she realises it, gripping Poppy's shoulders, shaking her like a rat. "You bitch! You filthy, whoring, two-timing little bitch! I hate you! I hate you!"

Poppy shrieks, curling up into a ball, her hands over her head. Emily flails wildly at her with her fists, grabs her hair, her clothes, sobbing. Vaguely, she's aware of someone coming in, feels strong arms pulling her off.

"You'd better go," Suzie says.

She can scarcely walk down the stairs. She can't stop crying.

"D'you want me to get a taxi?" Suzie asks. "Or shall I call Peter? Someone else?"

Emily shakes her head incoherently. "No, no. No one. Please. I'm okay." She manages a watery laugh at the absurdity of the statement.

"I'll walk back with you," Suzie says.

"No. Please. I'm better on my own."

"If you're sure…" But her gaze is already on the stairwell, and Emily knows she wants to get back to Poppy.

The fresh air hits her hot, wet face. She steps out more confidently than she feels, aware of people in the street and passing cars, people she may know.

Poppy, Poppy, she moans in her mind. *'I'm pregnant,'* she hears. How could she do it? After what they had, what she thought they had. And who? Who? She could've been seeing anyone when she wasn't with Emily: some fey youth, the step-brother back on the scene, maybe. God, even Simeon bloody Blackwood, who knows? From nowhere she hears another voice, *'Peter. There's another one under her spell.'* She thinks of the phone call, hears Poppy's voice. "Peter was here. He came to look at my new picture." The idea's so ridiculous she almost laughs, but once it's in her mind she can't dismiss it. Too many things add up: Peter's frequent absences, Poppy's acid little hints.

She's nearly home now. She sees the light on in the house. Peter's there. She feels a knot of dread tighten in her stomach. What can she say to him? She tries to picture herself saying casually, "I went to see Poppy. She's just found out she's pregnant." She sees Peter jumping, guiltily. She shakes her head, inwardly. She can't do it. She'll leave it, say nothing. Not until she has to. Maybe she won't have to. Maybe it's not true. And there's so much else to go through first. The dread deepens. She and Peter have to find a way forward. The enormity of it hits her like a huge wall she has to scale. The thought is exhausting, bewildering. Where will they start? Yet with the dread comes a certain sense of normality re-asserting itself. This is real life. This is what people do. Nothing like the fantasy world that Poppy lives in.

Epilogue

It's a brisk, sunny morning in late August. Lyme has scarcely looked better. The sun glinting off the sea, the curve of the bay, white breakers on the shore, children scurrying back and forth with buckets. The schools go back next week and the last influx of holidaymakers is making the most of it after a long, wet summer.

Grace hangs on to Emily's arm as they mount the uneven steps to the Cobb. The men are up ahead; Peter's pointing out something down in the bay, Matt's shielding his eyes against the sun, trying to see it. Peter leans into him, shouting something into his ear and they both laugh.

"Peter seems happier," Grace says.

Emily hasn't told her everything, of course, but she had to tell someone. Women have to have their confidantes even if men can bottle it up.

"Yes," she says, simply. "It's getting easier."

"All relationships go through bad patches," Grace says. "You just have to hang on in there and wait for the good times to come back."

"It was so difficult for Peter. The whole retirement thing. Not being useful any more. Important. I didn't understand. I didn't even try to."

It's five months since that awful night. When she got back, the whisky on Peter's breath told her where he'd been. He didn't question it when she said she'd gone out to look for him. He was too distracted, they were both too upset.

The days and weeks that followed have disappeared into a

great black pit, along with the endless restless nights. Gradually, time has given perspective. She doesn't blame Peter. How can she when she was just as much at fault?

She didn't need proof, would have gone out of her way to avoid the truth if she could, but she found the Christmas card and the pink Ann Summers carrier bag in the garage stuffed underneath the patio cushions. At first, she assumed they were for her. Peter never was very good at hiding things and he must have forgotten what he'd done with them. Or maybe he'd decided not to give them because they hadn't been getting on. 'To Someone Special' the card read. A glow of love and tenderness swept through her at the thought of him even considering a surprise present, the sort she'd longed for all those years. She realised her mistake the moment she held out the red and black g-string. It was huge. Even before she saw the size 16 label she knew Peter hadn't bought it for her. The knowledge that Poppy would have laughed at the card, with its hearts and flowers, didn't make it any easier. The double betrayal hurting deep in her chest.

Emily wouldn't want him to confess. If he does she might be tempted to confess too, and that really would be the end. This way they can carry on. And it's working, after a fashion. Peter's trying, she can tell. He's less grumpy, more caring, less likely to snap at her. She finds herself responding to it. She takes things more lightly, laughs things off where once she might have been upset. Of course, they still argue, but it doesn't feel like the end, just another silly disagreement that will blow over and be forgotten like all the others.

The Lyme Regis gossip spared her from having to tell Peter about the baby. It was at one of those boring Rotary dos Peter took her to. "Have you *heard*?" Pam's voice cut across the general hubbub of conversation, "About that artist girl, Poppy? Apparently, she's *pregnant*. I always thought she was… well, preferred women… you know…"

311

Emily's flaming face went unnoticed in the chorus of scandalised voices that followed, but when she risked a glance at Peter he seemed totally unperturbed. If she hadn't known differently she would have assumed he scarcely knew Poppy.

"I don't think it's true," Emily said the moment they got into the car.

"What?" Peter said, though of course he knew.

"About Poppy. She can't be pregnant. And if she is, she'd never keep it. Not someone like her. It would get in the way."

"Yes…" Peter said, distractedly. It's almost as though she's trying to reassure him. It's his worst nightmare, the thought that Poppy might turn up one day with a child in tow, demanding money. But as time goes by he convinces himself it will never happen. A small part of him, his masculine pride, is flattered by the thought he may have fathered a child at his age. But if Emily found out… the child she wanted but he didn't give her. Guilt settles on him, but he chases it away like he chases away all the other bad things: Anusia's infidelity, the separation from Jasmine, Zena's suicide attempts. He just wants to forget it ever happened.

Emily and Grace have reached the top of the steps now. They stop to get their breath. The wind snatches at their clothes, blows wisps of hair into Emily's face that she pushes impatiently away.

"Come on," Grace says, tugging Emily along.

Peter and Matt are waiting for them. Grace drops Emily's arm to grab Matt's and Peter holds out his hand to Emily.

"You okay?" he asks, squeezing her hand.

"Yes, fine." She smiles up at him, squinting into the sunlight. How did she ever lose sight of him? *This* is the person she knows, the man she loves, not the stranger he seemed to be before, the bad-tempered one, the one she grew away from.

They walk four abreast to the end of the Cobb. Conversation is impossible here as the strong wind from the sea blasts into their faces. They reach the end. Emily stretches her arms out like a bird. Grace stands staring out to sea like the *French Lieutenant's Woman* as she always does. The men squint out to sea, spotting boats or birds or some other interesting object. Soon they turn back, the wind at their backs now, hurrying them along, whipping their clothes around them, blowing the girls' hair into their faces, catching the men's bare necks.

Down the uneven steps again, Matt helping Grace, Peter holding Emily's hand until they reach the safety of the ground. Here in the shelter of the harbour wall they catch their breath, pull their clothes tidy, start to talk ordinarily again.

It's warmer down here. Matt stops to unbutton his cuffs, roll up his sleeves. It's crowded too: they steer past families with pushchairs, small children and ice creams; couples with fish and chips, the tangy mouth-watering smell preceding and lingering behind them; old people with walking sticks and slow, shuffling steps.

"I see that shop's reopened," Grace says suddenly. "The one that artist-friend of yours used to have."

Emily jumps as though she's been stung, her face flooding with colour.

"I hope they make a go of it," Peter says, quickly. "It's hard for that sort of small business nowadays…"

Emily's grateful to him for steering the talk away from Poppy, and on to the safer neutral topic of the big chains versus the independent business. She sees Poppy in a different light now. Distance has lent reality. Poppy feeds on people's needs. Does she mean to hurt them? Maybe not. But she has no idea of fidelity, loyalty, compassion, love.

She bumped into her in the street, one day, just before

313

they left. She tried to walk past but Poppy blocked her way and, dreading any sort of scene in public, she stopped. She couldn't help glancing down to Poppy's stomach. No obvious extra bulge under the usual voluminous clothes. But Poppy had seen the swift glance and her hand flew protectively down to pat it with a secret smile.

"We're leaving," Poppy said. "Selling up."

"I know." Emily had heard the rumours even before she had seen the 'For Sale' sign above the shop.

"Lyme isn't the place for a single mother," Poppy went on.

"Where are you going?" Emily found herself asking.

"Oh, I don't know. Back to France maybe. Maman will know what to do…"

She said it with such ease that for a moment Emily was taken in. Then she remembered. It was tempting to say something about the secretary-mother in Surrey, but she allowed Poppy this final innocent subterfuge. "And Suzie?" she asked instead.

"Oh, I don't know," Poppy said again, with that familiar Gallic shrug. "Suzie and I don't live hand in hand."

Suzie's words, *'Poppy needs me,'* came into Emily's head. She wondered how Poppy would manage without her support, her adulation, her money.

She must have said goodbye, wished her good luck maybe. She scarcely remembers now. She only remembers the sense of loss as she walked away.

The shop was on the market for months before it sold. The new owners have kept the name, 'Poppy Fields'. They've hung a picture in the window: a drawing of dried poppy heads, the poppy seeds blowing in the wind.